THE NICOLAS LE FLOCH AFFAIR

Jean-François Parot is a diplomat and historian. His Nicolas Le Floch mysteries have been published to much acclaim in French. The first three novels in the series, *The Châtelet Apprentice*, *The Man with the Lead Stomach* and *The Phantom of Rue Royale*, were enthusiastically reviewed on publication in English.

Howard Curtis's many translations from French and Italian include five novels by Jean-Claude Izzo, four by Marek Halter and three by Gianrico Carofiglio, as well as works by Balzac, Flaubert and Pirandello.

Praise for Jean-François Parot

'The period detail is marvellously evocative, Le Floch is brave and engaging . . .' *Economist*

'Parot succeeds brilliantly in his reconstruction of pre-revolutionary Paris, in splendid period detail.' *The Times*

'A solid and detailed evocation of pre-revolutionary France – the poverty and squalor, side by side with the wealth and splendour, are brought lovingly to life. And the plot has all the twists, turns and surprises the genre demands.' *Independent on Sunday*

'Jean-François Parot's evocation of eighteenth-century Paris is richly imagined and full of fascinating historical snippets.' *Financial Times*

'Parot's clever plotting and sharp eye for detail are, as ever, first rate . . .' *Mail on Sunday*

'. . . Le Floch is an engaging conduit for the reader through the teeming, phantasmagoric capital that is eighteenth-century Paris.' *Independent*

'The atmosphere is marvellous, the historical detail precise, and Le Floch and his colleagues are an engaging bunch . . .' *Guardian*

'An interesting evocation of place and period.' *The Literary Review*

THE NICOLAS LE FLOCH AFFAIR

GALLIC

Also by Jean-François Parot

The Châtelet Apprentice
The Man with the Lead Stomach
The Phantom of Rue Royale

THE

NICOLAS LE FLOCH AFFAIR

JEAN-FRANÇOIS PAROT

Translated from the French by Howard Curtis

GALLIC BOOKS

London

Ouvrage publié avec le concours du Ministère français chargé de la Culture – Centre National du Livre.
This work is published with support from the French Ministry of Culture/Centre National du Livre.

A Gallic Book

First published in France as *L'Affaire Nicolas Le Floch* by éditions Jean-Claude Lattès

First published in Great Britain in 2009 by Gallic Books, 134 Lots Road, London SW10 0RJ

A CIP record for this book is available from the British Library

ISBN 978-1-906040-22-2

Typeset in Fournier by SX Composing DTP, Rayleigh, Essex

Printed in the UK by CPI Bookmarque, Croydon, CR0 4TD

2 4 6 8 10 9 7 5 3 1

For Maurice Roisse

CONTENTS

Background to *The Nicolas Le Floch Affair* xiii

Dramatis Personae xv

The Nicolas Le Floch Affair 1

Notes 413

Background to *The Nicolas Le Floch Affair*

For those readers coming to the adventures of Nicolas Le Floch for the first time, it is useful to know that in the first book in the series, *The Châtelet Apprentice*, the hero, a foundling raised by Canon Le Floch in Guérande, is sent away from his native Brittany by his godfather, the Marquis de Ranreuil, who is concerned about his daughter Isabelle's growing fondness for the young man.

On arrival in Paris he is taken in by Père Grégoire at the Monastery of the Decalced Carmelites and on the recommendation of the marquis soon finds himself in the service of Monsieur de Sartine, Lieutenant General of Police in Paris. Under his tutelage, Nicolas is quick to learn and is soon familiar with the mysterious working methods of the highest ranks of the police service. At the end of his year's apprenticeship, he is entrusted with a confidential mission, one that will result in him rendering a signal service to Louis XV and the Marquise de Pompadour.

Aided by his deputy and mentor, Inspector Bourdeau, and putting his own life at risk on several occasions, he successfully unravels a complicated plot. Received at court by the King, he is rewarded with the post of commissioner of police at the Châtelet and, under the direct authority of Monsieur de Sartine, continues to be assigned to special investigations.

DRAMATIS PERSONAE

NICOLAS LE FLOCH : a police commissioner at the Châtelet
MONSIEUR DE SARTINE : Lieutenant General of Police in Paris
MONSIEUR DE SAINT-FLORENTIN : Minister of the King's Household
PIERRE BOURDEAU : a police inspector
OLD MARIE : an usher at the Châtelet
TIREPOT : a police spy
RABOUINE : a police spy
AIMÉ DE NOBLECOURT : a former procurator
MARION: his cook
POITEVIN : his servant
CATHERINE GAUSS : a former canteen-keeper, Nicolas Le Floch's maid
GUILLAUME SEMACGUS : a navy surgeon
AWA : his cook
CHARLES HENRI SANSON : the public executioner
MARIE-ANNE SANSON : his wife
LA PAULET : a former brothel-keeper
LA SATIN : a brothel-keeper
LA PRÉSIDENTE : a prostitute
JULIE DE LASTÉRIEUX : Nicolas Le Floch's mistress
CASIMIR : her manservant
JULIA : her maid
MONSIEUR DE LA BORDE : First Groom of the King's Bedchamber
COMMISSIONER CHORREY : a police commissioner at the Châtelet

COMMISSIONER CAMUSOT : a retired former police commissioner
GASPARD : a royal page
FRIEDRICH VON MÜVALA : a Swiss traveller
BALBASTRE : organist of Notre Dame
THÉVENEAU DE MORANDE : a French lampoonist living in London
THE CHEVALIER D'ÉON : a French secret agent in London
LORD ASHBURY : an agent of the British secret service
THE DUC DE RICHELIEU : a marshal of France
KING LOUIS XV
MADAME DU BARRY : the King's mistress
THE DAUPHIN, later KING LOUIS XVI
MASTER BONTEMPS : senior member of the Company of Notaries Royal
MASTER TIPHAINE : Julie de Lastérieux's notary
MASTER VACHON : a tailor
MONSIEUR de SÉQUEVILLE : the King's secretary with responsibility for ambassadors
MONSIEUR RODOLLET : a public letter-writer
NAGANDA : a Micmac Indian
MONSIEUR TESTARD DU LYS : Criminal Lieutenant of Police
MONSIEUR LENOIR : a State councillor

I

NEAP TIDE

The torch of discord lit by his own hand
Set off a hundred fires in the land.
The anger spread . . .
VOLTAIRE

Thursday 6 January 1774

The carriage narrowly missed him; leaping back, he landed with his feet together in a muddy, viscous puddle of melted snow. The splash sent a foul-smelling spray over him, which started dripping from the point of his tricorn. He cursed under his breath. Another good woollen cloak to take to the cleaner. Ever since his youth in Brittany, Nicolas Le Floch, police commissioner at the Châtelet, had liked to wear practical garments. These days, frock coats were all the rage in Paris, and the kind of warm, heavy cloak he liked was the preserve of cavalry soldiers and travelling merchants. Master Vachon, his regular tailor as well as Monsieur de Sartine's, despairing of his stubborn loyalty to old habits, had nevertheless managed to persuade him to accept a number of extravagances – a particular cut of the collar, buttons on the lower part, a wider flounce, no lining – hoping, without a great deal of conviction, that Nicolas, who was seen both in the city and at Court, would set the fashion.

Nicolas was sure that his low-fronted evening shoes were soaked, their fine gloss soiled, and that there were flecks of mud on his stockings. His cloak would have to suffer the outrage of an over-vigorous cleaning. That might not be too bad as long as the caustic mud did not leave indelible marks on the cloth; however, according to those in the know, it had an unparalleled ability to stick. Come to think of it, it might be better to leave the cloak to the meticulous, affectionate care of Catherine and Marion, the two guardian angels of Monsieur de Noblecourt's house. It was sad to think that Marion, her body twisted with rheumatism, now only presided in a symbolic manner over the household chores, although everyone strove to make her believe that her toil, however derisory, was as necessary as ever to the smooth running of the house.

This petty incident, so common in the streets of the capital, had briefly dispelled his unpleasant reflections. Now the reasons for his vexation, not to say his anger, came back into his mind. Better to think about it now than when he was trying to sleep. What a New Year season it had been! For days, he had been feeling a gnawing sense of anguish. He always dreaded, and never enjoyed, the transition from one year to the next, and should have become accustomed to it by now, but this year everything seemed to be conspiring to ruin it for him. Somehow, though, the old year had ended, and 1774 was here. Epiphany was being celebrated this Thursday, he recalled, but this detail merely increased his irritation.

A crisis in his relationship with Madame de Lastérieux had

been brewing for some time, but truth, like fruit, cannot be harvested until ripe. Anger welled up in him once more, and he stamped his right foot on the ground, again spattering himself with mud. His nose itched, a shiver ran down his spine, and he sneezed several times. That was all he needed: to catch his death of cold, running about like this in the melted snow! He remembered the evening's events . . . Everything pointed to the fact that this liaison had gone on for too long. The vessel of their passion had been drifting along, accompanied by all kinds of incompatibilities and irritations which for a long time had been overshadowed by their physical compatibility. It was a far cry from the harmony of their early days, when the woman had been transfigured in his eyes into an object of worship.

He remembered that evening in February 1773. He had been invited to dinner by Monsieur de Balbastre, the organist of Notre Dame, whom he had known for more than ten years via Monsieur de Noblecourt, a great music lover. Their first encounter, when Nicolas was a young man, had been a humiliating experience for him, but that had been followed by other occasions on which a love of music and a veneration for the great Rameau had drawn them together, despite the sarcastic tone the virtuoso loved to adopt. His drawing room was full of guests going into ecstasies over a Ruckers harpsichord, the pride of the host's collection. Every surface of the instrument, inside and out, had been painted, as meticulously as if it had been a coach, or a snuffbox belonging to a member of a royal household. The outside was decorated with the birth of Venus, and the interior of the lid depicted the story of Castor and Pollux, the subject of Rameau's best-known opera. Earth, hell and Elysium were all shown, and in the last of these the illustrious composer sat enthroned on a bench, lyre in hand. Nicolas, who had seen Rameau in the Tuileries some time before his death, had judged the portrait a fine likeness.

Against one wall of the drawing room stood a large pedal organ, on which Balbastre performed a fugue, all the while deploring the piercing sound of the instrument and the frightful noise of its keys. He needed it for his exercises, he said, adding with a laugh that it drove his neighbours to despair. A young woman with red-tinged hair and a fine, expressive face, made all the more striking by the grey and black widow's clothes she was wearing, cried out in enthusiasm at the organist's virtuosity. As a regular visitor, she was invited to try the harpsichord. She performed a particularly difficult sonata with a great deal of feeling, after which the host took over and played an air by Grétry. The sound of the instrument struck Nicolas as delicate and somewhat lacking in power. He asked the young woman about this, and she explained that the touch was very light because of the use of plectra made from quills. They continued talking, and both left the house at the same time. Nicolas offered to see her home in his carriage. By the time they reached Rue de Verneuil, where she had a large house, Nicolas was already a happy man, having completed the preliminaries. The moments that followed, after she had invited him in to admire a pianoforte in her possession, sealed their alliance. The next few weeks were a whirl of embraces and kisses and languor, and, although they were followed by long periods of absence and impatience, it did not look as though anything would ever put an end to the insatiable hunger that united them.

*

What, after all, did Nicolas have to reproach her with? Her beauty was undeniable: thanks to the young Dauphine – and despite the passionate efforts of Madame du Barry, the King's official mistress – blonde hair with a tinge of red had come back into fashion. Julie de Lastérieux's conversation was witty and ornate, and she charmed everyone with the range of topics she could speak on and the originality of the views she expressed. At a young age, directly after leaving her convent school, she had married a navy steward many years her senior, who had been appointed as a financial official in Guadeloupe. Entry into the King's service had ennobled Monsieur de Lastérieux, who had had the good manners to die almost as soon as he set foot in the West Indies. His widow had been left comfortably provided for, and she had returned to Paris in the company of two black servants.

Even though by nature she tended to wax enthusiastic about everything indiscriminately, when she was with Nicolas she took care to observe a certain reserve, tinged with tender admiration, which impressed him more than any assertion of will. Nevertheless, causes for irritation emerged between them. At first, while their passion was still aflame, these rifts were more than made up for by the delight of their reconciliations. As the months passed, however, these repeated skirmishes grew wearisome. The bones of contention were always the same. She would constantly proclaim that she hoped he would come and live with her. He would refuse, sensing behind this request another unformulated demand which he preferred not to acknowledge. Every time they quarrelled, she would complain about his absences, his enslavement to a profession which so often left him unavailable. He was also endlessly having to tell her not to introduce him as the Marquis de Ranreuil. What he, as an illegitimate son only belatedly recognised, could accept from the King and the members of the royal family as an honour, his pride and sense of decorum rejected from anyone else. He knew how desperate she was to appear at Court, and how much their relationship encouraged her pretensions, and this desire of hers embarrassed him, as if it were something unseemly, a lapse of taste. Last but not least, he could not conceal his annoyance and sadness at Julie's successive attempts to distance him from his closest friends, apart from Monsieur de La Borde, First Groom of the King's Bedchamber, to whom every virtue was attributed due to his access to the monarch and his personal prestige. A dinner at Monsieur de Noblecourt's house had proved a disaster. Despite the effort they had made for Nicolas's sake, neither the former procurator nor Doctor Semacgus had managed to cheer the young woman. It had taught him never to bring together those he loved, and he was tormented by the idea that his choice did not meet with their approval. As soon as this thought had insinuated itself into his mind, his devotion to her had suffered a fatal blow, and he had realised with a sense of dread that you could not continue to love someone if you were unable to excuse that person's faults.

The silent dismay of those closest to him had saddened Nicolas, although for a long time he had refused to draw the appropriate conclusions. But eventually he had had to accept that the relationship had been a mistake, and that Madame de Lastérieux was not worthy of him. He had immediately felt it as a blow to his pride that he had yielded to a creature he could not respect – for which there was nobody to blame but himself – but then, although ashamed of loving her, had told himself that she still loved him. What had happened this evening, though, had been the last straw. Why had he agreed to that intimate dinner? Of course, he knew perfectly well why . . . Accepting her invitation had obliged him to reject Monsieur de Noblecourt, who had planned to share a Twelfth Night cake this evening with some friends: Nicolas, Semacgus, Inspector Bourdeau, and even, if his duties to the King allowed him, Monsieur de La Borde. It was with a heavy heart that Nicolas had had to decline.

When he had arrived at the house in Rue de Verneuil late that afternoon he had found, much to his surprise, that a merry company had already gathered. He was irritated by the ironic pout with which Madame de Lastérieux expressed her dismay at seeing him arrive so early, and by the announcement that there would be a dozen people for dinner, some of whom were already there. Abandoning him, she ran, laughing, to turn the page for a young man who was playing the pianoforte. Balbastre came and greeted him, his plump, outrageously made-up face creased with irony, his dark eyes devoid of warmth. Four strangers, all young, were playing cards at a precious Coromandel lacquer table. Apart from the organist, who was a regular visitor, Nicolas was the oldest person there. He felt a twinge of bitterness, and then immediately reproached himself. It was absurd: why should a young woman in her twenties make him feel as though he were playing the role of some greybeard in a play, some Alceste surrounded by young dandies? He leant back against a window.

The angular face of the young man sitting at the pianoforte intrigued him: it seemed to conjure a vague, faded image from the distant past, like the face of a drowned man coming to the surface from the deep. Everything was conspiring to make him feel uneasy. And why hadn't she introduced him to her guests? One more wound to his pride, to be added to the growing list of daily snubs. Casimir and Julia, her two servants from the West Indies, served syrup, chocolate and macaroons, and a delicious beverage which Nicolas had enjoyed on other, more intimate occasions: a clever mixture of sugar syrup and white rum to which Julia added a slice of bergamot peel and a few drops of a special potion – whenever asked what it contained, she would always laugh loudly and refuse to divulge the secret.

Soon after he arrived, he saw the young man take a book of drinking songs from his coat. Could it be that he was feeling jealous? Julie leant over the young man's shoulder and threw her head back in a throaty laugh. She cast Nicolas a mocking glance and beckoned him to her. What did she want? When he reached her, she stood up.

'Monsieur, go and prepare some eggnog for me, my mouth is so dry and I need refreshment.'

She underlined her request by striking him with her lace fan. The aggressiveness of this gesture seemed to Nicolas to open a rift between them. It had happened in the presence of a witness – that provocative-looking young man – and the tone was quite unacceptable. Not to mention the fact that she had revealed a secret of their private life: the eggnog he had prepared for her every night in the early days of their relationship. He had been patient long enough. Now he lost control, unable to conceal his anger.

'Madame, I shall inform the servants of your wish. I bid you good evening.'

She was staring at him, the lower half of her face stretched taut in a half-smile, her eyes hard. The assembled company had fallen silent. Nicolas bowed and strode across the room so brusquely that he knocked Balbastre's glass out of his hand and did not even apologise. He threw his cloak over his shoulders, did not wait for Casimir to open the door for him, ran down the steps four at a time, and plunged into the cold and snowy Rue de Verneuil. He had no idea where to go, and stamped frantically on the cobbles. It was at that moment that a carriage had loomed up and he had regained a sense of reality.

His first impulse was to dash to Rue Montmartre and join his friends. He soon changed his mind: it was not fitting, either for him or for them, to make them feel that he was only seeking out their company so that his evening would not be totally ruined. Such an attitude did not sit well with the esteem and respect he had for them. He looked at his repeater watch. It had been a gift from Madame Adélaïde, the King's daughter, to thank him for retrieving her stolen jewels during an investigation. It was Monsieur Caron de Beaumarchais, watchmaker and factotum to the King's daughters, who had delivered it to him. A lively character, to whom Nicolas had taken a liking, he had explained the workings of the watch, which rang the hours and the minutes with two different chimes, and given him a great deal of advice: always close the lid – which bore a delicate portrait of the princess – carefully rather than snapping it shut, always wind the mechanism slowly, never leave the precious object on cold marble. Surprised by this, Nicolas had asked why, and had learnt that the cold froze the oil in the mechanism and stopped the cogs from moving. He pressed on a spring, and heard six deep strokes, followed by six crystalline strokes: it was six thirty. On the corner of Rue de Beaune, he was jostled good-naturedly by a group of musketeers out for a good time, who had just left the nearby barracks.[1]

He reflected for a moment, unsure where to go. No, he was definitely too unhappy to show his face in Rue Montmartre. For some time now, he had been wanting to see the rising new star of the Théâtre-Français, Mademoiselle Raucourt.[2] Her debut a year earlier in the role of Dido had been a sensation, and had been duly reported as such in *Le Mercure* and *La Gazette*. No other actress in living memory had made such an impression: she was not yet eighteen, and was pretty as a picture, with a voice that was said to be enchanting, an exceptional bearing and a prodigious intelligence in her approach to her roles. Nicolas would go and watch tonight's play: it would distract him from his worries, and no doubt he would glean in passing some spicy or edifying titbit which would delight Monsieur de Sartine the next day.

The snow had turned to freezing rain by the time he passed the dark mass of the Pont Royal water pump. The lanterns along the right bank of the river and the terrace of the Tuileries glowed feebly through the damp air. Having a permanent pass, he knocked at the window of the guardroom and identified himself. The guard, grumbling at being disturbed in his enjoyment of a mulled wine which had coloured his white moustache red, opened the gate. As soon as he was in the gardens, Nicolas regretted taking this short cut. Instead of making things easier for himself, he found himself in a vast snowy expanse in which all the paths had disappeared. Now he was going to ruin his shoes – a particularly annoying thought, since they were as comfortable as felt slippers, and allowed him to stand for hours on end without feeling any tightness or fatigue. It would have been more sensible to take the longer way round through the colonnades of the Louvre. In the calm of the evening, he could have got the measure of the improvements the city authorities were making in the area, clearing the square and driving out the market stalls that had cluttered it for so many years. The plan was that when the ground had been properly levelled, it would be covered with a series of enclosed lawns which would be pleasant to the eye and permit a clear view of the Point-du-Jour.

The great dark masses of the statues helped him to get his bearings, and he waded in a more or less straight line towards the gate to the swing bridge. At the end of the path, he bumped into Nicolas Coustou's great statue of Caesar. The octagonal basin faced him, its waters glimmering faintly in the darkness. He had to veer right to get to Passage de l'Orangerie and from there reach the Théâtre-Français. For many years, the company had performed at the Étoile tennis court in Rue des Fossés-Saint-Germain. In 1770, the building being on the verge of collapse, the theatre had moved to Servandoni's machine room in the Tuileries, left vacant after the Opéra had been rebuilt in the Palais-Royal. Nicolas shared the opinion of the many critics who judged the layout of this temporary theatre ill suited to its purpose.

The performance was about to start. He was greeted at the box office like a regular visitor: he was often on duty there, especially when the theatre was attended by members of the royal family or foreign monarchs who wished to remain incognito. In the foyer, his attention was drawn to an animated group dominated by the tall figure of his colleague, old Chorrey, the second oldest member of the police force. He walked up to the group. A sallow-faced man in a threadbare serge jacket was being held by two French Guards while Chorrey frisked him and placed his finds on a baluster console.

'And you claim to be innocent, eh? Your clothes are like a fence's shop in the Temple! Look, here's Le Floch! You've come just at the right moment, my friend. You're not on duty, though, are you? Or have I got it wrong?'

'No, my dear fellow. I'm here as a customer.'

'Well, you're going to get your money's worth! This blackguard has his pockets full. Two gold watches, one bronze watch, a double Barbette *louis*, six English guineas. These, too . . .' He held up some coins. 'Three ducats from Berne, a silver ducat from Venice, a few old French crowns. The whole of Europe seems to be here tonight to see La Raucourt. You're for the galleys!'

The man was shaking, as if stricken with a fever.

'Find me the lieutenant of the guards,' Chorrey said to one of the theatre attendants, 'and be quick about it.'

Nicolas was surprised that an old policeman with more than forty years' service should not make the distinction between a lieutenant of the guards, in other words, the bodyguards, and a lieutenant *in* the Guards, in other words, an officer of the French Guards. He immediately reproached himself for his judgement, realising that his colleague was not as familiar as he was with the Court and its subtleties. The lieutenant, an arrogant-looking fellow, arrived and listened nervously as the commissioner instructed him to take the culprit into custody and to inform the watch to come for him and take him to the Châtelet. Chorrey abruptly turned his back on the officer and drew Nicolas into the auditorium.

'That impostor infuriates me. I suppose he's too high-born to consider being polite. To think we have to suffer the snubs of a boudoir dandy like that!'

They took their seats in a box on the left-hand side, with a view of the whole of the auditorium, whose strange layout recalled its original purpose. Amidst a rustle of fabrics and creaking of floorboards, it was gradually filling up in the semi-darkness.

'Look, the Prince de Conti is here again. The old rogue! He has his eyes on the new girl. He wants her for his collection!'

'Yes, the young girls in the royal theatres are easy prey,' said Nicolas. 'They enjoy, as you know, a very particular privilege. They escape the authority of their parents, and the men who keep them are exempt from all prosecution.'

'You're telling me! I've lost count of those I have seen start like that and finish up amongst the criminal classes. For the moment, her air of decency and reputation for chastity have made her sought after by the greatest ladies, who smother her in jewels and clothes, overjoyed no doubt that this rare creature is no rival. Besides, her old father is still about, keeping his eye open for trouble. Will it last? Let's wait for the last act. In any case, she's a true prodigy, enough to make the most consummate of her rivals die of vexation.'

'You've certainly been around a long time,' said Nicolas. 'More than forty years, I believe?'

'Forty-three, to be exact. Time enough to get a little weary.'

'But what adventures! We're never bored in our profession.'

'Well, that depends,' said Chorrey, scratching his head under his wig. 'I've always preferred criminal work, much more diverting than civil cases. At the beginning of my career, I was constantly being sent to do house searches, day and night. After that, I seemed to spend all my time keeping an eye on usurers, swindlers and pawnbrokers, before they started the Mont-de-Piété. Some pretty terrible characters there, I can tell you!'

'But that's all routine!' said Nicolas. 'You must surely have seen some more extraordinary events?'

'Yes, of course. In 1757, the then Lieutenant General of Police, the worthy predecessor of Monsieur de Sartine—'

'Who holds you in great esteem.'

Chorrey blushed at the compliment. 'I'm pleased to hear it. As I was saying, in 1757 I knocked myself out going all over the Arras and Saint-Omer regions and the whole province of Artois, searching out and questioning the relatives of Damiens, the King's would-be assassin. In 1760, I constantly had to deal with thefts from theatres. That led me to a storehouse full of stolen goods in Briare: a mountain of purses, watches, snuffboxes and all kinds of coins. Finally, last year, I went with a company of grenadiers from Enghien, garrisoned at Sedan, to visit the printing works and bookshops in Bouillon and look for banned books.'

'Such is the cross we bear!' said Nicolas with a sigh. 'Constantly searching for a needle in a haystack!'

*

The footlights had just been lit, and the three knocks interrupted their conversation. The evening's play was *Athalie* by Racine. Knowing the work all too well, Nicolas soon found his attention wandering, the details of the actors' performances proving more arresting than the plot. The newcomer certainly had an attractive countenance, although it was her partner, Lekain, playing the role of Abner to perfection, who impressed him more with his supreme skill: through some miracle of artifice, his prodigious ugliness disappeared and his stern, forbidding expression grew softer. Part of the audience, however, seemed to resent Mademoiselle Raucourt for taking a role in which Mademoiselle Dumesnil and La Clairon had won fame. For weeks now, Monsieur de Sartine's spies had been reporting that a cabal had been organised by Mademoiselle Vestris. A member of the famous dynasty of dancers as well as of the Théâtre-Français, Mademoiselle Vestris was protected by the Duc de Choiseul, still in exile in Chanteloup since his disgrace, and by the Duc de Duras. These highly placed contacts were the basis of her self-importance and capacity to create trouble.

Suddenly, a cat was heard miaowing. Whether the cat belonged to the establishment or had been surreptitiously brought in, the effect of the animal's cry was extraordinary: the actors stopped in astonishment, and the youngest members of the choir were swept up in a fit of laughter that spread to the audience. The laughter reached its height when a young man in the stalls cried out in a bright, nasal voice, 'I wager that's Mademoiselle Vestris's cat.'

Hilarity swelled in the auditorium like a wave. Lekain imposed silence and was about to resume the performance when something else interrupted his flow. A man stood up in the stalls and leapt over the footlights on to the stage. There, shoving the actors who tried to drag him away, he declared that his name was Billard and that he had come to Paris to present a play of his own composition entitled *The Seducer*. This work, he said, had been praised by a number of men of taste but rejected by the ham actors in this theatre. The audience, amused by this second interlude, were listening so attentively that he was encouraged to continue.

He was so tired of being repeatedly rejected, he said, that he had decided to declare open war on the present company. He would denounce its bad taste, condemn its members to a thousand misfortunes, and pride himself on no longer having to depend on such judges. He appealed to the spectators in the stalls: he would read his play to them and, if they judged it worthy, that would force this unworthy assembly to accept it. When they tried to prevent him, he brandished his sword, which was soon torn from him by a French Guard. A confused mass of soldiers and theatre employees dragged him by force into the foyer.

The performance resumed immediately, in order to put an end to the commotion as quickly as possible, but a unanimous cry rose from the stalls, acclaiming the author. The clamour grew and the French Guards came back in force, arresting several spectators. There was an indescribable hullaballoo as members of the audience stood firm, and blows were exchanged.

Nicolas hurried out after Commissioner Chorrey, who had turned crimson and was puffing and blowing. They came out into the foyer to find the author standing on a chair, reading his play to the guards, who were highly amused. When the watch arrived,

Chorrey ordered the officer to conduct the culprit to the madhouse at Charenton, pending further information. This sequence of events had been a great distraction to Nicolas's wounded soul, chasing away the anger and resentment. There was no point in his staying any longer, he thought. He had seen and heard enough of Mademoiselle Raucourt. Certain rather unnatural vocal effects of hers seemed to him to spoil the charms of her appearance and the elegance of her acting. In fact, at moments, it became so rough, hoarse and excessive as to destroy the music of the verse. He took his leave of Chorrey, who made him promise to come to dinner as soon as possible at his little house in Rue Maquignonne, near the police pavilion at the horse market. Nicolas recalled having been present, a dozen years earlier, while still an apprentice in the profession, at the inauguration, by Monsieur de Sartine, of this elegant building. He recalled, too, that Chorrey had a solid fortune, which he had inherited from his father, a horse dealer.

The cold and damp of the night revived his anguish. Once again, as had so often happened in his youth, Nicolas found himself incapable of keeping his imagination in check. Left to itself, it would run wild, stubbornly heading down any path that presented itself, and he would be unable to rest until he had explored them all. It was a kind of mental itch, which he tried to dismiss, but in vain. The slightest upset or vexation, and it returned as strong as ever. If only he could take the middle way, see things in all their simplicity, and accept every fleeting moment of happiness for what it was! Monsieur de Noblecourt, being the honest man that he was, had promised him the cure: wisdom would come with age and the waning of the passions.

Nicolas forced himself to reflect coolly on the current situation. How absurd to make a drama out of a woman's caprice! A woman on her own, separated from her lover most of the time because of his work, as coquettish as the rest of her sex, susceptible to the attentions of idle young men, and perhaps driven to make him jealous as the only means of gauging the strength of his feelings for her. And he had flown into a rage at the smallest provocation as if he were her lord and master, and had over-dramatised what should only have been a little quarrel intended to reinvigorate their love for each other. He decided to give Julie a surprise and return unexpectedly. No sooner had this idea come into his head than the desire to see her again took him over completely. He hailed a cab in Rue Saint-Honoré, and was driven across a frozen, deserted Paris as far as Rue de Verneuil. He added such a generous tip to the fare that the astonished coachman called him 'Monseigneur'.

He looked up. The lights were still on in the windows of Madame de Lastérieux's house, and he could see shadows dancing. His ardour cooled: he had imagined that the house would be empty and dark and his lover tired and ready for bed. But perhaps there was still hope. When he got to the first floor, however, and opened the door with his key, he heard loud laughter and the clinking of glasses. Disappointment overwhelmed him like nausea. How wrong he had been to think that the party had been cut short simply because he had left in a hurry!

Casimir appeared, carrying a tray. Nicolas retreated into a dark corner. When Casimir came back out of the servants' pantry, his arms were laden with bottles. With an unaccustomed, but welcome, sense of pettiness, Nicolas remembered the bottle of old Tokay from Hungary he had acquired at no small cost from the Austrian ambassador's butler: the fellow supplemented his wages by selling wine from his country that had been brought in in his master's baggage, as well as supplying Monsieur de Sartine with interesting information. Julie loved that wine as an accompaniment to truffles, quail and *pâté de foie gras* in the manner of the Maréchal de Soubise. Nicolas decided to recover the bottle, which he had placed in the servants' pantry that afternoon. Fortunately, it was still there: doubtless, the veil of dust and spiders' webs that covered it and the dirty dishes piled around it had prevented it from being used during that evening's banquet. He slipped it into the inside pocket of his cloak: he had made up his mind to go to Rue Montmartre after all, and there was no point in arriving there empty-handed. He turned, and there, leaning on the doorpost, his right hand on his hip, looking at him mockingly, was the young man who had been playing the pianoforte. Where the devil had he seen that face before? Nicolas walked out past him, shoving him slightly as he did so. Casimir watched in surprise as he raced down the stairs like a madman.

He wandered for a long time along the *quais*, in the darkness and the mud, accosted at times by whores with toothless mouths uttering obscenities and disgusting propositions. In one of them, excessively made up and with her nose missing, he thought he recognised old Émilie, a ghost from his past, who cut meat from the carcasses of horses in the knacker's yard at Montfaucon to use in the soup she sold. The memory of the old woman cast him into a whirlpool of images and faces, amongst which the face of the young man in Rue de Verneuil kept coming back like an obsession. He stopped to drink some vile rotgut in a smoky tavern, and after many detours found himself in Rue Montmartre, outside Monsieur de Noblecourt's house.

The servants' pantry was so untidy, it was clear the party was a lively one. He shook his head bitterly. This, then, was what his evening boiled down to: rebuffs, escapes, visits to kitchens. A tremendous din of words and laughter was coming from the first floor, dominated by the bass voice of Guillaume Semacgus. Reaching the half-open door of the library, where the table usually stood, he stopped and rested his burning forehead against the wood, the smell of polish filling his nostrils, and listened to what his friends were saying.

'Faced with such a wonder,' Semacgus was proclaiming, 'it is necessary to proceed with the most consummate care. Making a long incision would let in too much air from outside and the contact with the air escaping might well upset a fragile equilibrium and cause the whole thing to collapse. I'm reminded of an operation I once performed in the middle of a storm off Ile Bourbon. It was a trepanation, and the meningeal part—'

'Pah!' said Monsieur de Noblecourt. 'There speaks the navy surgeon! Whatever is he about to tell us? I fear it may detract from our pleasure. What do you think, La Borde?'

'The King,' replied La Borde, 'excels at this kind of operation. He's both decisive and gentle. It's just like softening up a courtesan.'

'Hush now, you rogue!' said the former procurator, spluttering with merriment. 'There are ladies present. At my age, I'm not as firm as I used to be and my hand trembles.'

'Upon my word as a navy surgeon, there's a statement intended to be moral, but which makes the image all the saucier!'

'Nicolas would have opened it for you in no time at all,' said Bourdeau. 'You just have to make up your mind. To delay too long would spoil its excellence and soften the inner layers.'

'Ah, yes, we do miss our Nicolas,' sighed Monsieur de Noblecourt. 'But he's in love and, being so delicate in his feelings, *too much* is not yet *enough* for him.'

'Our friend,' grunted Semacgus, 'was a livelier companion when he was seeing the young lady in Rue Saint-Honoré.'

A silence followed this allusion to La Satin, the love of Nicolas's youth, who was now in charge of the Dauphin Couronné. The ties of tenderness that had bound them had never entirely loosened. Nicolas was surprised that they were so familiar with his private life, and comforted to sense no sharpness in their words, but on the contrary a thoughtful and indulgent demonstration of their affection for him.

'Come on, now,' said La Borde. 'While waiting for the return of the prodigal son who doesn't know what he's missing, let the magistracy do its work. Ladies, proceed!'

Intrigued by the noises he heard, Nicolas peered through the crack in the door. The scene which presented itself to his gaze reminded him of those so much admired by art lovers at the annual Salons: a vision of an enclosed interior, whose harmony seemed to enhance an enjoyment of the pleasures of nature and society. This charming moment of intimacy was softly illumined by the light from slender candles. In this fine room, three walls of which were covered in light wooden bookcases filled with precious volumes, the four guests sat at an oval table adorned with a silver centrepiece depicting the Abduction of Omphale. Poitevin always polished this object with maniacal care and grumbled whenever a public holiday or special occasion provided an excuse to display it on the table, like the monstrance in a dazzling culinary liturgy. Two candlesticks, also silver, flanked this showpiece. La Borde, Semacgus and Bourdeau were watching as Monsieur de Noblecourt, wearing a large Regency wig and a black coat with jet buttons, prepared to initiate a curious ceremony.

Poitevin stood motionless by the sideboard, holding in his hands a bottle just taken from a cooling pitcher, his eyes fixed on the monumental tower of golden pastry that had been placed before his master. Sitting on a *bergère* by the window, her chin resting on the pommel of her stick, Marion watched spellbound. Finally, like two Levites assisting the high priest, Awa, Semacgus's African maid, and Catherine Gauss stood holding between them a thin cloth which they gradually lowered over Monsieur de Noblecourt's head as he bent to find the best spot at which to cut into the golden splendour. The point of the sharp knife entered the crust, and the religious silence was broken by a kind of hiss, followed by a deep intake of breath from the magistrate and an almost voluptuous moan of pleasure. A cheer went up from the assembled company. Marion, doubtless the inspiration if not the architect of this success, sighed with satisfaction. Poitevin brought the bottle and began serving. The two cooks carefully folded the cloth and the guests applauded the perfection of the ceremonial gesture. With a nimbleness of which he would not have been thought capable, the high priest cut a small hole in the pastry and was making ready to plunge the fork into the well of wonders when Semacgus, who was watching, stopped him.

'What were you planning to do? You wouldn't by any chance be thinking of digging into the soft crust to extract the splendours it contains, would you, Monsieur? What about your gout? Do you intend, in the teeth of the Faculty, to extinguish the fire of a good humour that delights your friends, all for the vain pleasure of a greed which will cause your hands, knees and feet to suffer for days? Do you set at nought the pain and sorrow of Marion, author of this bastion of succulence on which you are about to launch an attack as if you were a young blade? It can only lead to a resurgence of your rheumatism, followed by an attack of melancholy for which, Monsieur, I shall hold you entirely responsible. Was it not agreed that we would grant you the unique privilege of breathing in the first odours coming from this dish, a privilege that leaves us weak with envy, having ourselves to be content only with the heaviness of the quintessential products?'

'I would happily burden myself with that quintessence!' With a contrite expression, Monsieur de Noblecourt teased the hidden treasures of the culinary fortress with the end of his fork. 'This is really cruel,' he muttered, 'and reminds me of the old Parisian story about a seller of roast meats who, when he demands payment from a customer, is paid with the mere clinking of coins. Well, I just have to resign myself to this sacrifice, I suppose, but I do ask one favour: let me taste a tiny bit of this treasure. A little piece of truffle, for example. It's only a mushroom after all.'

'No, no!' replied Semacgus. 'Even a little piece of truffle can cause constipation! I suggest a piece of pastry, although even that's too much.'

'A curse on old age! It deprives us of everything. Even when the spirit is willing, the body is weak. Does that mean we have to renounce these delights, compared with which our neighbours' recipes are mere cheap nothings more easily tolerated amongst the Mangageats[3] than in a refined climate like ours where cleanliness, delicacy and good taste are, alas, the true object of our zeal?'

'Philosophise as much as you like, Monsieur, you won't win us round,' murmured Semacgus.

Monsieur de Noblecourt slowly savoured the spoils of war, as Catherine cut the smoking fortress into four.

'Why four pieces?' he asked in surprise. 'Have you forgotten that I'm condemned not to have any of it?'

'What?' Marion said, equally surprised. 'Have *you* forgotten the poor man's portion? A fine Christian you are! Church warden of Saint-Eustache, to boot! And besides, what if I wanted to keep part of it for Nicolas? I'll cover the plate and put it on a corner of the oven. That'll keep it warm but won't make it too dry. He needs something to sustain him with all the running about he does!'

'It's too much for an ingrate who so often deserts our banquets,' protested Semacgus.

Monsieur de Noblecourt threw him a stern look. 'Weren't you young once? And have we done all we could to try and understand him and support him in a difficult situation?'

To divert them, Marion spoke up, her face flushing. 'If Monsieur so desires, I'll tell you my recipe.'

'Go on. The telling is often as succulent as the eating.'

The old cook threw a sideways glance at Monsieur La Borde. 'First, I must tell you that I got the recipe from Monsieur there.'

The cries of the guest covered her voice. La Borde, feigning embarrassment, hid his face in his napkin. He assumed a pitiful tone. 'Merely an attempt to relieve the austerity of my host's life. And besides, this recipe is not even mine. Its author is His Royal Highness Louis-Auguste de Bourbon, Prince de Dombes, governor of Languedoc.'

'Good Lord!' said Bourdeau sardonically. 'A grandson of the great Bourbon, no less!'

'This promises a fine diversion!' said Monsieur de Noblecourt. 'After the aroma, the recitation of my cook's fine deeds, then my guests feasting, and all I get is a wretched piece of pastry!'

Marion smiled, allowed them their joke, then took advantage of a short silence to resume speaking, anxious to play a role in this celebration.

'I make some very thin shortcrust pastry,' she began, 'and while I'm letting it cool, I prepare the stuffing: *foie gras* with a lot of grated bacon, parsley, chives, mushrooms and chopped truffles. It's better to do this early, that way it'll taste better. I open a few dozen green oysters from Cancale, as many as I need, whiten them in their own water and drain them in a sieve to keep the liquid. Then I put the stuffing in the bottom of the mould, with a layer of oysters over it, and so on. I cover the whole thing with a sheet of pastry brushed with egg to make it turn golden. When the oven's quite hot, I put it in and let it bake as long as necessary. Meanwhile . . .' – and here she pointed to a silver sauce dish – 'I make a sauce with the water from the oysters, to which I add two pieces of bread with melted butter from Vanvres and finely chopped herbs. Then I season it with lemon juice. It's a matter of taste, but I find it makes the stuffing nice and moist and gives the oysters their natural flavour back.'

'And what's the name of this marvel?' asked Noblecourt, his eyes bulging with desire. 'I didn't know Marion could describe her culinary dexterity in such a poetic fashion.'

'Ungrateful wretch!' said Semacgus. 'She's been serving him for forty years and he's only just discovered how good she is!'

'Forty-three, to be precise,' said Marion modestly. 'But, to answer Monsieur, the name is *tour farcie aux huîtres vertes*. I should add that the secret lies in the shortcrust pastry, which is kneaded for such a long time that it appears quite light and flaky but is actually firm enough to hold the stuffing.'

'It's true,' said La Borde with a smile, 'that to hear it talked about is to eat it twice.'

'I wonder,' said Semacgus, 'if just hearing this recitation won't reawaken our host's gout? That would be the revenge of Comus!'

They all burst out laughing. Nicolas listened to them, feeling sad and happy at the same time. It was strange to be witnessing this feast without his friends being aware of his presence. He could not bring himself to open the door and cross the threshold into the light. The fever was building in him, making him shiver, clutching at his temples. He was assailed by contradictory feelings: the sadness which went through him in waves, a kind of nostalgia for a past which would never come again, and the temptation to sleep and forget. He tried to get a grip on himself by concentrating hard on the conversation, which was as lively as ever.

'For a long time,' said La Borde, 'His Majesty cooked dinner for his guests and served it himself in his small apartments. If Nicolas were here, he'd be able to confirm it. The King once served him a whole plate of chicken wings, delighted to see that young Ranreuil, as he's in the habit of calling him, shared his predilection for this delicious dish.'

'How is the King?' asked Noblecourt gravely.

'Both well and ill. He acts like a young man, but feels the fatigues of old age creeping up on him.'

'Come on, I'm ten years older than he is and I feel like—'

'Like a man whose friends protect him from the temptations and foolishness which would kill many stronger men,' said Semacgus.

'You're a fine one to talk!'

'Even I, Monsieur, have been forcing myself to be more careful. I hope to be able to enjoy life as long as you have.'

'There you have it,' said La Borde. 'The King is not reasonable, and the lady takes advantage of the fact, constantly arousing his remaining passions. She's not La Pompadour and has no political ambitions, but she places her influence at the service of those who do have them.'

This was a clear allusion to the First Minister, the Duc d'Aiguillon, and was greeted with applause. La Borde sighed.

Nicolas recalled that his friend had quarrelled recently with La Guimard, the mistress he shared with the Prince de Soubise. The prince had demanded an end to a situation which had previously suited everyone, on the pretext that Monsieur de La Borde had given the actress a venereal disease, and she had given it to the prince, who had transmitted it to the Comtesse de l'Hospital and she to someone else, the chain of cause and effect swallowed up in the complex web of Court and city liaisons. La Borde had confided to Nicolas that he had been treated, on the advice of the Maréchal de Biron, a colonel in the French Guards, with anti-venereal pills supplied by a quack named Keyser, a remedy which the old soldier had tried out on those of his men who had been corrupted by the city.

'Is it true,' asked Noblecourt, 'that Madame du Barry paid twenty thousand *livres* for a full-length Van Dyck portrait of Charles I of England, and placed it opposite the King's portrait to remind him of the fate in store for him if he yields to the *parlements*?'

'I don't know if that's the correct explanation. But the portrait is certainly there, and I have often admired it. The idea may have been d'Aiguillon's, hoping to appeal to my master's morbid tastes. Whatever the truth of the matter, the sight of the painting always makes me uneasy. The fact is, the King is weary. He needs a stepping stone to get on his horse these days. He's thinking of using that private carriage invented by the Comte d'Eu when he found himself physically unable to hunt: it turns on a pivot and allows the user to follow all the movements of the prey. And he's always filled with grim thoughts.'

'My friend the Maréchal de Richelieu,' said Noblecourt, tipping his wig slightly in honour of this great name, 'told me that last November, during a game of whist at the Comtesse du Barry's, the Marquis de Chauvelin, feeling unwell, leant back against the Maréchale de Mirepoix's armchair and made a joke. Suddenly, His Majesty noticed that his face was all twisted. At that very moment, he fell to the floor, dead.'

'That's right,' said La Borde. 'They tried to help him, but in vain. His Majesty was quite affected by it all, especially as his old friend was only fifty-seven. Soon after that, alarmed by some slight health problem, the King spoke frankly to his First Surgeon, in whom he has great confidence. He told him how worried he was about the sorry state of his health. "I see that I am no longer so young," he said, "I have to slow down." "Sire," La Martinière replied, "you would do even better to stop."'

A long silence fell, as if each man were weighing the gravity and implications of these words. Nicolas felt as if his whole body were sweating. That was what happened, he thought, when you rushed around madly in the cold and dark. Suddenly, he slid to the floor, and the venerable bottle of Tokay fell from his hand and smashed to pieces. Cyrus, the old water spaniel dozing at his master's feet, rose at this noise and started howling loudly. Everyone ran out, except Monsieur de Noblecourt who tried to rise from his armchair, his face pale, his body trembling, his eyes filled with panic.

II

SUSPICION

'Lord,' replies the knight, 'I see that I must talk of my shame and my pain . . . in order to prove my loyalty.'
BOOK OF THE GRAIL

Friday 7 January 1774

Through the misty clouds that enveloped everything, Nicolas vaguely distinguished the faces of three greybeards shaking their heads and looking at a fourth who was muttering indistinctly, his head covered with a towel. A little old lady, her features obscured by thick black lace, was cutting a Twelfth Night cake with what looked like a billhook. When they were served, the four guests got down to eating their portions of the feast, which seemed to be difficult to chew. This activity was punctuated with brief, inarticulate words. Suddenly, the man whose head was concealed let out a brief cry, plunged his hand beneath the towel, and took out a black charm. Nicolas was wondering about the meaning of this scene when the old man with the hidden face struggled to his feet, seized a crown in his gloved hand, and raised it to his cranium. At the same time, the towel fell, revealing, to Nicolas's horror, a death's head, now crowned, laughing and staring at him with its empty eye sockets. The old woman removed her lace and he saw, with an increased feeling of dread, that her emaciated body bore, as if detached from it, the exquisite powdered head of Madame du Barry. He cried out and closed his eyes to dismiss the image . . .

'Hold him still, Bourdeau, he's moving about so much he's going to fall.'

'He's having a nightmare.'

Semacgus took Nicolas's pulse and placed his hand on his forehead. 'Seems like it. The fever's fallen and the pulse is back to normal. Awa's herbs are invaluable when dealing with these violent attacks. I congratulate myself every day that I stocked up well before I left Saint-Louis.'

'All the same, he's been sleeping for twelve hours,' Bourdeau said, glancing at a large brass watch. 'It's nearly one in the afternoon. Do you think he's strong enough to bear the news?'

'Without any doubt. Given the situation, we can't just let him lie here. You said yourself we ought to wake him.'

'What else can we do, Semacgus? Monsieur de Sartine has asked to see him as soon as possible at police headquarters. All the same, I wonder if we ought to leave it to Sartine to tell him the truth.'

'That's a worse risk than the one we want to avoid, blunt as we are. I'm of a mind to ask Monsieur de Noblecourt to talk to him with his usual calm and wisdom.'

'At your service,' said the former procurator. He was standing behind them, out of breath from climbing the small private staircase leading to Nicolas's lodgings. 'Leave me with him, but first do me a favour and move this armchair closer to the bed.'

'He's opening his eyes,' said Bourdeau. 'We'll leave you to it.'

*

Nicolas regained consciousness, and the sight of the familiar setting brought him back to reality. Monsieur de Noblecourt's grave countenance told him that something was wrong. He remembered the expression on Canon Le Floch's face when he had announced to him, many years earlier, his final departure from Guérande, and saw the same worried expression, the same affectionate thoughtfulness on the familiar features bending over him.

'Hello, Nicolas.'

'Have I been sleeping long?'

'Longer than you may think. It's Friday now, and nearly two o'clock in the afternoon. You lost consciousness last night at the door of my library. My friends found you bathing in Tokay. I can think of better uses for a wine like that.'

'It was meant as a gift for you, to beg forgiveness for deserting the party. I know how ungrateful you must have thought me.'

'No such feeling could ever exist between us. You are at home here. The wind of Rue Montmartre liberates. I remember saying to you, when you first came to this house, that it was an annexe of the abbey of Thélème, where freedom and independence were revered.'

He underlined these words with a nod of the head. He gave a slight smile, and his large red nose wrinkled in satisfaction.

'What happened to you?' he went on. 'Your coat stank of cheap brandy, and was as dirty and as muddy as a stray puppy on Quai Pelletier. You must have been moving about a lot, to get yourself in a state so contrary to your habits and the dignity of your office.'

'Alas, you are only too right,' said Nicolas, feeling like a pupil before his master, 'and I shan't weary you with an account of my evening.'

Monsieur de Noblecourt was looking at him with eyes as sharp as they had been in the old days, when he was involved in a criminal investigation.

'To cut a long story short,' said Nicolas in a faint voice, 'I went to Madame de Lastérieux's house in Rue de Verneuil, where I was supposed to be having dinner. She showed me a lack of consideration, and I left. I went to the Théâtre-Français, where I watched the first act of *Athalie*. Having calmed down, I decided to go back to Julie's, but the party was in full swing and I realised I had made a mistake. Feeling angry and offended, I wandered around Paris a little before returning here, like the prodigal son.'

'For a man of your maturity and experience, you behaved like a child. Did you see anyone you knew at the theatre?'

'Yes, my colleague Commissioner Chorrey was on duty.'

Nicolas had replied without thinking, but it suddenly occurred to him that Monsieur de Noblecourt was asking him to account for his movements, as if questioning a suspect. 'May I enquire, Monsieur, why you asked me that question?'

The procurator stroked his mottled jowls with a hand as white as a priest's. 'I see you're getting your senses back, Nicolas. I'm afraid I have some bad news to tell you. I will understand if it distresses you, but I ask you to stay calm. You may have the most pressing need to keep your composure in the hours to come.'

'What is the meaning of these words, Monsieur?'

'Their meaning, my boy, is that this morning, at the stroke of ten, an envoy from Monsieur de Sartine came to fetch you. The Lieutenant General of Police wants to see you immediately.

Bourdeau was here – he'd come to find out how you were – and he managed to worm it out of him. Be brave! This morning, at first light, Madame de Lastérieux's servants found her dead. According to an initial examination by a local doctor, it seems she may have been poisoned.'

Long afterwards, Nicolas would remember that his first reaction, fleeting as it was – well before the grief went through him like a knife, a grief made all the more intense by the images of their passion that flashed through his mind – had been one of relief, almost of liberation. For a moment he was speechless, and so pale and haggard that Noblecourt grew worried at his silence.

'Poisoned!' Nicolas said. 'Was it some rotting food? Mushrooms?'

'Alas, no. From what we know, there is every sign that she was poisoned by malicious intent.'

'Isn't it possible that she killed herself?'

'If you have any evidence suggesting she was in such despair that she may have wanted to take her own life, you must reveal it as soon as possible to those whose task it will be to hear your testimony.'

Nicolas shook his head and said in a barely audible voice, 'The last time – oh, my God! – the last time I heard her voice – I didn't even see her, just heard her voice – she was laughing uproariously and there was nothing to indicate that she wanted to die.'

'You will have to say all that. Everything will require an explanation. Take this calmly, and confront one at a time the unpleasant ordeals which, I fear, await you . . . Now go and talk to Monsieur de Sartine, and give him my regards.'

Monsieur de Noblecourt adjusted the velvet skullcap covering his balding cranium, an occupation which seemed intended to conceal a growing embarrassment. Nicolas felt sick at heart: it was as if, behind his friend's outward affirmations, an unformulated question were being asked. No, he had nothing to reproach himself with. He realised at that moment that he had entered unknown and dangerous territory, full of obstacles and concealed traps. The slightest word, the most innocuous remark, a look, an expression of simple concern from a friend could cause him terrible pain, and he would not know if it was merely the result of his own imagination.

The former procurator, angry with himself, tried to make amends. 'Don't misunderstand me. You have to see things as they are. Put yourself in the position of an outside spectator, a commissioner at the Châtelet embarking upon an investigation. You will be expected to give a precise account of an evening which you yourself say was full of incident. Make a commitment to explain everything in detail. Monsieur de Sartine knows you too well to have any doubts about your loyalty or your innocence in this tragedy about which we know nothing as yet. And when I say Monsieur de Sartine, I also mean your friends. Don't think we are indifferent to your grief; it touches us more than you can imagine and from now on our only concern is to assure you of our support, have no fear of that . . .'

Monsieur de Noblecourt's voice was at once so tremulous and yet so full of warmth that it chased away any doubts Nicolas might have been harbouring about his mentor's feelings, even though he still shuddered at the mere mention of the word 'innocence'. But it made him all the more aware of the risks he would have to face from interrogators, adversaries, accusers, witnesses and judges less well disposed towards him. The horrifying thought struck him that not only had he lost someone dear to him, but that until this affair was resolved he would also have to endure being placed in the position of those who, in the course of his twelve years in the police force, had borne the brunt of his unrelenting determination as an investigator.

The door of the bedroom opened and Bourdeau reappeared, with a worried look on his face.

'A cab sent by Monsieur de Sartine has just arrived. You know how he is, he must be getting impatient. I'll let you get ready and then go with you.'

Nicolas smiled weakly. 'Afraid I'll try to escape?' There was such a look of pain on the inspector's face that he got up and threw his arms around him. 'Forgive me, Pierre, I shouldn't have said that, but I'm at the end of my tether.'

'Come, my children,' said Noblecourt, 'let's not get carried away. Nicolas needs to get ready. Promise to come and see me as soon as you get back and tell me everything.'

He withdrew, leaning on Bourdeau's arm. Nicolas made an effort to take his time, anxious to appear in the best light to a chief whose sarcastic eye was in the habit of deducing the state of a man's morals from the propriety of his costume. Any sign of neglect filled him with gloom and made him suspect the most extreme immorality. He took care not to cut himself while shaving, put on a black coat, recently made for him by his tailor, tied an immaculate lace cravat around his neck, combed his hair for a long time – there were a few white hairs starting to come through – and tied his ponytail with a dark velvet ribbon. He only ever wore a wig at Court or on solemn occasions when he was dressed in his magistrate's robe. He took a last look in the mirror, and realised that he looked younger now that his fever had passed: it almost made him forget the seriousness of the situation. Then he descended the small staircase, and the sight of Bourdeau and Semacgus waiting for him at the entrance brought him back to reality.

Semacgus walked up to him. 'Remember, Nicolas, that you can ask me for anything,' he said. 'I haven't forgotten that you once proved my innocence and gave me back my freedom.'

Nicolas shook his hand firmly and followed the inspector into the cab. He lapsed into morose brooding. Suddenly, he recalled the graceful figure of Julie, and the image took his breath away and made him feel dizzy. He withdrew into himself, shaking with sobs. Incapable of controlling his imagination, he could not prevent the terrible images that flooded into his mind: a body thrown on a slab in the Basse-Geôle and subjected to the indignities inflicted by those given the task of performing the autopsy, a body whose softness he could still feel . . . Bourdeau coughed in embarrassment. The city Nicolas loved so much sped past, its houses and its crowds like a stage set painted in faded colours, without life or gaiety. They did not exchange a single word. The carriage soon reached the Hôtel de Gramont[1] in Rue Neuve-Saint-Augustin. Entering the building, they saw the familiar faces of their police colleagues, and the footmen bowed before them with their usual deference. The elderly manservant smiled when he saw Nicolas.

'Don't be surprised if things are a bit different. Monsieur de Sartine only got back from Versailles at midday.'

As Bourdeau was about to sit down on a bench to wait, the servant indicated to him that his presence was also required.

They entered the Lieutenant General's vast office to be greeted by an unusual sight. A silent assembly of wigs stood on the table in serried rows, like soldiers on parade. Monsieur de Sartine, having spent the night at Versailles, had missed his morning appointment with his precious collection. And, as he could not bear the slightest interruption to his innocent obsession, it was only now that his usual inspection was taking place. That was what the porter had been trying to say. Nicolas, who on any other occasion might have been amused at the spectacle, was wondering anxiously where his chief was, when suddenly one of the wigs moved and Monsieur de Sartine's sharp face emerged from amongst his inanimate creatures.

Nicolas had grown accustomed over the years to the whole gamut of his chief's facial expressions, which varied widely according to circumstances; and had today been expecting the irritated, impatient countenance the Lieutenant General wore whenever he was about to show his displeasure with a subordinate. Instead, he was surprised to see Monsieur de Sartine looking at him in a relaxed, affectionate, almost paternal manner.

'Nicolas' – the use of the Christian name was also a good omen – 'where did your late father and my greatly missed friend the Marquis de Ranreuil buy his wigs? I seem to recall they were ideally firm yet supple.'

'I think, Monsieur, that he found them in Nantes, in a little shop near the dukes' palace.'

'Hmm! I'll have to find out more about it. But for the moment, we have an unfortunate matter to deal with. Very unfortunate, in truth, for it concerns you personally, and, as everyone knows the esteem in which I hold you and the confidence I have in you, some people would be only too pleased to gossip about an incident which might implicate the *éminence grise* of the Lieutenant General of Police.'

This was said in the pompous tone Sartine used whenever he invoked the dignity of his office. With his hands, he stroked two tiered wigs placed symmetrically like yew trees in a French garden.

'We need to consider, however,' he went on 'that for the moment there is no case. A young woman has succumbed to something that a neighbourhood quack says resembles poisoning. *Primo*, are we certain of the cause of death? *Secundo*, if the cause is proven, do we suspect suicide, murder or, quite simply, a domestic accident, which is always possible? When all these reasons have been duly examined, we will still have, *tertio*, to question witnesses. Eh?'

This interjection, Nicolas knew, did not call for any reply: it was merely there as punctuation, a pause for breath after which the argument would resume its course.

'According to the information I have received, the body is still in the state in which it was found and has not been taken away. Only the local commissioner knows of the death. Nothing has leaked out, and the two servants are in solitary confinement. Seals have been placed on the bedroom, the servants' pantry and the drawing room. We must lose no more time. Bourdeau, see to it that the body is taken discreetly to the Basse-Geôle, that it is abundantly salted, even though we are in winter, and that Sanson is summoned as soon as possible. As you know, the duty doctors at the Châtelet are quite incapable, and have given proof of their incompetence on more than one occasion. Ask Semacgus, who has proved himself in previous investigations, to help Sanson in this task.' He laughed. 'Those two are used to each other by now! Don't forget to confiscate anything which might throw light on this matter: glasses, crockery. Look in the servants' pantry for the leftovers from last night's dinner – apparently it was given in Nicolas's honour.'

He gave Nicolas a long hard look.

'Now, as for this gentleman . . .'

He pensively twisted a curl on his wig.

'Commissioner, if you have a statement to make, I am listening. Something you may have on your mind and which you would like to do me the honour of confiding to me. Take your time; what you say to me will determine the course we take, for I shall not depart from whatever line I adopt. In fact, if anyone has my trust, it's you, and, in my position, there are not many who enjoy it. Eh? What do you say?'

For Nicolas, the open-mindedness of this conclusion tempered the inquisitorial tone of the rest of the speech, a tone which could have been applied to any suspect.

'Your words do me great honour, Monsieur, and I can only answer as honestly as possible. Yesterday evening, I spent no more than fifteen minutes in Julie de Lastérieux's house until an unjust remark caused me to leave. Having calmed down, I returned two hours later. I did not see her again, as the party was at its height. I judged that my presence would cast a pall over the guests' merriment, and so refrained from showing myself. So . . .' – he paused for a moment – 'I wandered a little and then went back to Rue Montmartre.'

'Nothing else I might learn from any malicious third parties?'

'Nothing else, Monsieur. I met Commissioner Chorrey on duty at the Théâtre-Français and spent a little time with him.'

Sartine made an impatient gesture. 'As I'm sure you can imagine, I already know that! In any case, I need to make it clear to you that, being a party in this affair, you cannot be involved in any way in the investigation. Go back to work, but do not attempt to intervene, however remotely. It's enough that Inspector Bourdeau, *your* friend . . .' – he emphasised the possessive – '. . . should be given the task of dealing with this. Not to mention the fact that the two men who will be opening the body are also close to you. I could easily be reproached for all this, which means—'

'Nevertheless, Monsieur—'

'Nevertheless nothing! As I was saying . . . it means that I must keep you at a distance from this case. Don't imagine that I don't understand your feelings, your grief, your legitimate desire to participate in the inquiries into your friend's death. But circumstances force us to act in a certain way. You would do well to obey. As long as the mystery has not been elucidated, any move on your part would bring the legality of our procedures into question and would place me in a delicate position should we come up against one of those magistrates who share the fashionable tendency to challenge the authority of the King.'

Monsieur de Sartine stood up, walked around his desk – stopping one of the wigs from slipping as he did so – took Nicolas by the shoulder and pushed him gently towards the door.

'If you want my advice, I think you should take some time off. What would you say to going to Versailles and paying court to His Majesty's daughters? Only yesterday Madame Adélaïde was asking after you. Or else, visit Madame du Barry, go hunting with the King. In short, a little courtly spirit would not go amiss in the present situation. Versailles is a place where we have to show ourselves often lest we are forgotten!'

As Nicolas, followed by Bourdeau, was about to descend the staircase, he heard Sartine call the inspector back. They spoke for a few moments, but Nicolas could catch nothing of what was said. Bourdeau then rejoined him and walked with him to their carriage without saying a word. Nor did he open his mouth as they rode through the fog-shrouded streets in which people moved like vague shadows. Nicolas, too, remained silent. He did not care where they were going. He was once more in the grip of his perverse imagination, his mind filled with horrible images and interminable and fevered reflections on the causes and consequences of what had happened. Then, as if trying to break through his defences, Monsieur de Noblecourt's words came back to him, echoed by Monsieur de Sartine's instructions. They sounded within him like the repeated strokes of a funeral bell, like so many manifestations of the imperceptible dangers with which he suddenly felt surrounded. The cause of Julie's death had still to be established, and yet everyone was keen to give him advice and recommend him to be careful. The fact was, he told himself, that however friendly and trusting they all appeared to be, he was being treated as if he was presumed guilty. Guilty of what? It was difficult to tell. That was what aroused his unease, this diffuse anxiety, this impression of slipping down a slope without anything to hang on to. He threw a sideways glance at Bourdeau, who was so still it seemed as though he were sleeping with his eyes open. He would have liked to talk to him, but no sound emerged from his mouth, and besides, what would he have said? Solitude had been his companion since his earliest childhood, and now it had reasserted itself in the cruellest, most unexpected way.

The noise of the carriage and horses echoed beneath the sombre archway of the Châtelet. The old walls plunged him into a melancholy so profound that Bourdeau had to pull him by the arm. The errand boy looked at him without recognising in this grim, downcast man the brilliant horseman who usually threw him the reins of his mount with a great laugh. Nicolas walked his usual route like an automaton, and passed Old Marie, the usher, without greeting him or making one of those friendly remarks which the old man cherished as a mark of friendship. He somehow found himself in the duty office. Bourdeau glanced through the register of incidents, then looked Nicolas in the eye and pounded on the old oak table.

'That's enough now, you have to pull yourself together. I've never seen you in this state, although we've been through a lot together! You've been wounded, knocked senseless, abducted, threatened. You must have undergone far worse ordeals than this. We must do something.'

Nicolas smiled weakly. 'Do something? What do you want me

to do? I've been told to go hunting and pay court to the ladies!'

'Precisely! That's exactly what you're going to do. Or at least, that's what Monsieur de Sartine has to believe you're going to do.'

'What do you mean?'

Bourdeau had opened the wardrobe where, for years, they had been accumulating a whole carnival array of clothes, hats and accessories. This collection, constantly enriched with new finds, was used by officers whenever they had to follow a suspect or were engaged on a mission in a dangerous *faubourg* and wanted to pass unnoticed. The inspector took out a quilted waistcoat, handfuls of tow, a large shapeless black coat so worn and threadbare that the black was turning green, a pair of thick shoes with brass buckles, a round, wide-brimmed hat, a great antique wig the hair of which seemed to have come from the mane of a dapple-grey horse, a thick linen shirt, a cotton cravat of doubtful cleanliness and equally dubious stockings. He threw the whole lot willy-nilly on the table.

'Nicolas, get undressed and put on this stuff.'

The commissioner shook his head. 'What madness are you dreaming up?' he asked.

'Just doing what friendship dictates. It being understood – and I say this before knowing anything for certain about Madame de Lastérieux's death – that I believe you, and that I know you are innocent in this affair, I don't see why I should deprive myself of your help in an investigation to which you can contribute a great deal.'

'But how, for God's sake?'

'Let's say a man your height, dressed in your clothes, with a muffler over his nose, comes out, accompanied by your servant, and gets in the carriage. "To Versailles, and don't spare the horses!" Monsieur de Sartine will immediately be informed of your departure, and he'll be relieved to know you're doing as he asked. Meanwhile, you slip out, you meet up with me a few streets from here, and we proceed with the investigation together.'

'But what should I look like?'

'What does it matter? You can be an informer, an officer. Or better still, a clerk, there to note down my observations. A scruffy-looking fellow, with his eyes so tired he wears dark glasses.'

He handed him a pair of spectacles with smoked lenses.

Nicolas rose to his full height. 'I'll never allow you to commit this folly,' he exclaimed. 'If this case is a criminal one, you're risking your job, perhaps more. There's no way I can permit this.'

'What do I care about my job,' replied Bourdeau, 'when the man I accepted as my chief when he was twenty years old, the man I've followed everywhere, the man I've saved from death several times, whose conduct and honour I've learnt to respect, finds himself in a difficult situation? What kind of man would I be not to try and remedy it with all the strength at my disposal? And what kind of man would you be, if you rejected my devotion?'

'All right,' said Nicolas, moved to tears. 'I surrender.'

'Not to mention the fact that, should this affair become complicated, it will be your judgement and experience, as always, which will lead us to a solution.'

Bourdeau had been walking up and down, striking his right leg with his tricorn. Now he stopped to think.

'We have to find someone just your height, someone we can

rely on. Now I come to think of it, Rabouine has a similar physique.'

'He has a pointed nose.'

'That doesn't matter; his face will be hidden by the muffler. And there's another advantage in using Rabouine. I've just remembered he knows that page in Monsieur de La Borde's service at Versailles. Damn, I can't remember his name . . .'

'Gaspard! He rendered me a signal service in 1761, in the famous Truche de la Chaux case.'[2]

'That's perfect, then. With a note which you'll write for me, he'll welcome the disguised Rabouine with open arms, admit him to the palace and hide him in Monsieur de La Borde's apartments. We just have to decide on a price, the fellow's quite partial to coin of the realm.'

With nimble fingers, Bourdeau mimed a hand distributing coins.

'His master is in Paris tonight,' he went on. 'He told me last night that he isn't on duty. He is said to be smitten by a new conquest. Gaspard spreads the gossip: "My master's friend, young Ranreuil, you know, the commissioner, is resting, he's not well." Rabouine abandons your clothes and comes back to Paris in secret. Everyone thinks you're in quarantine in Monsieur de La Borde's apartments. Sartine is relieved. There we are, everything's sorted out.'

Faced with Bourdeau's almost violent enthusiasm, Nicolas realised that he had to suppress his feelings and do exactly what the inspector wanted. There was a certain revulsion, of course, as he put on these coarse, musty clothes. The breeches were several sizes too big for him, and they had to look for a kind of lace to serve as a belt. The quilted waistcoat made it seem as though he had a large paunch. The wig, a black skullcap and a pair of spectacles transformed the commissioner to such an extent that he did not recognise his own reflection in the window.

'Right,' said Bourdeau, 'I'm going to find Rabouine. He's never far away at this hour. As soon as he's dressed in your clothes, I'll go and distract Old Marie, and he'll slip past me. Meanwhile, you make your way to Monsieur de Sartine's office, which is never closed. All you have to do is push the gilded moulding on the third shelf in the bookcase. As you know, there's a secret passage there. Go down the steps to the little door that leads out to the curtain wall, over on the Grande Boucherie side. That's where I'll meet up with you. In the meantime, don't move. I'll run now and find Rabouine. To be on the safe side, I'm locking the door.'

Nicolas heard the key turning in the lock. Once alone, he found it hard to rid himself of a sense of anxiety, not for himself, but for Bourdeau. His deputy's loyalty and devotion was dragging him – a man with a family to support and a reasonable chance of continuing his already long career in peace – down a dangerous path. This doubt was joined by another: could he deceive Sartine so deliberately, when the Lieutenant General had been so honest and patient with him? Nicolas had a remarkable gift for finding himself in these moral dilemmas, which he only resolved through painful exercises in casuistry, vestiges of his Jesuit education in Vannes, which inevitably left wounds in his soul. There was another thought that kept coming back: would he, usually so indifferent, or rather, so accustomed to the terrible sights that were part and parcel of a criminal investigation, be able to bear the sight of Julie's corpse, or her house overrun by police? Would he be able to keep a cool head, the prerequisite for his capacity for clear thought, when he was so intimately involved? Wasn't Monsieur de Sartine right in wanting to keep him away from the case, and wasn't Bourdeau, carried away by his loyalty, setting them both on a very slippery slope?

By the time Bourdeau and Rabouine came for him, he had regained his composure. He was writing the note for Gaspard, which he sealed with the Ranreuil arms after slipping a few *louis d'or* inside the paper. Before that, not wanting to deceive an old friend whose support had never failed him over the years, he had written a message for Monsieur de La Borde. It was a gesture he considered doubly justified: it would both reassure his friend and cover Gaspard in his master's eyes. This desire to come clean led him to reflect on human turpitude. Why was it that he had agreed to disobey the Lieutenant General of Police and flout his express instructions, and yet at the same time considered it essential not to act behind La Borde's back? Doubtless, he thought, because his relationship with Sartine was one of inequality and subordination, and perhaps – although he did not dare think too far along these lines – his attitude was not unconnected with certain rebuffs he had suffered which had left a bitter taste in his mouth, despite his gratitude to, and admiration for, his chief. In the peculiar circumstances in which he found himself, it did not amount to much: a small disobedience, a simple little act of revenge.

'I've sent Old Marie on an important mission,' said Bourdeau. 'He's gone to fetch a pitcher of brandy – he can keep half of it for himself. The time has come. Rabouine knows what he has to do. Give him the letter.'

'I'd like him to go and see La Borde first and give him this note.'

Bourdeau looked in surprise at the paper, on which the seal was like a bloody stain. 'Do you really think we need to . . . ?'

'Yes, or I won't do it.'

Rabouine changed, gradually transforming himself, with the help of a short wig, into a very acceptable Nicolas. With a piece of black wool over his face, the collar of his cloak raised, and the tricorn pulled right down, the illusion was complete. For his part, Nicolas adjusted the spectacles and took a few steps.

'Don't swagger,' said Bourdeau. 'Bend your legs, stoop a bit more, let your shoulders sag. There, that's it . . . That's much better.'

He opened a drawer, took out paper, quills, a penknife and a portable bottle of ink, and gave all these objects to Nicolas.

'Don't forget your work tools, if you want to look the part. That's perfect! Perhaps still a bit too clean, though. Take off your glasses.'

Bourdeau passed his hand over the top of the wardrobe, then smeared the dust on Nicolas's face, until his complexion turned grey and weary.

'The coast is clear. Let's go our separate ways. We'll meet again where we've arranged.'

The inspector left with Rabouine, who was in high spirits and as proud as punch to be acting as commissioner – as an old partner in crime, he would have thrown himself in the Seine for him. Nicolas made his way to Sartine's office. The silence in the room reminded him of his first interview with the Lieutenant General of Police, when he had arrived fresh from his native province, and a thousand other comic and tragic scenes over the years. The gilded moulding sank back and the bookcase swivelled around, revealing a staircase. The noises of the city rose in the distance. Two floors below, he found the door. Walking out into the street, he was struck by how cold it was, especially now that evening was closing in. He did not have long to wait. A cab stopped, the door opened, and he jumped in.

'That Rabouine is amazing,' said Bourdeau. 'He knows as much of the ways of the world as a bailiff at the Palais de Justice. He'll fool everyone at Versailles, and by God, he cuts a fine figure in your clothes.'

Nicolas smiled. 'Thank you on behalf of the clothes! It's clear you don't get the bills from my tailor, Master Vachon! As for Rabouine, God save him, he knows what to do in every situation and never spares any effort.'

'You just smiled,' said Bourdeau. 'All is well. Recovery is near.'

The conversation continued in a light tone which gradually calmed Nicolas, making him forget what awaited him. In Rue de Verneuil, a number of officers were keeping a discreet watch on the house. They immediately recognised the unnumbered carriage and Bourdeau's familiar face. An inspector sitting outside the door, which had been sealed, tried to deny them access. The mention of Monsieur de Sartine's name smoothed things over: the man had only been trying to defend the prerogatives of the local commissioner. The seals were broken, and Bourdeau and Nicolas entered Madame de Lastérieux's house.

The shutters were closed, and the rooms were dark and silent. The deserted hall opened on to a corridor which led to the reception rooms. To the right, a door led to the servants' pantry. At the end of the corridor, a velvet door gave access to a large drawing room, to the left of which, at right angles, were a library and a music room. On the right was a short corridor leading to a circular boudoir, after which came Julie's bedroom. Adjoining the boudoir was a wardrobe room, then a series of service rooms, leading back to the pantry. The main rooms had a view of Rue de Verneuil, the others looked out on the dark well of the courtyard, where the servants had their quarters. The windows of the library and the music room looked out on Rue de Beaune.

'Let's start with the bedroom,' said Bourdeau.

He glanced round the drawing room. The table had been cleared, although eight chairs still surrounded it.

'Everything looks so tidy, despite last night's party.'

'The two West Indian servants are very good,' Nicolas said. 'Julie was a stickler for tidiness. Everything had to be cleaned and put away. She couldn't bear to see the house looking untidy in the morning.'

'That's rather unfortunate. Untidiness has one great merit: it increases the opportunities for observation.'

'But there's still a clue here. Parties in this house, as I well know, rarely lasted beyond one in the morning. The tidying must have taken at least two hours. Which means, and the servants will be able to confirm this, that Madame de Lastérieux did not call for help during that time. She could have done so easily from her bed by ringing the bell pull, which sounds in the pantry. Her maid would have come running.'

'That's useful to know,' Bourdeau conceded. 'Unless she lost consciousness before she was able to call for help.'

At any other time, Nicolas would have been amused by the way their roles had been reversed. Perhaps it was the effect of this ridiculous disguise, but it was Bourdeau who was having the last word – he certainly had the ability and experience for it.

'How terrible,' murmured Nicolas, 'that Julie's body has been left like that with no one to watch over it!'

Bourdeau responded with an indistinct grunt.

When they opened the door to the bedroom, a sickening odour seized them by the throat. At first, they could make out nothing: the curtains were drawn and the room was in darkness. Bourdeau fetched a candle from the other room and lit the bedroom candles. The flickering light illumined the room. Julie de Lastérieux lay there in her nightdress, her body arched, her legs bent and splayed apart. Death had seized her as she was lifting her hands to her throat. Her head was thrown back on the pillow and surrounded by her flowing hair, and her mouth was open, as if she were screaming. The front of her body was covered in orange-coloured vomit, flecked with blood, which had dripped on the sheets and the carpet. The eyes were bulging, the pupils already clouding over. Nicolas, assailed by memories, was profoundly shocked to see how horribly death had done its work. He had to force himself to carry on. Only by clinging to the idea of duty could he summon the will power to act as if the poor body lying in its own vomit was not that of a woman he had loved. He had to take charge of the operation. He had noted in the past that, however pusillanimous his emotional reaction to a situation might be, it immediately gave way to a cold determination, even – or especially – when he himself was personally involved.

'Pierre,' he said, 'don't take another step. You don't know this room. I do, in great detail – that's why I want to have a very careful look at it. It doesn't matter if the cause of death is as yet unknown. When we do know it, and if it does prove to be a case of criminal poisoning, we'll regret not having been more attentive now. Lift that candlestick so that I can see.'

He stood looking at the room, motionless, deep in thought. Bourdeau, growing impatient, touched his elbow as if afraid he had fallen asleep. 'Nicolas, we don't have all that long . . .'

'In such circumstances, it's sometimes useful to take our time.'

'And what observations have you made?'

'Some quite surprising ones, actually. First of all, the fire is out, but that's normal. It's nearly six o'clock. But the fact that the windows are closed and the curtains drawn – now that's not in keeping.'

'Not in keeping with what?'

'With Julie's habits. She always demanded a raging fire – which I hate, as you know – and, to make up for it, she kept the windows half open and the curtains half drawn. Now, unless things haven't been left in the state they were in when the body was discovered, which I don't believe to be the case . . .'

'Why?'

'Look at those candles on the chest of drawers. The doctor

who came examined the body by their light. They weren't usually kept there, any more than there were usually all these jewels scattered about. When there's a dead body and it's winter, it's best to let the cold in from outside . . . I also see a half-empty glass of white liquid on the night table, and a plate with what seems to be a chicken wing in sauce. Now that's impossible, in fact totally absurd.'

'Why do you say that?'

'Because Julie hated eating in bed. She would never have had food brought in to her. She never allowed me to satisfy my hunger at her bedside. That's why the presence of this plate bothers me.'

In the dark, he blushed at the thought of these intimate details.

'Another thing,' he went on. 'Why would she have wanted to eat in bed or during the night when she had just finished a sumptuous dinner? It makes no sense.'

He looked pensively at the little writing case that lay on a rosewood table, surrounded by scattered sheets of paper, along with a quill, a seal and a stick of green wax.

'So much for the room,' said Bourdeau. 'What about the body?'

'We'll have to take a closer look at it. It reminds me of the body of an old man who was stung on the throat by wasps in Chaville, one night last summer. The position of the hands was identical. At first sight, poisoning is an obvious conclusion, as is suffocation. The throat looks swollen, even seen from a distance. The autopsy will tell us more, I hope. We need to take the glass and its contents with us, as well as the leftovers on the plate.'

'There are a lot of footprints,' said Bourdeau. 'Muddy ones, too.'

'The police and the doctor. We won't get much from them.'

They walked around the room, looking for other clues. Bourdeau pointed to a concealed door in the partition wall. 'Where does that lead?'

'To the servants' pantry, by way of the wardrobe, the toilet and the service rooms.'

Bourdeau opened the door, and walked through a small room full of cupboards which led to a larger one furnished with a mirrored table and a *bergère*. He opened a second door and found himself in a long corridor with jute-covered walls.

'Through here, the prints are more distinct,' he observed. 'A man seems to have walked along it in both directions.'

Nicolas came and joined him. Bourdeau stared at the floor in amazement.

'That's quite strange,' he said. 'I'll be damned if these prints aren't the same as those your boots are leaving on the carpet. See for yourself.'

They both knelt. After a moment, Nicolas broke the silence.

'Identical. Absolutely and totally identical.'

Nicolas took a few steps, crouched, took a sheet from his little black notebook and a lead pencil, and noted down the pattern of marks on the parquet floor.

'In fact, they're not completely identical,' he said. 'There must have been a nail loose on the sole, and it's scratched the floor. Look.'

'And what's more, these prints are fresh,' murmured Bourdeau, embarrassed. 'Or at least, from last night.'

'I see what you're thinking. There is an explanation.'

He went back to the wardrobe room and opened one of the

closets. Hanging on a rail was a cloak which Bourdeau recognised as one of Nicolas's, and on a side shelf there were folded shirts and handkerchiefs. But something did not correspond to what the commissioner was expecting, and Bourdeau sensed Nicolas's dejection.

'Vanished! My second pair of boots, identical to this one, vanished. I always keep some of my things here.'

'Perhaps the servants took them away to be cleaned.'

'I'd like to see that!' said Nicolas. 'I learnt from my father, the marquis, never to entrust that task to anyone other than myself. Otherwise you'd never obtain the right polish and brilliance. The surface leather has to look like that of a well-rubbed horse chestnut.'

'All right,' said Bourdeau, unaccustomed to hearing Nicolas mention his father. 'But they could be the servants' prints!'

'Impossible, they always walk barefoot. Julie hated noise. She would have liked people to slide along the floor.'

'The fact remains,' the inspector went on hesitantly, 'that the only footprints found in this corridor are yours . . .'

He observed Nicolas's impatient gesture.

'Yours, or left by your boots . . . Let's follow them, shall we?'

The prints led them to the servants' pantry, which was spick and span. In a larder, they discovered the remains of a chicken dish, which intrigued Bourdeau, but which Nicolas recognised as having been prepared in the style of the West Indies – it was a dish of which he was particularly fond.

'We'll have to collect all this and take it to the Basse-Geôle. Semacgus can take a look at it, and even test it on rats.'

Bourdeau was stooped over, clearly in the grip of an inner

dilemma. 'I ought to report to Monsieur de Sartine . . .'

'Oh, of course!' Nicolas replied in a somewhat brusque tone. 'And why not also tell him that you were accompanied by a clerk, a man nobody knew, who was wearing a fine pair of riding boots? Who then told you that he kept another pair in a closet, where the said clerk – a stranger, as I said – pointed out clothes belonging to a police commissioner at the Châtelet he'd obviously never met, but whose breeches he recognised! I told you this was a dead end . . . Now here you are, caught in a trap, and me with you. Our machinations have rebounded on us. I should never have accepted your generous proposition.'

'Please, God,' said Bourdeau, 'let this death be from natural causes! Because if it isn't . . .'

Neither of them really wanted to consider the implications of that. What most hurt Nicolas was to think that he himself, in Bourdeau's place, would not have been able to keep from wondering about those troubling boot prints.

III

TRAPS

Jesuz mab Doue, n'eo bet kredet
Piv en e vro a ve profed?
Jesus, son of God, was not believed.
Who would be a prophet in his own land?
BRETON PROVERB

Instructions had been given, decisions made, and everything was proceeding methodically. Bourdeau was very much in control. Messengers had been dispatched to Doctor Semacgus in Vaugirard, and to Sanson, the Paris executioner, who lived outside the city walls in a house he owned on the corner of Rue Poissonnière and Rue d'Enfer. For a long time now, Monsieur de Paris – as he was known – had been lending his skills to the performance of autopsies in criminal investigations. He was a discreet, cultivated man, although one who could conceal – as Nicolas had previously discovered – unexpected failings. The friendship Nicolas felt for him was genuine and compassionate.

The two practitioners were to be brought to the Grand Châtelet by carriage and there, that very evening, an examination of Madame de Lastérieux's body would be carried out. It was not a formality: everything hung on the results of this autopsy. If the assumption of premeditated poisoning proved correct, the machinery of the law would immediately be set in motion, with all the measures and procedures that entailed.

With a pang, Nicolas had moved back against the wall to let the porters take the body down to the wagon. As there was a risk that the body might undergo changes as the vehicle jolted over the Parisian cobbles, they had placed it on a bed of straw with the head held in place with splints to withstand the shaking. Beforehand, Bourdeau had plugged all the orifices of the body with shredded linen in order to prevent liquid requiring analysis from escaping.

He had put off interviewing the servants and the dinner guests until later. It was not a priority for the moment. The two men watched as the wagon set off, had the seals put back on the front door of the house, and got back in their carriage. Bourdeau had with him, in a basket he had found in the servants' pantry, the remains of the food discovered in the bedroom and the kitchen, as well as the white beverage, which had been decanted into a small bottle that had been duly corked.

Nicolas thanked heaven for his disguise. It allowed him to sink into a kind of drowsiness, a mixture of stupor and grief. He felt a sense of foreboding, all the worse now that night had fallen. He looked out with unseeing eyes at the people passing by, all of them wrapped against the biting cold, their faces hidden behind the turned-up collars of their cloaks. A damp fog had descended, blurring the colours of the streets. The street lamps gave off hardly any light. The sight of the hurrying crowd reminded him of a Flemish painting he had seen in the King's collection, in which, against the background of a snowy sky, faceless people walked in procession towards a cemetery in the distance.

Bourdeau tried to suggest to him that they should stop at the tavern in the Grande Boucherie where they usually went to fill their stomachs before autopsies, but Nicolas did not feel like doing anything. The way he was dressed, he observed curtly, risked drawing attention to himself. The tavern-keeper had known them for years and liked nothing better than to chat with his customers: he was sure to see through his disguise.

The noise of the wheels echoing under an archway drew him from these reflections. The carriage came to a halt. With a fatherly air, Bourdeau lifted the muffler over the lower part of Nicolas's face and made sure that the smoked glasses were well adjusted, then had a careful look at the area around the entrance to the Grand Châtelet. The way was clear. No one was lurking in the shadows and even the errand boys had abandoned the place for warmer retreats. They descended to the Basse-Geôle. At the beginning of his career, Nicolas had organised autopsies in the ogival torture room, near the office of the clerk of the criminal court. Since then, as the number of autopsies had multiplied, a small cellar containing a stone slab with grooves in it had been pressed into service. It had the advantage that the morgue, which was open to the public, was close by. When Nicolas and Bourdeau entered, they were surprised to find Semacgus and Sanson already there, engaged in an animated conversation. But they had not been brought from their respective residences in such a short space of time: they had both been summoned to take part in a delicate gallstone operation on a patient in the Hôtel-Dieu, and when it was over Sanson had invited Semacgus to the Châtelet to admire some new instruments from Prussia, which had just arrived on the mail-coach.

'Good evening, gentlemen,' said Bourdeau, smiling.

The two men turned round. Nicolas held back, taking care not to stand within the circle of light thrown by the candles. He noted that Sanson was elegantly dressed in green. It was the first time he had ever seen him without his perpetual puce coat. It made him look younger and compensated for the solemn air his growing paunch gave him.

'Won't Nicolas be joining us?' asked Semacgus, peering inquisitively into the shadows where the false clerk was standing.

'Not this time,' said Bourdeau. 'Monsieur de Sartine did not think it right that he should be involved in an investigation, or rather, in a preliminary inquiry, which touches him so closely.' He made a sideways movement of his head to indicate Nicolas. 'Monsieur Deshalleux, clerk of the court. He will make notes on our conclusions.'

Nicolas bowed.

'Inspector,' said Sanson, 'our friend has told me the facts. I'd like you to convey to Commissioner Le Floch how much I feel for him in his hour of grief—'

He was interrupted by the arrival of the stretcher, carried by two men and preceded by an officer. The body was placed on the stone slab, and Semacgus and Sanson began preparing their instruments in silence. There followed a terrible ordeal for Nicolas. He would never know how he had been able to bear the scratch of the scalpel cutting into the skin, the cracking as the ribs were separated on either side of the trunk, revealing the nacreous tints of the organs, and the various noises and smells of the operation. More unbearable still were the comments and remarks which accompanied this work. This body, once so passionately loved, was nothing more than a wretched, bleeding scrap of flesh. Once they had sewn it up again, salted it and wrapped it in a jute sack, Bourdeau and Semacgus conferred for a long time, then spent more time debating politely which of them would dictate the conclusions. In the end, it was Sanson who took it upon himself to sum up their observations. Bourdeau nudged Nicolas with his elbow, to remind him that he had to note down everything that was said.

'"We,"' began Sanson, '"Guillaume Semacgus, navy surgeon, and Charles Henri Sanson, executioner for the viscountcy and seneschalcy of Paris, residing separately in this city and its dependencies, hereby certify and attest that on this day, 7 January 1774, in response to the summons issued this said day by Pierre Bourdeau, inspector at the Châtelet, we went together to the prison of the Grand Châtelet, and in a cellar situated near the Basse-Geôle performed an autopsy on the corpse of Madame Julie de Lastérieux and are now making a statement of this internal and external examination. We report in all conscience that we found the body of Madame de Lastérieux to be healthy and intact in all its external parts, without wounds or contusions, and in its natural state, apart from stiff joints and stretch marks on the thighs and legs, a natural effect of a violent death. Proceeding to the opening of the corpse, beginning with the lower abdomen, we found the organs healthy on the outside. From the interior of the stomach we took out about a pint of a brownish liquid mixed with clots of blood, the surface of this organ appearing irritated and tinged with a redness which could not be wiped away with a towel. As for the colour—"'

'If you'll allow me, my dear colleague,' Semacgus cut in, 'I fear you have omitted certain details.'

'You're quite right, forgive me. I'll resume. "The stomach appeared empty of all solid substances apart from a small amount of liquid. As for its strange colour, it was not found again in the first intestine, which was very healthy, as was the rest of the canal. We then proceeded to open the chest. The lungs were healthy, as was the heart. The oesophageal duct appeared very irritated. The muscular and mucous masses of the neck were very swollen. On examination of the mouth, we found no lesions, and no fractures of the teeth, which clearly indicates that no violence was used to make the subject swallow any harmful foreign substance. An examination of the sexual parts of the said corpse showed, from what we were able to collect, that coitus may have taken place not long before death. Accordingly, we salted the corpse of the said Madame de Lastérieux, in order to be able to preserve it for further examination. This statement hereby completed and signed this day, 7 January 1774, by Guillaume Semacgus, Charles Henri Sanson and Pierre Bourdeau, and countersigned by clerk of the court Deshalleux, who has faithfully copied it."'

Grief-stricken as he was, Nicolas was nevertheless aware that this had been a somewhat unusual session. Even though Bourdeau was conducting the case methodically and with great determination, the autopsy had been carried out with no commentary other than medical jargon. What had been missing as it went on were those ingenuous, commonsensical remarks which only he could make at appropriate moments. Admittedly, this time, the object of the operation was so close to him that he might not have been able to find the words to express his doubts and questions. It was as if he had been listening to a quartet which lacked one instrumentalist, the very one through whom everything was organised and made clear. Admittedly, judicial practice prevented those engaged in such examinations from expressing their opinions, their function being limited to making a certain number of observations which could later be used to help the detectives and the judges form their own opinions. The investigation could only be completed through the finding of further evidence and the interrogation of suspects, even involving torture in the most serious cases. The inspector, probably assailed by the same doubts as his chief, also seemed puzzled and disappointed by what he had just heard.

'Gentlemen,' he said, 'that's all well and good, but I find it hard to discern the most significant elements in what you have said. What of the causes of Madame de Lastérieux's death?'

Semacgus and Sanson looked at each other. The navy surgeon coughed and put his big hands together, making the finger joints crack.

'It is still too early to express an opinion,' he said. 'It is likely that this woman died as the result of poisoning. That would explain the irritant lesions observed in the organs, especially the curious oedema on the neck. I hesitate to consider it the principal cause of death, but it may have been a major contributory factor.'

'It's possible,' said Sanson, 'that the swelling of the skin caused her to choke. In which case the heart may have given way.'

Again, silence fell. Bourdeau stared at the body in the sack, apparently lost in thought.

'There are other observations we could make,' said Sanson. 'For example, it is likely that there was carnal conjunction, although the traces are ambiguous.'

Nicolas found this qualification nonsensical.

'The strange thing,' Semacgus said, 'is the absence of food in the victim's stomach. A few excreta and traces of liquid, and that's all.'

'Which makes it all the more vital,' said Bourdeau, 'to analyse the whitish beverage found on the victim's bedside table, a kind of milk. I am surprised, though, gentlemen, that no food was discovered, despite the fact that we know for certain that the victim had just had a large dinner.'

'Perhaps she rejected what she had eaten?' suggested Sanson. 'Does what you observed in her house bear that out at all?'

'No. The excreta were liquid. Nor did we find any traces on the clothes in her wardrobe. Doctor Semacgus, I'd like you to examine the liquid in question with the greatest care, as well as the left-over food in this basket.'

'So,' said Semacgus, 'it seems as though the solution lies in the liquid. I'll analyse it as soon as possible, along with the food you recovered. I think we've done all we can this evening. Let's meet again tomorrow at about three in the afternoon, and I'll let you know what I've found.'

Semacgus had cleaned his instruments under the water in a brass fountain, and was now putting them in a leather case. His haste indicated to those who knew him that he was late for a rendezvous and had no wish to linger. He bowed and disappeared beneath the arch of the staircase, his steps echoing in the distance. Sanson was also getting ready to take his leave when the inspector drew him into a corner of the cellar and whispered in his ear. They both turned to Nicolas, smiling.

'Commissioner,' said Bourdeau, 'I've found you a refuge for the night. Our friend has agreed to offer you accommodation in his house. No one would ever think of looking for you there.'

He coughed, embarrassed by the words he had just spoken, which might have appeared wounding to Sanson.

'I'll meet you at about midday tomorrow outside the Hôtel des Menus Plaisirs[1] and we'll continue with the investigation. For the moment, nothing seems in any way conclusive. Of course, we now know that the victim was poisoned, but the cause and the circumstances remain unclear.'

Nicolas removed his spectacles. 'I am reluctant to impose on our friend, for fear of getting him into trouble.'

'Monsieur,' said Sanson, 'it will be an honour for me. Have no fear, I shan't be running any risks. One cannot lose a position one does not hold. And even if one could, I wager there wouldn't be a large number of people fighting to claim it!'

'What do you mean?' Nicolas said. 'Isn't the position yours? Everyone knows you as Monsieur de Paris!'

Sanson gave a bitter smile. 'My father is still alive and has never relinquished a position which only His Majesty can authorise him to leave. If and when that happens, the King will confirm me in my functions with a *lettre de provision*.'

'I don't understand,' said Bourdeau.

'My father, Charles-Jean-Baptiste Sanson, was paralysed in the arm in 1754 and retired to the country. That's why, as I once told you, my uncle Gabriel, executioner of Rheims, joined me for the execution of the regicide Damiens in 1757. He never recovered from that appalling event.'

'I thought,' Bourdeau said, 'that your father still officiated at the execution of Monsieur de Lally, the Baron de Tollendal.'

'That's correct. My father had known the baron for a long time. When he was a young officer in the Royal Irish, he took shelter in our house after a torrential downpour. For some reason, he asked to see my father's instruments. As he passed his finger over the double-edged blade, he observed that the condemned man's head must be cut off at a single blow, and then uttered these striking words: "If ever fate were to place me in your hands, promise me you'll remember."'

'And what happened?' asked Nicolas.

'When he was condemned after the surrender of Pondicherry, supposedly for betraying us to the English, my father remembered the promise he'd made the young officer. He left his home in the country and returned to Paris. He was in despair when he realised that he no longer had the strength to lift the heavy sword of justice. He gave me that honourable but terrible task, but . . .' – Sanson bowed his head, his chest heaving with emotion – '. . . the condemned man was sixty-four years old and his long white hair came loose. When the blade came down, it slipped and cut through his jaw. The crowd on Place de la Grève jeered. Monsieur de Lally was writhing in pain on the ground. I no longer knew what to do. My father, with a nimbleness and a power that were quite unexpected in a man of his age, snatched the weapon from my hands, raised it, brought it down, and cut off the condemned man's head at a single stroke. Then, overwhelmed with emotion as well as failed by his strength, he fell to the ground in a faint.'

'I don't imagine you've had to perform that kind of execution again, have you?' said Nicolas.

'Alas, yes! The Chevalier de La Barre, accused of sacrilege for not taking his hat off when a procession passed, and for mutilating a wooden crucifix on the great bridge at Abbeville, had the misfortune to be placed in my hands. Even though the evidence was far from conclusive, he had been condemned to have his hand cut off and his tongue torn out before being burnt alive. He appealed to the Parlement of Paris, which commuted his sentence. He was to be decapitated before being burnt. The poor young man was nineteen . . .'

'Wasn't he the one whose rehabilitation Monsieur de Voltaire has been clamouring for?' asked Bourdeau.

'That's right. So far without success.'

'But surely Abbeville is not in your jurisdiction?'

'True. However, the local executioner of that town had fallen ill and, although there were colleagues in Amiens and Rouen, Chancellor Maupeou ordered me to officiate. He was no doubt hoping to lend more prestige to this execution and please the Church. It went off without mishap, but ever since I've been praying to heaven for the salvation of the unfortunate victim. People always imagine we exercise our profession because we like seeing lives destroyed . . . It's an absurd fabrication, and we should do all we can to combat it.'

'We all know that,' said Bourdeau. 'But it's getting late, and I think we must part. How did you come?'

'I have my carriage, driven by one of my servants,' said Sanson.

'Can we trust him?'

'As you trust me.'

As Bourdeau and Sanson were already moving away, Nicolas walked to the stone slab. With two fingers, he touched his lips then placed them on the shapeless sack, where the head was. He stood like that for a moment, his face expressionless, then joined his friends, who were slowly climbing the stairs. They passed Old Marie, who cast a curious glance at the false clerk.

'My dear Sanson,' Bourdeau hastened to say, 'perhaps you'd be so kind as to drop our clerk, Monsieur Deshalleux, in Rue Saint-Denis. It's on your way.'

'I'd be pleased to,' said Sanson, drawing Nicolas towards the entrance.

In the carriage, Nicolas was unable to find words to keep a conversation going. Respecting his silence, Sanson closed his eyes and appeared to doze off. The carriage turned into Rue Trop-Va-Qui-Dure, opposite the exit from Pont au Change, and went around the Châtelet by way of Rue de la Sonnerie before rejoining Rue Saint-Denis. Paris seemed deserted this winter evening: even the market and the cemetery of the Saints-Innocents, usually so animated, only made their presence felt through the mephitic odour that rose from the area in spite of the cold weather. Gradually, the windows of the carriage misted over with their breaths. Nicolas, too, closed his eyes, appalled by the horrible vision of a ravaged body superimposed over that of his mistress in all her ravishing beauty. He suddenly remembered one of the observations made during the autopsy. Julie had been with a man that night . . . Not only been with him, but made love with him, if the experts were to be believed. She had been deceiving him. He felt a retrospective pang of jealousy, which he hoped might dispel the grief of his loss. In vain: the two feelings – the bitterness of grief and the raging anger of betrayal – rather than cancelling one another out, simply combined. A pointless question crossed his mind: what would he have done if he had surprised Julie in his rival's arms? In truth, he did not know, but the uncertainty tortured him. He took a deep breath, making an effort to regain the calm and serenity appropriate to a police officer.

In his disguise, Nicolas had not been in a position to contribute to the discussion during the autopsy. But now his thoughts fell into place with the greatest clarity. If Madame de Lastérieux's stomach was empty, that was explained by her habits. In order not to further inflame a generous temperament, she never ate meat. What was more, she hated chicken, and in particular chicken cooked in the West Indian manner, with all its spicy seasoning. Eggs and dairy products, fruit and vegetables constituted the basis of her diet. The plate found at her bedside could not possibly have been intended for her. Everything pointed to the fact that she had not been alone. Logically, then, the dish in question would seem to have been intended to appease the hunger of her new lover. But Nicolas knew that this dish was usually prepared for him, and that its presence in the room could mean only one thing: that someone had wanted to make it seem as though he had spent part of the night with his mistress. That supposed a good knowledge of the customs of the house, and the aim of it all had evidently been to make him the prime suspect if the cause of death was indeed established as premeditated poisoning. Personally, he did not believe it had been an accident. There were too many curious details, too many things that had been done to create a web in which to catch him, the powerless victim of a mysterious, invisible predator.

The circumstances were highly unfavourable to him. For a long time now, the law of the land had considered poisoning to be the most serious of crimes, and had punished it with particular rigour, with the aim of putting an end to a form of murder of which the previous century had offered a number of examples still present in many people's memories. King Louis XIV had reacted with great firmness to this violation of the fundamental laws of nature, especially as the culprits had been so close to the throne. Nicolas knew how harsh the procedure was, as was the punishment: repeated torture, death at the stake, and posthumous infamy. He remembered that in his home province, Brittany, the suspect was made to wear sulphur shoes during questioning: a particularly horrible torture.

After Porte Saint-Denis, the carriage took the left-hand side of the boulevard as far as Rue Poissonnière. Nicolas noted in passing the dark mass of the Hôtel des Menus Plaisirs, where he had an appointment next day with Bourdeau. As they were heading for the corner of Rue d'Enfer, where Sanson lived, it struck Nicolas, as an old Paris hand, that there were actually two streets of this name in Paris, one within the walls, in the Montparnasse district, and the other in this suburban district known as New France, where the nouveaux riches built their houses around the vast holdings of the Saint-Lazare monastery. Monsieur de Sartine's attention had often been drawn to the frequent accidents along this perimeter.

'You see,' said Sanson, who had been thinking along the same lines, 'this is a highly dangerous place. It is where all the market gardeners come, mostly women carrying baskets full of produce for the city. Every week, several of them break their arms and legs on this narrow strip of muddy, slippery ground along which they're forced to walk if they don't want to be hit by the carriages.'

'I'm very well aware of it,' replied Nicolas. 'The monks are reluctant to pay for a decent pavement out of their own pockets.'

Nicolas could still hear Monsieur de Sartine, a Freemason and a Voltairean, ranting against the Priests of the Mission, who were immensely rich, owned some twenty streets in Paris and nearly twenty-five villages in the suburbs and, it was said, 'begrudged their *écus* without charity or any sense of the public good'.

As he was thinking this, Sanson's servant was lifting the heavy knocker at the carriage entrance of an opulent-looking house. It opened and they entered a cobbled courtyard. Sanson beckoned to him to climb the few steps leading to the front door of his residence. Entering the house, Nicolas felt, for the first time in two days, a sensation of well-being, as if someone sympathetic had hugged him. The place had a pleasant smell of wax and wood. Paris and its crimes were suddenly a long way away. Two children, the elder barely more than eight, were standing by the staircase. The elder was holding his brother close round the shoulders and scowling, as if ready to defend him against the intrusion of a stranger, clearly a rare occurrence in this house. Sanson took off his cloak, and burst out laughing when he finally got a good look at his guest's costume.

'In that disguise, you're going to scare away my sons!' he said. 'Children, I want to introduce a friend. Don't let his appearance mislead you about his station. It was absolutely essential that he pass unnoticed. Don't worry, he'll get changed. Monsieur, I present to you Henri and Gabriel. Now, come give your father a hug.'

Still intimidated, they bowed to Nicolas, then rushed to Sanson and clambered all over him, covering him with kisses.

'Come on now, behave yourselves! Run and tell your mother we have a guest. In the meantime, I'll show him his room.'

He led Nicolas up the stairs and into his quarters, a room redolent of rustic comfort and reminding the commissioner of his childhood.

Sanson left him for a moment, then returned with a shirt, stockings, a lace cravat and a grey cloak which, although a little large for him, made Nicolas look more like his usual self. One of Sanson's servants brought him a pitcher of hot water, which he poured into the porcelain bowl on the washstand. Beside the stand stood a swing mirror on wheels. The face which confronted Nicolas, once he had removed the layer of dust disguising his features, struck him like a sudden shock. It was no longer a young man's face. The ordeal he was living through had given his countenance a tragic cast, accentuating the increasing number of lines, and bringing out all the marks left by his open-air childhood and his eventful life as a man.

Sanson returned and they went down to the dining room together. In the doorway, a woman wearing an immaculate lace bonnet and a dark-red serge dress protected by a starched apron gave him a kind of curtsey. She was plump, slightly older than her husband, and with a welcoming air that did not conceal a real sense of authority. Nicolas soon realised that it was she who laid down the law to the members of the household, beginning with her husband. Nevertheless, there was a real look of kindness on her benevolent face.

'Marie-Anne,' said Sanson, 'this is you-know-who. Madame Sanson, my wife . . .'

'Monsieur,' she said, 'please believe me when I tell you how honoured I am to receive you in this house. I trust you'll forgive our simple family fare. We were somewhat taken by surprise.' She threw a stern look at her husband, who bowed his head. 'Monsieur Sanson should have warned me you would be coming this evening. He's told me so much about you over the years . . .'

She gave him a gracious smile, which made dimples in her round cheeks.

'Madame,' said Nicolas, 'I'm terribly sorry to impose on you in this way. However, I thank the circumstances that have given me the opportunity to meet you. It is a privilege for me to be received by my friend Sanson in the bosom of his family.'

He emphasised the word *privilege* and Marie-Anne blushed with pleasure.

'Well now, shall we sit down?'

Sanson took his place at the head of the rectangular table, with Nicolas to his right and his wife on his left, and the children on either side. Marie-Anne hesitated for a moment, then stood up, looked Nicolas straight in the eyes, and asked him if he would like to say grace. They all rose. Nicolas, moved to rediscover a custom of his youth in Guérande, recalled the words he had so often heard spoken by Canon Le Floch. This memory revived the shades of the past: his father the marquis, his half-sister Isabelle, Père Grégoire, the apothecary of the Decalced Carmelites – now recalled to God – and all his scattered friends.

'*Benedic, Domine nos et haec tua dona quae de tua largitate sumus sumpturi. Per Christum Dominum nostrum.*'

'*Amen*,' they all replied.

Madame Sanson again favoured him with a smile. 'It's a sacred custom in our family,' she said. 'I find it surprising that at tables where everything is in abundance, and where there is such a great variety of meats, people refuse to pay due homage to the Lord, from whom they have received all these things and to whom they should be indebted.'

The two servants brought in a steaming tureen, and the master of the house set about serving its contents.

'This is a soup made with capons, knuckle of veal and white onions,' said his wife. 'I spent the afternoon skimming it to make sure it would be thin enough.' She turned to one of the servants. 'Bernard, serve our guest some of my father's cider. I remember hearing that he likes it.'

Nicolas thanked her for her kindness. He knew that Madame Sanson's father was a farmer in Montmartre, and that it was while he was out hunting that Sanson had made the acquaintance of his future wife. Clearly, he was well known in this friendly house. After a moment's embarrassment, the conversation turned to matters of cooking. Madame Sanson told Nicolas that she knew his good taste and knowledge in this field. The soup was followed by eggs *à la Tartufe*. The name intrigued Nicolas.

Marie-Anne laughed. 'It's because the white conceals the black just as false devotion conceals hypocrisy!'

'And how on earth do you make this dish?'

'Oh, it's simplicity itself! I cut bacon into thin slices and cook it with a little water in a saucepan over a low flame. Then I throw away the juice, to get rid of the salt and the slightly rancid taste. I put it on an ordinary clay plate and add a little wine from a good bottle of red which I've first steamed. Over the whole thing, I crack a dozen well-chosen eggs and, for seasoning, add salt, thick pepper and grated nutmeg. The whole thing must be cooked over a low flame, taking great care not to over-cook the yolks, which should be eaten soft.'

'It's delicious,' said Nicolas. 'I love the combination of flavour and consistency.'

The meal continued peacefully. Nicolas observed that the host did not say much, but that his wife, who never lost her good humour, had an answer for everything. A dish of puréed peas accompanied by a braised pork loin chop was served next, followed by what was left of a huge Twelfth Night cake, and a pot of jam.

'Forgive the modesty of this dessert,' said Sanson, 'but—'

'But Monsieur Sanson will warn me in future when we have an important guest . . .'

Nicolas was intrigued by the jam. It was clearly made from cherries, but there was another flavour mixed in with it, giving a slightly acidic overall taste.

'What do you call this jam?'

She nodded her head, pleased to see his surprise. 'It's a family secret, but I don't mind telling you. It's made from raspberry-flavoured cherries. All you do is take the stones out of the cherries and replace them with raspberries. You also add the juice of squeezed raspberries and cherries, and make sure you divide the stuffed cherries from the cherries with stones. The ones with stones should be pinched in two places with a pin, to stop them bursting and the stones coming out. You cook them with sugar, as usual.'

'I shall preserve the memory of this delicacy, and I promise you, Madame, that I'll guard the secret jealously.'

The supper ended and everyone, including the servants and the cook, gathered at the staircase. Madame Sanson made them all kneel and recited the evening prayers in a firm voice. Then she distributed candles, with the usual instructions. Less timid now, the children came and embraced their father's friend. Nicolas went up to his room. The warmth of this family evening had calmed him. Now tiredness swept over him and he collapsed into the soft bed, which enveloped him so snugly that he immediately drifted into a dreamless sleep.

Saturday 8 January 1774

He awoke to a familiar smell and the noise of the curtains being drawn back. On a little table, one of the servants placed a pot of steaming beverage, a cup and a plate of rolls which Nicolas assumed were home-made. Doubtless accustomed to being discreet, the servant did not even look at him. As he was finishing his breakfast, the door opened and a small shape in a white nightdress crept up to him.

'Good morning, Monsieur. I'm Gabriel. I'm five. Did you sleep well?'

‘Very well thank you, and good morning to you.’

‘I’d like to ask you something . . . something . . .’ He hesitated, and Nicolas gave him a smile of encouragement.

‘You’re the first friend of my father’s I’ve seen here. Why is that?’

Nicolas felt quite embarrassed. How could he answer the child? Did the boy know his father’s occupation? It seemed unlikely that Sanson could have concealed the true nature of his work from his children, running the risk that they might discover it by chance later on and be doubly shocked. But Nicolas did not know that for certain. How was he to handle this?

‘I think your father is so pleased with his family that it’s the only thing he needs to make him happy. He has friends, but he only sees them in the city.’

The boy frowned, seemed to think hard about this, then relaxed. His eyes thanked Nicolas. The explanation, weak as it was, had no doubt answered an unformulated question. He left the room without saying a word, just as he had entered. Nicolas washed and dressed. He carefully disguised himself again as the clerk of the court, although he had difficulty in finding enough dust for the finishing touches. While waiting to leave, he leafed through some devotional books he had found in a little cupboard. This house, so peaceful, so distant from the horrors of the world, was nevertheless the home of the public executioner.

Towards midday, he went downstairs. Sanson had been called away on some dreadful task. His wife greeted Nicolas warmly. She told him how happy her husband had been with his visit, and made him promise to do her the honour of returning another time. She did not seem surprised to see him in his unprepossessing disguise. She was a woman of discretion and duty, and nothing could surprise her.

Madame Sanson let Nicolas out of the house through a little concealed door into Rue d'Enfer. He walked along the street a little way, then turned round and walked back towards Rue Poissonnière. He wanted to make sure he was not being followed. He had done enough tailing of suspects not to be caught out himself. He soon came to the Hôtel des Menus Plaisirs. He knew that this fine-looking building served as a storehouse for all the machinery, decorations and clothes used in Court celebrations. Visiting it one day, he had been taken aback by the juxtaposition of material left over from a grand ball with the remains of the catafalque from a princely funeral. He did not have to wait long for Bourdeau. While he waited, he was amused by the number of pretty young women coming in and out, some little more than children. A few winked at him impudently as they passed. He had to admit that his curiosity was aroused: his appearance was hardly calculated to stir such interest. Then Bourdeau's carriage loomed up, a door opened, and he leapt in.

'I hope you didn't wait too long,' said the inspector, in a jovial tone.

'Not at all. You're as accurate as the clock on the Palais de Justice.'

'You seemed puzzled.'

'Yes, I was wondering about all those pretty women going into the building. Some of them were far from shy.'

'Ah!' said Bourdeau, slapping his thigh. 'That's not unusual –

it happens every day. All the girls from the Opéra and the theatres, provided they have a protector, have letters of introduction.'

'Of introduction? To visit that establishment? For what purpose?'

'What purpose? Why, the most appealing purpose of all for a woman. It costs as much to repair all the material left over from royal celebrations as it does to buy it new. So it's left to the greed of these young madams. You should see them! They plunder whatever they find – satin, other fabrics. They just can't get enough.'

'At the King's expense!'

'The King's? At our expense! The leftovers from Court celebrations being thrown away like that should trouble any good citizen concerned about the use his taxes are put to. That's what happens when the strength of the State lies with the monarch alone. One of these days, another force will prevail, to provide a counterweight to these reprehensible excesses. Not to mention the King himself, who, they say, speculates on the price of grain to line his pocket.'

Nicolas recognised that vein of caustic criticism to which Bourdeau sometimes gave vent, often with some justification.

'Come now, Pierre, you're quite wrong. You're drawing rash conclusions from dubious premises. I can't let you say that. Can you honestly imagine His Majesty doing something like that? It's the kind of thing you read in the newspapers and lampoons published in London and The Hague. And what kind of counterweight do you mean? Are you now in favour of the *parlements*, who've so often rebelled against the authority of the King?'

Bourdeau shook his head, unconvinced. 'I'm not thinking about the *parlements*, but about the people. They have no voice, no one to speak for them.'

The carriage suddenly swerved violently, throwing Nicolas on to the inspector. They heard oaths and cracks of the whip. The coachman's window opened.

'I'm sorry, gentlemen, it was a delivery boy who was day-dreaming as he crossed the street. We almost knocked him over.'

The carriage set off again. To their right, Nicolas saw a curly-haired young man with an alarmed expression on his face, wearing a tight white apron and carrying in one hand a silver coffee pot and in the other a tray with a bowl and a pyramid of cups he had miraculously saved from disaster. When they reached the Châtelet, Doctor Semacgus, his face tense with annoyance, was waiting for them in the duty office.

'What can you tell me?' asked Bourdeau. 'Have you finished your research? Can we close the case?'

'Far from it,' replied the surgeon. 'There was indeed poisoning . . .'

'We already knew that.'

'Yes, but I've now established premeditated poisoning. All my observations – and of course I checked everything several times – lead me to this assertion.'

Nicolas felt a chill descend on him, and he had to sit down on a stool. So, what he had suspected from the start had at last been confirmed.

'And what are your reasons?' asked Bourdeau.

'Oh, two rats! Or rather, six, because I did the experiment three times, which makes twelve, because I used one group for the liquid and the other for the food. The chicken didn't produce any result, but the liquid – what a massacre! I tell you, that poison's more effective than arsenic if you want to get rid of rats. At first the animals seemed confused, then the symptoms started coming thick and fast. Yawning, spasms, abundant sweating, squeals of distress. When they were shown water, they immediately ran to drink it, but as soon as they'd drunk it they rejected it and started crying out in pain. In the end they brought up phlegm tinged with blood. Within a quarter of an hour they were dead.'

'And what kind of poison was it?'

'That's the problem. I have no idea.'

'What do you mean?'

'That we still have to identify the corrosive ingredient in the beverage.'

'You know it exists, then.'

'I finally managed to precipitate it. By reducing and drying the traces of humid material, I ended up with some tiny fragments of crushed seeds.'

'What kind of seeds? Can't you see I'm on tenterhooks?'

'That's just it. I don't know. I don't recognise them at all, even though I've travelled in many regions of the world. In some ways, I'm reminded of the plant poisons whose effects I witnessed in the Americas: lianas with poisonous seeds which cause convulsions. I was up until late last night looking through my library, consulting every author I could think of. Even Pouppé-Desportes in his work on the common plants of Santo Domingo doesn't describe anything similar. I'm off to the Jardin du Roi now to question my colleagues and to look at their collection. As you know, I'm currently putting together a herbarium of exotic plants, so I do know something about the subject. But this business has defeated me.'

'Keep us informed,' said Bourdeau. 'But before you go, I'd like to ask you one last question: could this poison have been administered to Madame de Lastérieux by one of her two black servants from the West Indies?'

Semacgus thought this over for a moment. 'It's possible. The flora of those regions is highly diverse and therefore little known. But in that case, they would have had to bring it with them when they travelled to France. To what purpose? It would have had to be a long-premeditated crime, which seems to me quite a rash assumption to make! I must leave you, my dear Bourdeau. By the way, is Nicolas still at Versailles?'

Bourdeau looked at him in amazement.

'Don't be surprised, I went to Rue Montmartre this morning. He'd sent a message to Monsieur de Noblecourt saying he was at Versailles, staying with his friend La Borde. He must be fishing in the Grand Canal, the lucky fellow!'

Bourdeau and Nicolas both reacted worriedly to the mention of this mysterious messenger whom neither of them had dispatched.

Semacgus left without a glance at the clerk, who was stubbornly keeping his head down. Bourdeau waited a few moments for his steps to fade before he turned to Nicolas.

'I'm sorry about what we've just heard,' he said. 'So, here we are, ready to get down to the job. The real investigation begins here, and I think the first thing we should do is question our two tropical birds. What do you think? Madame de Lastérieux's servants must surely be our prime suspects. This business with the poisoned seeds could well be their doing. Do you know them well?'

'Fairly well. I've been seeing them for the past year at Madame de Lastérieux's house. They're good servants. They can speak French, and have always struck me as being docile and discreet.'

'Did Madame de Lastérieux treat them well?'

Nicolas's momentary hesitation did not escape Bourdeau.

'I think so . . . Although Julie could be harsh to them. She was rather influenced, during her stay in Guadeloupe, by the customs of the Creoles, who treat their slaves, for better or worse, like pieces of furniture. I got the impression, from the occasional complaint I overheard, that her two servants were hoping to be freed, but that she obstinately refused. She was very comfortable here, but wouldn't have tolerated being abandoned by servants she had complete control over and only had to feed and clothe.'

'Would being freed have brought an improvement to their situation?'

'To them, it represented a hope that they might see their country again. Once freed, they couldn't legally stay in France. They would have been forced to take passage at Le Havre. I'll have to have another look at the legislation and then talk to you again. For example, our dear Awa, who prepares us such delicious suppers, was freed by Semacgus well before the edict of 1762; that's why she's allowed to stay on at his house in La Croix-Nivert.'

'She wouldn't abandon our friend for anything in the world,' said Bourdeau, smiling. 'She'd probably prefer to go back to servitude if that was the only way she could remain here. How old are they?'

'Hard to say,' replied Nicolas. 'These natives tend to look young for a long time, then suddenly age. But Casimir can't be more than twenty-five, and Julia about twenty.'

'Are they married? Can they be?'

'They can, being good Christians, but I'd swear they've never said vows before a priest.'

'Do you think them capable of such a terrible crime?'

This time, Nicolas did not hesitate. 'I cannot imagine those two dreaming up or even flirting with the idea of such an insane plan to get rid of their mistress. The means used, those mysterious foreign seeds, would have immediately given them away. I should also mention that Julia was recently baptised, and Madame de Lastérieux was her godmother. A relationship like that would make the crime even more unthinkable to these people.'

'Open your eyes, Nicolas. You don't seem aware of the gravity of the situation. I shan't hide from you the fact that, if those two turn out to be innocent, your position wouldn't look good to any magistrate who gets hold of the case. In fact, you'd make an ideal culprit. A deceived and rejected lover, they'd say, driven by jealousy to take an extreme course of action. They'd also observe that you knew the customs of the household and were in a position to throw suspicion on the servants. They might even go so far as to insinuate that you were after Madame de Lastérieux's fortune . . .'

'Stop it, Pierre. You're worse than a procurator. I'm not in the dock yet.'

'What I'm trying to say, Nicolas, is that we must be prepared for the worst. Do you know if Julie had made a will?'

'She was still rather young to be thinking about it, though I do vaguely remember her mentioning the matter to me once. Her only relatives, she said, were some distant cousins. She thought it best to leave everything to a number of charities. It was her husband's sudden death that had given her that idea.'

'Do you know the name of her notary?'

'It shouldn't be too hard to find out. Someone relatively new to the city, like her, would usually choose the nearest one.'

'If we find out who it is, we'll have to talk to him. You know from experience how much useful information a will can sometimes contain. But the most urgent thing is to question the servants and the dinner guests. Do you think you can draw up a list?'

'I can tell you how many there were without any problem. But who exactly they were will be more difficult to find out. When I arrived for the first time, late that afternoon, the people there, apart from Julie and the two servants, were Monsieur Balbastre, the organist of Notre Dame, a musician who was playing the pianoforte, and four young men playing whist. All a bit vague, as you see.'

'Monsieur Balbastre may be able to tell us more,' said Bourdeau. 'Let's draw up our plan of campaign. First, question Julia and Casimir, who are at the police station in Rue du Bac. Commissioner Monnaye's in charge there. Have you ever met him? He's always seemed to me to have rather a sharp tongue.'

'That's an understatement. I've heard of some very unfriendly remarks about me and some caustic writings in prose and verse about Monsieur de Sartine. If he'd seen them, it would have made his wig fall off.'

'There's no time to waste! Adjust your false belly – it's dangling on the right-hand side – you look all lopsided!'

The door of the office suddenly burst open, and the Lieutenant General of Police appeared.

'I don't know if my wig's likely to fall off,' he cried. 'But I'd like to point out that the position of Commissioner Le Floch, who is supposed – note that word, gentlemen – supposed to be recovering from his grief in a cocoon-like retreat within the royal palace, is definitely lopsided, not to say compromised.'

He came and stood in front of Nicolas.

'Just look at this get-up! What a sight you are! A disguise like that wouldn't look out of place on the stage. Anyone would be taken in by it. You ought to walk up and down the boulevard or display yourself at Ramponneau's.[2] Your career would take off immediately!'

Suddenly, his face creased, and he grabbed a stool, sat down, and began gasping with laughter, while the two men looked on – Nicolas anxiously and Inspector Bourdeau quite unruffled.

IV

DARK DEEDS

Experience began to take the place of age, it had the same effect on us as years.

Abbé Prévost

Never, thought Nicolas, had Monsieur de Sartine let himself go like this in front of those closest to him. The object of his hilarity must really be worth it. Every time he looked at the stunned expression on Nicolas's face, not to mention his absurd costume, his laughter started up again, louder than ever, lighting up his face and fleetingly making him look his real age. His usual gravity and composure were cracking like a veneer, revealing a rough sketch of a happy adolescent. But gradually he calmed down, grew serious again and anxiously adjusted his wig.

'I imagine, Commissioner,' he said, 'that you were expecting some fit of anger on my part. It would certainly have been justified. There are many things I could say about your thoughtlessness – if that is not too weak a word. It's beyond my understanding that you should have heeded the poisoned advice of a friend acting on my orders. To give Bourdeau his due, he was not at all happy at the idea of deceiving you.'

Nicolas cast an indignant glance at Bourdeau, who did not flinch.

'Oh, you can forgive him. He defended you tooth and nail, being more convinced of your innocence than anyone, even before it had been established that this was a criminal matter. No use looking at me with that air of dismay. You've been with me for nearly fifteen years. Have I ever struck you as being so naïve as to take a suspect purely at his word? For, whether you liked it or not, that was what you were, potentially, even though my natural inclination and my warm feelings towards you led me to believe you innocent. Those feelings, anyway, were the man's, not the Lieutenant General's. You know my love of secrecy. I wanted to see you at work on an investigation where you would be free to do as you wanted, knowing that Bourdeau would keep me informed of everything.'

'Monsieur,' said Nicolas, taking advantage of a pause, 'one question, just one question. Why has this test – not that I'm complaining about it—'

'I should hope not! You are hardly in a position to do so, and I note that you don't exactly seem overcome with remorse.'

'Why,' Nicolas pressed on, 'has this test suddenly come to an end? If you'd let it continue, you'd have been able to back up your judgement even more conclusively.'

'Now he's giving me advice! Reason away if you must, but I have my own reasons for acting as I do, and I don't need to give an account of them to you. Try not to provoke me. I have every justification to be angry with you for your lack of honesty.'

'But what should I have done, Monsieur?' protested Nicolas. 'Should I have come to you and denounced a friend who had thrown me a lifeline? In not doing so, I wasn't betraying you. I was discreetly helping justice to do its work, since I was best placed, because of my intimacy with Madame de Lastérieux, to sift the truth from the lies.'

'There speaks a pupil of the Jesuits in Vannes,' said Sartine. 'But all I'm concerned with is the facts. Bourdeau's reports have certainly tipped the balance in your favour. There remains one factor, which will be decisive in restoring the trust I fully concede to you as a man and would like to restore to you as the Lieutenant General of Police too, Nicolas.'

'I am at your service, Monsieur.'

'I want you to tell me in as much detail as possible about your second visit to Julie de Lastérieux's house on the night in question.'

'That's easy, Monsieur,' replied Nicolas. 'I went back after my visit to the Théâtre-Français, determined to patch things up with Julie. As soon as I let myself into the house, I heard a lot of noise and realised that the party was still going on. That made me angry again and I decided not to show myself. As Monsieur de Noblecourt was giving a Twelfth Night dinner and I didn't want to go back to Rue Montmartre empty-handed, I went into the servants' pantry to recover the bottle of old Tokay I had bought for my mistress. On the way out, I bumped into someone I didn't know, a musician I'd seen for the first time that afternoon playing the pianoforte. As I was in a hurry, I shoved him aside. Then I passed Julie's servant Casimir and went downstairs.'

'I can bear witness to the fact,' said Bourdeau, breaking his silence, 'that when Nicolas returned to Monsieur de Noblecourt's house, he lost consciousness and broke the bottle in question.'

'Thank you,' said Sartine, handing him a letter. 'You have the Lieutenant General's trust and his certainty of your innocence.

May it please heaven that everyone is as convinced as I am! An impression, however strong, is not proof, especially to some of our magistrates.'

Nicolas opened the letter. What he read filled him with anger and dread.

7 January 1774

Monsieur

I owe it to myself and to my sense of moral rectitude as well as to the kindness you have always shown me to inform you of the following facts. I have just learnt of the death of Madame Julie de Lastérieux, a close friend and a distinguished harpsichordist, in conditions I cannot find words to describe.

However, rumours are circulating that she may have been poisoned. It so happens that last night I was invited to her house to dine with friends. Your clerk Monsieur Le Floch arrived late in the afternoon and had a violent argument with our hostess. He pushed me aside and ran out like a madman, much to the surprise of everyone present. Two or three hours later, as we were dining, I was told that he had come back and had crept secretly into the servants' pantry. Far be it from me to make accusations, but it seems that he was surprised tampering in some mysterious way with the dishes.

Whatever the affection I have for him, and all too aware at my age of how human passions may lead us astray, I was determined, Monsieur, to do my duty. I remain at your disposal and assure you that I am, more than ever, your very humble and obedient servant

Balbastre

'I've seldom read anything more ignominious and more hypocritical!' cried Nicolas. 'I have always known that the man has borne me a grudge since the very first time we met, without being sure why. Your clerk! He's always called me that, and in his mouth it's a genuine insult. As for this "secretly" and "mysterious" . . .' Nicolas was waving the letter. 'The nerve of the man!'

'Calm down,' said Sartine. 'I agree the letter is somewhat sickening. But make no mistake, it contains enough elements to condemn a suspect in a court of law. Imagine for a moment that you had concealed from me the fact that you had gone into the servants' pantry. What conclusions would I have had to draw from such an omission? We will of course have to look into the reasons for such rank hatred. It's too well founded not to conceal something else. The organist of Notre Dame truly hates you.'

'What are we going to do?' asked Bourdeau.

'There is no time to lose. We must question the servants. I've had them brought here from the police station in Rue du Bac. They're in my office, under guard. Nicolas, keep your disguise on for a moment. Rabouine, who never went any further than the Jardin de l'Infante, has left your clothes in Old Marie's box room, so you'll be able to change later and at last abandon this ridiculous get-up. I intend to carry out the interrogation myself.'

'Monsieur, one thing more,' said Nicolas. 'I don't quite understand why you are so personally interested in this affair. I don't dare think that my involvement is the only explanation for your concern.'

Sartine nodded his head with satisfaction. 'It seems that reason is gradually returning to that mad head of yours. I'm therefore going to answer you as frankly as possible and tell you something which I fear may come as a shock to you. What did you know about Julie de Lastérieux?'

Nicolas opened his mouth, but Sartine did not give him time to reply.

'Nothing, Monsieur! You knew nothing about her. You merely accepted blindly what she told you. For example, her husband did not die of fever in the West Indies. Pursued for trafficking in accounts and embezzling the King's money, he took his own life to escape justice. His fortune was confiscated and his property sold. However, a large proportion of this was ceded to his widow for reasons that will soon become clear. You saw her three or four times a week, sometimes less. What do you know of her activities outside those evenings? Very little.'

'But—'

'No buts! I know everything about her and you know nothing. Commissioner, imagine a woman who is received in the best houses in Paris, and who receives in her own house, several times a week, courtiers, men of letters, men of the world, and those idlers who are seen everywhere and put their noses into everything. She gave dinners, and the police – my police – paid for them. Her house in Rue de Verneuil – a meeting place for men of all conditions, both good and poor company – was not quite an open house; there were few women and no gambling, and it was a place where everyone spoke freely. I was the only person to know Madame de Lastérieux in her private role. She was very skilful at keeping all this from you. I was informed of what I wanted to know, and in a much more subtle fashion than I would have been by ordinary spies.'

Nicolas was stunned. 'And she never told me!'

'She was under strict orders not to, and she knew it was in her own best interests to obey them. I have to admit in your defence, Nicolas, that even in bed, where so many men pour out their secrets, you never divulged any, even though you were privy to so many. And the lady . . .' – he laughed – '. . . had been given instructions – forgive me, my dear Nicolas – to ask you many questions. You never yielded. It's very satisfying for the head of the police force to be so sure of the loyalty of his closest officer.'

'But, Monsieur,' said Bourdeau, 'if she had ever been suspected or denounced, this role would have exposed her to terrible reprisals.'

'That's a very sensible remark, Bourdeau. It was a risk we ran, certainly. But there's nothing for the moment to either invalidate or confirm the theory you're putting forward.'

Was it conceivable, thought Nicolas, that this woman he had loved so passionately had been deceiving him all that time, that he had been a mere plaything to her?

Sartine was looking at him sympathetically, guessing where his train of thought was leading him.

'You weren't part of the game, Nicolas. She was very fond of you and hoped one day to escape the constraints within which we kept her. That explains why she was so obsessed with the idea of your marrying her. She hoped that appearing at Court would free her. But rules are rules. To maintain order and serve the King, the ends justify the means, even when those means may be morally reprehensible.'

'Or may cost a human life?'

'Sometimes, yes, although there's nothing so far to indicate that this was the reason for her death. All the same, we need to throw some light on it. The very salvation of the State is at stake.'

The Lieutenant General led them to his office. Huge logs, specially brought from Vincennes, were blazing merrily away, with much crackling and throwing out of sparks: as usual, when Sartine was at the Châtelet, Old Marie had lit a fire in the great Gothic fireplace. In the centre of the room, Julia and Casimir stood waiting. They were in shackles, and two officers were guarding them. Sartine took up position in front of the fireplace, raised his slender figure to its full height, ordered Julia to be taken outside, and began interrogating Casimir.

In a somewhat singsong voice, the man stated his identity. He was a native of the island of Guadeloupe, about twenty-five years of age, Roman Catholic by religion, and served in Madame de Lastérieux's household as a slave. He described Thursday evening, when his mistress had held a dinner. There were eight guests. Monsieur Nicolas had dropped by late that afternoon, but had immediately left again. He had no explanation for this departure. The other guests were unknown to him, apart from Monsieur Balbastre, who was a regular, and a young musician who had been coming to the house for the past two weeks, and had even visited Madame de Lastérieux alone several times – staying very late on one occasion. The dinner had passed without incident. As was her custom, Madame had eaten very little. Asked whether he had seen Nicolas again during the evening, he unhesitatingly replied in the negative. He had seen his mistress for the last time when she retired to her boudoir to show the young musician a particular perfume. Julia and he had tidied everything and had gone to bed. Yes, Julia was his wife, even though no priest had blessed their union. He did not know if the young man had left or, if he had, at what time. The next morning, Julia had entered her mistress's bedroom and found her dead. She had screamed and he had come running.

Sartine then handed over to Bourdeau, who asked the slave if he had been well treated in the house. After a moment's hesitation, Casimir replied that he had never been mistreated and therefore had no reason to bear a grudge against his mistress. However, she had always refused to give them their freedom. For the dinner in question, he had prepared a chicken dish in the manner of the West Indies, using seeds from his country which he would be unable to find again as he had exhausted his stock of them.

Julia's interrogation confirmed what her husband had said. Either they had agreed on a story, or they were quite simply telling the truth. Sartine ordered them to be placed in solitary confinement in the dungeons of the Châtelet until the matter had been clarified.

'What did you make of that, Nicolas?' he asked.

'I found it quite puzzling,' Nicolas replied. 'There are several observations I might make. Firstly, for whatever reason, Casimir forgot – or omitted to mention – that he saw me the second time I left the house. Secondly, there is nothing in these testimonies to indicate that the unknown young man left Julie, which places him on the list of possible suspects.'

'I can well understand you might wish that,' said Sartine. 'We still have to identify him before we can bring him in for questioning.'

'It might be useful to speak to Monsieur Balbastre,' said Bourdeau. 'Musicians tend to know each other.'

'I fully intended to summon him,' replied Sartine with an ironic smile, 'to thank him for being such a good citizen and sending me that letter.'

'I have an observation to make, too,' said Bourdeau. 'Don't you think it's strange that Casimir should mention that the chicken dish was seasoned with a particular kind of seed, when we know that the poison came from seeds? If he's innocent, that's understandable. But if he's guilty, he must be very sure of himself and convinced that the substance in question won't be found.'

There was a timid knock at the door and Old Marie entered, a letter in his hand. Sartine looked at the seal, opened it, read the letter. He was silent for a few moments.

'It's as I feared . . .' he said at last.

He reread the missive and tossed it angrily on his desk.

'This Balbastre of yours is a viper, the kind that strikes more than once! Not content with writing to me to denounce you, he also wrote to Monsieur Testard du Lys, the Criminal Lieutenant. You know what he's like – every little shadow scares him and sends him shrinking into his robes! Fortunately, we've known each other for years, he trusts me, and ever since the Galaine affair[1] he's been singing your praises, Nicolas. But he hasn't only heard from that damned organist, he was also contacted by the young musician, who's no longer nameless: his name is Friedrich von Müvala, and he's a Swiss national. Before leaving – for apparently he left Paris yesterday – he saw fit to accuse you of threatening Madame de Lastérieux, and to mention that he found you engaged on some mysterious task in the kitchen at Rue de Verneuil.'

'"Mysterious!"' said Nicolas. 'The same word Balbastre used in his letter.'

'It's obvious the two of them have joined forces. But why? Bourdeau, I'm the head of the best police force in Europe. I want you to look at the register of foreigners as soon as possible, and find out who's arrived in the past six months and who left yesterday.'

Bourdeau hurried out of the office. Sartine was walking up and down.

'And what does the Criminal Lieutenant want?' asked Nicolas.

'What he wants, once you've got past all the usual convoluted courtesies, is nothing less than this: that, even though you are a police commissioner, I should remove my protection from you and authorise your arrest, so that you can be conducted to a place of confinement, where you will be interrogated with due process of law. That's what it's come to, and we shall have to find a way out. It's all my fault: I should have foreseen the dangers for you in that relationship. In trying to satisfy my need to control everything, which is both the prerequisite and the defect of my office, I have compromised my best officer. Yes, Nicolas, I regret it and I take full responsibility.'

In his anger, he brought the poker down on a log, breaking it to pieces. Nicolas was astonished to see such passion in a man reputed to be cold and insensitive. It was a justification, even a reward, for all the work he had done for him over the years. Nicolas was reassured to know that Monsieur de Sartine was so determined to save him, at the risk of jeopardising his own position, which was always at the mercy of Court intrigue, especially now that the current reign was drawing to an end.

Bourdeau reappeared, carrying a large register with grey covers. 'Since June 1773,' he declared, 'one hundred and seventy-two Swiss have entered Paris. The name of our musician is nowhere to be found. I've had a look at the alphabetical list of foreigners in furnished accommodation and hotels, and he's not on that either. We are going to have to rely on Balbastre for more details, since apparently he knows him.'

'Find Balbastre,' ordered Sartine. 'I assume he's at Notre Dame in the afternoon, either rehearsing or teaching. Nicolas will go with you in his clerk's costume. For my part, I'm going to give this case a great deal of thought. Come to me at police headquarters this evening, and we'll see where we stand. Nothing's going to happen before then. It's Saturday. Testard du Lys will wait for my answer – he won't make a move, knowing that I have a private audience with the King every Sunday evening. Hurry up now, and beware of that organist, he knows how to pull out all the stops!'

Sartine nimbly picked up a large cape, its edge trimmed with sable, wrapped himself in it, donned a grey tricorn with black braiding, and left the room. When Bourdeau and Nicolas left, Old Marie lifted a finger to his mouth and gave them a shameless wink. Now there was a man, thought Nicolas, who had grasped the situation quickly. In the carriage taking them to Notre Dame, the two men were silent for a while. It was Bourdeau who spoke first.

'The thing that makes me feel especially bad,' he sighed, 'is that you only responded with loyalty to the sham that I was under orders to force upon you. You even rejected my plan at first because you were afraid it would get me into trouble . . .'

Nicolas half turned to the inspector and gave him a thump on the shoulder. 'Let's not talk about it. The main thing is that

Monsieur de Sartine and you, Pierre, are convinced of my innocence at a time when fate seems to be against me. As for Balbastre, our first encounter at Monsieur de Noblecourt's house has stayed in my mind as a hateful memory. I was twenty, a young provincial newly arrived from my native Brittany, and couldn't tolerate anyone behaving arrogantly or contemptuously towards me. We've often met since then, but our relations have never grown cordial. The man's about fifty, but still struts like a dandy in his fine clothes and blond wig. He was a regular visitor to Julie's house. Don't trust him, he'll try and lord it over you. Make sure he knows from the start that you're acting on behalf of Monsieur de Sartine. I'll cough every time I think you should be on your guard.'

Throughout the short journey from the Châtelet to Notre Dame, Nicolas made an effort to make sense of the many thoughts assailing him. Julie, then, was no longer merely a desirable young widow, she was one of those paid agents thanks to whom the Lieutenancy General of Police kept track of everything happening in the capital, one of the conduits of information who made it possible for Monsieur de Sartine to say, 'Whenever four people talk amongst themselves, at least one of them is mine.' Reality was built on pretence, appearances were deceptive, and he had been a puppet in a kind of shadow play. The question of whether or not the feelings Julie had claimed to have for him were genuine was of little importance compared with what he had just learnt. By an incomprehensible kind of retrospective jealousy, the fact that the unknown young man had evidently seduced his mistress obsessed him as though it were happening now. From there, his reasoning led him on to blacken Madame de Lastérieux's character, to treat her as a creature who had been anybody's, as if by doing so he could assuage a grief he could not shake off. He hoped, too, that this devaluation of her memory would carry away all the rest, just as water thrown on the road washes away the rubbish. He saw himself as a man who had been led blindly, an ox ready to be a beast of burden, as his father, the marquis, would have said. It seemed to him that he had been walking on the edge of a precipice without being aware of the danger, and had taken vice for virtue and worshipped it accordingly. With the self-deprecating irony that always came out when he examined his own actions, he told himself that he was perhaps a little bit of a Jansenist, and consequently a little naïve. He had certainly been blind, and that was a lesson he would have to absorb.

They came off the Pont au Change and were in the Cité. Nicolas tried to dismiss his torments. He thought of their destination, Notre Dame, and of a conversation he had had with Monsieur de La Borde, a great lover of art, who scorned the 'vulgar work of the Goths'. The commissioner, who loved the old cathedral, had modestly countered with the views of Père Laugier,[2] author of an *Essai sur l'architecture* in which he sang the praises of the Gothic churches, despite the grotesque ornaments which disfigured them like the sediment of the ages. He had quoted the writer's thoughts on Notre Dame 'which strikes the imagination with its length, its height, the space above the nave, and the majesty of the whole'. The same author, much to the outrage of Monsieur de La Borde, found Saint-Sulpice to be highly overrated: there was nothing there, he wrote, 'but thickness and mass'. There had ensued an interminable evening during which each of them, expanding on his own ideas, had ended up cheerfully conceding the other man's point of view.

When a spot of traffic congestion held them up at the corner of Rue de la Lanterne, Bourdeau, who, once again, seemed to have been following Nicolas's train of thought, asked, 'Do you still love the cathedral as much as you did?'

'Of course. Why do you ask?'

'When I first met you, you frequently attended services and choral concerts there in the company of a friend of yours, a seminarist at the college of the Thirty-Three.'

'Pierre Pigneau. Good Lord, you're right! How long ago all that seems!'

'Come now, you're still a young man. What's become of him?'

'According to the latest news, which in his case is never very recent – in fact, it's probably at least six months old – after many adventures he'd ended up in Pondicherry. I believe that after the death of Monseigneur Piguel, the bishop of Canathe, Pope Clement XIV appointed Pierre his successor. So there he is, mitred and the coadjutor of the apostolic vicar of Cochin China. It's what he'd always dreamt of. To think that we used to gorge ourselves on rum babas from Stohrer's, the King's pastry maker in Rue Montorgueil!'

'You surely know the latest fashionable dispute?'

'No, but I'm sure you're going to tell me.'

'They're talking of whitewashing the interior of Notre Dame to make it brighter. Bring it up to date, so to speak.'[3]

'It would be a grave mistake. The building's patina of age and impressive darkness are what give it a sense of religious awe.'

Bourdeau lowered the window and leant out. Then he sat down again with a sigh. 'Another dead animal being cleared off the road and sent to the knacker's yard! They work these poor nags to their last breath. It shouldn't be allowed.'

'Write Monsieur de Sartine a memorandum entitled *Obstacles to Traffic*. He loves any excuse for making new regulations.'

Bourdeau laughed. 'That reminds me of something. In 1759 – I don't know if you were in Paris yet – Monsieur de Lalande, the astronomer, read a paper on comets at the Academy of Sciences, in which he said it was quite possible that one of these heavenly bodies would come crashing into our planet and reduce it to powder. The rumour that the world was about to end soon spread. Crowds rushed to the confessionals. I was given the task of keeping order around Notre Dame. Now that was impressive. Imagine a nightmarish crowd flocking to be heard by the Grand Penitentiary, the only man authorised to hear confessions of the worst cases. I can still see those terrifying faces, real gallows birds all of them. Quite a time, I can tell you!'

The traffic started moving again, and at last they reached the cathedral. The winter sky was so low that the smoke from the chimneys merged with the fog and the old church was invisible above the level of the frieze of Old Testament kings. As soon as they entered the cathedral, Nicolas was, as always, impressed by the monumental statue of St Christopher. The air was vibrating with snatches of organ music from the gallery. So Balbastre was there. They asked their way of a passing canon, who was so stooped that his chin touched his chest and he had to lift his head with his hand to look at them. He pointed them in the direction of the staircase leading to the gallery, and then let his head drop again. By the time they reached their destination, Nicolas was sweating beneath his false belly and Bourdeau was red in the face and panting like a bull. They glanced at the enemy flags lining the circumference of the building and the hats of dead cardinals hanging by threads from the vault. They heard a familiar voice, both shrill and pompous.

'Would you like to tell me what the *tremblant* is, Monsieur? . . . It may be the state into which my question plunges you. The *tremblant*, Monsieur, is the system which alters the rate of flow of the emerging wind in such a way that it comes out through the pipes in regular bursts and produces a trembling sound. Redeem yourself, you ignoramus. What is a strong *tremblant*?'

'I think, Master,' came a small voice, 'it's the one we use in the great stop.'

'That's better. But don't think you've got out of it. Define the great stop.'

'The great stop . . . is the stop . . . which . . . where . . .'

'Nothing! You're just a stupid ass. The great stop is the name given to the principal keyboard . . .'

They heard a fist beating wood.

'Without the great stop, there's no jubilation, no brilliance, no dialogue between the different resonances.'

Bourdeau coughed. Half a dozen terrified faces turned to him. The protagonist of the scene did not even deign to move his head.

'Who takes the liberty of disturbing Monsieur Balbastre when he's teaching?'

'I'm terribly sorry, Master,' said Bourdeau. 'Monsieur de Sartine, the Lieutenant General of Police, asked me to come as soon as I could. He's extremely grateful to you for the letter you were so good as to send him concerning the sad events in Rue de Verneuil, but requires some further information. Inspector Pierre Bourdeau, at your service.'

Bourdeau bowed, sweeping the floor with his tricorn. Nicolas thought the gesture a trifle exaggerated, but it was probably necessary in order to assuage the organist's wrath. Balbastre turned stiffly on his swivel chair until he was facing Bourdeau. His round, pale face was framed by a curly blond wig and covered in ceruse to conceal the wrinkles. The cheeks were spotted with rouge in an apparent attempt to hide the fact that he had no cheekbones. His ill-assorted garments – a daffodil-yellow waistcoat and mottled breeches with gold threads – made him look all the more like an automaton perched on its mechanism.

'Inspector? Am I only entitled to an inspector? I won't speak to anyone but the Lieutenant General.'

'I'm sorry to have to contradict you,' replied Bourdeau. 'You'll have to speak to me first. Monsieur de Sartine is at Versailles.' He turned to the pupils. 'And first of all, gentlemen, it's break time. Monsieur Balbastre is allowing you to go. Come on now . . .'

He waved his hands, and the pupils scattered like a flight of sparrows.

The organist got down off his chair and waddled towards Bourdeau. He reminded Nicolas of some exotic guinea fowl engraved on a Coromandel screen.

'What gives you the right, Monsieur?'

'Monsieur de Sartine has given me full authority to question you,' said the inspector. 'Now sit down and listen.'

Balbastre obeyed.

'In the letter in question,' began Bourdeau, 'you make a

number of serious accusations against Monsieur Le Floch. I would like to hear from your own mouth the arguments on which you base these.'

'Far be it from me to accuse anyone!' the organist cried. 'I merely reported the facts. And sometimes it is the facts that accuse—'

'How long have you known Commissioner Le Floch?'

'Commissioner? That little notary's clerk? What kind of age are we living in, when false values take pride of place? I first met him some fifteen years ago at the house of my friend Monsieur de Noblecourt. We've met occasionally since. Your "commissioner" wormed his way into the trust of that honourable magistrate and took up residence there, plundering the house and spending the inheritance of his benefactor, who didn't see through his game. I'm convinced he also had his eye on my lovely friend Madame de Lastérieux's inheritance, the master deceiver that he is.'

Bourdeau glanced anxiously at Nicolas, who stood with his head bowed, seemingly lost in contemplation of the inscriptions on a Pomeranian standard.

'Are your assertions based on specific facts?'

'Who needs specific facts? The lovely Julie had no secrets from me, let me tell you.'

Nicolas coughed, and the organist looked daggers at him.

'Are you suggesting you had a liaison with Madame de Lastérieux?' asked Bourdeau.

Without replying, Balbastre shook his blond wig triumphantly, and his head was immediately surrounded by a cloud of scented powder.

'So you won't answer? Very well, others will be more

talkative. Despite your lack of esteem for Monsieur Le Floch, it is well known that you were on speaking terms with him.'

'If we refused to be on speaking terms with all those we despise, we'd never leave our houses. I deigned to respond to his greetings. I'm sure he was afraid of me. After all, I do have some influence at Court and in the city. The Dauphine often requires my services.'

'A man as well connected as you must have been familiar with the regulars at Madame de Lastérieux's house.'

'Of course! Although on the evening of which we are speaking, most of them were strangers.'

'Most or all?' asked Bourdeau.

'There were four young people there, all very handsome, who had been introduced by that Swiss gentleman, Monsieur Friedrich von Müvala.'

'Ah, yes. Tell us a little about him. What do you know of him?'

For a moment now, Bourdeau had been trying to attract Nicolas's attention. Nicolas remembered that he was supposed to be taking notes of what was said. For fear of arousing suspicion, he had to give some substance to his role as a clerk.

'An interesting gentleman,' said Balbastre. 'A native of the Valais, travelling around Europe. Quite an artist, paints beautifully and plays the pianoforte quite well too. He's also interested in botany, and is trying to put together a herbarium from the different regions of Europe.'

'Where did you meet him?'

'He accidentally knocked into me one evening at the Opéra, and then apologised so graciously and displayed such knowledge of my work that—'

'So he knew you?'

'After we had introduced ourselves, obviously. I invited him to one of my musical afternoons, in order to hear him on the pianoforte. It was on that occasion that I introduced him to Madame de Lastérieux. That was two or three weeks ago.'

Nicolas handed Bourdeau a little piece of paper. He read it and stuffed it in his pocket.

'Tell me, Monsieur, you wouldn't invite someone you despised into your house, would you?'

'Never,' said Balbastre, laughing. 'I might acknowledge him in the street, that's all.'

'I happen to know for certain that you have invited Commissioner Le Floch several times. Dozens of times, in fact, over the past fifteen years. He once even demonstrated the bombard, an instrument from his native province, in your house. I shan't hide it from you, Monsieur, there are some very contradictory elements in all this which might be thought to throw doubt on the rest of your testimony. You despise the man, you slander him, you belittle him: that all makes perfect sense, but then you invite him to your house dozens of times. Don't you think that's strange?'

Balbastre went over to a cast-iron brazier filled with glowing coals, as if suddenly aware of how cold the cathedral was.

'Inspector, I'm going to tell you everything. I don't know if I can . . . if I should . . . and what risks I'm running . . .'

The organist had lost some of his arrogance. He looked round him like an animal at bay, peered towards the top of the staircase, and slunk the length of the organ case, as if trying to merge into the darkness at the far end of the gallery.

'To tell the truth,' he resumed, 'I have nothing against Monsieur Le Floch, whom I admit I have often invited. Just a touch of jealousy, perhaps, towards a young man who seems to succeed in everything he does, but nothing malicious. Nevertheless, I received orders from someone highly placed, very highly placed, to introduce him to Madame de Lastérieux a year ago.'

'Who gave you that order?'

'I can't say, on my life.' He was still standing in the shadows, in an attitude of dejection.

'The fact remains,' said Bourdeau, 'that you have made serious allegations against Monsieur Le Floch.'

Balbastre bridled at this. 'That may be what you think, but you're wrong! All I did was report what happened. Everyone saw the altercation with Madame de Lastérieux. He was so angry that he bumped into me as he left the room and spilt my drink over my silk doublet, which was completely ruined. He's a madman, I'm not exaggerating.'

'What about what happened next?'

'Well, I have to be honest and say I didn't see it myself. It was Monsieur von Müvala, coming back from the servants' pantry where he'd gone to look for a bottle, who told me that Le Floch had come back in the house, doing God knows what in the kitchen, and that when he was surprised, he'd quickly fled.'

'Did anyone else witness that?'

'Not to my knowledge.'

'What's your personal opinion of Madame de Lastérieux's death?'

'I wouldn't dream of having one, as I have no idea of its true cause.'

'And if I told you it was murder, what would your reaction be then?'

'The same, Monsieur. I'm not trying to accuse anyone. All I want is for the truth to come out and justice to be done.'

There was a short silence, then Bourdeau said, 'One more thing. What time did you get home?'

'I'd given my coachman the evening off. It wasn't easy to find a cab at that hour. It was about midnight.'

'Can anyone testify to that?'

'Now you're accusing me!'

'I'm not accusing you, but all those present at that dinner are suspects by definition. I don't suppose you remember the number of the cab?'

'I wasn't in a fit state to notice, even supposing such a detail might interest me – I don't have a detective's eye.'

'No, just a detective's pen . . . Thank you, Master, you've been a great help. I shall inform the Lieutenant General of the details you've been so good as to provide. I have the honour of bidding you good day.'

Bourdeau walked back down the stairs, followed by Nicolas, who still maintained his stooped position. On the square in front of the cathedral, they had to disentangle themselves from a mass of beggars demanding alms before they could get back in their carriage. The horse stumbled in alarm, and it was only the coachman cracking his whip that finally dispersed the crowd.

'Strange character,' said Bourdeau as the carriage set off. 'Is it possible to make so many malicious accusations without actually believing them, without being driven by some deep-seated hatred?'

'To ask the question is to answer it,' said Nicolas.

'What did he mean by that order from above? Why would anyone want you and Madame de Lastérieux to be introduced? What interest could there be for this unknown person in throwing you into her arms? In fact, the plan succeeded only too well. After what we heard earlier, I wonder if this could have been another of Monsieur de Sartine's little tricks?'

'I don't think so,' replied Nicolas. 'He would have told us. He's already revealed that, in his determination to know everything, he was having me spied on. That was the main thing. Why would he have omitted a detail such as the fact that he had had me introduced to Julie?'

'Who, then? The First Minister, the Duc d'Aiguillon? Monsieur de Saint-Florentin, Minister of the King's Household? He and Monsieur de Sartine are very close. The King?'

'Why not the Pope or the general of the Jesuits? Don't get carried away. Balbastre seemed terrified. Do you think he could be a Mason?'

'Sartine is.'

'Yes, but there are rival lodges and different obediences. What if someone wanted to get Monsieur de Sartine into trouble?'

'We'd still have to resolve an equation. The police have a hold over Julie. Balbastre has influence and authority over her. How is all that linked, unless there's a connection between her secret activities and the pressure exerted on her?'

'The best thing might be to ask Monsieur de Sartine.'

Bourdeau nodded and looked at his watch. 'Let's go back to

the Châtelet. You can get rid of that disguise and dress as yourself again. Then we'll go to police headquarters.'

Nicolas was lost in thought again. What Bourdeau did not know, and what he could not tell him, was that both he and Sartine belonged to a select group of men trusted by the King and involved in secret diplomatic activities. Even the Duc d'Aiguillon, the Minister for Foreign Affairs, for all the esteem in which the monarch held him, had not been deemed worthy of penetrating its mysteries, or perhaps it was more convenient for him to be kept apart. In his secret study in the small apartments at Versailles, the King received information from foreign capitals, some of it sent by his appointed ambassadors, but some sent in coded dispatches by his secret agents. There were a few ambassadors who combined both functions, but they were the exception. The information, coming as it did from two kinds of sources, often tallied but was sometimes contradictory, giving the King much food for thought. Nicolas himself received information from a native of New France named Naganda, a chief of the Micmac tribe who had remained loyal to France after the defeat in Canada, and had been recruited after a particularly grim affair[4] to keep an eye on the English and secretly monitor their activities. Since then, Nicolas had been involved, both directly and indirectly, in a number of different missions. It was possible that these had come to the attention of someone wishing to thwart the King's policies. Many people were involved in shadowy intrigues around the throne: foreign powers, the Duc d'Aiguillon in his desire to hold on to his position, Maupeou in his struggle with the *parlements*, and finally Choiseul, who had arranged the marriage of the Dauphin, and who hoped to reap benefits from the gratitude of Marie-Antoinette.

Nicolas was delighted to get back into his own clothes. By the time he left the Châtelet, night was falling. The fog was so thick that nothing could be seen beyond twenty paces. A shadowy figure emerged from the entrance to the old prison. Nicolas heard a brief whistle and turned, recognising Rabouine's signal. Rabouine came away from the wall and told him that their carriage had been followed by a cabriolet, and that an unknown man had got out of it, but that it had been too dark to make out his face. It could all have been a coincidence, so for the moment Nicolas did not take too much notice of this information. He did not even mention it to Bourdeau, who was waiting for him in the cab, half asleep.

At police headquarters in Rue Neuve-Saint-Augustin, Monsieur de Sartine, who was receiving visitors, joined them for a moment in the antechamber. He gave no indication of the impression Bourdeau's account made on him, merely observing that the early stages of the investigation had done nothing to strengthen Nicolas's position, and that the King had to be informed of the threat hanging over the head – he smiled graciously at Nicolas – of *his* servant. Nicolas was to come back at six o'clock in the morning, and they would go to Versailles together in his coach. They would attend mass in the Saint-Louis chapel, after which Monsieur de Sartine was hoping to bring forward his private audience with the King. Not that Nicolas should feel too conceited, he added: there was another affair, a very serious one, requiring an urgent decision, which had to be put before the monarch. He bade them both good night.

Bourdeau accompanied Nicolas to Rue Montmartre. Nicolas, remembering Rabouine's information, ordered the coachman to stop the carriage in the vicinity of Saint-Eustache. Bourdeau understood that something was the matter and asked no questions. He simply told Nicolas that the coachman would come and pick him up in Rue Montmartre the following morning. Nicolas plunged into the night. Once the cab was out of sight, he turned and walked back the way he had come until he was outside Saint-Eustache. From somewhere close by, he heard the sound of clogs, and the breathing of a horse. But the fog had grown thicker, and he could not make out a thing. He found the entrance to the church and went in. The huge nave was dimly lit by candles. He crept along a shadowy side aisle as far as a chapel which he often used when he wanted to make sure he was not being followed because from it he could see all the entrances. A few moments later, a figure wrapped from head to foot in a voluminous cloak came in and started looking around. The figure approached the chapel, brushed against the pillar behind which Nicolas was hiding, then continued on its way round the church. When it was on the opposite side of the central bay, Nicolas took advantage of the distance and the shadows to creep to the little door at the back of the building. He came out into a dead-end street which led to Rue Montmartre, close to Monsieur de Noblecourt's house. On reflection, it seemed to him that the person who was following him probably did not know him, or he could have saved himself the trouble and simply waited for him outside his dwelling. There were clearly threats against him coming from different sources, but he was still no clearer as to what they might be.

Nicolas found Monsieur de Noblecourt sitting by the hearth in the servants' pantry, wrapped in a madras and sipping a calming herb tea which Catherine had made for him.

The former procurator demanded to hear a detailed account of his day. The one thing that reassured him in what he heard was that the King was offering Nicolas his protection. He went back up to his apartments leaning on Nicolas's arm. Cyrus barked weakly but reproachfully when he saw them, not understanding why the regularity of his master's bedtime had been disrupted.

'As you've witnessed several times,' said Noblecourt, 'I sometimes have a kind of sixth sense that allows me to get to the bottom of complicated cases without being sure why. Age is turning me into a prophet. This seems to me a particularly difficult affair, because it conceals something else, and probably not just one thing but several.'

He saw a kind of incomprehension on Nicolas's face.

'Do my words seem confused to you?' he asked. 'Let me explain. Just as a river is the result of the convergence of several streams, this crime is the outcome of a number of different plots. Of that I am sure. Think about it and sleep peacefully.'

Thinking about this enigmatic remark, Nicolas prepared his Court clothes and went to bed in the silence of this friendly house.

V

VANISHING TRICKS

You have made me pass through the fire of the crucible, and have found in me no impurity.

Psalm 16: 3

Sunday 9 January 1774

Cardinal de La Roche-Aymon, the Grand Chaplain, had just intoned the *Domine salvum fac regem*. It was taken up in canon by the white-clad choristers grouped on either side of the organ gallery above the choir, barely visible in the waves of incense wreathing the high altar and the two gilded bronze angels tilting towards the tabernacle. The incense rose in spirals towards the half-dome of the apse and the skies in Charles de Lafosse's painting of the Resurrection of Christ. A strong emotion, an almost religious sense of loyalty, came over Nicolas as he gazed at the grey form kneeling on his *prie-dieu*: his master, King Louis XV.

The solitude of the man came home to him. Beside the King, the Dauphin and Dauphine, as well as his grandsons Artois and Provence, represented the hopes of the future. Since Nicolas had arrived in Paris, the Grim Reaper had cut a swathe through those surrounding the throne: two daughters of France – Anne-Henriette and Madame Infante – their mother, Queen Marie Leszczyńska, too soon gone, the King's son and his wife, the princess of Saxony, the good lady of Choisy[1] and many others whose faces he could still recall. This thought added to Nicolas's sadness. The unfolding of the liturgy had reminded him of the advice of his guardian and adoptive father, Canon Le Floch. 'You mustn't disperse your energies because you see torment and death everywhere. You know that everything is a test. Mourning and patience must engender the hope and impassivity through which one dies to the world.' Alas, he had not yet attained such wisdom!

Nicolas and Sartine had arrived just in time for the beginning of the service. Positioned behind his chief in a side gallery, he had been able to observe the personalities of the Court at his leisure. Beside Sartine was the shrunken form of Monsieur de Saint-Florentin, Minister of the King's Household. He could not think of him by any other name, even though the monarch's favour had raised his properties at Châteauneuf-sur-Loire to the status of a duchy and he now bore the title of Duc de La Vrillière. The best-informed man in France could see no end to the favours bestowed on him by the monarch: when he had lost his hand in a hunting accident, the King had provided him with a silver prosthesis, which he usually concealed with a silk glove.

Some distance from him was the Duc d'Aiguillon, Minister for Foreign Affairs and War, happily ogling all the women present with scant concern for his wife's feelings: he knew she would not hold it against him, accustomed as she was to the handsome duke's infidelities. She herself, Monsieur de Saint-Florentin's niece, was an example of piety, devotion and resignation to the rest of the Court. It seemed to Nicolas, as he looked at her, that they had not lied about her. He noted the sunken mouth, the lopsided nose and the distant gaze, not to mention a fishwife's figure with a huge chest and arms. The general effect, though, was not unpleasant, and he had heard her compared to 'a performance full of machines and decorations, with some marvellous features in no particular order, admired by the stalls but jeered from the boxes'.

The service was ending. The organ played a joyful fugue. The murmuring of the faithful grew louder. Everyone stood and repeated the words of the blessing. The officiating priests saluted the royal gallery and left the chapel in procession. The nave emptied. The King rose and took his gloves and hat from the hands of a chaplain. The doors of the chapel were thrown open and the Swiss Guards presented arms to the sound of a drum.

Monsieur de Sartine was whispering something in the minister's ear. The minister made a face and Nicolas heard him agree to speak to the King immediately. They waited a long time for him to return, which Sartine filled by examining a statue depicting *Glory Holding the Portrait of Louis XV*. A page appeared and summoned them to the council chamber, which was where, unusually, the King would receive Sartine today. The page bowed to Nicolas, who recognised him: it was Gaspard. Once in the service of Monsieur de La Borde,[2] Gaspard was now in the monarch's internal service. It was the King's trust in La Borde that had got him this flattering promotion. Although the man had performed a signal service for Nicolas in the past, he did not think the choice was an especially judicious one, and would not himself have advised it: the fellow was too partial to the lure of gold, and there were many temptations in the corridors and antechambers of the palace. They crossed the Hall of Mirrors, still filled with the Sunday crowd. Nicolas, who for a long time had been responsible for providing security for the royal family, particularly dreaded these days when anyone, provided they were properly dressed, with a hat in their hand and a sword by their side – a sword that could be rented at the entrance to the palace – could approach the King and his associates. Sartine signalled Nicolas to wait on a bench and entered the council chamber.

The commissioner could remember the days when there had been other furniture in the hall, before the taste for novelty had swept it away in 1769. He admired the gilded pedestal tables representing groups of women and children holding horns of plenty. Above, the cartouche in the central tableau proclaimed: *The King Rules by Himself*. Mercury was descending from the clouds, his caduceus in his hand, hovering over Louis XIV in Roman dress.

'Aha!' came a sarcastic voice. 'Young Ranreuil, sitting and gawping!'

Nicolas stood up and bowed respectfully to a little old man dressed in white satin, his face excessively made up, who was looking at him with an ironic expression.

'All hail, Monsieur,' Nicolas said. 'I was lost in the stars on the ceiling, with glory all around me. You are right to mock. I am unforgivable, and would deserve a blow from that stick of yours decorated with fleur-de-lis.'

'Oh, I've left it at home,' replied the Maréchal de Richelieu with a laugh. 'In truth, it's too much of a hindrance. One could not be more gracious than you are: a good pedigree hunting dog. The marquis, your father, had such repartee . . . Is it the marquis or the commissioner who is waiting on this bench at the door of the council chamber?'

He sighed, with all the bitterness of an old man who had never been admitted to the King's councils.

'To tell the truth, Monsieur, I still don't know that myself. His Majesty is receiving Monsieur de Sartine, and as you have so well observed, I am waiting.'

'But this isn't the usual hour for their weekly meeting. Some exceptional case, some salacious scandal likely to distract the King's melancholy soul? No matter. I wish you, Monsieur, a good wait. I am off now to pay court to the divine comtesse.'

The maréchal was a friend of Madame du Barry's, and was still hoping, through her, to satisfy his political ambitions. He had no compunction in recalling that his help had been indispensable to her when she had wanted to be presented at Court. Like it or not, it was thanks to him that enough sponsors had been assembled.

At last, the mirrored door of the council chamber opened and Monsieur de Sartine put his head out. Without a word, he looked at Nicolas with a pious air. Nicolas knew what that meant, and he followed him in. The King was tapping with one finger on the face of a bronze-trimmed rocaille clock that glittered between two Sèvres vases in the centre of the griotte marble mantelpiece.

'Commissioner Le Floch, at Your Majesty's service,' announced Sartine.

He had drawn Nicolas into the centre of the room, halfway between a console table and the end of the desk. The King turned and smiled. He was more stooped than ever, and his paunch filled out his grey, gold-embroidered coat. His face struck Nicolas as even more marked than usual, puffy in places, mottled in others. Only the brown, almost black eyes recalled the monarch of old. Louis took a few steps towards the table and leant on it with both hands, so that the ribbon of the Holy Spirit across his chest came loose. Then he turned his head and looked at the busts of Scipio the African and Alexander the Great.

'Who can tell me where Scipio defeated Hannibal?'

'If I may be so bold, Your Majesty, I believe it might have been at the battle of Zama.'

'Yes, that's it!' The King sighed. 'Ah, a Jesuit education . . .'

Nicolas knew that the monarch never approached a subject directly. Like a ship tacking against a contrary wind to reach port, the King, either through shyness or a concern not to rush his interlocutor, always took a roundabout route towards whatever he wanted to say.

'The Lieutenant General of Police has told me everything,' he said at last. 'You may rest assured that we consider you innocent in this affair. Now is not the best time to keep the matter quiet. The tragedy is already public knowledge and such censorship would only create even more of a stir. I do, however, insist on hearing from your own lips your word as a gentleman.'

'Sire, you have my word as the son of the Marquis de Ranreuil and your servant that I have no connection with the death of Madame de Lastérieux in any way, shape or form.'

'That is good enough for me, Monsieur.'

Showing little consideration for Nicolas's sensitivity, the King, with that delight in morbid subjects which was one of the strangest aspects of his nature, then asked for a detailed account of the autopsy on the victim. When he had heard it, he reflected for a long time.

'Do you understand English, Monsieur?'

'Yes, sire. Without taxing Your Majesty's patience, I can tell you that when the English fleet entered the estuary of the Vilaine, the Marquis de Ranreuil captured a detachment, including a naval lieutenant. This officer stayed at the Château de Ranreuil for one year as a prisoner on parole. At my father's request, he taught my sister Isabelle and myself his language.'

'That's very good.' There was another silence, then the King asked, 'Do you know anything about conjuring, Sartine?'

'Sire, there are several forms of—'

'The one I refer to is the most agreeable. The other evening, to amuse me, my grandsons the princes introduced me to a strange fellow, an English Jew named Jonas, who arrived in Paris four months ago—'

'Four and a half months,' said Sartine, with a smile.

'If you say so! He quickly became fashionable by deploying his talents for performing conjuring tricks and today there is not a single elegant dinner in Paris to which he is not summoned to serve up one of his own dishes. He earns a fair living, so they say.'

'Your Majesty is right, he takes four *louis* per session.'

'He is said to be superior to his colleagues,' the King went on. 'Especially Comus. He is finer, while the other is simply a quack. The fellow has an oafish air and a plump figure, which makes the distance between his appearance and the wonderful vanishing tricks he performs all the more impressive. You see where my train of thought is leading me. Marquis, you will have to vanish for a while. I am counting on your intelligence and devotion.'

The King took a document from a tortoiseshell writing case.

'Take this safe-conduct, it will be useful to you. It makes you my plenipotentiary. Sartine will tell you the rest. I wish you good hunting. A lady friend of mine who knows you well will be grateful to you . . .'

He held out his hand, and Nicolas pressed his lips to it respectfully.

Despite the cold, gloomy weather, Sartine had drawn Nicolas into the deserted park, and they had walked as far as the border of the Orangerie. Here, near the basin, the view was so open that no one could have approached them without immediately drawing their attention. The gravel crunched beneath their feet. With an inscrutable expression on his face, the Lieutenant General of Police was pondering his opening gambit, while Nicolas looked at him closely.

'I hope you are aware, Commissioner,' he said at last, 'that you enjoy His Majesty's particular trust and belong to that select group who are privy to his most confidential activities. I say this to impress upon you that the words I am about to utter must be consigned to the innermost recesses of your mind.'

Nicolas agreed.

'You know the impossible, constantly renewed struggle we wage against all those who try to weaken the King and the State with their endless slanders, all those pamphlets and lampoons we keep pursuing. For every one destroyed, how many others are widely distributed!'

All that was well and good, thought Nicolas, but he wasn't the one who turned fifty printing works upside down to find just one of those rags that had so obsessed Madame de Pompadour and now also angered the current royal mistress. At the beginning of her influence, Madame du Barry had suspected Sartine, who was a friend of Choiseul, of not moving energetically enough against these writings, and he had had to justify his actions.

'When they are printed in Paris,' Sartine went on, 'it's fairly easy.' He noticed his assistant's doubtful expression. 'Or at least, possible . . . We have the means to deal with them. On the other hand, what tricks we are obliged to resort to when these slanders are brought in to the country clandestinely! I am coming to the point. An adventurer who has long been known to the service, a refugee in England, publishes a scandal sheet by the name of *Le Gazetier cuirassé*. He calls himself, quite fraudulently, the Chevalier de Morande. His real name is Théveneau, and his father was an honest doctor from Burgundy who died of sorrow at his son's misdemeanours.'

'But if he's in England, Monsieur—'

'I'm coming to that, don't interrupt me, otherwise we'll catch our deaths in this high wind!' He folded the tails of his old-style wig over his throat. 'Encouraged by the success of his lampoons, this modern Aretino, has thought up an easier and less dangerous way to earn money. He chooses his victims, preferably rich. He makes it known that he's in possession of scandalous information about them, and that he believes it his duty to warn them and to find out if they would be upset to have these things revealed to the light of day and public opinion. He adds that, for a certain sum, he will spare them this unpleasantness by not publishing the information.'

'That's pure blackmail!' exclaimed Nicolas.

'The word hardly suffices. The shameless fellow, not content with applying to private citizens in this country, is now attacking the famous. For example, he dared to write to the Marquis de Marigny, until recently the director of the King's buildings and brother of the late Marquise de Pompadour, threatening to distribute a scurrilous lampoon about his sister. Then, to make matters worse, he made contact with Madame du Barry and threatened to publish what he describes as her secret memoirs. Imagine the King's indignation at the thought that not only may the reputation of a woman whose memory is dear to him be tarnished, but at the same time his current mistress is threatened with slander.'

'That's truly disgraceful! To attack a dead woman!'

'Finally he wrote directly to Madame du Barry, to try and get as much as he could from her. She complained to the Duc d'Aiguillon, the First Minister. D'Aiguillon consulted secretly with the English ambassador, who sent word to his own Court. His Britannic Majesty raised no objection, apparently, to this monster, this plague on society and scourge of the human race, being abducted from his territory. Albion would shut her eyes, provided everything was done in the greatest secrecy, without openly infringing the rights of the British nation. In consequence of which, the King gave his friend every latitude to act on her own initiative, which she did, unfortunately rather in haste.'

'Were you involved, Monsieur?' asked Nicolas.

'I wasn't even consulted! A man named Marie-Félix Dormoy, a bankrupt horse and cattle dealer, who'd fled across the Channel to escape his creditors, offered his services. With that, and in accordance with the agreement reached with the English, Monsieur d'Aiguillon, urged on by the comtesse and anxious to please her, organised an armed expedition to England of a group of officers led by a self-styled infantry captain named Béranger, who's actually a police spy and informer and was recommended to him without my opinion being sought and without my being involved in any way. As I'm sure you know, the Duc de La Vrillière, Monsieur de Saint-Florentin, is a relative by marriage of the Duc d'Aiguillon.'

'If I may be permitted to advance an opinion, I'm not sure it's a good idea to trust the English!'

'Spoken like a true Breton! But I fear you're right. A letter arrived two days ago. Nothing is going as planned in London. A series of traps laid by this demon Morande have ensnared our men led by that idiot incompetent Béranger. Great causes cannot be defended with small means. We have to find a solution urgently. At my suggestion, the King has chosen you for this mission. It has the added advantage that it will keep you out of Paris for a while, at a time when there's an ill wind blowing for you. These, then, are the King's instructions. *Primo*, shroud your mission in the utmost secrecy and try to settle the situation without causing a scandal. *Secundo*, bring back the members of our expeditionary force safe and sound. The prestige of the Crown and the maintenance of peace are at stake. In order to do this, you have his full authority to negotiate on equal terms with a representative of the Court of St James. *Tertio*, make contact with Morande, even if you obtain nothing from him . . .'

'It's always worth a try. I promise I'll do the best I can.'

Sartine smiled. 'Where that rogue's concerned, making a promise and keeping it are two different things! Now listen to me carefully. I need to warn you. Many people are interested in this business, for many reasons. It will be in all their interests to try and intercept you, including the English, who are skilful at playing a double game, negotiating with you in public while secretly trying to get rid of you. Above all – and I think you will understand me without my having to spell it out – great interests are at play within France. The King is getting older, you've seen as well as I have how tired he seems. The young lady with him distracts and . . . exhausts him. Be careful and come back to us.'

Nicolas, following up a thought that had occurred to him, asked, 'Has the Duc de La Vrillière been informed of the mission with which His Majesty has entrusted me?'

The response was an eloquent silence. Sartine took a few steps to the side, looking anxiously at the damp clouds lowering over the surrounding countryside.

'Well . . . The thing is . . . The possibility of a rescue mission was brought up, at least in its broad outlines. What does it matter if it's you or someone else? The important thing is that you're covered by the King and by me.'

It was a clumsy reply, and Sartine was being shamelessly evasive. It could mean only one thing: that the Minister of the King's Household was not in on this audacious plan. And that was not all.

'I must also tell you,' Sartine went on solemnly, 'that there is reason to believe that the writings in question, those concerning the lady of Louveciennes,[3] may interest many people. D'Aiguillon of course, for the reasons I've given you, but others too. You know I have a relationship of trust with Choiseul: it does not override my concern for the State. Behind his pagoda at Chanteloup, I am not unaware that he remains ever alert to the circumstances that might put an end to his removal from office. As for the parliamentarians, anything that threatens the throne and avenges them for their exile is fair means to them. That makes many beasts of prey prowling around the innocents. Oh, and another thing. The reason Madame de Lastérieux was given the task of sounding you out, unbeknown to her, was that His Majesty intended including you amongst his few faithful servants handpicked to deal with his most secret affairs. That necessitates, as I'm sure you can understand, certain precautions.'

'No doubt,' said Nicolas, not very convinced. 'I await, Monsieur, specific and detailed instructions.'

Sartine suddenly perked up. 'Now that's the kind of language I like to hear, the language of action, not the hot air of council chambers. You are to go back to Paris and spend the night at home. Pack your bags. Find an excuse to justify your absence, ten days at the most. Disguise it with a few gestures towards the truth. A one-horse carriage will come and pick you up at nine o'clock tomorrow morning. No one would imagine that you were leaving on a long journey in such a vehicle.'

'All the same, it seems a bit risky. If I'm being watched—'

'Let me finish. The carriage will take you to the Palais-Royal district. You're always telling me how congested with vehicles the area is in the morning! And you're right: Paris is a large city in which six thousand carriages circulate every day in the streets and squares. You urged me to remedy the situation, and I listened to you and posted sentries and guards on Place Louis-le-Grand and Rue Neuve-des-Petits-Champs to make sure the traffic flows smoothly. But tomorrow, I'm going to make sure it doesn't flow smoothly and that your carriage gets into a spot of congestion. You'll take your baggage and jump out of the one-horse carriage and straight into a travelling berlin. One of my men will take your place. No one will see a thing in the middle of all those coachmen, carters, rubble removers, chair carriers and barrow boys.'

He was rubbing his hands at the thought of the trick about to be played.

'Come now, Monsieur,' he went on, 'take that disapproving look off your face! You'll travel to Calais, where you'll take a ship. In London, you will go to No. 4 Berkeley Square, where you will find the instructions for your mission. What a relief it will be for me to know you are there!'

'And the King's minister in London?'

'Our ambassador, the Comte de Guines? He's at odds with His Majesty for the terrible job he's been doing, and his total lack of skill and finesse. You won't be troubled by the level of his talents: his vanity is equalled only by his vacuity.'

Nicolas recalled the rumours of a scandalous quarrel between the ambassador and his secretary, who accused his chief of stock-market speculation based on confidential information. It was also rumoured at Court that the ambassador had been challenged to a duel by Lord Crewen, who had imprisoned his own wife. Monsieur de Guines had contracted the pox in a house of ill repute in London and had seduced the mistress of the cuckolded husband, in order to pass the poison on to him. The poor confined woman, informed of the adventure, had taken her revenge by proclaiming out loud that she was being kept prisoner in her tower to avoid her talking about the illness with which her husband was afflicted.

'And who is to give me my instructions?'

'The Chevalier d'Éon.' Sartine grinned. 'I don't know if he'll be doing so in a coat or a dress.'

Nicolas remembered that this strange character's gender was

just as ambiguous as the role he played in the King's secret diplomacy. Those in the know claimed that he, too, had indulged in a little blackmail concerning a document, the divulging of which might have harmed Anglo-French relations. The chevalier was holding out on his master, changing position constantly while never quite severing his allegiance. His attitude swung between open revolt and conditional loyalty.

'And what should I tell Inspector Bourdeau?' asked Nicolas.

'So many questions! You don't tell Bourdeau any more than you tell the others. In any case, there's no reason for you to see him before you leave and, if you do, you must observe the most total discretion. This is a secret mission, and no one must know. I myself will put up a smokescreen of nonsense to keep him quiet.'

Sartine tapped his feet on the ground, either from impatience at the questions he was being asked, or more likely, discomfort at the cold and damp gradually enveloping them, leaving them chilled to the marrow.

'Ah! One more thing; and this is important.'

He rummaged inside his coat and took out a crimson velvet purse and a bundle of papers which he handed to Nicolas.

'Here they are, the sinews of war! It's a tidy sum in guineas and in gold *louis* for your travel expenses. Use it wisely and sparingly. Exchange the gold for currency as soon as you can, in order not to draw attention to yourself. As for the papers, they are bills of exchange for an unlimited sum, negotiable in every bank in London. I want to provide for every eventuality and not leave you without means. Make sure Morande doesn't try to extort an exorbitant sum from you, should you conclude negotiations. Dangle bait in front of a bird of prey like that and he'll cling to you and never let go. He'll eat you alive, asking for larger and larger amounts. Let's leave it there, you have to get back to Paris now and pack your bags. A royal carriage is waiting for you in the last courtyard. Don't forget to arm yourself when you go. I will see you soon.'

Nicolas walked off, and Sartine watched him, pensively. He made a little gesture of farewell, and the wind snatched his last words.

'Beware of tricks, mirrors that are too reflective, open doors, and the fortunes of the sea. Come back to us, the King needs you, and . . .'

Nicolas was now too far away to hear his chief's final words, but he thought he heard him say, '. . . and so do I.' It mattered little if it had really been said, all that mattered was that he thought it had, and he valued the man's esteem so highly that it filled him with a fierce joy.

Monday 10 January 1774

Without the inconvenience of travelling in one of the King's coaches, Nicolas's satisfaction would have been complete when he had returned to Paris the previous evening. But bad habits continued to prevail at Court, and the privileged users of these official vehicles never hesitated to relieve their bladders on the bodywork or to soil the velvet padding. And so it was surrounded by a pervasive odour of urine that Nicolas, with all the windows down, had travelled the few leagues separating Versailles from Rue Montmartre. He made an effort not to think of what awaited him, but he was shaken by an almost wild feeling of jubilation at the prospect of the mission with which he had been entrusted. Just as a horse left in the field shakes itself and prances, his mind was already wandering beyond the sea. This feeling accompanied him all the way to Monsieur de Noblecourt's house, where he arrived numb with cold, his heart thumping, his stomach empty. His last meal seemed like a childhood memory. He had a look in the servants' pantry and discovered an earthenware plate containing a pork stew preserved in aspic by the layer of congealed fat over it. He cut himself some long slices of bread, sprinkled them with thick grains of salt, and spread them with fat. He then attacked the meat in its tremulous amber casing. This impromptu feast was washed down with what was left of a bottle of cider and finished off with a few spoonfuls of quince jam from the latest batch.

He went up to his room and prepared his portmanteau, putting in it a spare coat, two shirts, a few pairs of breeches, two pairs of stockings, a pair of buckled shoes, a portable translation of Ovid's *Metamorphoses*, a small bottle of Carmelite water – a souvenir of Père Grégoire – and his miniature pistol, small enough to be fitted into the wing of his hat, a useful gift from Bourdeau. He cleaned his sword and carefully waxed his boots. Finally, he brushed his fine black woollen coat and his travelling cloak. He added some gloves and placed everything on a chair. Nor did he forget to sharpen his razor so that he did not need to bother with a strop, or to add a spare bar of soap in case he did not find any during the journey. Then he recited his childhood prayers and, trying not to think, fell asleep.

His departure went off without too many tears. He told everyone he was leaving for the provinces for about ten days.

Monsieur de Noblecourt was clearly not taken in by this. Nicolas got into the one-horse carriage he had been promised, the driver cracked his whip, and the horse set off at a jog trot. When they reached the Palais-Royal district, Nicolas became aware that some subtle manoeuvring was going on around him and that his carriage had been surrounded by others. The faces of the drivers were not unfamiliar to him. They were the faces of informers, officers and other police agents, all working for the Lieutenant General.

It was as if the whole of the police force and its cohorts had arranged to meet in these narrow, animated streets in order to create a chaotic merry-go-round. A heavy carriage, a shiny dark green in colour and edged in gold, stopped right up against Nicolas's frail vehicle. The door opened a little and a figure slipped out, jumped lightly to the ground, and made a sign to Nicolas to open his door. Nicolas took his portmanteau and slipped out, not without difficulty as there was barely any room between the two carriages. Once on the ground, he recognised Rabouine, dressed so like him that the two could easily be confused. This was clearly becoming a habit. He got into the berlin. The window curtains were half drawn. A letter bearing Monsieur de Sartine's seal of three sardines was clearly visible on the bench. A note on the front of it said that Monsieur Le Floch was to read it, absorb the contents, and burn it at the earliest opportunity. He put the document against his chest, between his shirt and his coat: he would read it later, once he had passed the city limits.

Miraculously, as if at the behest of some invisible ballet master, the congestion came to an end. The way now was clear, and the coachman cracked his whip against the rumps of four sturdy horses.

They passed through the tollgates without hindrance, the postillion having been provided with passes. Once past the *faubourgs*, Nicolas broke the seal on the letter. It contained a number of reports, one on the general situation of the British kingdom and the other on the position of the British cabinet towards George III's policies. Much mention was made of the difficulties of the British in India and the misconduct of the East India Company. The unrest amongst the American colonists was also discussed, especially those in Massachusetts whose judicial system was again to be administered from London and whose trade was to be burdened with the most tyrannical restrictions. This unrest had caused tremors in Parliament and brought to the forefront of the anti-ministerial phalanx a brilliant newcomer named Charles Fox. In the cabinet's estimation, the charter of the colonies was not so sacrosanct that it prevented England from making new regulations to prevent sedition. There followed some portraits and notes on the French in London. Nicolas stopped the coach beside a patch of waste ground, stretched his legs a little, struck a light and set fire to the papers. When they were nothing more than a heap of black ashes, he let the wind scatter them.

He discovered other papers stuck to the wall of the coach with sealing wax. One listed the various post houses on the route from Paris to Calais. From the *faubourgs* of Paris, he would proceed to Amiens by way of Saint-Denis, Écouen, Luzarches, Chantilly,

Clermont, Saint-Just, Wavigny, Flers, Breteuil and Hébécourt. From the Picard capital, he would then get to Calais by way of Pecquigny, Flixecourt, Ailly-le-Haut-Clocher, Abbeville, Nouvion, Bernay, Nampont, Montreuil-sur-Mer, Cormont, Boulogne, Marquise and Hautbuisson. In terms of cost, it implied that he would have to pay at forty-nine post houses. He calculated mentally that this mission by private post berlin drawn by four horses would cost the Lieutenancy General of Police about nine hundred and eighty *livres*, that is, twenty *livres* each post, or, he noted with amusement, the equivalent of about a hundred chickens bought ready-roasted or three good-quality wedding dresses – he knew this last detail because of a recent remark by Master Vachon, his tailor. A small leaflet informed him that the English did not accept French money and that he would have to change his gold coins as soon as he arrived in Dover: at the current rate, a *louis* was worth one guinea, or twenty-one shillings. But he already had a not inconsiderable number of English coins at his disposal.

His foot hit an object, which rang at the impact. He bent down and discovered a chamber pot with a white porcelain lid decorated with little flowers, the interior lined with fragrant dried herbs. This thoughtful touch, he decided, was there to tell him that he should not linger on the way: if he needed to relieve himself, he should use the pot, and when it became too full he could simply lower the window and throw out the contents. In this arrangement, he thought he detected the taste for childish pranks that sometimes showed through in Monsieur de Sartine. This was not the only utilitarian object in the carriage: there was also a little metal and wood foot-warmer filled with hot coals. Once again, he appreciated the thoughtfulness of it, and slipped the foot-warmer under the travelling blanket, where it started to give off a gentle heat.

The swaying of the carriage gradually induced a drowsy torpor. This half-sleep did not, however, stop him from thinking, and his tired mind went over and over the stages of the drama he had lived through since the death of Madame de Lastérieux and the new developments which had led him to become involved in this unexpected mission. A nagging pain resurfaced: not so much the pain of knowing that Julie had been deceiving him as that of not knowing how genuine their relationship, which he now missed, had really been. Desperately, he tried to think of anything that had happened that could explain this betrayal. At other moments, he saw the King's face, and remembered his elegant ability to maintain his distance while at the same time showing his kindness to those who enjoyed his trust, a kindness accentuated by those dark, gentle and still surprisingly young eyes. In the midst of his distress, Nicolas realised how lucky he was to be able to count on the indulgence of the monarch.

To get away from Paris gave him a sense of freedom. Like a bird fleeing a storm, he was escaping the cruel torments that had surrounded him for days. He was about to sink into a serene sleep when the carriage came to a halt in a great screeching of hand brakes and scraping of the wheels, as well as the strident neighing of the horses. Before he was able to move an inch – he was somewhat restricted by his blanket and foot-warmer – the door was thrown open, making the curtains fly, and a rider in a hunting costume the colour of dead leaves jumped in and sat down opposite him. When the visitor's head, which was concealed by a large felt hat with a white feather, was raised, Nicolas was surprised to recognise the almond-shaped blue eyes and gentle oval face of the Comtesse du Barry. She took off her hat, revealing a small white wig tied with an amaranthine ribbon.

'Good morning, Marquis. Forgive the disguise, I hope you remember me.'

Her nose crinkled and she gave a mischievous pout.

'May it please God, Madame—' He sat up and banged his head on the roof of the carriage.

She burst out laughing.

'How could anyone who has ever had the privilege of meeting you ever forget you?' he stammered in confusion. 'But to what do I owe this honour?'

'It's not a question of honour, Monsieur. A close friend, concerned about my interests, revealed to me the mission with which you have been entrusted. The success of your journey to London interests me greatly and I wanted to make sure that my fate was in good hands, that you would take up the cudgels on my behalf and give me back my peace of mind, in short, that I could count on your loyalty.'

'Madame,' said Nicolas, dumbfounded by this flood of words, 'that goes without saying. Let me set your mind at rest. As I had occasion to tell you some years ago, I—'

She raised her hand to interrupt him. 'Four years, Monsieur, four years! I haven't forgotten. I was convinced then that an opportunity would one day arise when you could be of service to me.' She seemed to be questioning herself rather than him.

'I promised you then that you could count on my zeal and my devotion,' replied Nicolas. 'I am your servant.'

She looked deep into his eyes, and he trembled, sensitive to the seductive power that emanated from the comtesse. She held out her hand, and he kissed it.

'Marquis, my eyes will go with you. Remember that you are amongst my friends now. Don't forget!'

She left the carriage as quickly as she had entered. He leant out of the door in time to see her disappear in a Court coach escorted by two bodyguards. His amazement faded and gave way, as the berlin set off again, to a kind of irritation. What was Madame du Barry doing, meddling in his business? Why couldn't she believe that he was content with what the King had ordered him to do without having to pursue him publicly? How could she imagine that these few minutes would encourage him to accomplish his task better? Then he realised that this irritation of his concealed a real sense of apprehension. This supposedly secret mission wasn't a secret any more. Madame du Barry, a coachman, two lackeys, two bodyguards, and God knew who else had had wind of his departure for London. Who had informed the comtesse?

He found it hard to believe, having been close to the King for fourteen years and having on many occasions observed his love of secrecy, that it could have been he who had informed his mistress: he would have risked compromising an enterprise he himself had devised to save the reputation of 'the beautiful Bourbonnaise'[4] from slander. Nor would Sartine, who always took care to pay court to the lady, have done something like that, aware as he was of the need to protect his officers' safety at all times. Saint-Florentin apparently did not know of the mission: Sartine's embarrassed response when he had questioned him on the subject had convinced him of that. Who, then? The Duc de Richelieu? It couldn't be him: no one would have dared tell him, with his reputation for not being able to keep a secret. What about the Duc d'Aiguillon? That was beyond the realm of probabilities, as the King preferred to keep things moving in parallel and never meeting. Nicolas wondered suddenly if the interview between Louis XV, Sartine and himself in a place as public as the council chamber could have been overheard. The crowd of lackeys and ushers must surely contain a few black sheep in the pay of those whose interests lay in knowing the secrets of those in power in order to ensure their position and increase their influence. Nicolas, moreover, was a little disappointed by his conversation with the comtesse, when he compared it with those he used to have with Madame de Pompadour, a jouster of quite another calibre and a much more subtle intelligence.

Tuesday 11, Wednesday 12 and Thursday 13 January 1774

The average time it took to get from Paris to Calais, depending on the season, varied between six and eight days by regular mail-coach. It had been calculated that this time had to be reduced by half: he wasn't travelling, he was flying. Nothing on this journey corresponded to the immutable rules of the mail. He changed coachmen several times: they all had the same surly appearance and the same respectful discretion. Fresh horses were waiting, stamping the ground, at each post house for the arrival of their exhausted predecessors. The most forbidding masters of post houses did their best to change his teams of horses as quickly as possible, however much they were kicked. Nicolas would stop at whatever inns he came across, plundering their reserves and eating in the berlin. He spent his time reading in the sad winter light or, at night, by the dim light of a lantern inside the carriage. In the morning, he would take advantage of a change of horses to wash himself thoroughly in the wells and fountains by the post houses, laughing at the sight of his skin, which was blue with cold, and provoking sidelong glances of delight from the local housewives and maids.

At Ailly-le-Haut-Clocher, on the way to Abbeville, a pig crossed the road and was hit broadside on by the speeding carriage. The team of horses stumbled and the carriage hit a milestone hidden in a thicket. One of the wheels broke. It had to be repaired and one of the horses, which had dislocated a leg in the accident, had to be changed. The wheelwright and blacksmith had been called away to a nearby hamlet. Weary of waiting beside a stable which was more like a covered dungheap, under the sardonic and curious eyes of the ostlers, Nicolas decided to spend the night in the local inn, which served as a post house. The repairs would take several hours. Night was falling and snow was in the air.

He insisted on paying a decent price for the pig that had been killed. It was a benevolent gesture – the animal should have been kept locked in and not left to wander on the public highway – and it unleashed a flood of goodwill on the part of the pig's owner, the innkeeper, who roused the servants to attend to the traveller's every need. The fire was immediately stoked and a table was laid near the fireplace for dinner. Before long, Nicolas was telling himself that, when conditions were like these, a traveller could be very happy in France. The most wretched inn always concealed something good to eat. His culinary curiosity was soon satisfied. He was brought an earthenware vessel containing a wrapped pâté. Its taste would haunt him all his life and he would strive in vain to rediscover its aroma. He tried without success to obtain the recipe. The host assured him that it was a family secret, which each father handed down to his son on his deathbed. The rest of the meal consisted of offal from the martyred pig, roasted on the hearth, and a robust cabbage soup. This improvised feast was washed down with a pot of beer, which was very bitter but with a lovely white foam, and concluded with a few bruised apples and a comforting glass of genever.

On the other hand, the room he was offered as being the best in the establishment left a lot to be desired. With its wobbly wooden furniture, its rough whitewashed walls hung with a few old scraps of tapestry, its spiders' nests and half-eaten moths, it was similar to many others he had encountered in the French provinces. The door was almost impossible to close and its hinges squeaked unbearably. Icy air whistled through the cracks in the shutter, which took the place of a window pane. It was not easy to open – nor, once this feat had been accomplished, to close again. The condition of the sheet convinced him not to get into the bed. The horror its population of creepy-crawlies inspired in him drove him to settle as comfortably as possible in an armchair covered in almost threadbare Utrecht velvet. He would stretch his legs on a stool. It did not take him long to fall asleep, but in the early hours of the morning he was awakened by the creaking of the door. Who could it be? He kept completely still, huddled in his cloak, his heart pounding, not wanting to raise the alarm. A shadowy figure approached the bed, and an arm was raised and came down twice. He heard an exclamation of surprise, hurried footsteps and the door banging. He stood up, grabbed his sword and ran out after the intruder. On the circular balcony, with its view over the central room of the inn, he stopped and listened. No sound disturbed the heavy, almost muffled silence, which reminded him of something long ago. The first light of dawn was starting to chase away the shadows. It suddenly occurred to him that there might be other travellers occupying the other rooms on the upper floor. Cautiously, he opened the doors one after the other: the rooms were empty. The last room was the innkeeper's. The man was genuinely alarmed that there had been an intruder. He went downstairs with Nicolas. The fire was rekindled and the candles lit, while the innkeeper's wife warmed up a little soup from the night before. Nicolas went to the open door and looked out. Now he knew why the place was so strangely silent: snow had fallen in abundance during the night. In the pale light of the new day, he saw a man's footprints on the ground, going in two directions, to and from the inn. He followed them for a long time across the fields, as far as a little copse. He advanced cautiously, listening out for any sound, and came to a clearing where the trail ended beside a great oak, in a confusion of other prints: clearly, a horse had been waiting here for its rider. The intruder seemed to have ridden off in the direction of Abbeville. It was at that moment that Nicolas, numb with cold but his consciousness sharpened, finally realised that someone had tried to kill him and that once again he had narrowly escaped death.

He went back to his room and discovered a scene of desolation. His open trunk had been tipped on the floor, his effects rummaged through and turned upside down. The bindings of the few books he had brought with him were slashed, the pages torn. Yet nothing had been stolen: the marauder had clearly been looking for something else. He must have been hiding in some corner. Luckily, Nicolas still had on him the gold, his bills of exchange and his papers of accreditation, but this latest incident proved that he was not dealing with bandits, who were always to be feared in open country, but that the attack was connected with his mission and that his attackers would stop at nothing to prevent him from carrying it out. He noticed that his shutter was open. He leant out of the window, but the area to the north was still plunged in darkness and he could not make out anything on the ground. He knew what he would have discovered: other prints leading to another copse where another horse must have been waiting. He folded his spare clothes and his coat as best he could, packed, and paid the grim-faced innkeeper for his board and lodging. His coachman was waiting for him at the nearby wheelwright's. He had already paid for the repairs. A new wheel had been fixed. The horses were brought and harnessed. No sooner was he settled in the berlin than the team, throwing up a cloud of snow, set off full tilt along the road to Abbeville.

VI

LONDON

> We are the only nation the English do not despise. On the other hand, they do us the honour of hating us as cordially as possible.
>
> FOUGERET DE MONTBRON

The wind was chasing away the morning fog, pushing the clouds in an easterly direction, and the sun was gradually coming through. Nicolas looked out, deep in thought, towards the horizon of a flat, ugly landscape whose monotony was broken at times by great forests with serried ranks of trees. Having given up the idea of sleep, he was on his guard and had told the postillion that, if there were the slightest alert, he was not to spare the horses. He continued to speculate on the reasons for an attack evidently intended to kill him. He recalled Monsieur de Sartine's warnings. The interests involved were so powerful that, now that his mission was no longer a secret, the threats that hung over his head had accumulated. He could understand that – his job had taught him all about the power and hidden influence of certain factions within the State – but what he could not grasp was the connection between the death of Madame de Lastérieux and this hunt in which he was the prey. From now on, his salvation and the success of his mission would depend on his skill in anticipating danger and avoiding it. They were trying to hurt him, to dishonour him, to deliver him into the hands of the law, which, as he well knew, could decide a man's fate speedily and sometimes indiscriminately. The trap in Rue de Verneuil and the murder attempt at Ailly could not be dissociated, but he was unable as yet to make sense of the context or disentangle the bizarre chain of cause and effect: the thread common to these two incidents escaped him. Monsieur de Noblecourt's prophetic words echoed in his head like a sinister warning: 'Just as a river is the result of the convergence of several streams, this crime is the outcome of a number of different plots.'

He changed horses at Abbeville, which surprised him with its antiquity, its old, poorly built houses of wood and cob. Night was falling, but he gave orders to continue. He then had to change horses again at Montreuil, where he rode past peat bogs that reminded him of the area around his native Guérande. Here, he had to insist in order to obtain the best horses, which another traveller, generous with his money, was demanding for himself. It was only by invoking the King's name that Nicolas managed to sway the innkeeper, despite the other man's threats, but it was an uneasy victory, as Nicolas could see his own anonymity gradually unravelling.

Friday 14 January 1774

Boulogne came into sight just before dawn. Nicolas ordered the berlin to be stopped. He had decided to modify his route. He asked the coachman to adopt a more moderate pace from now on and get to Calais, the original destination, without undue haste. This would make it seem as though the traveller was ill or exhausted. The curtains would be drawn and the coachman would have to ask for provisions in order not to attract attention at the last post houses before Calais. Once the carriage reached the port, he would trust the coachman to use his skill to disappear without revealing that his passenger had already gone. Meanwhile, Nicolas would enter Boulogne on foot through the *faubourgs*, and try to embark on the first boat leaving for Dover. He hoped that this ruse would throw his pursuers off the track.

Despite the still-bitter cold, Nicolas waited for daylight, leaning against a big tree on the top of an open hill. In this dominant position he could be sure not to be surprised from behind. The sun at last emerged behind him, setting the landscape aflame. It looked like being a fine day. Boulogne lay before him, squashed within its ramparts. Near the city, the River Liane widened as it approached the sea, flooding the low valley, where it shimmered, half-frozen. Flocks of motionless birds indicated the places where the water had turned to ice. The river finally plunged into the sea between two cliffs. In the distance, he made out a vast shore and oyster-coloured waves flecked with foam.

He walked down towards the city, through the poor *faubourgs*, and entered a tavern, where he drank a warming bowl of mulled wine heavily laced with brandy. Nicolas won the innkeeper round by offering him a few glasses. The man confirmed that it was possible to take a ship from Boulogne to Dover: the service had existed since the peace treaty of 1763 between the two countries. As well as taking passengers, these ships also transported bottles of French wine to England. Preserved in the cellars of Boulogne, this wine was the property of the British, who had it brought over as and when they needed it. Enquiring as to the reasons for this unusual system, Nicolas was told that, through this arrangement, the English wine lover paid only a percentage proportionate to his consumption of the considerable duty levied on French wine entering the United Kingdom.

Having obtained clear directions to the place of embarkation, Nicolas entered Boulogne, whose gates had just opened. The sentry on duty was surprised to see someone so well dressed coming on foot, and let him through without hindrance. The ship was due to set sail at about nine o'clock. He decided to go for a stroll. Although he avoided the busier streets, he was struck by the number of English people he passed. It was the difference in costume which distinguished them. He saw high-society women from across the Channel with their fashionable dresses and their little hats, and Boulogne women recognisable by their closed bonnets and full-length cloaks. Something about him attracted the attention of a local citizen standing outside his door taking the air, who proceeded to hold forth about the invasion of the English: Boulogne, he said, had long been a place of refuge for those from the other side of the Channel who, because of business difficulties or scandals aroused by their behaviour, found it more convenient to live abroad than in their own country. Time was passing, and Nicolas walked back to the harbour, where the office selling tickets for the ship to Dover was now open.

The moment he set foot on board, he felt very moved. It was the first time he had ever left France. He had always entertained the idea of going to sea, and now it was happening without his really having sought it. The ship, the *Zéphir*, was an old merchant vessel, of which a part of the interior had been converted to sleeping quarters. But there were only makeshift beds for a dozen people, a figure well below the number of possible passengers. The captain greeted Nicolas and informed him that for several days the weather had been stormy and ships of all nationalities had been forced to remain in the English ports. But, in his judgement, the wind was variable and, by following its direction, it should be possible to gain three hours on the duration of the crossing. They would be casting off very soon. A few passengers ran to take shelter in the interior of the ship, but most remained on the poop deck in order to watch the departure without disturbing the vessel's manoeuvring.

Nicolas surreptitiously observed his travelling companions. There was a French merchant with his clerk, both talking loudly, and near them, two young Englishmen, whose appearance, words and nonchalant attitude indicated that they had just completed the Grand Tour, which any son of a reasonably well-off family owed it to himself to make in order to get to know Italy, Germany and France, however superficially. The naval officer who had once been a prisoner on parole in the Château de Ranreuil had told him that the new world had to be known in all its variety. He recalled some words of Monsieur de Voltaire's, from his *Essai sur les Mœurs*: 'Everything that is intimately linked to human nature is alike from one end of the universe to the other. All that depends on custom is different and is alike only as a result of chance.' The other passengers included the young men's four servants, a stout woman in widow's weeds whose ceruse make-up reminded him of La Paulet, his old accomplice at the Dauphin Couronné, two other servants and the crew. No one suspicious at first sight.

Sailors were bustling around the capstan, pulling the hawser to raise the anchor. The ship was advancing on its cable. He heard the boatswain announce that the cable was now vertical and that the anchor was dragging. The decks and catwalks were alive with cries and commands. As the vessel continued to manoeuvre, men scrambled aloft to unfurl the topgallants. Nicolas watched anxiously as they walked along the yards. The sails flapped, making a sound like a whiplash. The ship seemed to tremble. The pulleys squeaked, the sails swelled and the *Zéphir* set off, close to the wind.

Nicolas remained on the poop deck, glad to breathe in the sea air and with little inclination to go down into the cramped passenger room. From the pale faces of those he saw coming up again, he deduced that the stench must be unbearable. An hour after casting off, the wind had turned and was now definitely blowing from behind them. After a few minutes' observation, the captain decided to brail some of the sails in order to allow the front ones to catch the wind more easily. The spanker was lowered first, followed by the mainsail, but that did not suffice to give the ship a decent speed. It became clear that the captain's calculations were out by nearly four hours. The ship had not made enough headway to catch the tide. A swell moved the *Zéphir* in every direction. Soon afterwards, within sight of the English coast, whose cliffs could be made out in the distance, the anchor was dropped. They would have to wait for the right moment. The sails were struck and the ship headed into the wind, the prow pointing towards France, which was where the prevailing – and increasingly cold – wind was blowing from.

The situation became difficult for the passengers below deck, since the movements of the ship, already so noticeable at top speed, were almost more so on a becalmed vessel subject to the caprices of the waves. From the upper deck, Nicolas watched the array of ships, freed now from the English ports, all emerging together and heading across the waters towards the continent. It struck him that there was a strong risk of a collision. Every minute, it seemed, some large vessel would loom up, apparently making straight for the *Zéphir*. But at the last moment a skilful move of the helm avoided disaster, and shouted greetings were exchanged.

Night was falling by the time the order to cast off was given. Nicolas, weary of being splashed with sea spray, was standing on the poop gunwale. Suddenly, he felt himself being seized by the legs and thrown into the void. He barely had time to realise that he was falling towards the sea when he hit an obstacle. He found himself lying in a hull that smelt of tar – but never was a smell sweeter. He lay there on his back, bruised and motionless. He could feel a coil of rope beneath him. He understood now what had happened: the little skiff hanging in the stern had broken his fall, but in the darkness his attacker was probably not aware of this. If providence had led him here, then it was probably advisable to stay where he was. He was not worried about his baggage: he had left it locked in a cupboard of which only the captain had the key. It was in this way that he finished the crossing, fearing nothing but seasickness, although he was not prone to it, having often as a child gone out with the fishermen of Le Croisic. Two hours later, the *Zéphir* entered the port of Dover.

Nicolas waited a reasonable time, then picked up his tricorn from the bottom of the skiff where it had fallen, put it between his teeth, and, with the help of the cables and the carvings on the poop, he managed, hampered somewhat by his sword, to clamber back on deck, watched by two alarmed sailors. He hurried to get his portmanteau from the captain, who had been waiting impatiently and somewhat anxiously for him. He took the portmanteau without offering any explanation, jumped on to the quay and set foot on the shore of Old England.

Immediately, a horde of boys and grooms clustered around him, offering him transport, lodgings and all kinds of services. He got away from them quickly enough once they realised that he spoke their language and could answer them. A badly dressed man came up to him and asked to inspect his baggage. Not wishing to plead his status of plenipotentiary, he agreed to the search, which in any case was conducted in a polite manner. He had to pay the customs officer the equivalent of an *écu* to discharge something called a viscountcy tax. Then he entered the town and searched for an inn where he could eat and sleep. He was struck by the size and highly decorated appearance of the signs outside these establishments. The town was inundated with travellers, and it was only with some difficulty, and jostling, that he managed to obtain – after much haggling and at a high price – an awful bed in a mediocre hostelry. In order to dine, he had to go himself to the servants' pantry and grab a few pieces of beef from the steaming brazier. Nothing else was available, and the innkeeper seemed to spend all his time blowing on the fire to keep it alight – the coal being half choked with the grease from the meat – and putting new pieces of beef on the fire to replace those which the guests of the establishment had taken.

As he was about to go to bed fully clothed, Nicolas took off his cloak and noticed some big white marks at thigh level, obviously left by the hands that had grabbed him to throw him into the sea. By the light of the candle, he examined them closely and sniffed them: ceruse. There was no doubt about it: the heavily made-up widow he had noticed when they cast off must have been a man in woman's clothing, and it was he who had been responsible for this new attempt on his life. He realised with dread that his pursuers had an efficient team at their disposal, that his ruse had failed, and that all of his movements seemed to be anticipated by an invisible enemy. The net was closing in on him and it would not be easy to escape it.

Saturday 15 and Sunday 16 January 1774

At about four in the morning, a servant came and shook him awake. He was expected to vacate his bed for a newcomer who was standing at his door, cursing and stamping his feet. But Nicolas refused to budge, and did not leave until six. His back hurt so much, it was not easy to get out of bed. Catherine was not there to administer one of the old wives' remedies she had brought with her from her native Alsace, which could restore a man or a horse in the twinkling of an eye. He thought nostalgically of the house in Rue Montmartre. Could it be that he was already homesick?

As he left the inn, he was accosted by a boy who hopped around him and kept crying, 'One shilling, sir!' He asked him the quickest way to get to London. The boy grabbed his portmanteau and informed him that London was twenty-eight leagues from Dover and that the best way to get there was to take the mail-coach as far as Gravesend, on the Thames, and from there take a boat along the river. He was immediately urged to reserve his place on one of the coaches: there were so many people travelling, they were sure to fill up quickly. He got a seat beside the postillion: he would be in the open air and have a view of the landscape. The weather looked cold, but fine. He could have hired a carriage, but that would have attracted attention. He would be safer amongst normal passengers, he told himself.

In the sun, the landscape looked tranquil and surprisingly green compared with France at this time of year. He lunched in Canterbury. Beef seemed to be the staple diet of this nation. At Gravesend, he left the coach. As the tide was again unfavourable and it was impossible to go up the river at night, he decided to take a room in a yellow-brick inn which surprised him by its cleanliness. The washed and waxed floorboards shone. The room he was offered was small but pretty, with furniture of varnished mahogany and fresh linen on the bed. The efficient, discreet service was provided by young people of both sexes who smiled as they bustled about. He dined on a dish of piecrust with beef and pork kidneys in a thick sauce, which he was told was called a steak and kidney pie. He spent a peaceful night and, early in the morning, embarked on a barge heading for London.

The weather remained fine, and the banks of the river offered many pleasant and varied views. Fine houses appeared on the slopes of the hills, surrounded by ornate gardens. He became aware that the Thames was one of the widest rivers in Europe and that even the largest vessels could enter it. The English capital was near, and the river at this point was so covered in ships that there was only a small lane left for those going upriver. The barge found itself surrounded by a forest of masts through which the wind blew, rustling in the yards and shrouds. The tide being favourable, it took only a few hours to arrive beneath the Tower of London. Disembarking, Nicolas had no difficulty in finding a carriage to take him to the district where he had been instructed to go. Was he still being followed? He no longer trusted his own vigilance: it was too easy to be distracted by incongruous details, unknown faces and new impressions.

Berkeley Square was a beautiful rectangular square surrounded by residences that were pleasant if a little repetitive in style. These brick buildings had only two or three floors, and all possessed a kind of basement occupied, as far as he could see, by kitchens and pantries. These low rooms opened on to a kind of ditch, some three feet wide, which separated the houses from the street. The pavement was cut off from this ditch by iron railings. He easily found the number he was looking for, and as he raised the knocker he felt a kind of apprehension: he was about to enter a house that was both unknown to him and foreign. After a few moments, the door was opened by an elderly woman. She was austerely dressed in a black dress with a shawl across her chest, and her grey hair, pulled back tightly from her forehead, was covered with a kind of mantilla. There was something of the nun about her, thought Nicolas, an image accentuated by the heavy bunch of keys hanging from her belt. She fixed him with her piercing little eyes set deep in a plump face. Her small, tight mouth contrasted with the folds in her neck, around which she wore a ribbon adorned with a cameo. She was looking at him as if he were a poisonous species which had to be handled with caution. The fact that he introduced himself in her language seemed to surprise her, and she forced a smile.

'I need to ask you a question, sir.'

'Please go ahead, madam.'

'Can you tell me the name of your tailor?'

'Master Vachon,' replied Nicolas, surprised by the question.

'Where is his shop?'

'Rue Vieille-du-Temple, in Paris.'

'How long have you been his customer?'

'Since 1760, precisely.'

Nicolas would have sworn that all this was pure Sartine. His answers clearly reassured the woman, and her face gradually brightened. She made a slight forward movement with her chest which could have been taken for a curtsey.

'Mrs Williams, at your service. If you would be so good as to follow me, I will show you to your rooms.'

They climbed a carpeted staircase, and she admitted him into a suite of three rooms, comprising a sitting room that doubled as a library, a bedroom and a toilet. He accepted the suggestion of a bath and asked if his clothes could be brushed and ironed. Mrs Williams eagerly seized those he took from his trunk. A few moments later, a butler appeared, carrying some pitchers of hot water. He returned several times, on the last occasion handing him a dressing gown of Indian cotton. Before she withdrew, the woman told him that tea would be served and that 'the lady' would pay him a visit at six o'clock.

With a feeling of voluptuousness, Nicolas stepped into the copper bathtub. The pain of his fall into the skiff on the *Zéphir* was fading. This, he thought, was what his father, the Marquis de Ranreuil, must have called *comfort*. He had not previously enjoyed this pleasure except on brief occasions, at the Russian baths in Rue de Bellechasse or in the private rooms of the 'floating woods' on the banks of the Seine, all places closely watched by the police on the lookout for licentious behaviour. He fell asleep in the scented steam, only waking when the water had grown cold. He shaved and brushed his hair. In the bedroom, he found his clothes, cleaned and ironed. His waxed boots gleamed in the light from a coal fire burning in a kind of shell in the fireplace. He took the time to admire the silk and cotton pagoda-patterned wall coverings, which reminded him of the fabrics on sale in the fashionable shop in Rue du Roule in Paris that specialised in *chinoiserie*. Mahogany dominated everywhere. He was struck by the number of framed prints on the walls, depicting pastoral scenes and naval battles. Freshly dressed, he went into the sitting room, and there, set out on a little gaming table, were a pot of tea, butter, bread and several bowls of jam. The bread was unlike anything he had ever eaten before. He found it delicate, white, soft, but not very tasty – and it had no crust. The clock on the mantelpiece struck six, and Nicolas heard a noise on the stairs. His visitor – 'the lady' – was on her way up. Her hurried steps, though, struck Nicolas as unlikely to belong to a member of the fair sex. They clumped on to the landing, sharp and heavy at the same time, making the parquet creak. There was no knock. The door opened, and a figure swished into the room and simpered in a rasping voice, 'Charles Geneviève Louis Auguste André Timothée de Beaumont, Madame d'Éon, wishes to speak with the Marquis de Ranreuil.'

Nicolas found both this third-person introduction and the ambiguous list of Christian names somewhat outlandish. He was not sure how to behave towards this androgynous and distinctly faded beauty. He would have had to make out the person's contours and features, but they were far too distorted by an accumulation of artifice. Without waiting for an answer, the figure collapsed into a *bergère*, and struck hard at all those flounces and ruffles with both filoselle-gloved hands to stop them inflating. The person was wearing a wide-sleeved grey dress from Valenciennes, with a bodice that went all the way up to a thick neck surrounded by a wide black ribbon. Nicolas noted the red cross of Saint-Louis, memento of a brilliant military career under the Maréchal de Broglie. The excessively painted face reminded Nicolas of actors he had seen before they went on stage, their features made to look disproportionately large. The whole was surmounted by a hat of fluted lace. The creature shifted in its seat until it felt comfortable, then stretched its legs, revealing a pair of military boots: the Chevalier d'Éon had been – had never ceased to be – an officer in the dragoons.

'Will you take tea?' Nicolas asked.

'Oh, no. A stronger beverage would suit me better, but it's neither the hour nor the moment. Let us be clear with one another. We both know what affairs have brought you here, and there is no need to harp on about them. I shall therefore come straight to the point. I believe you know the background.'

'I can confirm that. Monsieur de Sartine has told me everything.'

'There are two reasons you've been sent to London. The first requires urgent action. Everything must be done to rescue a group of wretched incompetents led by an imbecile, who have fallen into every trap laid by our English friends. I understand that you have the powers of a plenipotentiary. It is up to you to be convincing, even if you are not convinced, and above all more skilful than the most skilled . . .' Éon gave a forced, high-pitched laugh. 'You will be up against a tough opponent. I have played my game for you. It wasn't easy, I can tell you. A representative of Whitehall is to meet you this evening, I don't know where. A cab will come for you at the ninth hour. Be careful, I've been dealing with these people for years; they're sly and they like to play tricks. How can we struggle against so many merits!'

The chevalier expanded on this theme at great length, making the conversation heavy and wearying, only occasionally enlivened by bursts of harsh sarcasm and bad taste.

'In short, they will treat you coldly and politely, but they'll hide their ulterior motives. Our people, or rather, those rogues sent by d'Aiguillon – Captain Béranger, two officers and four archers – are being held at Bow Street police station, watched over by the agents of justice, as well as by the lowest elements of the populace, who would be only too inclined to manhandle a few Frenchmen while the police looked on indifferently. And now I have to talk to you about Morande.'

'Do you know him well?' asked Nicolas.

Éon rummaged in his bodice and adjusted his blouse. 'Every day God makes, the rascal pesters me with letters and appointments. I listen to him and meet him and try my best to make him see reason – so far without success, I have to admit. It's a waste of breath. The only people the man feels any pity for are his children. Thanks to him, his father died of grief and his mother was nearly hanged. After a long prison term in Armentières, he found a comfortable refuge in England. Mark my words, he'll end up at Tyburn, where his big feet will give their blessing to the scum of London who've come to see him stick out his wicked tongue!'

'How would you describe his character?'

'The man is wholly without qualities, a wicked fellow. He has a hundred debts and doesn't know which way to turn to improve his lot. At the same time, I repeat, a good father and a good husband. But the mixture of ambition and mediocrity in him has led him to wade in the mire and now he's drowning in it, and is impervious to all arguments. He never pushes home his attacks, but makes little thrusts, provoking and annoying like a dog with a bitch . . .'

Éon stretched out a leg and leant towards it as if trying to see his face in the boot.

'He told me all about the episode of the men who came from Paris to kill him,' he went on. 'I told him right out that it didn't surprise me, that I'd predicted it for a long time and that he himself was the main cause of anything dangerous that occurred. Then I asked him if he couldn't choose other objects of censure than the King's official mistress, not to mention the one before her, on which to vent his poisonous slanders.'

'And how did he react?'

'Like a madman, Marquis. I shan't go into details, you'll be able to judge for yourself. He dismissed me, telling me to inform the Duc d'Aiguillon and "the whole clique" at Court that he didn't give a damn about them and all their intrigues and henchmen. I again exhorted him to put an end to this insanity, but he wouldn't budge an inch. Would you believe, he sent an account of his adventures to the *Morning Post and Daily Advertiser*, which published it on 11 January. He plans to involve the law to right the wrongs that have been done to him. I was exhausted by the time I left him, and I told his poor wife to beware of the consequences of her husband's actions, because he seemed to me quite deranged and she should blame him for whatever calamitous repercussions befall her and her children.'

'And what am I supposed to do about this mess?' asked Nicolas, with a laugh.

The chevalier's response was a bawdy slap of the thighs. 'Just take it easy, and don't despair. With a character like that, everything remains possible. Not that others haven't tried, but . . .'

'But?'

'Despite appearances, the man is far from mad. He can laugh at that lamentable bunch, even though the episode left him shaken and anxious. Talk to him. If you don't get anything from him straight away, at least you'll break down his defences in readiness for later offensives. Apart from that, he's quite aware, because I took it upon myself to tell him, that you are not the Duc d'Aiguillon's emissary, but the King's. I have my sources of information, he has his, and sometimes they overlap. According to rumour, Marquis, the hounds are after you. That'll make him feel sympathetic towards you. But even in England the fox sometimes escapes! That's what I wish for you. By the way, are you armed?'

'Yes, I have a good sword and a pistol.'

'If not, I would have got you what you needed. My swords are the best in London. Did you know I was the pupil of

Dumonchelle and Rousseau, the Parisian fencing masters?' The chevalier's small frame proudly straightened. 'Beware of everyone and everything. Morande will show you respect and be lavish with words, but don't let yourself be taken in. He's caught up in a fatal game of dice, and it won't let go of him, absorbing and blackening all his thoughts.'

'When will I see him?' asked Nicolas.

'Probably tomorrow. Mrs Williams will let you know. He wanted you to come to his house. Too conspicuous. I'm organising something else on neutral ground.' Éon gave Nicolas a half-smile full of a kind of friendly pity. 'Take care of yourself. Fear can be a good counsellor, and it would be dangerous not to feel any. There are not so many of us fighting to help His Majesty, the best of kings, my illustrious and secret protector . . .'

Nicolas was surprised at this strange character's visible emotion.

'Oh, I almost forgot,' said Éon. 'I'm dealing with another affair which our embassy also has its hands on. If it's left up to them, I fear the whole thing will be ruined. You'll see the King when you get back from London. Tell him from me that Mr Flint, who travelled to China in 1736 and crossed the Great Wall in 1759, but was unable to enter Peking and was imprisoned by the Chinese for several years, is still hesitating about our proposal. He's told me that, since he landed, he hasn't come across anyone who's ever heard of the hundred-ton English vessel with a crew of twelve on which he sailed during that expedition.'

'I shan't fail you,' replied Nicolas, although he had no idea what this was all about.

'That's not all,' Éon went on. 'I conclude that the observations which the English were able to gather – observations so vital to our interests – have now been lost apart from what's in Mr Flint's head. He claims to have studied that region and those seas even before he embarked on the vessel in question.'

'But what is the object of your negotiation?' asked Nicolas. 'Excuse me for pressing you.'

'We need to compensate him for any risks he and his family may run through dealing with us, all the more so if he is unable to avoid exile. The Lords of the Admiralty have their eyes on him. The last time I met him, I impressed upon him that it was right for a great ruler and a government such as ours to seek out men of rare talent or knowledge. In order to convince him, I reminded him of the days of Colbert, when merit was rewarded in whatever nation it was found. You see, my dear fellow, this may be more important for the King's future reputation than all the Morandes in the world. Marquis, I bid you good day and reiterate my concern: take care of yourself.'

'Mademoiselle,' said Nicolas, 'I am grateful to you for your solicitude: the recent past speaks in favour of my heeding your advice.'

The chevalière held out a hand, and Nicolas shook it. The grip was firm and heartfelt. In a great gathering of fabrics, Éon hurried out.

Nicolas's feelings about Éon had gradually changed in the course of their conversation. The way in which the chevalier spoke of the King could not help but move him, nor could his concern for the triumph of the kingdom. Of course, he remained aware that

Éon was blackmailing his master, holding on to certain documents as a safeguard. But in his present situation, Nicolas could well understand the extreme measures to which a person could be driven in difficult and unusual circumstances. On balance, he felt favourably disposed towards the chevalier – or chevalière – which was not something he had foreseen. As for the substance of what Éon had told him, it merely confirmed to him the complexity of an affair in which the interests of the State and some very murky intrigues mingled and clashed.

He knew that he would have to beware of the Englishman he was due to meet, who had already shown his bad faith by allowing Captain Béranger's men to fall into the trap laid for them. As for Morande, the prospects were decidedly uncertain. If the description given by Éon bore any relation to reality, what could he hope to obtain from such a deeply immoral individual? What kind of pressure could he put on him to move him in the direction desired by the King? Would he have to alternate persuasion and threats in order to break down defences based on lies and slanders?

Last but not least, Nicolas recalled with a shudder his visitor's repeated warnings. They were as ambiguous as the man, or woman, who had uttered them. That he was under threat, he had never doubted. The question lay in knowing where the threat was coming from and whether or not this chain of events had a single origin. His confusion centred on that fatal evening of 6 January, when a lovers' quarrel – a mere domestic tiff – had shattered the course of a life, led Madame de Lastérieux to a terrible death and had plunged him, Nicolas, into the snares of suspicion and the perils of a murderous chase. In his sadness, he had almost forgotten the ambiguous role she had played towards him.

The clock struck seven thirty. The butler entered, cleared away the tea things, and put a place-setting on the gaming table. Nicolas was sighing with pleasure at the sight of these preparations when Mrs Williams glided into the room like a high-sided ship, with an indignant look on her face.

'Sir, there's someone downstairs asking to see you. I told him you weren't here, but he insists. He says you were supposed to meet him at nine, but he wants to bring your meeting forward.'

'What kind of man is he?' asked Nicolas.

'An honest-looking gentleman.'

'Good. Be so kind as to show him up and bring us two glasses and whatever it is that people drink before dinner in London.'

She left the room, looking annoyed, and came back accompanied by a short, potbellied man of about sixty without a wig, his bald skull surrounded by a crescent of white hair. He had a pale face, with roughly cut bushy eyebrows, a red, pointed nose and a long chin encased in a white gauze cravat. He wore a green coat that was too tight for his shapeless body, a pair of immaculate white cashmere breeches, black stockings and shoes with silver buckles. The man drew himself up on his little legs, took in both hands a kind of lorgnette hanging on a black ribbon, and looked round the room, seeming to approve its fixtures and fittings, and finally at Nicolas. Without having been invited, he sat down facing Nicolas, looked him up and down once again, then began speaking in an aristocratic English accent.

'Marquis,' he said at once, 'did you ever ask yourself if we were happy to receive you?'

Nicolas had no intention of letting himself be thrown like that. 'Before anything else,' he said, 'to whom do I have the honour of speaking? Although you appear to know who I am, I myself do not have that pleasure.'

'I'm Lord Ashbury, Robert Ashbury. They were supposed to bring you to see me this evening, but I anticipated you. I have no desire for an envoy as distinguished as yourself to be subjected to these frightful obligations. I will add that I am not especially happy *for our mutual friend to organise our entertainments for us*.'

He had said all this in a self-satisfied tone, waving his lorgnette. Nicolas got up and went to stoke the fire, amused to recall that this was a habit of Monsieur de Sartine's when he wanted to give himself time to think. The acrid smell rose to his throat and made him cough. That helped him to gain a few seconds and to calm his mounting irritation.

'My lord, do you have any papers on you that would assure me you are indeed who you say you are?'

His guest laughed. 'Commissioner, you will have to take my word for it. I'm not asking you for the letters your monarch signed to accredit you as his plenipotentiary and which, no doubt . . .' – he pointed at Nicolas's chest – '. . . are warming your heart. Affairs such as these, as I'm sure you'll learn, are a matter of trust – or mistrust, if you so wish.'

Mrs Williams came in with a bottle of an amber liquid and two glasses, which she placed on the gaming table. Lord Ashbury immediately poured himself a large glass, which he knocked back in one go, clicking his tongue in a manner which Nicolas found quite plebeian.

'Excellent sherry! My compliments to your sponsor.' He sat back in his *bergère*, shaking his head sardonically. 'So, Mr Plenipotentiary, what have you to tell me?'

'I'll come straight to the point. Your ambassador in Paris, Lord Stormont, gave his assurance that a French police mission could land on British soil and stop Monsieur de Morande doing harm with his indecent writings, which gravely slander His Very Christian Majesty and those closest to him.'

'You mean the ladies closest to him.'

Nicolas ignored the provocation. 'And what do we see? This mission – a difficult one, I grant you – found itself from the first hampered by underhand manoeuvres. The members were denounced, the populace were roused against them, and now our people are imprisoned and liable to the full weight of your laws. The commitment made by your government has not been respected. We don't want this affair to bring about a lasting deterioration in the relations between our two countries, which have been at peace for eleven years. We are faced with a genuine obstacle, a stumbling block, as you call it.'

Ashbury smiled. 'Your knowledge of our language is more impressive than the quality of your reasoning. Your argument would be admissible, sir, if your emissaries had displayed the requisite caution and skill for such an unusual procedure and if the laws of the land had been respected.' He puffed out his cheeks, and breathed out and in again. 'But what do we in fact see? A bunch of wretches who confide indiscreetly in a certain Madame de Godeville, a Frenchwoman without honour, a common harlot. Thanks to her good graces, everything was revealed, which we – please note – being faithful to our promises, had no wish to see happen. Your men visited the lampoonist in question, and he set about extorting thirty *louis* each from them. After which, he sounded the alarm in such a nasty manner that your negotiators –

if we can apply that word to such hoi polloi – became the object of a manhunt. The English people, so upright, so just, so attached to their freedoms, became incensed against them after Morande excoriated them in our press, which is free. Your men were besieged in their hotel, and one of them was seized, tarred and thrown in the Thames, then fished out by our police and confined in a lunatic asylum. The others threw themselves into the arms of the law. They are now being protected, but they will be tried and, if the accusations against them prove to be true, convicted.'

'Whatever blunders they committed,' said Nicolas, humiliated by this arrogantly proffered lesson, 'nothing in your words demonstrates the consideration with which your government should have treated a mission of whose aims and importance you were well aware.'

'It would have been treated in such a way, naturally, if everything had been conducted in secrecy, without publicly damaging the rights and customs of the English nation. You'll just have to accept it and bide your time. You can get them back in a few years.'

He poured himself another glass of sherry. His cheeks were gradually turning redder.

Nicolas rose to his feet, deep in thought. 'My lord,' he said at last, 'I fear we have nothing more to say to each other. I shall inform my master of the failure of a procedure which was only authorised because of the commitments made by your embassy in Paris. No doubt this result will please those in my country who observe your country's difficulties with the stated aim of taking advantage of them. The fortunes of war are changeable. The Duc d'Aiguillon, who has been anxious to maintain the peace, may, after such an affront, change the direction of his policies. As for

Monsieur de Choiseul, who, as you know, dreams only of returning to office and is driven by the spirit of revenge, he is sure to turn this business to his own advantage.'

Lord Ashbury had turned red with outrage. 'My country's difficulties? What do you mean?'

'I've read your free press. It's full of the problems your government is encountering in India and in your colonies in America.'

Nicolas felt extremely pleased now that he had read so carefully the documents with which Sartine had provided him. He could sense Lord Ashbury's dismay.

'Are you suggesting that—'

'I'm not suggesting, I'm merely observing, in my role as plenipotentiary, how impossible it seems to resolve to everyone's satisfaction a deplorable situation which would never have existed if a person as harmful as Monsieur de Morande had been duly prevented from causing harm, instead of finding refuge, support and sustenance in your country. Equally—'

'Come now, Marquis, you have the passion of youth, but you still have to acquire the self-possession which is considered the most desirable quality here. Please sit down.'

Nicolas pretended to do so reluctantly.

'The government of His Gracious Majesty,' Lord Ashbury went on, 'has no wish to turn this affair into a *casus belli*. We will pass over our inviolable rights, the freedom of our press and the independence of our courts. In two days' time, at six in the morning, you will get your men back and be able to take them home. There you have it, sir. I bid you good evening. I doubt we shall ever meet again.'

Lord Ashbury gave a forced smile and stroked his crown of white hair with one hand. Nicolas was not convinced he had carried off the prize by his own efforts. His arguments had merely confirmed the English in their belief that this trivial episode risked triggering a serious crisis that would impugn the honour of the two nations and tarnish the throne of France, thereby making any solution impossible. The game was not worth the candle. Had the English hoped to obtain something in exchange? If success there was, it was in that direction that it had to be sought.

The Englishman rose. 'Marquis, Commissioner, Plenipotentiary, you are as diverse and multiple as your Chevalière d'Éon. I take my leave of you.'

With these words, and without holding out his hand to Nicolas, he took a few steps towards the door. Then he stopped and turned, making his lorgnette spin.

'Above all, don't stay too long in London. My fellow countrymen can be cruel and vindictive. I have reason to believe that a price has been placed on your head by persons unknown. God save the commissioner. Goodbye.'

Lord Ashbury left the room with small steps. The door opened at his approach. He gave a start on realising that Mrs Williams had probably been listening to their conversation. Nicolas told himself that his own ingenuousness and inexperience were no match for this strange new world. What an improbable situation: this Englishwoman at the service of a French spy, known as such, who was himself working in league with men from the English secret service. How did she see her way through such an imbroglio, and on what did Éon base the trust he seemed to have in her? Nicolas added a further observation to this reflection:

everyone, friends and enemies alike, seemed to know about the threats concerning him. The adversary was nowhere, but for Nicolas the danger was everywhere and would jump out at him one day when he least expected it.

A dish of roast beef and Yorkshire pudding, washed down with a good-quality Bordeaux, dispelled these gloomy thoughts. At the end of his dinner, he was surprised to see the butler bring in a dusty bottle and place it carefully on the table. It was a fine wine from Portugal, called port, he said, usually served at the end of a meal and drunk exclusively by men. The liquor shimmered amaranth and amber in the candlelight. Breathing in this nectar proved to be a rare treat, drinking it was an enchantment. Its velvety smoothness seemed to gain in strength and warmth as it suffused his chest. Nuts and squares of dry cheese set off this sumptuous beverage. Unable to resist its pleasures, he finished the bottle, putting off until the morrow the task of untangling the web of thoughts and theories cluttering his mind.

Monday 17 January 1774

Nicolas woke at dawn, but did not have time to laze in the gentle warmth of the bedroom before the appetising smell of toast roused him completely from his sleep. Once again, he found the eternal pot of tea. Mrs Williams waited for him to finish washing and dressing before she appeared. She was impatient to tell him that a cab would take him into town, to an unspecified location, and that he should not be surprised by the precautions taken during the journey, at the end of which he would meet 'you know who'. The driver would explain what was required. He could rest assured that everything was being done to keep his movements as discreet as possible.

He did indeed find a cab waiting for him outside the door, and as soon as he had sat down it set off. Traffic in London was as heavy as in Paris. He was unaware of anything suspicious, trusting entirely in his English accomplices, the arrangements made by Éon, and fate. After half an hour, the cab came to a halt. The driver got down calmly from his seat and beckoned him to enter a wig-maker's shop. The sight of the most diverse types of wig on display would have driven Monsieur de Sartine mad with envy. A young girl took him by the hand, led him behind the counter of ebony and polished brass, and preceded him down a dark corridor. A door was opened. He felt a cold draught on his face and stony ground beneath his feet. Soon daylight appeared, a second door opened, and the girl handed him over to a little boy who was waiting for him, his face half hidden by a woollen cap somewhat too big for him. The boy pulled him by the sleeve and led him to another cab with a new driver.

The cab rode on for a long time, turning several times at right angles, and fifteen long minutes went by. It stopped at last. The door was opened and the coachman asked him to enter a church which he called Queen's Chapel. He handed him a Catholic missal in French and told him that, as he knew his address, he could find his own way back. The person he was looking for, he said, would offer to describe the monument to him. He shouldn't talk to anyone else.

*

The chapel was not large but admirably proportioned, with a carved and coffered ceiling. As Nicolas approached the altar, he heard someone come up behind him. Turning, he discovered a man of medium height, draped in a cloak with a high collar, a wig on his head, his tricorn in his hand. He had a plump, smooth face, but inquisitive eyes.

'Perhaps,' the man said in French, 'Monsieur would like to know the history of this monument?'

He took Nicolas's missal, opened it, checked something, then put it in his pocket.

'Yes, I'd like that,' said Nicolas.

'The architect Inigo Jones built it in 1627 for Princess Henrietta Maria of France, the wife of Charles I. I recommend the altar decorated by Annibale Carracci. Does that satisfy your curiosity?'

'Monsieur,' said Nicolas, 'you know who I am and who sent me. I've been authorised to propose any arrangement that may help to put an end to a situation which is prejudicial to everyone, but especially to you, and which can only be the result of a misunderstanding.'

'That's all very well for you to say,' the man protested. 'Look how I'm treated! What about the bandits who were sent after me to kill me? How can I accept just any old proposition? As sure as my name is Morande, I want revenge! I'm going to lodge a complaint, and as a victim of despotism I'm bound to obtain something.'

He suddenly calmed down, and adopted a honeyed tone.

'I have nothing against you,' he said. 'Come and meet my wife and children. I beg you very humbly to come to my home and eat a head of salmon I've been given as a present and which is worth all the fish in France. There'll be fried oysters with it. What do you say? Enough to satisfy the heartiest appetite. My wife is very ill, she often loses blood. Have pity on her, be kind.'

'I'm willing to help you in any way I can,' replied Nicolas. 'I haven't come all this way without having a solution to propose which would allow all the interested parties to obtain satisfaction.'

'No,' retorted Morande. 'It's too late for a deal. I'm being attacked, so I counterattack.' He stamped his heel on the floor. 'I've consulted lawyers. I'm going to write another article in the newspapers about those rogues from the Paris police that d'Aiguillon sent here to abduct and kill me.'

'Monsieur,' replied Nicolas, 'it's all well and good making accusations, but you yourself are the cause of your tribulations. Can't you find anything better to do than tarnish the reputations of people of quality who don't know you from Adam?'

'And what would you have me do? Can you tell me what better subjects there are than the Court whores to help me reach the goal I've set myself, which is to obtain money. If I wrote plays or novels, no one would read them or buy them! Thanks to the subjects I choose and the manner in which I treat them, I'm assured of buyers and readers all over Europe. Let the people in Versailles who've sent you dispatch assassins. I don't give a damn about poison or knives, and if I died that way I'd escape hanging, and that would dishonour those who sent the murderers.'

He had grabbed hold of Nicolas's cloak, and was now shaking it in his frenzy, while also gnashing his teeth and frothing with rage.

'I'm not threatening you, Monsieur,' said Nicolas. 'On the

contrary, I'm offering you an honourable way out of this business, giving you the means to feed and cherish your family without all this torment; in short, I'm holding out my hand to you, and yet you refuse to listen to me! Accept my proposals and destroy those scandalous writings, which provoke tears in a woman who genuinely cares for those less fortunate than herself and who, on many an occasion, has shown that she can respond with pity to the signs of a generous temperament.'

Nicolas had the impression that these sensitive words had touched Morande. He seemed to hesitate for a moment, kneading his tricorn in his hands. But his pride finally got the better of him.

'I want them censured in a public court! Oh, you don't know the English judges! Béranger and his officers are in their clutches in Bow Street. I shall crush them, those vile serpents of the Court! As for you, please take advantage of my hospitality, and you can judge my style.'

Nicolas bade him farewell and left the chapel in disgust. The cold air did him good. He decided to walk aimlessly: he could always take a cab if he felt tired. As Éon had predicted, the man was too driven by hatred to give in easily. Had he even shaken him? Absorbed in his thoughts, he bumped straight into a woman in a striking red dress and a short rabbit-skin cape.

'Throw me to the ground, why don't you?' she cried out in French. 'What a brute!'

Suddenly her painted face froze in an expression of surprise.

'I can't believe my eyes! Monsieur Nicolas! You're the last person I'd have expected to meet in London! Don't you know who I am? Don't you remember? La Présidente, the friend of La Satin! I used to work at the Dauphin Couronné!'

He did indeed recognise, beneath the make-up and the impasto, the former resident of the brothel in Rue Saint-Honoré. 'What have you been up to, my beauty?'

'I crossed the Channel in 1770, taking advantage of the peace. Frenchwomen are very sought after here. You could meet a whole flock of charmers from our shores. It's much easier, we don't have the police on our arses so much. We use the beer shops as boudoirs and their back rooms as bedrooms. We don't have to hide, everything's perfectly free – they even publish a list of girls, with names, addresses and the liveliest details about their size, their figure, and their particular talents. What's more, the list is revised with every fresh consignment.' She winked.

'So the police are more indulgent here?' said Nicolas.

'Not better, but less money-hungry, except in the *bagnios*. The fools are the same everywhere. No offence intended, Nicolas.'

'None taken. The *bagnios*, you say?'

'Yes, they're the places where amorous parties are organised. The owners don't like too many scandalous scenes. Besides, business would be bad if they allowed people to insult the girls.'

'So you're happy in London, then?'

'Oh, I miss Paris, but there's work for wenches who aren't too choosy. I'm building up a nest egg so I can get back to Faubourg Saint-Marcel and open up my own business. I still pay my way, but I'm no spring chicken any more. How's La Satin?'

'Fine. She took over from La Paulet.'

'Really? Now there's something! The sweet La Satin, a brothel-keeper! I can't get over it. Are you two still lovers?'

Nicolas did not reply.

'I know how close you are. How's your son?'

'My son?'

'Yes, little Louis, the spitting image of you. You can't deny that.'

Nicolas felt his whole body turn to ice, and he had to lean against the wall. The blood drained from his face, so much so that La Présidente noticed.

'Oh, that's just like me. Always talking too much. You look so pale. What did I say? My God, you didn't know! I could kick myself, old fool that I am . . . She begged me to keep quiet. I was coming to England, she didn't think she'd ever see me again.'

Nicolas hurried away, leaving her standing there. He was walking like a madman, his thoughts feverish. When, in 1761, La Satin had told him that she had had a baby, he had questioned her, anxious to know if the child was his. Her answer still echoed in his ears. 'I did my accounts, and it was a long time after we were last together.' He had taken her at her word. Her evident embarrassment he had put down to modesty and shame. Now he felt like a fool. A moment later, he had convinced himself that it couldn't be, that La Présidente was imagining things, that she had put it together from scraps of brothel gossip. He would have to investigate this new mystery when he got back to Paris. For the moment, he would have to try not to think about it.

He looked round him at London. Its filth rivalled Paris, despite the enormous tipcarts used for taking away the rubbish. Thanks to the use of coal as the only fuel in kitchens and apartments, the sun was constantly veiled by smoke and fog. Nicolas finally took a cab back to Berkeley Square, where Mrs Williams, reassured to see him, sighed and handed him a sealed letter without arms or signature. The unknown writer informed him, in a tall sloping hand, that because of the tide the evacuation of his protégés would take place that very evening. Nicolas had to be at Bow Street police station at five o'clock precisely. He and the men would immediately be conducted to the Embankment, from where a rowing boat would take them to their ship. Nicolas went upstairs to pack his portmanteau, and gave a few guineas to the butler, who was greatly surprised. Mrs Williams simpered, but finally accepted some money, too. Nicolas had won her over, and her surly attitude had gradually faded. She gave Nicolas a cake with raisins and Indian spices: the house was still suffused with the smell of baking. They parted good friends.

The welcome he received from the English authorities revealed their annoyance. A shifty-looking magistrate explained how he intended to proceed. The police carriage would approach the front steps of the Bow Street station and let the Frenchmen get in, trying, as far as was possible, to prevent any hostile move from the crowd. Nicolas had encountered this ugly rabble, the dregs of the port and the street, when he arrived. The sight of him had unleashed cries and insults, and a clump of mud had narrowly missed him.

He found his countrymen in their cells, gaunt and distraught, their clothes in tatters and their beards bushy. Captain Béranger was trembling, and it was immediately obvious to Nicolas that he had been the wrong man for such a delicate mission – quite apart from the information given him by Sartine, which had already warned him against this officer and adventurer, who risked everything because he had nothing to lose, was well known in the gambling dens for cheating at faro[1] and was ready to do anything for money. One of the officers was lying on the floor, and seemed to be delirious. Another started to cry, and all of them grabbed Nicolas's knees, imploring him to save them.

Their departure from the police station was tumultuous. Projectiles rained down on the carriage. The hatred of the populace for the French was all too clear, which struck Nicolas as a bad omen for future relations between the two kingdoms. He gave up the idea of getting back to his cab and squeezed in with the prisoners, even though he was worried about losing his baggage. When they reached the quay, he was grateful for the presence of mind of Éon's servants: the cab driver had preceded them and now gave him his portmanteau, with a smile. He received a guinea, and shook Nicolas's hand warmly. Why was this Englishman, who had no stake in the matter, so sympathetic towards him? But there was no time now to think about these things, and he jumped in the rowing boat.

The ship waiting for them was in fact a large fishing boat, and the skipper, fearing to miss the tide, immediately cast off. A favourable wind took them all the way to Calais. Throughout the crossing, Nicolas had to suffer the officers' incoherent stories, punctuated by screams from the one who was delirious. Early next morning, he again set foot on French soil, older, wiser in the ways of secrecy, and the possible father of a boy of thirteen who, he suddenly realised, bore the first name of his own father, Marquis Louis de Ranreuil, as well as that of his master, the King. Abandoning the members of the sad company to their colleagues in the port, he asked for the best charger at the post house and set off at full tilt, hoping to get back to Paris as soon as possible.

VII

CONFUSION

It is the hour of ice for the truth
And the hour of fire for lies.
La Fontaine

Tuesday 18 January 1774

Nicolas's return journey to Paris had been a nightmare. The horses supplied at the post houses were of variable quality and had twice thrown him, landing him in potholes of mud and ice. It was not that the horses were defective or temperamental, and he had spoken to them with skill and tenderness, but they had slipped on patches of ice, startled by the ghostly clouds rising from the road after a constant succession of rain and fog, which seemed to their weary eyes like so many threatening obstacles. During the brief halts, he had scoffed down a little food and immediately resumed his journey, determined to reach his destination come what may.

On Saturday morning, he had at last reached Rue Montmartre and dropped from the saddle. The boys from the bakery on the ground floor had carried him, almost paralysed, up to his room. Everyone had done what they could, Poitevin had cut open his boots in order to take them off, Marion had stoked the fire and heated water, and Catherine, a former canteen-keeper, who had learnt her trade on the battlefields of Europe, had undressed him and rubbed him down like an animal, with a soothing mixture of schnapps and peasant ointments. He had fallen into a sleep that lasted two days, and had not woken until Monday morning. Feeling refreshed, he had come through the servants' pantry half naked, bounded out into the courtyard, and vigorously worked the lever of the pump until he was covered in cold water, singing at the top of his voice, before raiding the kitchen and teasing an alarmed Marion and Catherine. Then he had gone to see Monsieur de Noblecourt, who was delighted at the return of the prodigal son, and they had chatted away about trifles: more serious subjects could wait. Newly shaved, combed and dressed, he had walked to the Grand Châtelet, knowing he would find Bourdeau there at that hour. He was like a man reborn, all his passion and appetite for living revived.

It was not until he saw the familiar outline of the royal prison that the dread reality of the situation came back to him: he was still the prime suspect in a terrible murder. None of those closest to him thought him guilty, but everything seemed to have been contrived to confirm the suspicions of a great many others. He was still lost in conjecture as to who could have been behind the various attempts on his life. What did seem clear, though, was that some mysterious coalition of powerful interests was intent not only on tarnishing his honour but on doing away with him altogether. How would Sartine and, above all, the King judge the very moderate success of his mission to London? And, to add to this ominous prospect, he also had to investigate the past of a child, now an adolescent, whose future might be of great personal concern to him. But that, he thought, could wait a while: thirteen years of silence were justification enough for proceeding with caution.

Bourdeau was sitting in the duty office, looking through the book in which the previous night's incidents had been noted. It was a comforting scene, redolent of everyday routine. And Nicolas was deeply touched when his friend leapt from his chair and came and gave him a thump on his back, crying joyfully, 'By God, it's good to see you again! Where on earth did you get to?'

At the same time, Nicolas felt embarrassed. How to explain his absence? Bourdeau wasn't supposed to know anything.

But it was Bourdeau himself who said, 'I know, I know. Affairs of State! Monsieur de Sartine told me just enough, so I'm not going to ply you with questions. As for the rumours . . .'

'I missed you!' cried Nicolas, relieved. 'One day, I'll tell you all about it. But what's new here?'

'Hats keep getting taller and taller,' replied Bourdeau, as serious as a pope. 'To be more specific, I can reassure you about the rumours. Madame du Barry's people kept going on about an encounter on the road north with a certain marquis who's also a commissioner . . . When the Lieutenant General heard about it, he flew into a rage, tore off his wig and promised the rack to those gossips – he used a stronger word – who had endangered the life of his best commissioner. So you can understand how anxious I've been and how happy I am to see you alive and well.'

'I see. But enlighten me: how far have we got with the case?'

'*Adagio ma non troppo*. In order, and briefly: *primo*, you are Madame de Lastérieux's heir; *secundo*, we received an anonymous letter implicating you in a mysterious act; *tertio*, Casimir, your friend's slave, underwent torture but didn't tell us anything – though I'd like to know what you think of the interrogation.'

'Right, let's look at all that in order.'

'I found the name of Madame de Lastérieux's notary. As you predicted, he's quite close by, even if not in the immediate vicinity. His name is Master Tiphaine, and his practice is in Rue de la Harpe, opposite Rue Percée. I went to see him, and he produced from his files a will written, dated and signed by your friend, making you her sole legatee.'

Nicolas, overwhelmed, bowed his head.

'That's nothing, there's worse to come! The document was signed three days before her death.'

'In what circumstances? Did she visit the notary? Did she summon him to Rue de Verneuil? Was the seal intact?'

'All good questions! No visits, no witnesses, and the will was deposited at the notary's office by an unknown bearer.'

'What about the signature?'

'There are several, apparently genuine according to an expert at the Palais de Justice, and the red seal was intact. You know as well as I do how easy it is to make a mistake in such things. To tell the truth, we can never be certain. The will may be genuine or a fake. If it's a fake, it may throw suspicion on you as the person who benefits . . . But if it's genuine, well, the same thing.'

Nicolas thought this over. 'A genuine signature isn't enough,' he said. 'The document itself must be entirely written by hand, and the date, too. All three conditions are required for this particular category of will to be legally recognised. That's been common law in Paris since an amendment brought in by the Parlement in 1581 to curtail the prerogatives of the Notaries

Royal, who were the only people authorised to draw up wills. In any case, my dear Pierre, I suggest you find out more about this notary. I'm an old Paris hand, but this is the first time I've ever heard his name.'

'You've put your finger on the dubious part of all this,' replied the inspector. 'This Tiphaine has only just been admitted to the Company. Nobody knows how he was able to get the money together to buy a practice that had been suddenly abandoned by a family that had held it for centuries. That kind of takeover is quite rare, and usually only happens when someone marries into the family. It's quite an awkward process and takes a lot of diplomacy. But how come you know so much about the subject?'

'Don't forget it was my intended profession. I was even a notary's clerk before my exile to Paris.'

They both laughed.

'What do you advise me to do?' asked Bourdeau.

'It might be an idea to approach Master Bontemps, the senior member of the Company of Notaries Royal. He'd be able to tell us more about this Tiphaine. We can talk to Monsieur de Noblecourt, they're more or less the same age and I know they're good friends. Now what about this anonymous letter you mentioned?'

Bourdeau opened a register and took out a small stained sheet of paper, covered in printed characters.

'This was thrown into Monsieur de Sartine's carriage. Handwriting disguised to look as featureless as possible, common paper and ink. No usable clues.'

He read the missive aloud. '*Ask Nicolas Le Floch what he threw in the river at the corner of the quai by Pont Royal, opposite Rue de Beaune, on the night of 6 to 7 January 1774. May justice be done!*'

'That doesn't make any sense,' said Nicolas, who could feel that morning's sense of elation gradually fading. 'Who on earth is so determined to destroy me, and why? The murder of Julie, other things I can't tell you about, the will . . . When is there going to be an end to all this?'

'When we've arrested the guilty party or parties. About this latest point, though, I've had an idea. While you were away, Monsieur de Sartine asked me to be present on his behalf at an experiment presented by an inventor to a commission of the Academy of Sciences.'

'And what has that experiment to do with this case?'

'Let me explain. The inventor will demonstrate a new machine which he claims allows him to stay underwater for at least an hour, without any communication with the surface. He maintains that he can reach a depth of thirty feet. Do you follow me? The bed of the Seine isn't as deep as that. I know what you're going to ask. Yes, we've already dragged the river at that spot, without any result. The experiment is due to take place in two days' time. We simply have to request that it be performed at the corner of the Pont Royal.'

'Extraordinary as it is, your idea seems to me an excellent one. I'd like to be present.'

'There's no reason why not. Monsieur de Sartine has decided, with His Majesty's agreement, that you can accompany me during this investigation, without any disguise this time – although, come to think of it, carnival's on its way.'

'You mentioned a third thing,' said Nicolas with a sigh.

Bourdeau handed him a sheet of paper covered with the spidery scrawl of a clerk of the court. 'The transcript of the interrogation of Madame de Lastérieux's slave Casimir.'

Nicolas shook his head. 'We don't regard these people as free men, but when it comes to torture they're no different from their masters. We listen to what they have to say, and their word's as good as anyone else's!'

'There speaks your good heart,' said Bourdeau, 'and I share your sentiments entirely. I should tell you that since this affair came to light, your name hasn't been mentioned, but the same can't be said for Casimir! Someone informed the Minister of the Navy, and there was a great fuss and a demand that light be thrown on a crime they consider exceptionally serious. Just think, a murder of a white woman, the widow of a financial official in the navy, by a black slave – and on French soil, to boot! Think of the salutary effect on the colonies if news of the episode was held back until a severe punishment had already been meted out! A great deal of pressure was put on Monsieur de Sartine to act firmly – and you know his enlightened views on slavery, and on torture.'

'I assume he resisted!'

'Of course. He gave Sanson instructions to go gently on Casimir, and our friend, being the humane person that he is, observed these instructions to the letter. The torture was done only faintly. It was more a matter of scaring the prisoner into telling the truth than hurting him for the sake of getting him to say just anything. The torture instruments are impressive enough in themselves to break down the resistance of a poor slave accused of a crime a thousand leagues from his native island!'

Nicolas took the document and read it aloud. '"In the year 1774, on 15 January in the royal prison of the Châtelet, I, Pierre

Bourdeau, inspector of police, by extraordinary authority of the Criminal Lieutenant and in the presence—"'

'You can skip all that,' said Bourdeau. 'Mostly, he repeated word for word what he'd said before. I've underlined in pencil the passage where there are a few new details.'

Nicolas resumed reading. '". . . for the second time, said Casimir was subjected to torture. Questioned as to whether or not he had attempted to poison his mistress, he answered that he had not, and stated that she had never mistreated him, but confessed that he had often asked her to set both him and his companion free, and that she had always refused, which made said suspect very unhappy. Questioned as to whether he had spoken of this to a third party, he answered that he did not want to reveal the identity of the person who advised him to go back to the West Indies, that the only unknown factor had been having sufficient money. Questioned as to whether he knew that such an action would amount to desertion and that he was exposing himself to being pursued and severely punished if he was caught, he answered that he did know that but that his freedom had no price. Questioned as to how he obtained the spices he sometimes used for cooking, he answered that they were seeds from Santo Domingo called *piment bouc*, which were commonly consumed in his native country. Questioned again on the presence of Monsieur von Müvala on the evening of his mistress's death, he answered that he knew nothing and had seen him for the last time that evening when his mistress was showing him the perfume about which he had enquired. Questioned as to why he was called at that moment by his mistress, he answered that she had asked him to post a letter, that he had done so immediately and that he did not know to whom it was addressed, being unable to read or write. Questioned as to whether his mistress was having carnal relations with Monsieur von Müvala, he answered that he was certain she was not and that his mistress was too besotted with Monsieur Le Floch to look for pleasure elsewhere.'

Bourdeau handed him another paper. 'This is the procurator's indictment.'

'"In the name of the King,"' read Nicolas, '"I demand, in expectation of the results of the investigation and the gathering of evidence, that said Casimir, a black slave, be sentenced to be burnt alive on a pyre, which will be built and lighted to this effect on Place de Grève in this city. Said Casimir to be previously subjected to ordinary and extraordinary torture in order to reveal his accomplices."'

'Obviously, all this is just routine, to speed things up. Some people just can't wait to see the prisoner convicted and punished! The only problem is, there's no evidence against him. When it comes to poisoning, extreme measures have often been advocated. One magistrate we know[1] has said that when the condemned man arrives at the place of execution and mounts the scaffold, he should be lowered into a cauldron of boiling water.'

'The horror of it!'

'What do you think of Casimir's testimony?' asked Bourdeau.

'A mysterious person giving advice, an unknown poison, uncertainty about Julie's feelings for Müvala, a letter sent in the middle of the night, why and to whom? This interrogation raises more questions than it answers! It's a paltry thing, really.'

'Exactly. I've organised an unofficial war council for this evening. Semacgus has agreed for us to go to his house in

Vaugirard. For once, Sanson has accepted his invitation. We'll examine the case calmly, from all angles – if you agree, that is. Catherine will come and help Awa with the cooking, so it's sure to be good! Monsieur de Noblecourt would happily have come, too, but his presence might have scared off Monsieur de Paris.'

'I'm happy to fall in with your plan. I need as many friends around me as possible right now. Not to mention the pleasures of French cooking.'

The words had escaped without his volition. He bit his lip: what an idiot he'd been! Bourdeau made no comment, but his eyes creased with suppressed irony. To create a diversion, Nicolas stood up and looked in the pigeonhole where mail that had arrived for him at the Châtelet was kept. His heart missed a beat: on a square little envelope with a red seal, he had recognised Madame de Lastérieux's handwriting. But this first feeling was followed by incomprehension when he saw that the address read: *To Monsieur Nicolas Le Floch, Commissioner of Police at the Châtelet, Rue Montmartre, at the house of Monsieur de Noblecourt opposite Passage de la Reine de Hongrie.* Why, despite such specific directions, had the letter come to the royal prison? Forgetting that Bourdeau was there, he opened and read it.

Nicolas, he who will not marry us exposes himself to the risk that the object of his passion will make him feel her displeasure, so great is her despair at this desertion. My love will even wish for you to fall. I am not claiming to justify an all too real mistake, nor to minimise it. Believe me, I despise myself as much as it is possible to do so for having yielded to a momentary impulse and given you the impression that I was so weak as to take advantage of the presence of that young man who means nothing to me and who is the least likely person to take me from you. Whatever the fate you have in store for me, so frightened was I by your reaction, in which I saw all the tenderness you have for me, that you can be sure I will never feel punished enough, for I admit that there is nothing more unbearably odious than a woman who flirts for no reason. Come, I beg you, as soon as you can; one can only raise oneself above those whom one misses by forgiving them.

Your loving and faithful Julie.

Her voice had reached him from beyond the grave. He should have been moved, but the affected style struck him as strange and inappropriate. Without thinking, he handed the letter to Bourdeau. The inspector glanced through it, looked at the address, and turned it over several times in his hands, seemingly lost in thought.

'To be honest,' he said at last, 'the mystery appears to be deepening. So many assumptions, but so few certainties! Let's be clear and direct about this. First of all, we have the physical evidence gathered by our friends during the autopsy on Madame de Lastérieux's body, which was not very conclusive. Now, unless the woman was lying – which, let's not forget, she'd been doing ever since she met you, by concealing her secret activities from you – this letter throws a new light on the evening of 6 January and the events that followed. It seems strange that she should have written it and given it to Casimir in the presence of Müvala. In addition, I'm puzzled by what happened to this letter. According to the servant, it was placed in the box that very night. The first thing to do is check where the nearest post box is.'

He opened a drawer in the desk and, after rapidly sifting through the contents, pulled out a small printed poster.

'Let's see, now . . . This notice was authorised by Monsieur de Sartine on 13 October 1761 and was intended to inform the public about the workings of the postal service. The office . . . Ah, here it is. The office corresponding to the residence of Madame de Lastérieux covers the whole of the Faubourg Saint-Germain area, and the box is situated in Rue du Bac, between Rue de l'Université and Rue de Verneuil. On every item of mail three stamps have to appear. The first is a letter distinguishing the different offices and the boxes dependent on them.'

He pointed to a letter above the address.

'Here it is, the letter *F*, which does in fact correspond to that area. The following figure indicates the postman who received the letter and is mainly used to check the history of that delivery when necessary. As you know, the post office is often blamed for things that aren't even its fault. The number of people who take invitations to the post office only after the hour when the particular ceremony was supposed to take place! Or who, in order to avoid trouble, say they've sent letters when they haven't even written them! Or, for one reason or another, deny they ever received them!'

Nicolas leant over Bourdeau's shoulder. 'And the other stamps?'

'On letters which are going out of the area, we find the day of the month. If it's inside the area, it would have the same letter in a circle, and would be delivered within two hours at the latest – sometimes within half an hour. The others go to be sorted, but the time for delivery is never more than four hours. Now what do we see here? *F*, that's the Rue de Verneuil area, *7*, the date, and *1*, meaning the first of the nine daily collections, which takes place at six in the morning. Therefore, Madame de Lastérieux's letter should have got to Rue Montmartre by midday at the latest. Why did it never reach Monsieur de Noblecourt's house? I note that your friend, no doubt automatically, underlined the part of the address which mentioned that you were a commissioner at the Châtelet. The mail must have been sorted too quickly, and the letter ended up here. And there you have it. I think you're in a hurry to report to Monsieur de Sartine, so I'll leave you now. We'll meet at five. Sanson will be with us by then and we can go to Vaugirard together. A carriage is waiting for you downstairs.'

Nicolas made a gesture to stop Bourdeau.

'No,' the inspector said. 'You go alone. Secrets should remain secret.'

On the way out, Nicolas said goodbye to Old Marie. He found a carriage at the entrance. The snow was beginning to fall vertically, gradually transforming the mud in the streets into a dark river in which the pedestrians splashed about. He rode past the black-clad hosts of the law heading for the Châtelet and the Palais de Justice. Their comical procession, a jumble of bands, robes and case files, skidded on the slippery ground, followed by a crowd of litigants, their noisy chatter rising to the upper floors of the houses. Here and there, hired men carried terrified ladies on their backs across the flooded streets. A worker carrying a huge oval mirror on his back stumbled and almost fell and, as he did so, Nicolas saw the swaying reflection of his own carriage on the polished surface.

It had not taken long for the case to obsess him again. It had become so complicated that it was impossible now to deal with each of its elements by itself. They were all linked in a web of crime and dissimulation. What would they discover in the Seine, if they discovered anything at all? What was the meaning of that letter with its bizarre, affected style? Did its tortuous sentences truly express his mistress's last feelings towards him, or . . . He did not dare formulate the absurd theories jostling in his mind. And what of that nameless person who had given Casimir advice? Why was the slave, so eloquent on other matters, obstinately refusing to reveal his identity, even if it meant drawing further suspicion on himself, and perhaps sending him to the scaffold?

When he reached Rue Neuve-Saint-Augustin, he was, as usual, admitted without delay to the office of the Lieutenant General of Police. Monsieur de Sartine was writing. A blazing fire crackled in the hearth: an indication that the magistrate was feeling the cold. Absorbed in his correspondence, he did not look up for several minutes. Nicolas realised that it was already well into the morning, past the hour for the presentation of wigs. He regretted the fact that he had not had time to bring back some new model for his chief, perhaps one of those he had glimpsed in that splendid shop to which he had paid a lightning visit during his stay in London.

Sartine's gaze came to rest on him. 'Monsieur,' he said, 'we are pleased with you, and even more pleased to see you safe. Perhaps you now have some idea of how difficult these secret affairs are. You seem pensive.'

That 'Monsieur' had been neither aggressive nor sarcastic, but full of restrained affection.

'To tell the truth, Monsieur,' replied Nicolas, 'I was thinking what a pity it is that I saw a wig-maker's shop in London but that the King's business did not leave me the opportunity to choose one for your collection.'

The Lieutenant General's eyes creased with irony. 'Your servant, Monsieur! The very idea of such thoughtfulness fills me with gratitude. Give me the address and Monsieur de Guines, the ambassador, will see to it.'

'Alas, the affairs you mentioned—'

'Didn't give you time to make a note of it. The Chevalier d'Éon will find it for me. In the meantime, tell me all about your adventures.'

Monsieur de Sartine was in such a good mood that Nicolas was encouraged to launch into a lively and colourful account. He was good at finding the appropriate words to describe things: it was a gift on which he had staked his career, one day in 1761, in the small apartments at Versailles, before the King and Madame de Pompadour. The memory of that first day had been the basis of the monarch's appreciation of 'young Ranreuil'. Did he owe this talent to those evenings in his childhood in Brittany, spent gorging on pancakes and cider, listening enthralled to an old fortune teller? Now it was Sartine who listened patiently and attentively, his chin on his fist.

'My one regret,' concluded Nicolas, 'is that I failed with Morande.'

'Don't complain, my dear fellow, you narrowly escaped death. It's easier to accumulate dangers in our profession than resounding successes. You don't yet know the best of it: Morande finally yielded.'

'What?'

'Yes, a letter sent from London at about the same time you left arrived yesterday, informing me that the little crook, impressed by your firmness and your reluctance to bargain – I don't think you made any actual proposal, did you? – said he was ready to compromise. If you'd tried to deceive him, you would have spoilt everything! Instead, you mounted a direct assault, without prevarication, just like your father.'

Nicolas nodded, touched by the comparison.

'It made the fellow so anxious, so racked with dark thoughts, so convinced, in a word, that your determination meant terrible reprisals were on their way, that he immediately made contact with our agent to say that he was prepared to admit that he was at fault. He agreed to receive a new emissary, provided the latter had some monetary propositions to make, in particular the paying-off of his debts and, possibly, a pension. In return, he would undertake to burn all copies of his pamphlet, with all the guarantees which have to be made when one has a fish like that at the end of one's line!'

'I'm very pleased.'

'His Majesty, with whom I spoke last night, is singing your praises, as is a lady who, alas, saw fit to meet you in the woods at Chantilly. Anyway, thank God, here you are! But don't expect me to tell you who was behind those attempts on your life. That's all shrouded in a fog of mystery, and I know quite a few people who'd like the fog to be even thicker. The King wasn't at all happy to hear that you, his representative, had been attacked. He's going to look into the matter.'

'Let's hope he finds out something,' sighed Nicolas. 'The Chevalier d'Éon gave me a message for His Majesty about Mr Flint and his affairs in China.'

Sartine nervously adjusted his wig – a movement that suggested to Nicolas that his chief did not like being confronted with a matter about which he knew nothing.

'You'll see the King yourself,' he said. 'He needs distracting, and I'm sure you can do that. That said, what of the sad affair of Rue de Verneuil?'

It seemed to Nicolas that his chief had passed rather quickly over the attempts on his life, but he knew that Sartine also had to safeguard his own position, subject as he was to the vicissitudes of favour and the threats posed by secret cabals. He commented on the latest developments without going into detail, since the Lieutenant General was not especially interested in the nitty-gritty of an investigation. Only results mattered. The last thing he mentioned was Madame de Lastérieux's letter. He held it out to him, but Sartine waved it away.

'There's no point, I already know the gist.'

'Inspector Bourdeau is always very quick off the mark!' said Nicolas, a touch sourly.

Sartine smiled. 'How unjust you are! I don't have my information from him. Even if I had, what of it? It's his duty to tell me everything. But the fact is, as you should know, I'm in a position – a unique position – to be able to look at private correspondence for the good of the State and the security of His Majesty. It's a privilege and a burden.'

He had risen and was striding up and down his office, suddenly irritable.

'It so happens that it was my own office – what a shallow populace calls the *cabinet noir* – that brought me this intriguing letter. Intriguing on two counts – firstly, because it was from an agent in the pay of the police – Madame de Lastérieux – and secondly, because it constituted an important piece of evidence in a secret procedure currently in progress in which a man who enjoys my trust finds himself, whether he likes it or not, heavily implicated. You have nothing to prove to me. I'm not like the Criminal Lieutenant, who as usual, as you have seen, is being . . . let's say, cautious. Had you omitted to mention this letter, either inadvertently or out of a deliberate desire to conceal the truth, neither the King nor myself would have been able to continue protecting you. But we were right to do so, as your attitude confirms. Even Monsieur Testard du Lys, who, in view of your position, has been making this into an affair of State, will give his *nihil obstat* to your participation in the ongoing investigation. Unless,' he said with a laugh, 'this is only the Machiavellian ploy of a guilty man calculating that it's to his advantage to feign honesty. Don't make that face, I'm only joking.'

'I spoke without thinking,' sighed Nicolas.

'That's what's so delightful about you! I can well understand how the past two weeks might have tested the most steadfast of men. In my opinion, you've conducted yourself extremely well and I'm overjoyed to have reduced the Criminal Lieutenant to silence. Continue your investigations and keep me informed.'

*

Leaving Monsieur de Sartine's office, Nicolas passed a man climbing the stairs four at a time, whistling an opera aria. He recognised him as Monsieur Caron de Beaumarchais, factotum to the King's daughters and a man very much in fashion. They had already met at Madame Adélaïde's. He made him promise to have dinner with him one evening at his convenience. He felt spontaneously drawn to this frank and amusing figure. He got back to his carriage. He had decided not to eat anything, in anticipation of the evening at Semacgus's house. Instead, he would go and see Master Vachon, his tailor, in Rue Vieille-du-Temple. His eventful journey to England had taken its toll of his clothes, which would otherwise have had a long future ahead of them. He was fond of his clothes and always found it heartbreaking to part with them. To make up for this inconvenience, he would now order two of each garment.

Master Vachon was the same as ever: increasingly stooped and diaphanous, but still talkative and still manifesting that authority which allowed him to reign, half cantankerously, half paternally, over a troop of apprentices who mocked him but were ready to pull their needles in the right direction at the slightest stern look from the master. While taking Nicolas's measurements – and remarking ironically that he was getting bigger – the tailor related various pieces of Parisian gossip. Nicolas chose his fabrics, a lustrous russet satin for the coat and a darker wool for the cloak. The two colours went well together. After a while, Master Vachon drew him for a moment into a corner of his shop where no one could hear them.

'Commissioner,' he began, 'in these difficult times of ours I get to hear many things. There is increasing discontent with His

Majesty, and terrible rumours being spread about him. Oh, I can guess what you're thinking. It isn't that: the people are accustomed to the King's private conduct, and are no longer shocked by it. No, what they're saying is that he has his own private treasury and that, in order to give his mistress all she asks for, he's increasing it by speculating on stocks like a merchant, but with fewer risks because, having inside knowledge about the state of the finances, he knows when the rises and falls will occur. They say these speculations revolve around the market in wheat and that His Majesty has established a secret monopoly, which is why there are shortages and price rises. I think you should tell Monsieur de Sartine. I felt obliged to bring this to your attention, as a good citizen and a loyal subject.'

Nicolas thanked the tailor, who walked him wearily to the door. What he had heard did not surprise him. He noted sadly that they confirmed what the informers and spies of the Lieutenancy General had been reporting for months without being able to silence the rumour or determine its origin. Every evening, he knew, the items of gossip gathered in public places and drawing rooms were carefully sorted, put in order and written down in Monsieur de Sartine's back office, to be conveyed later, in extract form, to those ministers who might be interested by such tittle-tattle.

The narrow network of alleyways situated between the Marais and the central market, where even a single carriage had difficulty passing, slowed down his journey back to Rue Montmartre. Some alleys were so narrow that Nicolas would have been able to touch the houses and read, each time he stopped, the countless posters on the walls: decrees, advertisements by charlatans, decisions of the Parlement, verdicts of the Châtelet, auctions of property seized by the law, monitories, appeals to find lost dogs and cats, death notices, the poster for a special performance of Ariosto's *Orlando Furioso* by a Sicilian Teatro di Puppi, and, finally, ten copies of the address of a maker of elastic trusses. Monsieur de Sartine's agents made sure that most of these were torn down by the following day, to make way for others and to avoid them ending up littering the roadway. In this way, the hands that put them up undid their own work a few hours later by tearing them down.

As he rode, cataracts of snow and water fell on the cab, frightening the horses, which swerved, thus happily avoiding the fragments of tile, plaster and even lead which had fallen from the roofs during the storm. Despite the atrocious weather, Nicolas was amused by the Parisians' habit of stopping and staring at any object that caught their interest as they walked. A man in the street only had to look up at some vague point above his head for several others to do the same, searching for whatever might have drawn his attention. The people of Paris might be touchy and quick to take offence, thought Nicolas, but deep down they were happy and easily amused.

For a moment, he was tempted to order the coachman to turn on to Rue du Faubourg-Saint-Honoré so that he could make an impromptu visit to the Dauphin Couronné. He saw himself, with all the dignity of a man wounded by a lie, asking the crucial question of a panic-stricken La Satin. So vivid was his imagination that he was able to experience scenes from his life before they had even taken place. He heard himself speaking and listening to his friend's replies. These mental images sometimes became so complex that his tormented mind would choose variations, carefully sorting the elements like those in a police file, triggering changes of tone, unexpected turns, happy or calamitous conclusions. He would imagine these fictions with such intensity that sometimes the scenes merged together depending on his mood or his unconscious desires. Worried about his growing excitement, he finally persuaded himself to cease a cruel game which was rubbing salt into a private wound he did not yet recognise as such, even though the pain of it was real enough. Once again, he suppressed deep inside himself this nagging desire to know that had been with him ever since his conversation with La Présidente in a street in London. He would have to do something eventually, but not now.

In Rue Montmartre, he found Monsieur de Noblecourt in his library, sitting in a large tapestried armchair, leafing through a calfskin-bound folio he had set down on a gaming table. In his grey coat, his hair combed and powdered, he seemed rejuvenated. He smiled when he saw Nicolas.

'How angry I am with myself for being born so late!' he sighed.

'That's a strange statement,' said Nicolas. 'What's the reason for it?'

'If I'd been born fifty years earlier, I could have seen Molière act in *Le Misanthrope*! I find today's plays so insipid, apart perhaps from those of Marivaux, so true to life in their delicate portrayal of human passions, but even they are already of another time, the time of my youth. And even with Marivaux, I have my reservations. I find him too inclined to fling ideas together in such a way that the effect is needlessly subtle. I agree with Monsieur Rousseau: we shouldn't try to make life too subtle, for then all ends in tears.'

'You would probably have been disappointed,' replied Nicolas. 'I've been told the divine Molière veered towards the comical in his performance, with a lot of grimacing and buffoonery, and that he soon handed the role over to young Baron.'

'No, don't destroy my illusions!' protested Noblecourt. 'Listen to this perfect fusion of form and content:

Oh, nothing can compare to what I feel for you,
And in its ardour to declare itself to all,
My love will even wish for you to fall.

Don't you feel it? The man who wrote that really lived and suffered. So much truth can only lead to perfection. There's a kind of moral music in that piece. But what's the matter? You look so pale! Sit down.'

Nicolas had taken Madame de Lastérieux's letter from his pocket. In a low voice, he told his friend all about the latest developments in the case.

'This letter,' he said, 'puzzled me when I read it, because it was so unlike what I knew, or thought I knew, of Julie. I found it affected and full of hand-me-down phrases. I've just realised the reason why. There's one sentence in it – "My love will even wish for you to fall" – which is shamelessly borrowed from Molière.'

'I suspect you're wrong,' replied Monsieur de Noblecourt. 'It might just be a coincidence. The idea is an unusual one, I grant you, but your friend was refined enough to have thought of it for herself. Or perhaps it was buried deep in her memory and she copied it without realising.'

'Say what you like, you won't convince me. A woman writing to her lover in the heat of passion wouldn't start looking for quotations. Either this letter reveals a treacherous woman with a heart of stone, or it's a fake, and I incline to the latter hypothesis. Nor is that the only suspicious document.'

He told him about the will which made him the victim's sole heir.

'Are you telling me,' said Noblecourt, 'that both the will and that letter are forgeries?'

'There are plenty of people in Paris skilled enough to do that kind of work. Even the King is surrounded by secretaries who write and sign letters in his place, and you'd have to be very clever to spot the difference between the original and a copy!'

'If I understand you correctly,' said Noblecourt pensively, 'you'd like me to facilitate your introduction to Master Bontemps, the senior member of the Company of Notaries Royal, the famous "cat man".'

'Cat man?'

'You will understand when you climb his stairs. He's an original. We're old cronies, even though he's appreciably older than me. I shall write to him immediately.'

Monsieur de Noblecourt rose nimbly from his chair, disturbing poor Cyrus, who had been dozing at his feet, as he did so, and took a sheet of paper from a writing desk. He filled it with his small, rapid handwriting, dried the ink with a handful of sand, folded it into a letter, lit a candle, held a piece of red wax in it, spilt a few drops on the paper, and pressed in his seal.

'Don't be surprised by his welcome. He affects a certain incivility which it's best to ignore. As for your mysterious journey,' he said, sitting down again, 'don't worry, I'm not going to pry. Curious as I am to know what happened, I will never pry into State secrets. Bourdeau warned me.'

Nicolas smiled at this chain of warnings, passing from Sartine to Noblecourt via Bourdeau, imposing discretion and reserve on friendship.

'On the other hand,' the former procurator went on, hitting the armrests of his chair, 'I am indignant that my friends – my children, rather – are going away and leaving me all alone in Rue Montmartre, where I shall be sitting full of envy, imagining their sumptuous banquet this evening!'

Nicolas laughed. 'You're hardly the one to complain. You're surrounded by friends who are concerned about your health and who, knowing your natural appetites, wanted to spare you temptation. It would only have brought on a massive attack of gout, whereas here you are, strong, lively, fresh as a daisy, talkative, looking twenty years younger . . .'

'Flatterer!'

'Not at all, I describe things as I see them. And anyway, the main reason we didn't invite you was not to scare off Sanson. He has so much respect for you that your presence would paralyse him. And we need him in order to discuss our case.'

Noblecourt smiled. 'That's a rather more persuasive argument, Jesuitical as it is. But I'll get my revenge in Lent. I shall serve you all fish smelling of herring barrels!'

Laughing, Nicolas left the room and went back up to his apartment to get ready. He was about to leave when he suddenly remembered his keys. He searched in the pockets of the cloak he had worn in England but did not find them. This was worrying: his keys, which included those to Monsieur de Noblecourt's house and Madame de Lastérieux's apartments, had been tied with a blue ribbon his mistress had given him. Could they have slipped out when he had fallen into the arms of the baker's boys after his mad ride back to Paris? He went down and asked Poitevin, Marion, and the baker's boys. None of them knew anything about the keys. So, unless Catherine, who was already at Semacgus's house in Vaugirard, could throw some light on the matter, they were well and truly lost. With a chill, he remembered the incident at Ailly-le-Haut-Clocher. At the time, nothing seemed to have been stolen. He could not recall the last time he had held the bunch of keys in his hand. Was it after his last visit to Rue de Verneuil? He made an effort to remember: on that terrible night, he had come back to Rue Montmartre and had found the door open, as it usually was when Monsieur de Noblecourt had guests. Had the keys gone missing when he was wandering the streets on the night of the murder, the details of which still escaped him, or when he had fallen from his horse on the road from Calais to Paris? Suddenly, a detail came back to him. When he had changed vehicles in Rue Neuve-des-Petits-Champs, he had been afraid of losing his keys and had clutched them in his hand inside his pocket to stop them falling out. That narrowed it down to his journey to England. He asked Poitevin to leave the key to the little staircase leading to his room in the corner of a window where nobody would think of looking for it.

In any case, he did not want to wake him when he came back late from Vaugirard.

His carriage took him back to the Châtelet. There was a lull in the bad weather, and the lights of the city were coming on. Sanson in a green coat and Bourdeau in mouse grey were waiting for him at the entrance. With them was Rabouine, who informed Nicolas that he was still trying to find out more about Müvala: so far, there was nothing to indicate that he had left France. The carriage set off, taking the same route Nicolas had travelled several times a month since he had first met Semacgus. The Pont Royal, the great mass of the Invalides and the Vaugirard tollgate sped past. A few stars began to show through the gaps in the cloud cover, but the heights of Meudon were still shrouded in thick, inky-blue clouds. The slate-grey sky stretched as far as the *faubourgs* to the west. The snow had not settled, and the wheels of the cab splashed black mud on the few pedestrians hurrying home.

Semacgus's massive residence came into sight, a haven of peace. Lanterns illumined the exterior. Through the windows, they glimpsed a household busying itself for the arrival of guests. The tall figure of the navy surgeon was framed in the doorway of the servants' pantry. The neighing of the horses had alerted him to their arrival. He had taken off his coat and was wearing an apron. A particularly warm welcome was reserved for Sanson, who immediately emerged from the silence he had observed throughout the journey.

'I was just giving Catherine and Awa a hand,' said Semacgus.

'And what operation are you performing?' asked Sanson, bending curiously over the dishes being prepared.

'Ah, the delicate operation of poaching black pudding made from *foie gras* and capon! It's poached in milk, which shouldn't be brought to the boil but has to be left to simmer gently to avoid destroying the harmony of the ingredients and above all to stop the delicate casing from bursting.'

'That sounds promising,' said Bourdeau, his nostrils flaring and his head lifted like a pointer. 'And what do you put in these fragile marvels?'

'A finely chopped quarter-pound of pork fat, a mince made from *foie gras* and capon meat in equal quantities, herbs, chives, salt, pepper, nutmeg, ground cloves, and six raw egg yolks. I mix the whole lot together and put it in the little pork casings.'

Semacgus led them into his study, where the table had been laid. They sat down by the fire which was roaring in the big stone hearth. The room was cluttered with curiosities collected by their host on his voyages across the seas: exotic stuffed animals, minerals, primitive fabrics, herbariums and many other objects. Nicolas always felt transported a long way away when he was in this room: it gave him the same feeling of strangeness as when he read tales of the exploits of travellers and navigators, and aroused in him a hunger for the open sea.

Catherine brought in a bottle of ratafia and served it to the guests.

'A reminder of the good old days at the Dauphin Couronné,' said Semacgus. 'La Paulet used to regale her customers with ratafia that she'd been sent by one of her admirers in the West Indies.'

This allusion brought Nicolas's obsession back to the surface. He recalled with a pang in his heart that the navy surgeon had briefly been La Satin's lover when she was a resident of the brothel. But then he remembered that the child had been born long before, and his anxiety subsided.

'Gentlemen,' said Bourdeau, 'we are gathered here to celebrate our friendship and at the same time to help Nicolas elucidate this sad business with which you are all familiar. You've all had time to think about it. What new ideas have you come up with?'

'I made a discovery that may interest you,' said Semacgus. 'Tell me what you think. As you know, I am engaged on a large-scale project, putting together a general herbarium. I therefore often visit the Jardin du Roi and its excellent collections. Some time ago, I met a man I greatly respect, an expert on the subject: Monsieur Duhamel du Monceau,[2] who is both a herbalist and the most eminent practitioner in our navy.'

'How did you come to meet him?' asked Nicolas.

'He is the author of a work on how to ensure good health on the King's vessels, and he was keen to benefit from the experience of a navy surgeon who had travelled widely. During our meeting, I happened to mention our famous seeds. He's quite positive: if it was *piment bouc*, it couldn't have caused the toxic effects we observed. He suggested to me that perhaps the seeds were used to conceal another, more poisonous substance.'

'Casimir's testimony is making us go round in circles,' said Bourdeau. 'He cooks a chicken, but the poison isn't in the chicken, it's in the eggnog prepared for Madame de Lastérieux. Casimir sees Nicolas when he comes back to the house, but claims that he didn't. He tells us Müvala spent the whole evening there, yet seems unwilling to accept that his mistress might have been having a relationship with the man. That's a lot of contradictions!'

'Well, I questioned him,' said Sanson, 'and my modest experience – or rather, my intuition – leads me to believe he was lying.'

'But why?' asked Bourdeau. 'It's as if someone is forcing him to conceal the truth.'

'Let's sum up,' said Semacgus. 'It seems to me that Bourdeau is asking the right question. In whose interest is it to make sure that all the evidence points to a commissioner at the Châtelet? A jealous colleague, a rival, a criminal convicted in the past as a result of our friend's efforts?'

Nicolas felt powerless, unable to put his friends on the right course by revealing to them the hidden aspect of the case: the fact that Madame de Lastérieux had been working secretly for the police. It was quite likely that she had been the victim of blackmail. And what of the attempts on Nicolas's life, whose connection with the crime in Rue de Verneuil was yet to be proved? Why did his invisible enemy hate him so much, accumulating false evidence against him, as if wanting not only to destroy him but to dishonour him on the way to the scaffold? What would have become of him without the help and trust of his friends and of the Lieutenant General of Police, not to mention the King?

These reflections were interrupted by a great burst of laughter. Catherine, draped African-style in an undulating mass of yellow and red, her broad snub-nosed face surmounted by a superb knotted madras, had come in to announce that dinner was ready. Behind her, beating her sides with amusement at the guests' surprise, was Awa. The men took their seats at the little table that had been placed near the window. Semacgus took a paper from his pocket.

'Gentlemen,' he announced, 'here is the menu. A galantine of sorrel and beans, Breton style, in your honour, Commissioner. Then ears of pork *à la barbe Robert*, followed by black puddings of *foie gras* and capon. Last, but by no means least, a great fish stew prepared by Catherine Gauss, former canteen-keeper to the King's armies. A dessert of cauliflower with Parmesan, a Bavarian cake and a brioche stuffed with rosehip jelly.'

There were cries of enthusiasm.

'And what nectars will water all that?' asked Bourdeau.

'A Bordeaux claret from Fronsac, a gift from the Maréchal de Richelieu to Monsieur de Noblecourt, who gave me a few bottles as a way of being present at this dinner despite everything. They will be drunk to his health. And . . .' – he took out a long bottle from a cooling pitcher – '. . . a Rhine wine, an *Eiswein*. Imagine the grape forced to ripen by the autumn mist: what is known as a *Traubendrücker*. A sudden frost, and the water reduced to ice remains on the press, leaving an extract of sweet and scented oils in the vat.'

'And where is this marvel found?'

'In the German Rheingau, near Johannisberg.'

'I didn't know you spoke German,' said Nicolas.

'There are many things you still don't know about me,' replied Semacgus, enigmatically.

The dinner unfolded like a well-constructed symphony. After his initial reserve, Sanson proved a very talkative guest, much more so than when his wife was present. The smoothness of the ice wine and the alacrity of the Fronsac helped to keep the conversation lively. Awa whirled around them, her hand resting occasionally with unfeigned tenderness on Semacgus's shoulder. Their new complicity was obvious to all: the incorrigible libertine seemed to have settled down at last. Nicolas assumed that worry about his health had made the navy surgeon rethink his way of life and convinced him of the charms of a welcoming home, where his temperament found freedom in the pleasures of a relationship with his maid. The results of this conversion could clearly be seen on the features of a man long accustomed to nights of abandon: his pink, relaxed face shone with a new dignity, without the marks of the old days. The summit of the dinner was reached with the appearance of the fish stew. Catherine was summoned to recite the recipe.

'Well, gentlemen, first you make a mince of eel and carp. Awa kept the carp in a tub of water for a week to get rid of the smell of silt. Then you season the mince with salt, pepper and nutmeg and put it in a little clay pot with a lid, the sides of which have been smeared with fine butter. You place the carp skins all around the inside, you cover the bottom of the pot with the mince, to a height of half an inch, and then you fill the rest of the pot with truffles, morels, pike livers and carp tongues, kneading the whole thing with butter. You cover the whole thing with the forcemeat, put a silver plate on top and cook it in front of the fire, turning occasionally. Finally, you tip it over on to a hollow plate and sprinkle it with lemon juice and shelled pistachios.'

There was a round of applause, which turned Catherine's face red with pride.

'What's really delicious,' said Nicolas, always a lover of contrasts in cooking, 'is the crustiness of the surface and the softness of the inner layers.'

'I think it's the tongues and fish livers,' said Bourdeau. 'They thicken the mixture without making it too heavy and really bring out the aroma.'

'Let's drink, let's drink!' sang Sanson, who had taken off his beautiful green coat and was brandishing his glass. 'Here is the veritable nepenthe[3] which makes us merry and delivers us from dark thoughts!'

They chatted away about the latest fashionable entertainments and the gossip currently doing the rounds. Semacgus mentioned the rumour that a number of police officers had been arrested in London for trying to assassinate the notorious pamphleteer Théveneau de Morande. Nicolas made no reaction. Later, as they sipped, as was the custom of the house, an old rum from Semacgus's collection which had been round the world at least twice, the conversation once again touched on the affair of the murder in Rue Verneuil. It was Bourdeau who brought their wandering minds back to the subject.

'Gentlemen, there's a detail I'd like to see clarified for the sake of the investigation and Commissioner Le Floch's peace of mind.'

The solemnity of these words jolted them out of the drowsiness induced by too much eating and drinking.

'Did Madame de Lastérieux,' he went on, 'have carnal relations on the night of her death? Neither of you made a clear statement one way or the other during the autopsy.'

Sobering up, Sanson and Semacgus looked at each other. Neither seemed to want to speak first.

'The thing is,' the navy surgeon said at last, 'nothing is certain as far as that's concerned.'

'Is that a yes or a no?' said Bourdeau.

'To tell the truth, both possibilities exist.'

'The state of the organs did not rule out either hypothesis,' added Sanson.

'Can't you be more specific?'

'You have to bear in mind,' said Semacgus, 'that there are various factors which may make it seem as though intercourse took place when it didn't in fact do so . . .'

'I insist,' said Bourdeau. 'It's a crucial point. The mystery of what happened on that evening and its consequences largely centres on what the unseen puppet master is trying to make us believe: that Nicolas spent part of that night with his mistress.'

'In all conscience,' concluded Semacgus with Sanson's approval, 'it's impossible for us to express an opinion. It's always possible that someone arranged things to look that way . . .'

They all fell silent. At that moment, muffled sounds were heard outside the room. Awa came in and said that a man was asking for Inspector Bourdeau. He rose and followed the cook out of the room. He came back almost immediately.

'Gentlemen, the dance of death continues. The slave has been found dead, poisoned, in his cell at the Châtelet.'

VIII

DEAD END

Strange accidents, those of the past and those of today,
The eddies of fate whirl us from joy to sorrow.
EURIPIDES

Wednesday 19 January 1774

It was just after midnight. They decided to return to Paris at once. Semacgus insisted on going with them, as he wanted to examine the victim with Sanson. They were all still stunned by the news of Casimir's death. The temperature had risen unexpectedly, and a fog had formed, shrouding the gardens in increasingly dense clouds. In the city, where the dampness combined with the smoke from a thousand chimneys, the phenomenon was worse, making the carriage's progress difficult. As they approached the river, the dangers multiplied. It was impossible to see anything, not even the lanterns and torches carried by the few people still out and about at this time of night.

For a while, the coachman was reduced to getting down from his seat and leading the horses, feeling out the ground with his hands and feet in order to find the corners of the streets. To break the oppressive silence that had fallen inside the carriage, Nicolas reminded his companions that, a few years earlier, winter fogs had become so dense that people had taken it into their heads to hire blind people by the hour from the hospital of the Quinze-Vingts to guide pedestrians and carriages in the middle of the day. So precise was their knowledge of the topography of Paris, superior even to that of the draughtsmen and engravers of city maps, that they were offered five *louis* as a reward. No one responded to Nicolas's remarks, and silence fell once again. Once they came off the Pont Royal, it was easier for them to orient themselves. The coachman got back up on his seat and followed the *quais* as far as the Pont au Change, near the Châtelet.

Grim-faced officers, guards and jailers were running about in all directions in the old royal prison. Nicolas and his companions were led up to the first floor where the prisoner had been kept in solitary confinement in a large cell, quite unlike the usual wretched dungeons, rotten with damp, where the only light and air filtered in through little barred windows at ground level. A fetid odour greeted them as they entered. By the light of the torches, they made out a shape huddled on the straw mattress. It was Casimir, lying on his side in a pool of blood and vomit, his legs bent, his hands clenched over his stomach, his head thrown back, his eyes open and bloodshot. While Sanson and Semacgus busied themselves with the body, Nicolas and Bourdeau carefully examined the cell. Nicolas hated situations like this – there had been two others in his career – and blamed himself when a prisoner died, especially by his own hand. The image of an old soldier driven to crime by poverty rose to the surface of his mind and plucked at his conscience.[1] The first thing he noticed now was an earthenware plate on a stool, containing what remained of a dish of saveloys and beans. There was also a clay jug, which he picked up and sniffed: from what he could tell, the wine had been of good quality. This was all so different from what was usual in prison that he pointed it out to Bourdeau and asked him to find out everything he could about the provenance of the food and drink.

'Look at the spoon,' said Bourdeau. 'Silver, damn it! It couldn't be more obvious!'

'I agree: everything indicates that he was given special treatment. To think we put this prisoner in solitary confinement to avoid contact with the outside world, and this is what happens! A vital witness, the one solid thread in a tangled knot, snatched from our hands!'

Two guards appeared, carrying a stretcher. The body was laid on it and immediately taken to the Basse-Geôle, escorted by Sanson and Semacgus. Nicolas and the inspector spent most of the next hour questioning the jailers. It transpired that, at about eight o'clock, a man of indeterminate age, so nondescript that nobody would be able to recognise him if they saw him again, had presented himself, dressed like a kitchen servant, to deliver a meal intended for Casimir. Whatever surprise the guards may have felt, no doubts had crossed their minds. The case in connection with which the slave had been imprisoned was already mysterious enough and his treatment unusual: why had he been given such a comfortable cell? The thing that had clinched it was that the man had mentioned the name of Commissioner Le Floch, which had swept away any possible reservation. Soon after the meal had been taken in to the prisoner, they had heard moaning. By the time the door had been opened, the poor man was already in his death throes. A few minutes later, he was dead.

What skill, thought Nicolas, in the pursuit of evil! What could be simpler than an unknown man, presumably in disguise and giving an official name as his password, delivering, as sanctioned by custom, a meal bought and made outside the prison? This is given to the guard, who is told that the price has been settled. There isn't even any need for direct contact with the victim. Surprised by this unexpected treat and quite unsuspecting, the victim throws himself on the food. What a cowardly, treacherous act! Nicolas trembled at the thought, sure that new accusations would be made against him to add to those already made. In this case, though, there was nothing to link him directly to the crime, since he had been with his friends for the whole of the evening. The odds were that the unknown murderer had not known that, which suggested that he had stopped following Nicolas, at least for the moment.

The autopsy on Casimir's body took place early the next morning, as soon as Semacgus and Sanson had gathered together the necessary instruments and a few rats. The operation was rapid and conclusive: the prisoner had been poisoned by an unknown substance contained in the food. But this time, the poison had not contained any spices. To Nicolas, this confirmed what he had been thinking: the only reason those crushed seeds, harmless in themselves, had been added to Madame de Lastérieux's eggnog, was to throw suspicion on Casimir and, through him, on Nicolas. Now that there had been a second death by poisoning, everything pointed to the fact that the same person was responsible, even though, in this latest case, the culprit had not tried to conceal the nature of the poison. As for tracing the supposed kitchen servant who had come right into the heart of the prison, that, said Bourdeau, would be like finding a needle in a haystack. If Müvala and the other young men present in Rue de Verneuil had already vanished so completely into thin air as to cast doubt on whether they had ever existed, then it would surely be impossible to track down Casimir's killer.

Nicolas asked Bourdeau to question the dead man's companion Julia, who had been in a prostrate and almost imbecilic state since their arrest, and to put every last police spy and informer in the capital to work, but especially Tirepot, whose skill and foresight always worked wonders. Rabouine would coordinate the operation and centralise all incoming information at the duty office in the Grand Châtelet. As he was giving his orders, a fleeting thought crossed his mind on the subject of the *piment bouc*, a thought he could not quite seize. It seemed to him that a crucial element, which he had thus far ignored, was trying to rise to the surface of his consciousness. He made no attempt to force it: as so often happened, it would come to him when the moment was right.

He left the Grand Châtelet to pay a visit to Master Bontemps, senior member of the Company of Notaries Royal. The wind had risen, sweeping across the river and driving away the clouds and fog. Patches of blue appeared in the sky, forming a kind of chessboard over the city. Like many old men, Master Bontemps probably got up early, but seeing him when he was only just out of bed would have far exceeded the rules of decorum, and it was important for Nicolas to win him over, eccentric as he was, if he was going to get what he wanted from him. He set off on foot, and soon found himself wading through almost liquid mud: he was glad he had kept his riding boots on. The mud was already invading Quai de Bourbon, Quai de la Mégisserie and Quai de l'École, and he had to walk quickly to avoid it. He turned left to reach Rue Saint-Honoré by way of Rue des Poulies. Rue Saint-Thomas-du-Louvre descended towards the galleries of the palace, its tall buildings clearly visible at the end of the street. Master Bontemps lived in an opulent-looking house situated just opposite the Longueville mansion. This mansion had been acquired by the Farmers General as an annexe to their administrative offices. Monsieur de Sartine had spoken to him about the power that Company wielded within the State. The number of buildings it owned was multiplying. According to Monsieur de La Borde, the Farmers General were unstoppable: they were the future. Their administrative department numbered seven hundred people, far more than served the King's ministers. Thirty thousand employees throughout the kingdom worked for them, directly or indirectly. Nicolas had been surprised to discover that the administrators were recruited through competitive examinations, received training in their work, were assessed throughout their careers, and were paid retirement pensions from a fund to which both the Company and its employees contributed.[2] The common people were constantly complaining about this institution, which they held responsible for the burden of taxation and the harshness of the times.

Nicolas presented himself at Master Bontemps's practice, pleased to have Monsieur de Noblecourt's letter of recommendation in the cuff of his coat sleeve. Walking through the offices brought back memories of his youth in Rennes: the musty smell of ink and parchments and mildew, the unwholesome sweat of young men spending all day indoors drafting documents, the irritating scratch of quills on paper. The adolescent faces that looked up sharply as he passed were like reflections of his own past self. As he climbed the staircase, a pervasive odour of cat's urine struck his nostrils, and he had to take a pinch of snuff, a habit usually reserved for autopsies at the Basse-Geôle. He was greeted on the first floor by an elderly servant, dressed all in black, with a ruff so often folded and washed and rewashed that its white was close to grey.

Monsieur Bontemps's living quarters were vast, dark and dusty. Nicolas was instantly surrounded and hemmed in by dozens of cats who sprang out to inspect the intruder. Some rubbed up against him, while others kept a mistrustful distance and spat at him angrily. The antechamber made him feel as though he had found himself inside a painting from the beginning of the previous century. Tall, dark oak dressers standing against walls covered in embossed leather accentuated the comparison. He was shown into a study whose walls were lined with shelves filled with folios. A gigantic church lamp-holder, all dripping with wax, lit the room.

A small form sat huddled in cushions on a stiff-backed cathedra, entirely wrapped in furs apart from a bald, toothless head. Eyes stared out at him through spectacles with enlarging lenses, in a strange, stern gaze full of suppressed rage. From here and there beneath the furs, cats' heads peered out, contemplated the visitor, then retreated back into the body that housed them.

'To what do I owe this visit?' came a grating voice.

'Master,' said Nicolas, 'your friend Monsieur de Noblecourt asked me to give you this letter.'

He took a step towards the notary, and a huge black cat sat up and started growling, its fur bristling and its tail twisting with slow, serpentine movements.

'Quiet, Ajax, there's a good boy!'

The cat moved slowly back, looking offended. The notary took the letter and read it.

'The old brigand only remembers I'm still alive when he needs me!' he grunted. 'I'm still good enough to do what he requires of me. What do you want? Sit down.'

Nicolas looked round and noticed an upholstered stool. He was about to sit down on it when the notary screamed, 'Not there, you wretch! That's Friquette's place, she has her litter there. She'll scratch your eyes out.'

Not knowing where to put himself, Nicolas preferred to remain standing. The room seemed to come alive. Regiments of cats jumped from the *bergères*, appeared under the cushions, emerged from behind the books and climbed down the brocade curtains, scratching them as they did so. The smell was overpowering. A fight broke out, and the cats launched into a free-for-all, which continued until the master of the house cracked a small whip to restore order, and each animal went back to its hiding place, striking out with its claws as it went.

At last, Nicolas was able to get down to business. 'In the course of a criminal investigation,' he began, 'I've had occasion to wonder about the brief but brilliant career of one of your younger colleagues, Master Tiphaine.'

'Viroulet, what a scoundrel you are! Go and do your doings somewhere else, not on your master.'

From beneath his furs, the notary brought out a kitten. Holding it by the neck, he kissed it on the nose and flung it away from him. It landed on the carpet. He wiped his hands and stroked his furs.

'These,' he said to Nicolas, 'are the perfectly tanned skins of their grandparents. It gives me great pleasure to wear them. They soothe my pains, and they're so warm I don't have to spend too much on firewood. Master Tiphaine? Why should you think I want to talk about him? Why don't you find out what you want to know from your police spies?'

'It seems to me a sensible thing to do,' said Nicolas humbly, 'to turn first to the senior member of the Company. I'm sure that he can but approve of an approach so in accordance with the service of the King.'

'You're a smooth talker, aren't you? You remind me of Croquet when he wants his lights. Senior member! I'd do quite happily without that, believe me. It's a matter of survival. They're waiting to see how long I last. Fortunately, my cats keep me alive. Though I'd prefer to be young again, like I was in the days when Noblecourt and I would go wenching every night . . .'

Nicolas vowed to himself that he'd repeat those words to the former procurator.

'Tiphaine . . . Hmm! A nonentity with lots of contacts but not much substance, quite unsuited to our venerable Company. Apparently the rules were relaxed in his case. He's not even twenty-five yet, and didn't do his five years as a notary's clerk. He must have obtained a royal dispensation, which isn't easy. As for the fellow's morals, you'd have to visit every brothel and gambling house in town, and question the madams, pimps and girls and every other dispenser of the clap! Not to mention the faro players! Oh, yes, a fine notary, with lots of experience – of trifles!'

A big, grey, thick-furred Chartreux cat was scratching with one paw at the tip of Nicolas's boot. Fortunately, the mud had covered the leather with a protective layer.

'I was told by some colleagues . . .' – Master Bontemps leant forward and beckoned to Nicolas to come closer – '. . . that the money he needed to buy his practice was provided by a highly placed individual who was keen to have a notary under his influence and owing him his position. The sum arrived miraculously, all in *écus*, in sacks bearing the seal of the Comptroller General . . .'[3]

'So you're saying—'

'I'm not saying anything, I'm not surprised by anything. That's how the times are. I think you understand me. I don't have to spell it out for you. Now forget about me and go, my children need feeding.'

The servant appeared, carrying plates loaded with various meats. A terrible hullaballoo ensued, with a lot of squealing, and further fighting. Nicolas bowed and, without any further ado, withdrew. Thinking about this brief interview when he was in his carriage, he observed that it had confirmed everything he and Bourdeau had feared. Master Tiphaine's practice, acquired in dubious circumstances in violation of the normal rules, was his reward for selling his loyalty and being ready for any kind of compromising act. In which case, descending on his residence and questioning him would probably not have the desired effect. He would show the will to a handwriting expert in order to establish, if not for certain, then at least with a degree of probability, whether or not it was a forgery, and he would place the young notary under strict surveillance to get a better idea of his movements and associates. Only then would they interrogate him and get him to admit the truth.

When Nicolas got back to the Châtelet, he sought out Inspector Bourdeau and asked him to set up the surveillance. Nicolas looked so tired and wild-eyed to Bourdeau that he persuaded him to go back to Rue Montmartre as soon as possible. His earlier sense of exhilaration had given way to a great weariness and a clear need for sleep. Nicolas was still suffering from the after-effects of his English adventure.

Catherine, who had got back from Vaugirard, found Nicolas's listlessness quite worrying. When Monsieur de Noblecourt pressed him with questions about his interview with the 'cat man', he replied distractedly, merely reassuring him that his letter of recommendation had achieved its goal. Then he went upstairs to bed. The bells of Saint-Eustache had just struck four.

Thursday 20 January 1774

A huge black cat was pawing his stomach, making it increasingly difficult for him to breathe. He started to panic, especially as the cat was speaking to him, its yellow-flecked green eyes gleaming with a vaguely human look, and he could not understand any of the hoarse sounds the beast was making. He tried to escape its embrace. Suddenly, the mist cleared, and he gasped, coughed, and opened his eyes to discover Bourdeau's good-natured face.

'Ah, at last the commissioner consents to wake up! I've been shouting myself hoarse for ages.'

Nicolas yawned. 'I was just finishing off the night.'

'My God, I wish I had nights like that! From four in the afternoon to nine in the morning, that's seventeen hours! I hope you're feeling refreshed?'

'Wonderfully,' cried Nicolas, leaping out of bed. 'I thought you were a cat.'

With these words, which left his friend dumbstruck, he ran to wash himself. It was not long before he returned, to find Bourdeau with Marion, drinking a milky coffee. It struck Nicolas, who preferred chocolate, that this beverage had now reached all levels of society, being enjoyed as much by fishwives in the central market as by duchesses. As Bourdeau was burning his tongue, Marion advised him to take the bowl with him and finish drinking it at his leisure.

'This beverage is only good when made at home,' said Bourdeau as their carriage was setting off.

'Monsieur de Noblecourt likes it. He says that when he was a young man the first café was set up at the Saint-Germain fair by Armenians. Later, a Persian opened a second establishment in Rue de Buci. But the thing that really started the current craze for it was the superb establishment in Rue des Fossés-Saint-Germain, near the Comédie-Française, founded by a Venetian named Francesco Procopio di Coltelli.'

'Hence the name Procope, that mecca for wine lovers and chess players.'

'And talkers – that's why we keep a good half-dozen spies there on a permanent basis!'

'In fact, their coffee isn't bad, and they have it delivered all over Paris.'

'I've never taken to it,' said Nicolas. 'When I first arrived in Paris, the *bavaroise* was in great demand. That used to be delivered, too.'

'You haven't forgotten our appointment at the Pont Royal, I hope?' said Bourdeau. 'If the experiment is successful, what do you think we'll discover?'

'We shall see,' said Nicolas. 'To tell the truth, this is hardly the best season for diving. But with everything the city throws into the river, there are really only a few moments in summer when the water is a little clearer. In January, there's all the mud and snow to contend with, not to mention the current.'

'I pity the poor inventor,' said Bourdeau. 'I fear he may get into trouble. But we have people there to rescue him if he does, and to deter onlookers.'

By the time their carriage crossed the Pont Royal, the sun had returned and was intermittently lighting up Quai des Tuileries. Against the other bank, boats and barges rose and fell on the choppy water, and from them porters were unloading wood and other building materials for the construction sites of the rapidly expanding Faubourg Saint-Germain. Beyond the bridge, the tall white façades of the Mailly and Belle-Isle mansions rose over

Quai d'Orsay and Quai des Théatins. A small crowd had gathered at the entrance of Rue de Beaune, but were being kept at a distance. A row of carriages had drawn up near the bridge, and beside them a group of officials stood waiting at the top of the steps leading down to the river, stamping their feet to keep warm. A chain of boats moored in a semicircle demarcated the small space reserved for the experiment. The watch let Nicolas and Bourdeau through the cordon. A man in a military-style cloak, still young, held out his hand warmly to Nicolas.

'There's no mistaking you, you're Commissioner Le Floch. May I introduce myself? I'm the Chevalier de Borda, naval lieutenant, member of the Royal Academy of Sciences and the Royal Academy of the Navy. And these are my colleagues.'

One by one, apparently in order of age and office, he introduced Monsieur Leroy of the Royal Society in London and the Philosophical Society of Philadelphia, Monsieur Petit, professor of anatomy and inspector of military hospitals, and a priest with a childlike face, wrapped in an otterskin pelisse to keep out the cold.

'Abbé Bossut, Examiner of Engineers. We are the special commission of the Academy of Sciences, appointed to evaluate the interest of this new invention. Monsieur de Sartine asked us to combine the scientific with the practical and lend our help to your investigation. We were glad to oblige.'

'And we're grateful to your learned company,' said Nicolas. 'May I introduce my deputy, Inspector Bourdeau? One question, though: you appear to know me. Have we met before?'

'I had the honour,' said Monsieur de Borda, lifting his hand to his tricorn, 'of serving with your father, the Marquis de Ranreuil, during the Seven Years War. Sailors sometimes fight on land. You bear a strong resemblance to him, I thought I was seeing him again. He was a soldier and a wise man . . .'

Nicolas trembled with emotion at this mention of his father. It was always a surprise to him that everyone knew his personal history, but secrets never stayed secret for very long, either at Court or in the city, and everything was discovered in the end, provided the object of curiosity occupied a certain rank in society and therefore aroused interest in his case. How much longer, he wondered, would people be judged by their origins and their birth?

Near the parapet, in a coarse shirt and shiny woollen breeches, with a sheepskin over his shoulders, stood a man with a face like a peasant's, who reminded Nicolas of the rough fishermen of his native Brittany. He was waiting with an inscrutable expression and inquisitive eyes for the 'gentlemen' to give the signal. A servant, as coarse as his master, was preparing a strange costume which for the moment looked like nothing but a shapeless heap of leather and metal.

'My dear colleagues, Commissioner Le Floch, may I have your attention, please?' said Borda. 'Our friend here, being unaccustomed to public speaking, has asked me to present his invention. This is a new machine which makes it possible to remain underwater for at least an hour without any communication with the outside world. It consists of a kind of leather sheath shaped exactly like a man. The person attempting immersion, who is wearing a shirt or nightshirt, gets inside the sheath through an opening made in the neck. Thus attired, he puts on a brass helmet . . .'

The servant handed him a large, shiny metal ball which the scientists considered with great curiosity.

'. . . which encases his entire head, and which is fitted to the wide collar of the same metal at the top of the sheath and screwed on tightly. You will observe that there are three glass openings, two for the eyes and one on the forehead. At the top of the helmet are two pipes, one on top of the other, each attached to a leather tube the diameter of a thick candle. These two pipes, which are about four feet long, end in a brass ball. This ball, so I've been told, possesses a spring which can be lifted with a wrench. The air contained in it is pumped through the lower tube to the diver's mouth and then, rarefied, is carried up through the upper conduit, where it is purified in the ball before going back to the mouth.'

'But my dear fellow,' said Monsieur Leroy, 'these leather tubes can easily be crushed or get stuck together under pressure. What happens then to the unfortunate diver?'

'That has been taken into account,' replied Borda. 'The tubes are strengthened at regular distances by iron rings which make it possible to avoid the disadvantage you so rightly raise, my dear colleague.'

'But what is in the brass ball,' asked Abbé Bossut, adjusting his gloves, 'that can purify the carbonic air corrupted by the diver's breathing?'

'I cannot tell you that. Our friend claims that he will prove the efficacy of his machine before consenting to reveal the mystery of its invention.'

There was a discontented murmur. The man raised his head defiantly, and for a moment Nicolas thought he was about to withdraw.

‘But what is the point of this apparatus?’ asked Monsieur Leroy. ‘Will it help our enlightened century to progress in a way that is useful to the human race, for it is that, and that alone, which opens doors and . . .’

‘God protect us from long-winded philosophers!’ Borda whispered in Nicolas’s ear. ‘He’s a good man, and fortunately he never finishes what he has to say.’ Then, turning to the audience, he explained, ‘Apart from the fact that it will help us to examine the condition of our ships’ hulls without having to take them into dry dock, it should also allow us to study the bottom of the sea and its flora and fauna. These are only some of the objectives which come to mind. No doubt other prospects will present themselves. I’m sure our friend here has thought of some.’

The man, clearly assuming that he had been called upon to say something, launched into a speech in his low, urgent voice.

‘I was a navy blacksmith for twenty years,’ he said. ‘I didn’t design and make this machine just to go ferreting about underwater for trifles. Far be it from me to try and deceive gentlemen as learned as you. Let me tell you about it. I used to live on the coast near Cherbourg, and we had loads of shipwrecks round there. All those fine boats smashing up. I told myself we were really stupid to let the cargoes go, it was a crying shame to leave all those riches in the sea. So if we had a way when the weather was good to go down to the wreckage that wasn’t too far from the surface, we’d surely recover something. Times are hard and—’

Monsieur Leroy struck the ground impatiently with his cane. Foreseeing an outburst, the Chevalier de Borda thought it best to cut short the good fellow’s speech.

‘I think we should get down to work now,’ he said. ‘You know what the police are expecting from you. That's at least one thing that will justify your invention.'

The man took off his shoes and his breeches. The leather diving suit was lying shapeless on the ground. Helped by his servant, he first put on the part containing the legs, then, with a great many contortions, plunged first one arm, then the other, into the sleeves. He now looked like a knight in armour before battle. The brass helmet was placed over his head and screwed to the collar. Just imagining how the man must feel enclosed in that shell made Nicolas feel suffocated.

'I may be completely wrong,' he could not help saying to Monsieur de Borda, 'but surely there's a strong likelihood he'll tip upside down as soon as he's in the water.'

'That indeed is what would happen if the feet of the suit were not filled with ballast to keep him upright. He'll balance like the keel of a ship.'

The servant stood on tiptoe and carefully lifted the spring on the brass ball with the help of a small wrench. The noise of it echoed in the cold air and silenced the crowd on the *quais*, who ceased their talk and laughter and became suddenly attentive. Ready for the experiment, the man clumped heavily towards the steps which began directly above one of the supports of the Pont Royal, descended all the way to the river and vanished below the surface. A rope was tied round his waist. It would be used to hoist him up in case of danger. He had only to tug on it for his servant at the other end to understand that he needed to bring him up as quickly as possible. In his hand he held another rope, also tied to the servant, and a kind of coarse net, with which he would collect any object he might find on the river bed. Slowly, the man disappeared into the yellowish water and everyone leant over the parapet. The moments that followed seemed very long. Five minutes after he had gone under, there were several tugs on the rope. The servant hauled it up. Nicolas and Bourdeau walked down as far as the level of the water. The net came up with a small brown mud-covered object caught in it. Bourdeau grabbed it and handed it to Nicolas, who cleaned the sides of it roughly. It was a small metal box, open and empty.

'It's just a trinket, without any interest!' said the inspector. 'The things we'd find in the river, if ever we drained it!'

Nicolas moved the object closer to Bourdeau's eyes. 'But we might not find this every day. A pewter jewel box . . . with Julie de Lastérieux's initials engraved on the side.'

Monsieur Leroy, exasperated by their whispering, tapped Nicolas on the shoulder with the pommel of his cane, and Nicolas stopped speaking. The experiment continued in a silence disturbed only by the lapping of the water. Almost ten minutes had gone by since the beginning of the experiment when suddenly there was such a strong tug on the rope that the servant almost fell in the river. He asked for reinforcements, and Nicolas and Bourdeau, his closest neighbours on the narrow platform, rushed to him. It took two minutes to bring up an inert body. The brass helmet was nodding as if the person it was supposed to be protecting were already dead. He was lifted up on to Quai d'Orsay, and the helmet was quickly unscrewed. Monsieur Leroy came running, but made no attempt to take off the suit. The man had lost consciousness and his face was almost blue and quite lifeless. Monsieur Leroy took a little phial from his pocket and passed it several times under the inventor's nose. The effect of the salts was to revive the man immediately. After a few moments, his breathing resumed its normal rhythm and he opened his eyes.

'I'd have made it,' he said, spluttering, 'if that damned spring hadn't broken.'[4]

'It's already quite something to have stayed underwater for ten minutes,' said the Chevalier de Borda, glancing at his watch. 'But the experiment wasn't conclusive. Improve your apparatus and we'll again give you all the attention you deserve, won't we, my friends?'

The academicians nodded their approval. The man shook his head, muttering, 'Well, it was conclusive enough to drag that box from the mud. The commissioner seems very interested in it.'

Nicolas took a few *louis* from his fob and held them out to the man. 'And the commissioner is grateful to you. May this little contribution help you to perfect your invention.'

The gold was pocketed avidly. Nicolas and Bourdeau took their leave of the commission and got back in their cab. The crowd that had gathered at the entrance to the Pont Royal moved aside and muttered as they passed. A woman rushed forward, climbed on to the footplate and hung on, her grimacing, toothless face framed in the window.

'Tight-fisted bastards!' she cried. 'Treasures belong to the people!'

She spat and jumped off, nimbly dodging a blow from the driver's whip.

'What was the matter with her?' said Nicolas.

'The common people always see evil where it doesn't exist,' replied the inspector. 'They saw us recovering something from the river. Tongues are already wagging.'

'There's hatred in the air these days.'

'Oh, the people have been filled with hatred for many centuries,' said Bourdeau, ironically.

He was about to go on when he had second thoughts. It was not the first time that Nicolas had witnessed these moments of bitterness in his deputy. Of course, Bourdeau's attitude could be explained by his humble origins, the tragic fate of a father sacrificed to satisfy a King's pleasure – he had been fatally wounded by a boar during a royal hunt – and the existence in him of a diffuse mixture of criticism, acrimony and sympathy for the interests of the poor. There was a kind of contained violence in him which might well explode one day.

'Is there any particular reason she called us tight-fisted?' asked Nicolas.

'Haven't you heard the rumours that the King is filling his coffers by speculating on wheat?'

Nicolas remembered how worried his tailor, Master Vachon, had been about the same thing. 'Don't tell me you give credence to such slanders?'

Bourdeau shook his head, as if pitying the commissioner's naivety. 'I don't give anything; I simply obey and do my duty. Haven't you read the *Almanach royal* for 1774?'

'I never read it,' replied Nicolas. 'I may occasionally consult it to find a name, a position or an address.'

'Others do it for you. If you'd read it, you'd have been surprised to discover on page 553 a reference to a man named Demirvalaud, treasurer of grain in the King's employ.'

'Where's the harm in that?' said Nicolas, irritably. 'It must be a financial position. God knows they've multiplied lately!'

'Financial! Precisely. You've put your finger on it. Position or not, everyone read the news in his fashion, and it spread like wildfire in every direction and through every level of society. The whole kingdom is laughing it to scorn, especially now that—'

'Now that what?'

'Now that the order has been given to seize all copies still on sale, fine the printer, and close his workshop pending further information. These accumulated blunders have convinced everyone that the reference was included out of malice, its aim to accuse, and the 1774 *Almanach* has become a rare item, now much in demand from collectors who are willing to pay a hundred times what it cost before it was seized. It's even become the subject of a song:

Now everyone knows what before was just theories
The master is trafficking the gifts of Ceres
And to show that he has nothing to hide
He even takes a certain pride
In putting in his Almanach no less
His fortunate agent's name and address.

And that, Commissioner, is why we, as the King's men, now have the advantage and privilege of being called these names by the people.'

Pensively, Nicolas stroked the pewter box, which, although small, was very heavy. It must have fallen like a rock when it was thrown from the bridge, and then hit something, presumably a stone on the river bed, and opened, causing the contents to spill out.

Bourdeau must have been following the same train of thought and had reached the same conclusion. 'If this is a jewel box,' he said, 'where are the jewels?'

'There were jewels all over the place in Julie's bedroom when we searched it. I pointed them out to you on the sideboard.'

'Yes, I remember. What do you deduce from that?'

'That there was something else in this box. That whatever it was had been put there with the one aim of getting me into trouble yet again, by implying that I had thrown it in the river. That this thing got lost when the box opened and is probably either lying buried in silt, or has been carried off by the current.'

Bourdeau turned to Nicolas. 'And does nothing come to mind as to the nature of this thing?'

'What's the point in playing at riddles? It's not my business. Let the author of these base deeds explain himself. It's clear that a hidden enemy is pursuing me. But we should not be misled by slander and accusation without evidence. In criminal matters, it is through the facts that we discover the intentions, not the other way round. This enemy is using so many means to discredit me that one is tempted to say to him, "Monsieur, you're overdoing it."'

This convoluted reply was neither very sincere not very skilful: it even came close to dissimulation. But it seemed to satisfy Bourdeau. In fact, Nicolas was pursuing an idea that had been nagging at him for some time without his being able to pin it down. Like a panic-stricken bird, it was fluttering around in his head without direction. He would catch it when the moment was right.

*

A surprise awaited them at the Châtelet. Semacgus was pacing the corridors of the old fortress, talking to Old Marie, who was finding it hard to keep up with him. He heaved a sigh of relief when he saw his friends and drew them outside, a finger to his lips.

'I'm delighted to see you haven't missed me. I have some surprising news for you.' He looked at his watch. 'The hour for sustenance approaches and this timepiece is urging me to answer its call. What would you say to a little visit to your usual lair, I mean your countryman's place, Monsieur Bourdeau?'

They set off at a good pace, both curious about the navy surgeon's information and their mouths watering at the prospect of taking a break over a dish in a tavern. They headed for Rue du Pied-de-Bœuf, where this favourite establishment of theirs was situated. The host found them a table in a quiet corner, and they sat down, feeling very cheerful.

'This place,' said Nicolas, 'brings back memories of a reprehensibly heavy drinking bout, into which I was dragged by the inspector here and Tirepot.'

'Go on, complain. You were recovered half dead[5] and the infusion you were served put you back on your feet and made you a real chatterbox.'

'Enough of this foolery,' said Semacgus. 'What shall we have for dinner?'

'A leg of veal the way my grandmother used to make it at Montsoreau,' said the innkeeper. 'To wit, a saucepan of fresh bacon rinds with three big handfuls of sliced onions and carrots. In it, I lay the meat like a baby in its crib. I cover it, heat it and let it sweat in its juices for half an hour. Then I sprinkle it with half a bottle of white wine and level it off with a few ladlefuls of stock. After that, I put it to one side on the stove, go about my business, chat to my customers, drink five or six glasses, and two or three hours later, I'm reminded of the veal by its delicious aroma. I'll carve it for you over a purée of onions and serve it with a few jars of the usual Chinon. Finally, to make it all go down, a pâté of prunes that'll make you sing Hallelujah.'

'That all sounds fine,' said Semacgus, radiantly. 'Something to keep the chilblains at bay in any case.' He let the host go and, raising his voice, addressed his friends in the tones of a female vendor at the central market. '*Six sous, six sous, see my purslane, see my lettuce!*'

'What's put you in such a good mood?' asked Nicolas, serving the wine which had just been brought.

They stopped to take their first sip. It was so satisfying that a second serving followed immediately.

'Here's the thing,' said Semacgus. 'As I was continuing my researches at the Jardin du Roi and exploring its collections—'

'What kind of collections?' asked Bourdeau.

'Large cabinets with drawers containing herbariums and boxes of specimens – flowers, dried leaves, seeds – all learnedly presented and referenced. I'd been opening drawers for some time, examining the contents and reflecting on them when I suddenly discovered an empty box. It was obvious that it hadn't always been empty. That intrigued me, especially as the label read . . . well, I'll let you guess . . .'

'*Piment bouc*,' breathed Nicolas.

'Ah, how do you do it?'

'It seemed only natural,' said Nicolas modestly.

‘I haven’t finished yet,’ Semacgus resumed, with an impatient gesture. ‘You should know that the curator of the collections, Monsieur Bichot, the assistant of Monsieur de Jussieu, the demonstrator at the botanical exhibition, is a man very much in love with his treasures, indeed somewhat obsessive about them. He notes the names of visitors in a register with numbered and initialled pages, like a notary’s minutes. It’s a habit he adopted after a number of petty thefts by collectors. In fact, he has not only the names but also the addresses of the visitors and, better still, the details of which herbariums and boxes they specifically asked to examine. Apart from that, you may not be aware that the Jardin is only open to the public on Tuesdays and Thursdays.’

‘That’s what I call good work!’ said Bourdeau, emptying a third glass in his enthusiasm.

‘Now,’ Semacgus went on, ‘the last person to visit that section did so . . . on Tuesday 4 January 1774, that is, exactly two days before Madame de Lastérieux was poisoned!’

‘You’re going too fast for my poor brain,’ moaned Bourdeau. ‘Either that, or this Chinon’s going to my head. Look, we already know she wasn’t poisoned by *piment bouc*, which isn’t even poisonous—’

‘True,’ Nicolas cut in. ‘But we’ve discovered – or rather, Semacgus has demonstrated – that seeds of *piment bouc* were ground into the eggnog to conceal the presence of a strong poison we haven’t been able to identify.’

‘Why go to the trouble of stealing it?’ insisted the inspector.

‘Because Casimir didn’t have any more,’ Nicolas explained calmly. ‘He’d exhausted the stocks he’d brought with him from the West Indies. An indisputable connection had to be established linking the concealed poison to a household product to which someone familiar with the house – myself, in fact – had access. As for what the role of Casimir was in all this, we may never know. Dead men tell no tales.'

'Gentlemen, gentlemen!' Semacgus cut in. 'This is all conjecture. Just let me finish my story. On Tuesday 4 January 1774, a man named Charles du Maine-Giraud asked to look at the collections from the West Indies. Monsieur Bichot remembers him as a young man of quality to judge from his clothes, very polite and with no distinguishing features. It was only after he'd gone that the curator noticed the theft.'

'And the address?'

'There's the crux of it. This gentleman lives in a furnished apartment in Rue Saint-Julien-le-Pauvre.'

'Then let's pay the fellow a quick visit,' roared Bourdeau.

'Especially,' added Semacgus triumphantly, 'as he is lodging – I have this from Rabouine, who has already sniffed around the area for me – in an apartment belonging to . . .'

They all looked at him, hanging on his words.

'. . . Monsieur Balbastre, organist of Notre Dame and sworn enemy of Monsieur Nicolas Le Floch, commissioner of police at the Châtelet.'

When the host came in with a large clay dish straight from the oven, he found his customers looking dazed. He put it down to admiration and hunger. The leg of veal was steaming, its tender meat subsiding gently on its bed of onions.

IX

HUNTING

We all touch the infernal shore in our lives.

CRÉBILLON

The meal turned into a war council.

'This is what we're going to do,' said Nicolas. 'Bourdeau will go to this young man's lodgings. If the bird's in the nest, he'll bring him back to the Châtelet, and we'll immediately proceed with a preliminary interrogation. As for me, I need to examine Julie's will. I have some genuine letters from her which I intend to show to an expert. I've heard of a clerk at the Ministry of Foreign Affairs who's skilled at opening letters diverted, bought or stolen from the mail of other countries. He might be able to help us. I have to go to Versailles in any case, to . . .'

He stopped himself just as he was about to reveal the fact that he was due to give the King an account of his mission to London.

'. . . to get help from Monsieur de La Borde, who will, as usual, be more than willing. I hope I'll have a much clearer idea of the matter by the time I get back to Paris. Depending on what I've found out, I'll go to see Master Tiphaine and force him to come clean. As a last resort, a few threats may encourage his honesty. As for Monsieur Balbastre, the inspector's inquiries will provide plenty to question him about when we have that pleasure. He already has a lot of explaining to do. He's been turning up everywhere in this investigation, much too often for it to be mere chance.'

'Let's not forget,' said Bourdeau, 'that, for all his arrogance, Balbastre has no alibi.'

As he dug into his portion of pâté of prunes, Nicolas reflected on the connections, known and unknown, between the organist of Notre Dame and himself. It was at his house that he had first met Julie. He knew the mysterious Müvala. He was suspected of belonging to certain secret circles. Under questioning, he had been forced to admit that a highly placed individual had a hold over him and was forcing him to perform certain actions. Although nothing was known of his private life, it could not be ruled out that he, too, had fallen under the spell of Madame de Lastérieux. Something had struck Nicolas during the interview with Balbastre beside the organ case at Notre Dame, a detail whose nature he was unable as yet to determine, but which, like a piece in a jigsaw puzzle, had somehow to be slotted into the general picture.

By the time they had finished eating, they were a good deal less cheerful than when they had started. It was as if an extra weight had fallen over the three friends' thoughts. Nicolas went back to the Châtelet to consult the *Almanach royal* and find out the name of the clerk at Foreign Affairs he was hoping to meet at Versailles. Unable to discover it, he decided to turn to Monsieur de Séqueville, the King's secretary with responsibility for the ambassadors, who lived in Rue Saint-Honoré, opposite Rue Saint-Florentin. He decided to stretch his legs, as walking helped him to think: there was something about physical movement which allowed him to forget everything and concentrate on the essentials. The unceasing spectacle of the busy streets and the multiplicity of faces and sounds also acted as much needed stimulants.

Monsieur de Séqueville was at home. After the customary compliments, he listened to the commissioner's request and, having thought it over, told him that the thing he wanted was feasible but that there was no point in turning to a clerk at the Ministry of Foreign Affairs, who by definition had little experience with private correspondence. Lowering his voice, he admitted that he knew a public letter-writer and high-class calligrapher who lived deep in Faubourg Saint-Marcel. His voice now almost inaudible, he explained that *they* had had occasion to call on his services in the past to check certain dubious papers and signatures suspected of being forgeries, and that it could well be that this Monsieur Rodollet would be able to help Nicolas. Nevertheless, the man being rightly suspicious, it would be risky to approach him without taking prior measures. Nicolas needed a letter of recommendation, and he, Séqueville, undertook to write one for him immediately. But all Nicolas was given as a letter, much to his surprise, was a little square of paper on which he had been able to make out, before it was folded and sealed, a pen drawing without any writing. Monsieur de Séqueville's good-natured face, creased with amusement, dissuaded him from asking any questions. All he asked for was the address, which he was given, accompanied by a shrill little laugh.

*

Impatient as he was to settle this crucial question as quickly as possible, Nicolas allowed himself to be carried away by an impulse in which his will played little part and which led him to the Dauphin Couronné. The pretext was to say hello to La Satin, who was now mistress of the place. Arriving outside the house, which evoked so many memories, both pleasant and tragic, he knocked at the door. After a moment, a well-dressed young maid opened and, with a smile, asked him what he wanted. The establishment welcomed customers from early evening onwards, she explained, but, she added with a graceful curtsey, she was at his disposal for any information he might require. Nicolas asked after the mistress of the house. She was out visiting some of her suppliers, he was told, and would be away until the evening. He was about to leave when he heard hurried steps, and an impatient hand pushed the maid aside. It was a young man, not much more than a child, wearing a black coat and white cravat, and with a tricorn in his hand, who excused himself and asked if he might be allowed to get to the front door. Nicolas was turned to stone. It was as if he saw, in this boy's face and bearing, an image of himself as he had been twenty years earlier reflected back at him. He was so overcome with emotion that he remained in the doorway and let himself be pushed gently aside. The young man threw him a curious glance as he passed, but Nicolas was standing against the light, his face in darkness. Almost running out, the apparition vanished. Recovering his composure, Nicolas could not help asking the maid about this fleeting vision.

'That's Madame's son, Louis,' she replied, blushing. 'He's still at school, where he's doing very well. He doesn't come here often . . .' She turned scarlet. 'Madame wouldn't be happy to know he dropped by. Given his conduct, his determination and his excellent work, she's hoping he'll get a position, a position . . .'

She broke off, on the verge of tears.

There's a young man who'll break hearts, thought Nicolas with a sigh, equally moved. His face will get him a long way. He gave the girl a *louis*, much to her surprise, and walked out into the street, in a daze. There was no longer any room for doubt, if there ever had been. He was so overcome that he seemed not to see other pedestrians coming in the opposite direction and bumped into them, provoking curses. He felt a mixture of joy and anguish. In a world where birth was of such importance, what would his child's fate be? He himself had suffered a great deal from being illegitimate, even though the advantages had made themselves felt over the years. What would happen to the bastard son of a police officer and a prostitute? True, at the time the child had been conceived, she had not yet taken up that career. What should he do? Once again, he put off making a decision. This was a serious issue, he knew: he was quite aware that it would change his life and that nothing would ever be the same.

He hailed a passing cab and returned to the Châtelet, where he picked up Madame de Lastérieux's supposed will, as well as the mysterious letter, then went on to Rue Montmartre, where everyone noticed the unaccustomed gravity of his demeanour. Here, he found Julie's old letters. He ordered the driver to take him to Faubourg Saint-Marcel. Once past the city limits, his carriage drove along Rue Mouffetard as far as Rue du Fer-à-Moulin and the Scipion mansion, on the right-hand side of which was the little street of the same name, leading to the outbuildings of the monastery of Saint-Marcel.

Apart from monasteries and hospitals, this district, the poorest in the capital, was home to a populace that was kept at a distance from the main life of the city. Amongst them were a few studious, misanthropic sages living isolated lives. The whole *faubourg* had a reputation for being difficult, quarrelsome and easily inflamed, more susceptible to popular unrest than any other. Monsieur de Sartine always advised moderation in dealing with it, saying that sedition could be reduced but never entirely suppressed. His police force handled the population of the area with kid gloves, for fear of provoking an extreme response. In the course of their investigations, Nicolas and Bourdeau often frequented the infamous tobacco shops of the *faubourg*, where unemployed workers whiled away their days, with smoke and contraband brandy taking the place of food. Such places also attracted deserters from the army, porters and refuse collectors, as well as the lowest prostitutes. He could not help asking himself what real difference there was between these poor creatures wallowing in the mire and La Satin in her lace and velvet. He refused to answer his own question, aware of the injustice he was committing, even if only in thought. He looked at these poor houses of cob, these wan faces, these children freezing with cold, their bare feet in the icy mud. It was a place of total degeneration, a place dominated by straw bread, poisoned oil, vinegary wine and purpuric fever. With such a reputation, it was easy to forget the discreet, tranquil presence of modest, well-established craftsmen who devoted themselves to the arts of furniture and textile making and, above all, printing and bookbinding.

*

Monsieur Rodollet's little house in Rue Scipion, with its ivy-covered front, stood next to a printing shop. Above the windowed door, a discreet but elegantly adorned sign indicated the occupant's activity. Nicolas was received in a kind of workshop that doubled as an office. Illuminated manuscripts and calligraphy models hung from pegs attached to wires slung across the room, and there were pigeonholes containing many different kinds of paper and a large number of pens. Bottles of ink and shiny, soluble squares of paper were heaped up in every nook and cranny. The proprietor, a fat, middle-aged man with a few faded wisps of hair poking out beneath a grey bonnet, looked at him circumspectly, slowly rubbing his hands. Nicolas would have put his age at about fifty. He was wearing a kind of chasuble tucked loosely into black breeches and a pair of comfortable-looking leather slippers. The man saw Nicolas looking at them.

'I wear these,' he said, 'so that I can put my feet on the foot-warmer when the weather is cold. How can I be of service, Monsieur?'

'I have a particular job that needs doing, one that requires discretion. I'm a police commissioner at the Châtelet, and I'm investigating a case of forgery. It was Monsieur de Séqueville who pointed me in your direction. I have some serious doubts regarding the authenticity of a will, and he assures me you are the ablest man in this field.'

The man did not say a word, but looked at Nicolas through narrowed eyes.

'Our mutual friend,' the commissioner went on, 'gave me this to give to you.'

He handed him the little square of paper. One glance was

enough for Rodollet, which confirmed Nicolas's impression that this was indeed a recommendation. The paper was immediately placed in a candle flame and burnt, as if it was important not to leave any trace of it. The little seal sputtered, giving off black smoke, and a smell of resin filled the room.

Rodollet turned to Nicolas. 'Now then, Commissioner, what can I do for you?'

Nicolas took out Julie's letters and the will and gave them to Rodollet, who examined them for a long time through a magnifying glass. Then he arranged a number of candlesticks in a row and placed the will over one of the letters. He repeated the operation with all the correspondence, then examined the documents again. Nicolas was biting his lips with impatience and annoyance: it was humiliating to see his private life scrutinised by a stranger. But then he told himself it was a reasonable price to pay if it led to his mistress's killer, and he calmed down.

'Hmmm . . .' grunted Rodollet, and he took off his bonnet, revealing a bald patch surrounded by a fine weave of white hair. 'Of course, I may be wrong, but here are my conclusions. Handwriting, even uneducated handwriting, is an instructive thing. Of all the movements of the body, there is none as varied and diverse as those of the hand and the fingers. Imagine, Monsieur, a hundred identical copies of a master painting by a hundred different painters. They would all resemble the original, and yet they would each have, to the eyes of an enlightened art lover, a particular character, a nuance, a touch which would make them distinctive.'

'So, for you . . .'

'For me, each and every one of us possesses his own handwriting, which is individual and inimitable, or which can only be counterfeited imperfectly and with great difficulty. There are very few exceptions, and they merely prove the rule. Another thing: a person's handwriting can change, under the influence of different states of mind. We write differently if we're penning a love letter or a solemn document such as a will. In writing, as in other things, there is a physiognomy of the emotions.'

'And in this particular case?'

Rodollet looked at Nicolas with a kind of commiseration. 'In this particular case, I don't understand how letters burning with the fires of passion – please forgive me – where the thought naturally runs faster than the quill, could be so similar to a legal text such as this will. In short, I believe this will is a forgery, closely modelled on the person's genuine handwriting.'

'And the signature?'

'Forged, too, I'm sure of it. There are several signatures on the document, and they are identical and can be superimposed one on top of the other, which is scarcely credible. That, Commissioner, is all I can tell you.'

Nicolas had kept to the end the letter that had been posted to him on the night of the murder. Rodollet took one quick look at it and confirmed that it, too, was a forgery.

'If I've understood correctly,' he said, 'my conclusions have resolved your doubts. Do you suspect anyone of these forgeries?'

'For the moment,' said Nicolas, 'all options are open.'

'Well, if this can be of any help . . . It's only a vague impression, mind you, but I think I should pass it on to you. It's something I came across in a previous case, an observation I made on the way a writer started a line . . . It may not make any sense and I'm reluctant to trouble you with it . . .'

'It doesn't matter, go on.'

'Well, the person responsible for this forgery could – and I repeat *could* – be a musician, or rather, someone who composes or copies music. When you place notes on a stave, you end up acquiring certain habits that come through in your handwriting. Give my regards to Monsieur de Séqueville.'

The man bowed and politely refused the money Nicolas tried to give him for the consultation. 'A thousand pardons, Commissioner. Monsieur de Séqueville and I are quits.'

Alone in his carriage, Nicolas was thinking so intensely that the blood hammered in his temples. So the will and Julie's letter were both false. That confirmed that a malevolent force was at his heels, striving by every available means to throw suspicion on him. Another, more insidious idea crossed his mind. Monsieur Rodollet's last remarks meant that the forger might have a musical connection. His first thought was of Balbastre, whose daily occupation was music, but Müvala was also something of a musician, and his disappearance after the murder was undoubtedly suspicious. A chill came over him: he had just remembered Monsieur de La Borde, a man of eclectic talents who had even composed operas. He recalled Madame de Lastérieux's indulgent attitude towards the First Groom of the King's Bedchamber. He alone, of all his friends, enjoyed her whole-hearted – and flirtatious – attention. He had long assumed this was due to his mistress's desire to one day take her place at Court. But he doubted now that she could ever have harboured such an ambition, being in the dishonourable position of a police agent.

Could there have been something between his friend, whose womanising was notorious, and the pretty widow from the West Indies? And wasn't Monsieur de La Borde the person best placed to know every detail of Nicolas's activities, including his secret missions? He dismissed the idea: after all, hadn't Monsieur de La Borde been at Monsieur de Noblecourt's house on the fateful night? It was all terribly confused, and Nicolas felt trapped in the snares of a plot against his life and honour that could surely only have been set in motion by an organisation with many ramifications.

By the time he got to Monsieur de Noblecourt's house, darkness was falling. He found the master of the house sitting in a large straight-backed armchair, reading a volume of Ovid which he had placed on the flap of his writing desk. Monsieur de Noblecourt claimed it was the only way he could read, as if such a strict habit expressed all the respect he had for books and the gentleness of the treatment he reserved for them.

'You seem very thoughtful,' he said, looking at Nicolas's inscrutable face through his spectacles.

He listened to the commissioner's account of his visit to Monsieur Rodollet without manifesting the slightest emotion. The candle sputtered, and went out. Monsieur de Noblecourt carefully closed his book and said, after a silence, 'Haven't you ever wondered, my dear boy, what led you to become an officer in the King's police?'

'A series of chance events and a recommendation from the Marquis de Ranreuil to Monsieur de Sartine.'

'Not at all! Listen to an old sceptic. You may be surprised by his words. It was providence that wished to make life difficult for criminals by confronting them with an honest man whom she trusted to carry out her arrests.'

'That's all well and good,' said Nicolas, cheering up, 'but it doesn't tell me the name of the man who's orchestrating this conspiracy against me.'

'Remember that the elements always come together in the end to reveal the truth. Sometimes in very mysterious ways.'

'Is it the twilight hour that has made you so pious, or your reading . . .' – he leant towards the book and managed to read the title – 'of Ovid. Oh, I see, nostalgia for lost loves . . .'

Monsieur de Noblecourt nodded. 'See how accurately you aim. Just before you came in, I was thinking about my wife, that noble, loyal heart. How heavy a burden my life would have been without her love, and how heavy it would be now without my friends, above all without you. I don't mind telling you that you have taken the place of the child I long desired and never had.'

This was an unexpected declaration: the former procurator had never before opened his heart like that. Was it merely a result of the darkness surrounding them? This confidence released the pain Nicolas had so long held in. His voice muffled by emotion – although sufficiently in control of himself to omit the fact that he had been in London – he poured out to his old friend the whole story of his love for La Satin, and the question of paternity that now hung over him. He expressed his fears and his indecisiveness about this child who had dropped out of the sky, unaware of his origins.

'I understand your emotion,' said Monsieur de Noblecourt,

gently. 'But don't worry. As someone who did not discover his own father until after his death, you are best placed to make the right decision. The fault lies more in your lack of confidence than in the spontaneity of an impulse which, I feel, is urging you to reach out to this son you do not know. Take your time, think carefully, and when you have made your decision, give this son a father and yourself a son. Offer him, while there is still time, the love and support he is entitled to expect from you. Reject the prejudices of birth in his case as you did in yours. I can foresee a day when such things no longer mean anything. Give this child what Canon Le Floch, the Marquis de Ranreuil and, dare I say it, I myself gave you. Act boldly. But I'm starting to feel moved . . . We'll talk about it another time.'

He stood up and groped in the writing desk.

'A letter arrived for you from Court this afternoon.'

Nicolas took the letter, which was sealed with the arms of France. He opened it after relighting the candle.

'His Majesty's secretary of commands has sent me an invitation to the King's shooting party at the Satory ponds tomorrow morning. I'll have to get my green coat ready, as that's the only thing allowed for hunting with rifles. When the weather's cold, the wildfowl fly over the ornamental lakes.'

'Now that is a skill,' said Monsieur de Noblecourt, 'which denotes a born gentleman, a fine tradition to be handed down from father to son.'

Nicolas thought it was high time he initiated his son. The conversation took a peaceful course, and they talked about different models of flute, an instrument Monsieur de Noblecourt played occasionally. Nicolas went up to his apartment early, anxious to get some rest: he would have to leave well before dawn in order to be on time for the King's hunt at Versailles.

Friday 21 January 1774

The sun was rising when the carriage emerged from Avenue de Paris on to the Place d'Armes. The light was cold and bright, promising a calm day. Frost and ice were everywhere. Stalactites hung from the golden gate of the last courtyard. Beneath Nicolas's boots, the cobbles slid and cracked. When he got to the park, he saw a long line of coaches outside the Princes' wing, waiting to take the King and his hunting guests to Satory and the flooded fields over which the migrating birds flew. Nicolas paced up and down to keep warm, exchanging greetings and friendly words with his acquaintances amongst the courtiers. He threw an indulgent glance at a few newcomers, looking stiff and starchy in their beginner's costumes, their young faces red with cold and emotion. A page from the small stables tugged at his sleeve and told him that it was time for him to be at the door of the King's coach, as the King had just finished his daily mass. This order was given loudly enough for a number of people to turn and look at him, intrigued, and whisper comments to each other. He greeted the bodyguards who would escort the coach and waited.

A noise on the gravel told him the King had arrived. Louis was in his hunting costume, with a matching fur-collared cloak. He was leaning on a lanky young man a good head taller than him, whom Nicolas recognised as the Dauphin. Monsieur de La Borde gave him a friendly wave. The King smiled, got in the coach and sat down heavily. The Dauphin was about to join him, when the King intimated that he was to give up his seat to Nicolas.

'Berry, take your carriage, I need to speak to young Ranreuil.'

The Dauphin went red, nodded to Nicolas, and waddled to his coach. Nicolas sat down facing the King. The procession set off for the great park. The King was silent, his chin in his hand, watching the landscape pass by. Nicolas studied him through half-closed eyes. He was looking older than ever: the great eyebrows were turning white, the nose was getting narrower, and the jowls more and more noticeable, destroying the balance of what had long been a harmonious whole. The dark, infinitely melancholy eyes had lost their sheen, and the bluish bags beneath them made them look larger.

'It's cold and sharp,' the King said at last. 'We'll see the wildfowl clearly. Did you shoot wildfowl with the marquis, at Ranreuil?'

'Yes, Sire, in the Brière marshes.'

'What kind of dogs did Ranreuil use?'

'Setters, Sire. Rustic water spaniels that were good at swimming and withstanding cold.'

'A good choice. I've been told many wildfowl fly over the Somme. Did you see any on the way to London?'

'I was trying hard not to be the prey, Sire.'

The King laughed. 'Tell me about it, it'll distract me.'

Nicolas adorned his account with a number of outlandish or extravagant details. He described the appearance of the Comtesse du Barry as if it were an episode from a fairy tale. The King burst out laughing. Everything was expressed lightly and without excess. It was Nicolas's great skill as a storyteller to avoid heaviness. He did not hesitate to mock himself and, knowing the King's irritation with the growing Anglomania, he described England and the English somewhat unfairly, having no words of admiration for London and its buildings. What a career he might have had as a courtier if his circumstances had been different, he thought as he spoke. He told his story in a succession of scenes that were so vivid and witty, they cheered the King up, and he even laughed uproariously at various points, making him seem younger. The procession was approaching the Satory ponds. At last the caravan came to a halt in the middle of an area of heathland surrounded by birches and poplars. The King lowered his window and called one of the officers.

'I haven't finished with young Ranreuil. Tell the Dauphin to start without me.' He turned back to Nicolas. 'I am sorry, Monsieur, that I exposed you to so many dangers. They might have deprived me of a good and devoted servant.'

'Your Majesty knows it was to save me from a greater danger.'

'Has that been averted now?'

'It's hard to say for sure. But what I can tell Your Majesty is that so much effort has been put into throwing suspicion on me that the very excess of it can only confirm my innocence.'

After a moment's thought, the King murmured, 'Troubling indeed, this accumulation of malign actions directed against you. Could there be a connection between your case and the mission with which I entrusted you?'

Nicolas nodded, assuming it was a rhetorical question that did not require an answer. Shots were beginning to ring out on all sides.

'The wildfowl have arrived,' said the King in his hoarse voice.

'I'll have to thank Mesnard for the accuracy of his predictions. He never seems to grow old. The Duc de Penthièvre knew him as a child! What knowledge of birds he has! Almost as good as Louis XIII, my grandfather's father . . . And what about the chevalier? Tell me what you think.'

'The Chevalier d'Éon was perfectly polite to me as your envoy. And if I may be so bold, I think I can tell Your Majesty that he does not have a more affectionate or more loyal servant.'

The King gave a little laugh. 'Affectionate, certainly! As for loyal . . . If disobeying my orders is a mark of that virtue, then yes. However, for all his faults, I think he is genuinely anxious to serve me and would be delighted to place his knowledge and contacts at our disposal. They were certainly useful in the affair you resolved so happily. You actually managed to convince this Morande to agree to our conditions. We are grateful to you, Ranreuil.'

Nicolas had the feeling that this royal 'we' included Madame du Barry.

'You have shown once again that nothing is too difficult or too risky for your talent. Sartine is lucky to have you!'

'Sire, the Chevalier d'Éon asked me to speak to you about the matter of Mr Flint.'

The King did not reply immediately. Every time they met, it was borne in on him just how resilient the man was: a monarch who could trust no one, or only a few handpicked individuals, plagued by scruples, dealing coolly with a hundred different matters without ever allowing himself to seem moody or impatient, and always extremely open towards those with whom he was on intimate terms. Why did his people so misjudge him, and why had appearances been against him for so many years?

'In your opinion,' said the King, 'can we trust this Englishman?'

Nicolas replied with his usual spontaneity – surely a constant surprise to a man accustomed to the cautiousness and guile of the Court. 'What trust can we have in a man who betrays his King and his nation? I think it is wrong to put ourselves in his hands without a guarantee and without having confirmed his information, or at least pretended that we can do so.'

'Well, that sounds wise to me! I'll see to it.' The King lowered his window. 'Let young Ranreuil be given my rifles. Call La Borde. Go hunting, Ranreuil, and talk to the Dauphin about Mr Flint. I want him to like you. One day, he'll need you.'

He held out his hand to Nicolas, who bowed and kissed it before stepping backwards out of the carriage. The King seemed to have recovered his serenity. A page walked Nicolas to the spot where the Dauphin was shooting. The birds were not flying over so frequently now, and the prince did not seem to mind Nicolas's intrusion.

'Fine weather, Monsieur!'

Nicolas was racking his brains about how to begin. 'His Majesty wishes me to report to you about a matter I dealt with secretly in London.'

The young man could not help reacting with pleasure and interest, a reaction which did not escape Nicolas.

The Dauphin handed his rifle to a page and leant back against a birch tree. He looked benevolently at Nicolas with his grey-blue, slightly blurry eyes. Nicolas dealt briefly with the preliminaries and insisted, knowing the prince's interest in cartography, on how advantageous it would be for the French navy to have new information concerning the coast of the great Chinese empire, from both a military and a commercial point of view. The Dauphin knelt, picked up a twig and drew the coastline of Asia on the ground, from memory. Warming to the subject, he expounded arguments so well founded and so well thought out that they surprised Nicolas. Although the decision remained with the King, he hoped that he would involve his heir.

'Monsieur,' said the Dauphin, 'I'm glad to have seen you again on a topic of such importance to the interests of the King. I imagine I will please you by giving you news of Naganda, the Micmac chief to whom you introduced me some years ago. His reports have been consistently interesting. The tribes with which he has made contact look upon him as a man who has come to help them against the English. You know how restless the American colonists are at the moment . . . He's making a lot of good contacts. For example, he's already spoken to the Tuscaroras, the Onondagas, the Senekas, the Mohawks, the Oneidas and the Cayudas. He's a real treasure, and we're very grateful to you.'

Nicolas was astonished at the prince's memory and knowledge. At that moment, the pages pulled them by the sleeve. More flights of birds had been sighted. For a while, the two men devoted themselves to the pleasures of the hunt, shooting up at the flocks that sped by overhead and seeing them scatter and re-form. Unlike venery, this was not a struggle with the noblest of animals, nor a dangerous game played against a fierce foe, but an entertainment whose interest lay in the abundance of the prey and the rapidity of their flight. The Dauphin complimented Nicolas good-naturedly on the fact that he was shooting with the King's rifles: an exceptional gesture, reserved for those whom His Majesty wished to distinguish. The birds fell one after the other, so quickly that the breathless spaniels could no longer gather them. Swiss Guards would load the rifles and pass them to the pages, who would hand them to the hunters. The amount of game collected would be totted up on tablets by the First Page of the Small Stable, who would then go to the King's office to receive orders concerning its distribution. The largest portion went to the pages, along with the traditional twelve bottles of champagne. The King had remained in his coach. His foot-warmer had been taken to him and he was talking to La Borde. The shooting party was coming to an end, and the Dauphin graciously invited Nicolas to his coach. Their conversation, quite relaxed now, centred on hunting, a subject on which the prince was unstoppable and the commissioner a mine of information.

Nicolas was duly present when the King's boots were removed, and was granted a happy smile by the monarch. Monsieur de La Borde, who was returning to Paris, offered him a lift. No sooner was he in the Court carriage than he lowered the window, despite the cold.

'Are you rather too warm?' asked Nicolas.

'My dear fellow, a plague on the Maréchal de Richelieu! I was next to him in the King's study. The old dandy measures his own youth by the power of the smell he gives off. He's always soaked himself in pure musk, and wherever he goes, the odours of the badger, the stag and the rutting boar go with him. In Paris they sing:

Whenever old Richelieu enters a room
Strengthen your heart and plug up your nose.

He has his breeches made from Spanish hide soaked in the same perfume. In the theatre, his scent is so strong that the boxes adjoining his quickly empty in the intervals. How did you find the King?'

Nicolas had noticed that, for some years now, the monarch's closest and most attentive servants had invariably asked the same question.

'To tell the truth, a little older . . .'

La Borde's face tensed and he let out a sigh, as if trying to rid himself of a fear that lay heavy on his heart.

'But he seems better as soon as he speaks. That livens him up.'

'If only you saw him more often!' exclaimed La Borde. 'It's enough to mention your name and his face lights up. I don't know where you get the gift which allows you to distract him. Many others try, but in vain. One conversation with you, though, and he's young again! How sad to see him huddled in his carriage against the cold. He so used to love hunting!'

He fell silent for a moment, as if lost in thought, and sighed again.

'At the time of Madame de Pompadour, hunting was followed by delightful little dinners where everyone enjoyed themselves. Now it's quite different . . . Madame du Barry is causing a great deal of anxiety and worrying the King's doctors. He feels it's his duty to respond to her ardour. Richelieu supplies him with strong stimulants, and he certainly takes too many of them. To tell the truth, he's scared of getting old. He's constantly trying to make sure his powers have not diminished. Stag's horn in powdered form and pills filled with cantharids[1] are his favoured remedies.'

'Semacgus has always warned me against such products.'

'Quite rightly. Alas, there comes a time when an old machine runs out of steam, its springs stiffen from overuse, and nothing we do can mend it. The worst of it is that the weaknesses we notice, instead of making us wiser, lead us to try even harder and more often.'

'But didn't His Majesty sell the deer park to Monsieur Sevin, the usher of Madame Victoire's chamber?'

'Yes, but the temptations remain. For some people, the more there are, the better. In the harem of the Great Turk, the most desirable girls are those who are not yet there.'

Nicolas wondered if his friend, who was a great libertine, would apply the same counsels of prudence and moderation to himself when he was older. Everyone led the life he wanted, and wisdom sometimes prevailed in the end. The change in Semacgus's behaviour was proof enough of that.

'Alas, my friend, as President de Saujac never stops saying, "We do not change our habits, it is our habits that change us."'

Nicolas decided on a frontal attack. 'What were your feelings towards Madame de Lastérieux?'

The use of the word 'Madame' seemed to implicate him less directly in the question. La Borde looked Nicolas in the eyes gravely and a trifle sadly. It was as if a whole lifetime's experience of love were in those eyes, and the difference in age between them was suddenly made clear.

'Don't be angry with me,' he replied, 'but I thought her flirtatious and quite unsuitable for you. It's a terrible thing to say, but I think her death has liberated you in a way, and has certainly spared you many disappointments. I don't deny that she was fond of you. But the question is, what was the basis of this fondness:

the love she claimed to feel for you, or her desire to succeed? I would incline to the latter hypothesis. These days, we are no longer content with appearing vermillion, we want to become crimson. I don't know if it was just an impression, but she seemed to treat me differently and was less arrogant in my presence than with other people. Her simpering was meant to enhance her charms and act as a bait.'

'And you think . . .'

'That she was only interested in me as a man of the Court. She was so anxious to get herself there, by whatever means . . .'

Faced with such honesty, Nicolas could not but dismiss the few suspicions that had crossed his mind, even though, as a professional, he knew that it was unwise to base a properly conducted investigation on feelings and impressions. A long silence fell between them, which La Borde broke suddenly.

'It was I who had you invited to the King's shooting party. His Majesty commented that you didn't need to be invited, as you were entitled to come by right. He added that he regretted not seeing you as often as he would like. Please come hunting more often, for his sake and for mine!'

Monsieur de La Borde dropped Nicolas at the Grand Châtelet, where a very agitated Old Marie informed him that something serious had happened and that Inspector Bourdeau had gone to Rue Saint-Julien-le-Pauvre, leaving a message that the commissioner was to join him as soon as he got back from Versailles. A police carriage was waiting to take him across the Seine. It was not very far, but the traffic was heavy this late in the afternoon and a spot of congestion blocked the carriage in Rue du Marché-Palu, as they were leaving the Cité. He had to abandon it, ordering his coachman to join him as soon as he got through. He went along Rue du Petit Pont, then Rue de la Boucherie, and finally entered the narrow Rue Saint-Julien-le-Pauvre.

An animated crowd surrounded a police wagon. French Guards were holding them at a distance from the door of an old house whose façade leant with age. Nicolas made his way through the crowd and identified himself. Bourdeau hailed him from one of the windows. In the hall, he also had to move aside a group of gossiping women, who swore at him. On the fourth-floor landing, he found the inspector and an officer. Bourdeau stopped him, took him aside and brought him up to date.

'Rabouine had been keeping watch on this house since yesterday. Nothing unusual happened until noon today, when Balbastre appeared. He went up to Monsieur du Maine-Giraud's apartment. He only stayed a few moments, then came out again looking distraught. Rabouine did not hesitate. He dispatched a messenger boy to inform me of the facts and followed the organist. I haven't heard from him since. As soon as I was reached – I was dealing with an affair of contraband wine in Montmartre – I rushed here. The room wasn't locked: the latch falls as soon as you pull the door. I found the young gentleman dead, transfixed on a sword that had been jammed between the bars at the back of a chair. Everything points to suicide. I avoided touching anything, as I wanted you to be the first to examine the body and the room.'

Without a word, Nicolas opened the door. At a single glance, the whole drama was revealed to him. The furnishings were so sparse that the room seemed empty: a white wooden wardrobe, a bunk with a straw mattress covered with a worn damask counterpane, a rickety table, a stool with holes in its straw seat, a half-folded screen made of oil paper, a dressing table with a washbowl. The window, presumably opened by Bourdeau, faced the door. To its right, at a slight diagonal from the entrance, a body in a shirt sat totally motionless, sprawled over a chair in a corner of the room, hair covering the face. Slightly to the left, beneath the shoulder blade, glinted the tip of a sword.

Nicolas approached the victim cautiously, like a pointer at a hunt. He examined the bloodstained floor, registering every detail. He stood up again and read the titles of the books on a small shelf. A few garments hung on nails above a pair of boots. Bending, Nicolas noticed a series of scratches on the floor. Some gashes on the flowered wallpaper also caught his attention, so recent that the plaster dust still lay on the floor. He took a step forward for a closer look at the body and pulled on one of the arms: it was not yet stiff. Clearly death had occurred not long before, a few hours at the most. That coincided more or less with Balbastre's brief visit, he calculated. He called Bourdeau and the officer. Together, they moved the body and laid it on its side, as Nicolas wanted to leave the weapon in its place, to be carefully examined during the autopsy at the Basse-Geôle. He was struck, like the others, by the expression of terror on the victim's still almost childlike face. But, distorted as the features were, he recognised him as one of the card players he had glimpsed during the party at Madame de Lastérieux's house. The body was then taken away on a stretcher, while Nicolas noted down the pattern of scratches on the wooden floor. Before leaving the room and having seals placed on the door, the inspector and he conducted a thorough search. Their task was made easier by the poverty of the place. It was Bourdeau, as he moved the clothes, who pointed out to him the pair of boots they had glimpsed earlier: they turned out to be Nicolas's, the very same boots that had disappeared from Madame de Lastérieux's house. One of the soles had a nail sticking out. That, clearly, was what had made the scratches on the floor, as it had in Julie's bedroom.

It was with this remarkable observation that they left Rue Saint-Julien-le-Pauvre. At the Châtelet, Nicolas gave instructions for the autopsy to be performed as soon as possible. He felt a few scruples at once again having to turn to Sanson and Semacgus, but he did not want to leave such an important operation to the prison's own, mediocre doctors. He next decided to pay a visit to Master Tiphaine, Madame de Lastérieux's notary, at his practice in Rue de la Harpe. There, he found the clerks in a panic and the notary's young wife in tears. She told him that her husband, after receiving a visit from a person she did not know, had thrown a few things in a portmanteau and hurried to his carriage. All he had said to her was that she was to write *poste restante* to his banker in The Hague: he would go regularly to collect his mail. Disappointed by this twist of fate, Nicolas returned to the Châtelet. In the duty office, he found Rabouine making his report to Bourdeau. Nothing had attracted his attention during his surveillance of the house of Monsieur du Maine-Giraud. Only a few common women had gone in and out, as well as a monk he had not seen again.

'A monk?' said Nicolas. 'Of what order?'

'A Capuchin,' said Rabouine. 'With his hood pulled down.'

'Don't look any further!' laughed Bourdeau. 'I thought you were a clever fellow, Rabouine. Well, you were had!'

The informer bowed his head. 'Later,' he went on, 'a young man came out, with a folded sheet under his arm. I took him for a laundryman's assistant. Finally, after an hour, Monsieur Balbastre, whom I know, appeared. He seemed very nervous, and kept looking around as if he was afraid he was being followed.'

'Did he see you?'

'Impossible, Monsieur Nicolas. He came out again five or six minutes later.'

'Was he carrying anything?'

'A package.'

'What happened then?'

'Well, I thought I should follow him. He took a cab back to his house – he lives near Saint-Gervais. He didn't stay there long. When he came out, he was walking quickly and reading a letter, which he tore up and scattered to the four winds.'

'Were you able to collect any of the pieces?'

'How was I supposed to run after him and pick up the pieces at the same time?'

There was nothing you could do, thought Nicolas, when bad luck played all these tricks on you, one after the other. You just had to endure them and wait for your luck to change.

'I hope you kept after him and didn't lose him?'

Rabouine lifted his angular profile. 'On the contrary, Monsieur Nicolas, I stayed with him all the way to his destination.'

'Tell me more.'

'His carriage turned into Rue de l'Université and stopped near the Palais Bourbon. Balbastre got out and went in through the gate of the Duc d'Aiguillon's mansion.'

'Now that is interesting!' exclaimed Bourdeau.

'And you didn't stay to keep watch?'

Rabouine winked. 'You seem to be doubting my abilities today. I have my contacts in all the best houses. And to see a case through to its conclusion, you only have to know human nature and how to exploit it.' He made a gesture of counting money.

'No,' said Nicolas impatiently, 'we don't doubt your abilities, but we don't have much time.'

'Well, then, to cut a long story short,' said Rabouine, 'I spoke to my contact a little while later. He told me that our man had a conversation with one of the minister's associates, who gave orders for lodgings to be made ready in the attic of the mansion and for the organist to be taken up there. That's where he is right now, apparently with a high fever and shivering all over.'

'Bravo, bravissimo!' cried Bourdeau. 'Rabouine, you're the best! You redeem your previous negligence with this latest feat!'

Once Rabouine had left, Nicolas and Bourdeau summed up the situation. They were in the presence of another death clearly linked to the murder of Madame de Lastérieux. What they had to do as soon as possible was determine the exact circumstances of Monsieur du Maine-Giraud's suicide. Added to that was a mysterious monk and the visit of Balbastre, who had come out of the dead man's lodgings with a package. The same man, clearly terrified, had run to seek refuge at the house of the First Minister, the Duc d'Aiguillon, where he had been received like a regular guest. Last but not least, why had Master Tiphaine left hurriedly on an overseas trip?

The two men again divided up the tasks. Nicolas would be present at the autopsy, which would be performed that very night, if possible, while his deputy would go and search Balbastre's house near the church of Saint-Gervais. After which, to obtain authorisation for more exhaustive investigations, they would have to apply to the Lieutenant General of Police, who usually left for Versailles on Saturdays to prepare for his weekly audience with the King.

Saturday 22 January 1774

The interview with Monsieur de Sartine had begun pleasantly enough. Preoccupied with his hobby, he first informed Nicolas that, after enquiries in London, a full chest of wigs was on its way to France, and he was dying with impatience to receive it. However, the commissioner was far from sure that this preamble did not conceal something else, and he knew his chief's character well enough to realise before long that the apparent gentleness of his tone hid a growing irritation.

Nicolas therefore made his report in a deliberately neutral manner, making sure that no exaggeration opened the floodgates to a torrent of reproaches. A vain hope: the news of Casimir's death, Semacgus's discoveries in the Jardin du Roi and the investigation into Julie's supposed letter and will, even though it did not occasion any outburst, nevertheless led to Sartine moving a number of objects about on his desk, a sign that he was growing impatient. The information about the death of Monsieur du Maine-Giraud and the possible involvement of Balbastre produced the same reaction. But then the announcement of the organist's escape to the Duc d'Aiguillon's mansion and above all the latest news of the night really did startle Monsieur de Sartine. The search of Balbastre's house had in fact led to the discovery of a pair of bloodstained shoes and, hidden at the back of a wardrobe, the Capuchin's robe, equally soiled. In addition, the autopsy performed by Semacgus and Sanson at the Basse-Geôle had made it possible to rule out suicide as the cause of death: Monsieur du Maine-Giraud had been murdered. An examination of the wound had revealed that a first blow had punctured the liver, provoking a fatal haemorrhage, and what had happened thereafter was pure make-believe. The body had been run through with a sword stuck between the bars of the chair, the point of the blade being driven into the original wound. This second penetration had followed a different route from the first. There was no doubt possible: the blood spattered around the room and the scratches on the floor, caused by boots whose soles had been cleaned before being put away, proved that there had been a violent attack. The threatened victim could well have struggled or have tried to parry the fatal blow. In conclusion, Nicolas requested authorisation to arrest Balbastre, who might not be the murderer but who certainly had information crucial to the progress of the investigation. This conclusion, although perfectly logical, unleashed Sartine's rage. He began striding up and down his office, ranting and raving.

'The progress of the investigation! How much more of this nonsense do I have to hear, Commissioner? The only crime I see here is that, thanks to your irrational liaison, you dragged us into this infernal affair in the first place!'

Outraged by his chief's bad faith, Nicolas tried to protest. 'Would I have become involved in that liaison if you yourself, knowing everything you did, had dissuaded me?'

Monsieur de Sartine, who was now by the fireplace, picked up the tongs and struck a pyramid of logs, which collapsed noisily. 'Be quiet! And, as is your unfortunate custom, now you're strewing corpses in your wake! Not only is your mistress murdered, but her servant, an unknown young man, and who else besides? You are wreaking havoc in the city, which makes me question how right I have been to extend my protection to you thus far.' He caught his breath. 'What is it you imagine? You should be well placed, Monsieur, to know exactly what you have escaped. In this kingdom, whether one likes it or not – and I was, don't forget, Criminal Lieutenant, at a time when you were still causing mischief at the Jesuit school in Vannes, no doubt wreaking havoc there, too . . . What was I saying? Oh, yes, the fact is that the aim of our procedures is to ensure the success of an accusation, whether true or false. And although we take meticulous care to establish the smallest piece of evidence, and are constantly concerned to observe the rules and gather as much proof as possible, we know that the judge always approaches a case with the idea that the person brought before him is guilty and that the aim of the procedure is above all to deliver a prey to be condemned by him and to impress the people with an example. Whatever the integrity, sensitivity and intelligence of the magistrates, that is their inclination. Do you understand? Do you?'

'But what does that have to do with—'

'My God, the man's a fool!' cried Sartine. 'Let us suppose, Monsieur, since you insist on appearing stupid, that a citizen has a dangerous enemy, who wishes to destroy him by accusing him of a capital offence, can't you see what a terrible predicament this poor innocent will find himself in? According to our edict of 1670, he is placed under the criminal procedure known as extraordinary, reserved for the most serious crimes. Have you no idea how difficult it will be for him to prove his innocence? First of all, his enemy denounces him in secret, and he has no way of discovering the person's identity. The Criminal Lieutenant produces witnesses, but naturally, only those provided by the denouncer. They are heard in the greatest secrecy by a single judge, for fear of being contradicted: a judge who may in addition – I don't like to think this, but there we are – be biased or corrupt. Where does that leave our poor innocent? The procedure takes its course, and our unfortunate innocent is taken to prison amidst public scandal or – which is worse – in secret, put in irons and sometimes thrown in a horrible dungeon where he is fed on bread and water and sleeps on straw, unable to communicate with the outside world.'

'But—'

'No buts. He is dragged from his cell to face interrogation. He is expressly forbidden to have a counsel present. The judge puts pressure on the accused, in accordance with the law, which presumes him to be guilty. He tries by every means – and I mean *every* means – to extract a confession to the crime which has been imputed to him. The more dangerous the crime, the fewer the facilities the law gives the accused to present his case. In addition, when the accused is confronted with the witnesses, he cannot even question them directly. Such, Monsieur, is the procedure which has already aroused many protests in favour of more humane treatment, has more than once led to fatal misunderstandings and has often compromised the interests of justice. And such is the procedure from which the trust placed in you and the power that protects you have allowed you to escape. Consider how lucky you have been, and then tell me if you really want to tempt fate by continuing doggedly on your present course.'

'Monsieur,' protested Nicolas, 'I am only trying to get at the truth, as you taught me to do.'

'Ah, the good disciple! But don't you understand that justice can only be exercised in so far as another force, in whose hands it resides, authorises it?'

'His Majesty wouldn't allow—'

'Don't involve the King in all this! Since you seem determined not to understand what I'm saying, I must tell you that this morning I was duly summoned by the Duc d'Aiguillon, who informed me, in that tone of his with which you are familiar, that Monsieur Balbastre is under his protection, that it is his wish that the man be left in peace, that to disregard these instructions would be to oppose him, and that he would never tolerate the Lieutenant General of Police protecting, and I quote, "a little bastard of a commissioner with whom the King has become besotted". Such were his words, and I'm sorry to have to repeat them to you. I'm also sorry to have to order you to abandon this case.'

Nicolas could not believe what he was hearing. For a moment, he said nothing, then ventured, 'Nevertheless, Monsieur, without

Monsieur Balbastre's testimony and an understanding of his actions, our investigation has reached a dead end, and I think Monsieur de Saint-Florentin—'

'Don't think! Above all, don't think! Do you have a hat pulled down over your head that stops you hearing and remembering that Monsieur de Saint-Florentin, whom I command you to call the Duc de La Vrillière, is the uncle of the Duc d'Aiguillon's wife? I would also add that your Monsieur Balbastre, around whom you are strewing corpses, is not only a highly regarded musician, a talented composer, the organist of both Notre Dame and the royal chapel at Versailles, but is also our Dauphine's harpsichord teacher. So you want to carry on, do you? Go on, then, carry on! No, no, let's be serious, go about your business as commissioner at the Châtelet and be glad about the turn this affair has not taken.'

Sartine slowly walked back to his armchair. Without a word, Nicolas bowed to him and turned to go out. When he was at the door, his chief almost shouted after him, 'It's not you I'm angry with. In truth, I'm not proud of myself . . .'

Nicolas closed the door behind him, half joyful, half alarmed at what he had just heard. As he descended the staircase, he recalled the first lessons Sartine had taught him, in particular Colbert's definition, so often repeated, of the eminent office of Lieutenant General of Police: 'He must be a man both of the cloak and of the sword. If the learned ermine of the scholar covers his shoulders, the spurs of the knight must jangle at his feet. He must be as impassive as a judge or an intrepid soldier, he must not pale before flooded rivers or raging plagues, nor before popular uprisings or the threats of courtiers.'

It seemed to Nicolas – and the thought was a melancholy one – that times had changed and that the King's power no longer supported the Lieutenant General as much as it had in the past.

X

THE KING

Here lies our much loved King
Who always looked so neat
And paid for everything
With what he gained on the wheat.
ANONYMOUS

Thursday 28 April 1774

Three months had passed, three months of everyday routine. Monsieur de Sartine, having regained his usual composure, had been treating Nicolas with particular thoughtfulness, as if hoping to be forgiven for having been forced to break off the investigation into the murder in Rue de Verneuil. Nicolas pretended that he had come to terms with the situation, while secretly hoping that one day, in more favourable circumstances, the law would resume its normal course. One thing cheered him and made him forget this failure: the King was inviting him more and more frequently to Versailles. Apart from his presence at hunts, his repeated attendance at intimate gatherings showed the degree of favour he was in, a favour strengthened by Madame du Barry's benevolent attitude towards him. She had been happy to listen to Monsieur de La Borde, who had suggested to her that young Ranreuil was better equipped than anyone else to distract the King and that his presence guaranteed a few smiles.

It was true that this seemed increasingly necessary. The King was now in his sixty-third year. He had gained weight and was less able to withstand excess of any kind. More and more frequently, his mind would go blank for short periods, as if he were intoxicated, thus fuelling much speculation at foreign courts. As had happened during his grandfather's last days, they were beginning to lay bets in London on how much longer his reign would last. He often fell from his horse, but refused to give up riding despite his doctor's repeated pleas. Always a lover of women and food, he had nevertheless finally agreed to a diet, drinking Vichy water and doing without dinner almost completely. He had always been obsessed with death, and now a series of sudden deaths amongst his entourage filled him with gloom. His every word was reported, and much comment was elicited by his vague desire to return to religious practice. It was noted that he was paying increasingly frequent visits to his daughter, Madame Louise, who was a Carmelite at Saint-Denis.

The Abbé de Beauvais, Bishop of Senez, had preached at Versailles on Maundy Thursday. Nicolas still remembered a terrifying moment which had struck all those present. The bishop had chosen death as the theme of his sermon. He began by destroying the illusion that the century had seen an increase in human longevity compared with previous centuries. He painted an eloquent picture of the miseries of the common people whose love for their monarch was diminishing. He then attacked the King in the transparent guise of Solomon. Nicolas remembered his words: 'Finally Solomon, sated with sensuality, tired of having exhausted every kind of pleasure surrounding the throne in his attempts to revive his withered senses, finished by seeking a new pleasure in the vile dregs of public licentiousness.' The prelate's final peroration had made the King turn pale and dismayed the courtiers. 'Another forty days and Nineveh will be destroyed.' As for Madame du Barry, cruelly hurt and full of sombre presentiments, she was unable to conceal her anxiety: ever since the clandestinely distributed *Almanach de Liège* had predicted the imminent fall 'of a great lady playing a role in a foreign court', she had been wishing for this 'damnable month of April' to pass.

Nicolas had arrived the day before, summoned to Versailles by a message from Monsieur de La Borde, who had mentioned, without going into details, that he had a surprise for him. During the hunt, though, La Borde had remained silent. The King, complaining that he felt cold despite the mild weather, had not left his carriage. He did not look well: he was suffering with his gums, which his dentist had examined a few days earlier. Nicolas had slept in La Borde's apartment. The next day, returning at about three to the Petit Trianon, he learnt that the King had felt unwell, had taken a few mild remedies without feeling any relief and, after a game of cards, had gone to bed, counting on sleep to ease his discomfort.

While waiting for news, La Borde and Nicolas went for a walk in the little French garden beyond the hothouses where the King was attempting to acclimatise coffee, fig and pineapple trees. They were approaching the little pavilion of Gabriel, where the

King often stopped to classify his herbariums or to take a collation of milk and strawberries, when suddenly the commissioner spied a figure at the top of the steps leading up to the pavilion and stopped dead. He could not believe his eyes. It was Naganda who stood there, smiling at him.

Monsieur de La Borde left them to enjoy their reunion. They had not seen each other since the summer of 1770, when Nicolas had accompanied the young Micmac chief to Nantes, from where he had set sail for Canada. They talked of the memories they shared, and the Indian asked for news of Bourdeau and Semacgus. He recounted the conditions in which he had succeeded his father at the head of his people, and told Nicolas that the sheer volume of information he had gathered, not only from the Indian tribes, but also from the American colonists, had led the administration at Versailles to ask him to come and explain everything in person, especially the sketch maps and strategic summaries he had been able to draw up. A fishing boat, tricking the English fleet, had secretly picked him up on the banks of the Saint Lawrence and taken him to Saint-Pierre-et-Miquelon, where a French vessel had been waiting for him. Proudly, he showed Nicolas the officer's uniform in which he was dressed. What he said about the American situation confirmed what Nicolas already knew from his recent conversation with the Dauphin. He would not be staying long: once he had been received by the King and the Minister for the Navy, he would set sail again with new instructions. He was staying in Versailles, at the Hôtel de la Belle Image on Place Dauphine. Nicolas suggested they go to Paris together: Monsieur de Noblecourt had always regretted never having met 'the man of the New World'. Their conversation was interrupted by an officer who had come to look for Naganda, and by La Borde, who, once Naganda had gone, told Nicolas what he had just learnt.

'The King had a very bad night,' he said. 'Headaches complicated by back pains. Monsieur Le Monnier, the First Doctor Ordinary, was woken up. He found the King in a fever. On the King's orders, Madame du Barry was sent for. Le Monnier, accustomed to his patient's squeamishness, is not unduly concerned by the symptoms. According to him, it's merely indigestion. The gentlemen in attendance have also made light of this indisposition.'

'And the comtesse?' asked Nicolas.

'She knows how scared the King gets at the slightest thing, and she's worried he'll ask for his confessor. She leans in the same direction as the others. She wants to be the only one to watch over the King and has asked that no one in the palace be told.'

'But everything soon gets known about at Court.'

'Precisely, my dear Nicolas. As you can well imagine, His Majesty's family were immediately worried. Not daring to appear, they sent La Martinière, his First Surgeon. He's just arrived. Let's hurry back to the new palace.'

La Borde had taken Nicolas by the arm. On the staircase leading to the first floor, where the reception rooms were, the servants were waiting. In the antechamber, leaning on one of the porcelain stoves, Gaspard the page greeted them. Several courtiers were waiting there, too, amongst whom Nicolas recognised Monsieur de Boisgelin, with whom he and his father, the Marquis de Ranreuil, had gone hunting in the forest of La Bretesche, near Guérande. The King's apartment was situated in the attic. A little staircase, at the foot of which he was in the habit of taking his coffee, gave him direct access to his bedroom. The two windows could be sealed at night by an ingenious system of moving sheets of glass that rose from the ground floor. A clock struck five in an adjoining room. The Prince de Condé appeared, coming down from the King's apartment.

'Monsieur,' he said to La Borde, 'the surgeon has told the King that he cannot stay at the Petit Trianon, and that if he's going to be ill it'll have to be at Versailles. The Duc d'Aiguillon has urged His Majesty, who has just given his orders. Let the carriages be called at once!'

Everyone started running in all directions. La Borde rushed up to the attic. Soon, the din of horses and coaches echoed on the cobbles outside, putting an end to the heavy silence which had fallen after the first orders had been given. Everyone was in a hurry. Standing at the foot of the stairs, Nicolas saw the First Minister coming down towards him, throwing him a sharp look as he did so, followed by a man in plain black clothes whom he took to be La Martinière. Almost immediately after them came the King, leaning on La Borde for support. He was wearing a dressing gown under a hunting cloak that had been thrown hurriedly over his shoulders. His face was red and puffy. Reaching the bottom, he gave Nicolas such an imploring look that, without thinking, the commissioner held out his arm. The King's hand rested on his wrist: it was burning hot, indicative of a high fever. The King walked to his carriage, supported by La Borde and Nicolas. He got in and cried out in a cracked voice, 'Make it quick!' He had not let go of Nicolas's arm, and Nicolas found himself obliged to follow him, just like La Borde. The carriage set off amidst a great commotion: cries, the cracking of whips, the creaking of wheels. The King, shivering with cold, pulled his cloak tighter about his body. For a moment, he stared at Nicolas as if he had never seen him before. His head nodded every time the carriage hit a bump in the road. In three minutes, travelling at breakneck speed, they were at the palace.

The carriage came to a halt beneath the archway of Madame Adélaïde's apartments. The two friends helped the King all the way to his daughter's drawing room, where he sat down. He had not been expected to return from the Petit Trianon that evening, and had to wait for his bed to be made up. The news spread rapidly that the King was ill. The princes and the most important officials came running. As soon as the King had been put to bed, the royal family were admitted, but only remained for a moment. Only the Comtesse du Barry and the Duc d'Aiguillon had the privilege of remaining and watching over him. Madame du Barry was still stubbornly insisting that it was only indigestion. At nine o'clock, the King received the cabinet, the Comte de Lusace, and the ambassadors of Naples and Spain, and gave the watchword as usual. La Borde went to find out what was happening, and reported that the fever had risen still further and that the headaches were getting stronger.

Nicolas waited for a long time on a bench in the great gallery. At about ten, La Borde came to find him. The most important thing, he said, was to ensure the sick man's security and tranquillity. The King's bed having been installed in his real bedchamber,[1] visitors and those who usually had access to his person would have to be turned away. They made arrangements with the pages and bodyguards to bar the bull's-eye antechamber and move back by one room all those reserved for persons of honour, the show bedchamber thus taking the place of the council chamber. La Borde informed Nicolas that the King, in a peaceful moment, had asked for 'young Ranreuil' to stay close to him and assist the First Groom. The Duc d'Aiguillon had tried to raise an objection, which the King had dismissed irritably. The comtesse, on the other hand, had been favourably disposed to the idea and surprised by the minister's hostility towards such a faithful servant. Nicolas dozed for part of the night on a bench in the council chamber.

Friday 29 April 1774

Early in the morning, he was woken by La Borde. It had been a very bad night. The King had been extremely restless, and neither dabbing his temples with opium nor any other remedy had succeeded in calming him. The morning passed in anxious expectation. At about nine, Le Monnier, in agreement with the First Surgeon, decided to bleed him. The operation was performed in public, and the three bowls of blood drawn were left on a console table in full view. Nicolas, standing in the shadow of the fireplace, could see, as could everyone present, that the patient did not seem in the least relieved. The two doctors withdrew to the council chamber to discuss the next step. Le Monnier, who had been so optimistic the previous evening, now contemplated calling on his colleagues' expertise. Nicolas, who had followed them, eavesdropped on a lengthy debate as to who would receive the honour of being consulted. Lorry, the Duc d'Aiguillon's doctor, and Bordeu, the Comtesse du Barry's, were chosen. From what the comtesse had been heard saying, Bordeu, who was considered a solid practitioner, seemed ready to be called if the indisposition were to become an illness. The Dauphine's doctor, Lassone, was added to this council, as were others. Gaspard, the page, came and tugged at Nicolas's sleeve: he was being asked for in the King's bedchamber.

The room needed to be cleared. Too many people were pressing in, and the space was becoming cramped and airless. The King lay on a little camp-bed in the middle of the room, bathed in sweat. He was speaking incoherently, in a hoarse voice, often calling La Borde, whom he finally sent to see Madame du Barry, and demanding that young Ranreuil stay there, 'above all, above all'. He repeated these words several times, his eyes searching for Nicolas. By midday, the doctors had arrived from Paris, and now they made their solemn entrance.

They examined the King for a long time, questioning him on his pains. His face was flushed, and he complained of headaches. No one seemed concerned to determine the true nature of his illness, and the Faculty held forth at length on the possibility of a catarrhal fever. The King was still restless and so, after much hesitation, the doctors ordered him to be bled a second time, and possibly even a third. The whole of Versailles was soon buzzing with the news, and the royal family again came running. The secret meetings and intrigues resumed with renewed vigour.

'Bled for a third time!' said the King. 'Bled for a third time! So I am ill, after all. It'll lay me low, I tell you.' He clung to this idea, questioning the doctors with his eyes. 'I don't want it done. Why a third time?'

In the rooms preceding the patient's bedchamber, Nicolas

watched, appalled, as the secret meetings went on. This bleeding was becoming an affair of State. The doctors, attacked on all sides and drawn alternately to both factions, wavered. What was at stake was clear to everyone. Depending on whether or not they were favourably disposed to the interests of Madame du Barry, one side feared and the other hoped for the verdict. Some described the King as being terrified at the prospect of a third bleeding, which would finally convince him that he was ill, and could have dangerous consequences for a man as weak as he was: specifically, recourse to the sacraments and the sending away of Madame du Barry. They pointed out to those as yet undecided the risks for themselves of making irreconcilable enemies of the King's mistress and his First Minister. Monsieur de La Borde sided with the comtesse's faction, as much out of genuine friendship for her as out of concern for his master's anxieties. The others, arguing that it was important for the King to be at peace with his conscience in the grave situation in which he appeared to be, were using the demands of religion as a pretext for their desire for revenge on Madame du Barry and the Duc d'Aiguillon. Nicolas did not know what to think. In the end, the doctors settled for a second bleeding towards evening. The King almost fainted and asked for vinegar. Deeply worried, he had his pulse taken every moment.

'You keep telling me I'm not ill and I'll soon be cured. You don't believe a word of it. You must tell me!'

At five o'clock, he received a visit from his daughters: they had been called by La Borde, who had thought it only fair, given that Madame du Barry had already been summoned. But Nicolas was upset to see so many people flooding into the room. Apart from the princes, the Gentlemen of the Bedchamber, the servants, the doctors, the surgeons and the apothecaries, an inquisitive crowd kept coming in and out, despite instructions to the contrary. Once again, there was not enough air to breathe. At about ten, the King was showing the doctor his tongue when La Martinière, about to give him something to drink, thought he saw some suspicious red blotches on his face. Without manifesting any surprise, he asked the servants to bring the light closer, on the pretext that the patient could not see his glass. All the quacks present observed the phenomenon with a surprise that was a confession of their own ignorance. Acting as if nothing had happened, they went into the adjoining room to confer. Like a shadow, Nicolas followed them.

None of them were keen to name the suspected disease openly, instead using convoluted terms to describe it. Some saw in it only a skin rash, others a fleeting attack of smallpox, although they did not dare utter the word. It was La Martinière who spoke up at last.

'What we are observing, gentlemen, is an acute fever, violent headaches, pains in the small of the back, dryness of the skin and a rash on the face. What are we to conclude?'

Again they all came out with meaningless words.

The First Surgeon reacted impatiently. 'What, gentlemen, can your science have failed all of you? Let me tell you, then: the King has smallpox with severe complications. For my part, I consider him lost.'

A profound silence followed this bombshell.

'That is a very careless comment to make,' said Monsieur de Duras, First Gentleman of the Bedchamber, who had been following the discussion.

'Monsieur,' replied La Martinière, 'my duty is not to flatter His Majesty, but to tell the truth about his health, and what I have just advanced cannot be denied by any of these gentlemen. They all think as I do, but I am the only person to say it because I regard it as a point of honour to present the whole truth.'

Murmurs rose amongst the gathering.

'So the King is lost?' said the Duc de Duras. 'What more can be done?'

'Take care of him and prolong his life as much as is humanly possible, that is all we can do. He tried to tempt nature, but nature wouldn't listen.'

'All the same,' said Le Monnier, 'are we sure it's that? I was always told that the King had already suffered an attack of smallpox, in 1728! And besides, look at his age!'

'His Majesty's age has nothing to do with it,' sighed Lorry. 'Last January, Monsieur Doublet, Chancellor to the Queen of Spain, uncle of the Marquise de Montesquieu and the Comtesse de Voisenon, died of smallpox at the age of seventy-eight.'

'What makes you conclude that the attack is so severe?' asked Lassone, the Dauphine's doctor.

'Alas,' said La Martinière, 'the symptoms reveal the most dangerous form, the kind where the rash is confluent. Did you observe the pustules, not separated, but joined together? The whole body will swell, especially the head, and there will be a great deal of salivation. This form of the disease is generally complicated by purpura and anthrax and the patient usually dies on the eleventh day after the onset of the disease.'

A terrifying silence followed this declaration.

'I'm sure we can do something,' said Le Monnier.

'We can try,' replied La Martinière, 'but for a person to recover using ordinary methods is more likely to be due to nature than the efforts of those who treat him!'

'There is much discussion of the treatment,' said Lassone, 'and opinions are very divided on the matter. The Germans don't go in for a great deal of bleeding, whereas Alsahavarius[2] prescribed bleeding the patient until he faints.'

'It is said,' murmured an apothecary – the doctors immediately glared at him for encroaching on their domain – 'that horse dung is an excellent medication, which provokes sweating and protects the throat!'

'The devil take all that!' said La Martinière. 'We have to apply vesicatories and ease the evacuations with a series of enemas. We must at all costs force the pustules to suppurate then dry out. We have to do everything we can to avoid any reflux of the purulent matter. We must give the patient plenty of cleansing, soothing and fortifying herb teas and apply rose ointment to the pustules. At the very least, we must immediately ease the rash with decoctions of black salsify, lentils and milkweed. It's equally important to give him lots of thinning and moistening drinks, and by way of sustenance, a plain clear soup to avoid stoking the fever.'

Immediately the consultation was over, Nicolas went to La Borde and whispered the Faculty's verdict in his ear. His friend turned pale. The royal family were advised by the doctors to stay away from the King's bedchamber. Although they had not neglected, in officially announcing his illness, to add that 'he was wonderfully prepared and that all would go well', fear of possible contagion immediately spread. The royal family, alone amongst the sovereign houses of Europe, had not adopted inoculation and not one of its members had yet suffered from the disease. The first concern was to force the Dauphin to leave the apartment: it was his wife who dragged him away. All the princes withdrew, except for the Duc d'Orléans, the Comte de La Marche, the Duc de Penthièvre and the Prince de Condé, who, having had the disease, declared that they wanted to continue to see the King. Then Adélaïde, Victoire and Sophie decided that they would be their father's nurses and installed themselves in his private office and the clock room.

As for the servants, they could not escape quickly enough. With a weak smile, La Borde urged Nicolas to withdraw: caution demanded it. Nicolas declared that he had been inoculated some years earlier, at the friendly prompting of Semacgus, who – arguing that the epidemic recurred periodically – had persuaded the whole of Monsieur de Noblecourt's household to undergo this preventive operation. Nicolas had not needed much convincing, having remembered that his father, the Marquis de Ranreuil, a fervent enthusiast for the century's innovations, had himself been persuaded of the effectiveness of the vaccine by the English officer who had been a prisoner at Guérande. He could therefore stay, much to his friend's joy. So could Gaspard the page, who declared that he had had the disease when young. The Comtesse du Barry arrived, to be greeted without any haughtiness by the King's daughters: it was as if the situation had drawn them together. Early in the morning, Nicolas went back up to La Borde's apartments to clean himself and write two letters informing Monsieur de Sartine and Monsieur de Noblecourt of what was happening and why he was being detained at Versailles.

Saturday 30 April, Sunday 1 May and Monday 2 May 1774

The illness was taking its course. The two factions watched each other closely. The day passed without any perceptible deterioration in the King's condition. While it was light, his daughters did not budge, giving way in the evening to Madame du Barry with a murmured exchange of polite greetings. When night came, the fever made noticeable progress and the King began to suffer a great deal. The next day, Sunday, the debate about the sacraments resumed with renewed vigour. The King's daughters joined forces with d'Aiguillon's party, out of concern for their father and to avoid provoking a violent shock whose consequences they dreaded. But the matter was causing increasing scandal, and feelings were running so high that Cardinal de La Roche-Aymon, the Grand Chaplain of France, gave orders to send for Christophe de Beaumont, archbishop of Paris, who alone had the authority to advise the King.

During their long vigil, Monsieur de La Borde had explained the various aspects of the problem to Nicolas. The archbishop was on his way to Versailles with the sacraments. That would clearly involve the expulsion of the King's mistress. But, secretly, the prelate owed it to his conscience to take into account the gratitude he felt for the services Madame du Barry had rendered the religious party, through the removal from office of Choiseul, the elevation of d'Aiguillon and the destruction of the *parlements*. The allies of the archbishop and the friends of the comtesse were openly against the sacraments. On the other side, the 'Choiseuls' were urging the King's officials as hard as they could to adopt their position. This would eliminate from Versailles the woman who had overthrown their great man. So it was that, in all the speculation surrounding the King's conscience, a strange thing happened: d'Aiguillon's party joined forces with the religious faction to prevent Louis XV from taking communion, while Choiseul's party, that of the philosophers and non-believers, were uniting to press for the sacraments. La Borde himself wished only to devote himself to the service of the King, and wanted nothing to do with these intrigues – except that he would not abandon the comtesse's ship in the hour of danger.

Nicolas wandered the great apartments in despair. He was looking, unseeing, at the splendours around him when he heard the sound of weeping behind him. Turning, he found himself face to face with Madame Adélaïde, her face swollen, her eyes red, dabbing her mouth as if this exercise was the one panacea to assuage her grief. He bowed to her. She was no longer the haughty, beautiful young woman he had met fourteen years earlier while hunting in the great park, but an ageing woman whose creased face lit up when she saw him.

'Ah, young Ranreuil, as Father always says.'

She again burst into tears. Nicolas did not know what to do. She seized his hands as if clutching a branch for support.

'Monsieur, I ask you,' she implored, 'what should we do? You who are a faithful and loyal servant of His Majesty, what should we do?'

'About what, Madame?'

She could not have looked more scandalised if he had insulted her. 'Do you not think it is time, Marquis, to lead the King to the idea of the sacraments? The Duc d'Orléans has been urging me to make up my mind. He told me we had to talk to the doctors.'

Nicolas, who had just read the latest bulletin on the King's condition, had judged it anything but reassuring. 'And what did they reply, Madame?'

'That ever since the illness started they had been suggesting the sacraments to the high officials, but that no one was willing to comply . . .' – and here she sobbed – '. . . for fear of displeasing the Duc d'Aiguillon, who has his eyes on them. They also consider that, while the King's wounds are suppurating, he might have an extreme reaction to strong emotion.'

'In other words, Madame, it is important not to act in haste.'

'Yes, I think you're right. We risk putting our father in danger. I insist on the archbishop being watched. He must not be left alone when he is in the bedchamber, in order to prevent him saying anything that might frighten the King.'

'Madame, I think it is in the hands of God, and I am sure that His Majesty will know what it is right to do when the moment comes.'

She thanked him with a weak smile and walked quickly to an adjoining room, where her sisters awaited her. Nicolas noted with a touch of pity that the heel of one of her slippers was coming away and that she limped as she walked.

The next day the archbishop arrived with ceremony. According to rumour, he was suffering from kidney stones and had given up two large ones the day before. In anticipation of a new attack, he had brought his bathtub with him. Having been kept waiting for quite a while in the guardroom – much to his annoyance, given the pain he was in – he was greeted by the Maréchal de Richelieu, who detained him with idle chatter in the bull's-eye antechamber.

Pinned down in a corner of the room with the maréchal's scent in his nostrils, he was subjected to an all-out attack designed to keep him away from his duty. The maréchal's loud voice attracted onlookers, who wished to see this indecent comedy for themselves.

'Archbishop,' the maréchal was saying, 'if you are so keen on hearing confession, come with me and I swear you'll hear some juicy stuff, if you're at all curious about my pretty sins! But don't say anything to His Majesty – you'd kill him as cleanly as if you'd shot him with a pistol, and for no valid reason would be aiding the return in triumph of someone who would do great harm to your Church.'

Alarmed by what he heard, Christophe de Beaumont finally managed to free himself. He caught only a brief glimpse of the King's daughters, but, entering the monarch's bedchamber, saw a woman bending over the bed. At the sight of him, Madame du Barry let out a cry and fled in fright towards the great recess, where she disappeared through a concealed door in the panelling. In the presence of the Duc d'Orléans, the King asked the prelate about his ailments, then turned his back on him. Christophe de Beaumont withdrew. As he crossed the King's study, he caught his foot in the carpet and stumbled. Nicolas ran to catch him before he fell. The archbishop looked at him with his bloodshot eyes. He had aged a great deal since their last encounter. His face was grey and the great lines of bitterness were etched even deeper around his sagging mouth.

'Commissioner,' he said, recognising Nicolas, 'the devil is never very far away when you appear. Yet the Lord wishes you to be the rampart and support of . . .'

All the way to his coach, he continued talking, and Nicolas was unable to tell whether this speech was addressed to him or was part of an inner monologue. The prelate did not respond to any greeting, but pontificated endlessly.

'He is always about us, and it is above all at the hour of death, the moment of transition, that he redoubles his vigilance and manifests the full extent of his malice. How can a man who does not take care of his own house be expected to take care of God's Church?'

The Maréchal de Richelieu, barely concealing his amusement, waved the archbishop goodbye. Once the prelate had gone, he turned to Nicolas and burst out laughing.

'How these churchmen do go on! He's leaving with his head down and his bathtub with him. He pisses blood in Paris and clear water in Versailles!'

Tuesday 3 May and Wednesday 4 May 1774

The doctors' bulletins continued to be issued, always with the same refrain: reassuring symptoms, effective vesicatories, moderate fever, calmer sleep, satisfactory evacuations, a perfectly straightforward rash. Nicolas, who was well placed to know the truth, could see the King getting weaker. On his camp-bed, up against the balustrade, he seemed peaceful enough, but all those who came near him were shocked by the swelling of his head, which had grown as big and red as an earthenware pot. While the King's daughters looked on wearily, d'Aiguillon and Richelieu continued to pull the strings and to conceal the gravity of their master's condition from him. The King began to have his suspicions: if he was not sure that he had had smallpox at eighteen, he remarked, he would think he was suffering from it now. He would ask Madame Adélaïde to undo his buttons and Madame du Barry to stroke his forehead in order to calm the itching. The whole entourage were ever alert for every eventuality.

The following day, despite his own sufferings, the archbishop reappeared and, as before, the Duc de Richelieu did everything he could to dissuade him from his duty, even threatening to throw him out of the window if he dared mention confession to the King. Early that afternoon, with the Duc de Noailles, La Borde and Nicolas in attendance, the King examined the spots on his hands closely.

'It's smallpox,' he said, as if stating an obvious fact. He turned to his companions. 'What a surprise!'

The doctors tried to get the idea out of his head, but it was no use. That evening, the King seemed normal again. The windows were open, the room was well aired and the spring smells of the park chased away the miasmas of sickness. The patient, who was very lightly covered, kept taking his hands out from under the sheet, against his doctors' wishes. He kept up the conversation in an even tone of voice, touching on macabre topics as was his custom. Seeing him so talkative, Nicolas regained hope. Suddenly, the King turned to the Grand Chamberlain, the Duc de Liancourt, and asked, 'This year, during the Christmas festivities, did you see the monk playing the violin in the middle of the river?'

'Yes, Sire,' replied the chamberlain.

They all looked at each other anxiously, as though fearing that the King was losing his reason.

Seeing their expressions, the chamberlain smiled. 'His Majesty has a very good memory,' he said. 'My ancestors gave a large amount of land to the monks on the express condition that every year at Christmas one of them would get in a boat in the middle of the river and play a melody on the flute or violin. The donation would be taken back if the beneficiaries failed to keep up the tradition.'

The King dozed for a little while, then became restless again and spoke at some length to La Borde. The latter approached the Duc de Liancourt, who announced that the King wanted to rest and asked everyone to withdraw. The grand officials and the servants left the room, and La Borde signalled to Nicolas to stay. The King looked round and, realising that everyone had gone out, beckoned the two friends to his bedside.

'How is the moon?' he asked.

'Last quarter today. New moon on the eleventh, Your Majesty.'

'Black moon in the *Almanach*?'

'Yes, Sire,' said La Borde.

Confused as he was by his illness, the King had not lost his habit of never tackling anything directly. He sighed. 'They'd like me to believe it isn't smallpox. They keep trying to convince me. But from the two of you, I want the truth. I not only want it, I demand it.'

The tone emanating from the large red head was that of a monarch in majesty concluding a *lit de justice*. Nicolas looked at La Borde, who bowed his head, his features tense, as if on the verge of tears.

'Sire,' he said at last, 'it has indeed shown itself. They are currently drying you out.'

The King fell back on the pillows. 'Thank you, La Borde. Ranreuil, are you ready to perform one last service for your King? Come closer.'

He looked at him for a long moment, then brought out a small inlaid box from beneath his sheet. With clumsy fingers, he pressed one of the bronze corners to release a spring. The lid popped up, revealing a velvet purse and a sealed paper.

'This box contains some stones of great value and a document of even greater value for anyone who possesses it. If I die—'

'Sire!'

'If I die,' the King went on in a firm voice, closing the box, 'you must take it, at whatever risk to your own life, to the Comtesse du Barry. It is her safe-conduct to the coming reign and her guarantee against any attempt at revenge. If God allows me to come through this crisis, you will give me back the box. Check that no one is at the doors.'

When Nicolas returned after trying the doors to the council chamber and the clock room, the King gave him the box.

'In the meantime, put it somewhere safe . . .'

His words became blurred and incomprehensible. The fever was returning, and his eyes stared out vacantly from his puffy face. He breathed heavily as if feeling suffocated, and his chest lifted, half opening his shirt and revealing his torso covered with spots.

Suddenly he began singing. '*Your King on the bloody bank / Sees Death before him / Flying from rank to rank* . . . Ah, Voltaire! . . . Yes, Maréchal, it is you who command here, and I am the first to give the example.' He sat up, crying, 'The house of the King will give . . . To arms! Ranreuil in the first row . . . We were happy, so happy. Do you remember, Ranreuil?'

La Borde whispered to Nicolas that the King, in his delirium, had taken him for his father, and that he should reply.

'Yes, Sire. Fontenoy was a great day.'

'Oh, yes, the greatest!'

He fell silent and seemed to fall asleep. Two hours went by before he woke again. Once more, he was quite alert, and his words were clear.

'La Borde, now that I am informed of my condition, we must not repeat the scandal of Metz.[3] I owe it to God and my people. Send for Madame du Barry. She must leave Versailles.'

Thursday 5 May 1774

Thanks to Gaspard, the page, acting on La Borde's instructions, Nicolas was able to obtain a horse from the large stables in the middle of the night. He was anxious to put the precious box entrusted to him by the King in a safe place. As he rode, he made sure that he was not being followed, using the usual stratagems to thwart any possible surveillance. Day was breaking when he reached Rue Montmartre at a gallop. His mare lifted her head, overjoyed to breathe in the cool morning. The baker's boys, to whom he threw the reins, looked on admiringly as Nicolas ran into Monsieur de Noblecourt's house. In his apartment, he shifted two books in his bookcase and slid the little box behind them. From the outside, nothing was visible. Who would think of looking for it there? This was where it would stay while there was still any uncertainty about the outcome of the King's illness. After washing himself at the pump in the courtyard, he shaved, combed his hair and changed his clothes. He was just finishing when Catherine knocked at the door and told him that Monsieur de Noblecourt, having woken and learnt of his return, wanted to see him as soon as possible. He followed the cook, accompanied by the yapping of Cyrus. The former procurator sat enthroned in bed in a blue-green dressing gown, his head hidden by a knotted madras. He smiled when he saw Nicolas.

'Back at last! The house has been quite sad without you. Any news?'

'Alas,' said Nicolas, 'the King is quite ill, and I have to return to Versailles immediately.'

'Well, we all knew that! But what are the doctors saying?'

Nicolas, feeling the burden of the secret he was carrying, did not like to deceive Monsieur de Noblecourt. 'They're not very sure.'

'What do you mean, not very sure? There's nothing unsure about smallpox, especially in a man of that age. It needs to be treated vigorously.'

Nicolas was astonished to realise that the whole country knew about the King's condition. In the seraglio-like confinement of the palace, he had assumed that only those closest to the King, including his family, were aware of the truth. The health bulletins that had been issued had never mentioned the fatal illness, although the symptoms had been described clearly enough.

'Cheer up,' said Noblecourt. 'Don't tell me you didn't know the nature of the King's illness?'

'Of course not, but I am surprised by how public it is.'

'That's the only thing people in the street are talking about. It's a great scandal. The archbishop has ordered every diocese to hold forty days of prayer, to display the Holy Sacrament and to recite the *pro infirmo*. And yet . . .'

'And yet?'

'The public who are being commanded to pray don't really understand why there is such equivocation concerning the King's confession. No one knows what's going on. People no longer believe the doctors' reassuring bulletins. Yesterday, a woman who took it into her head to criticise the contents of these was immediately arrested and imprisoned. Paris is filled with your police and their spies, who are eavesdropping on what people are saying and forcing even the most charitable to be more circumspect.'

'They're only doing their job, Monsieur,' replied Nicolas, with a weak smile.

'I'm not saying they aren't, but it only adds to the unease in the minds of the public. Not to mention what people are saying about the origins of this disease. It's so horrible, I can't bring myself to repeat it.[4] But people believe it, oh yes, they believe it as if it's the gospel truth . . . In any case, I thank heaven for having placed Guillaume Semacgus on our path. I'm sure it's his foresight that has saved you. The vaccine is protecting all of us, but you above all, being young. Run to do your duty and come back to us soon!'

Nicolas took his leave of Monsieur de Noblecourt, promising to keep him informed, and, after filching some brioches from the servants' pantry, went to retrieve his mare, which Poitevin had been spoiling by mixing a little old wine with her oats. He left at a jog trot, not wishing to exhaust his mount. This slow ride gave him time to think, something which the gravity of the past few days had prevented him from doing. The endless wait had been like a nightmare, in which nothing was certain any more, and the most stable foundations of his existence were being shaken. He felt genuine grief at the thought of the King's imminent demise: even though, as a mere subject, he was a long way from the majesty of the throne, the ties he had forged with the King over so many years could not be broken without breaking something in his own life. A new world was already emerging, in which everything would have to be rebuilt before the calm and tranquillity of everyday life could be restored.

There was an unusual amount of traffic on the road to Versailles. The Pont de Sèvres was cluttered with all kinds of carriages, and there was a long line of them as far as the entrance to the royal town. It was just after three by the time he reached the palace. He left the mare in the care of a groom. As he went in under the arches, a two-horse coach driven by a grey-clad lackey passed close by him. Inside it, he recognised a sad-faced Comtesse du Barry, accompanied by her two sisters-in-law and the Duchesse d'Aiguillon. The threat of contagion had emptied the apartments, and the odours of infection could be smelt as far as the bull's-eye drawing room. La Borde hugged him in his arms.

'The comtesse has just left for the Duc d'Aiguillon's house at Reuil.'

'I passed her coach under the arches. How is the King?'

'Silent most of the time, only opening his mouth to ask for what he needs. He's worried about whether the lady has left. I told him she left this morning, in order not to trouble him.

"What, already?" he replied. Tears appeared in his eyes, and he turned away from me. He's received the archbishop.'

The long wait resumed. In the evening, the King, feeling better, decided he wanted to get up. The doctors consented, and his trousers were put on. But when he tried to walk as far as his armchair, the pain of the spots on the soles of his feet and the vesicatories hurt him so much that he felt faint and had to be carried back to his bed.

Friday 6 May to Tuesday 10 May 1774

The King had a restless night, and was somewhat delirious. Madame Adélaïde sat on an armchair by the bedside, having taken over the nursing duties previously carried out by the Comtesse du Barry. La Borde and Nicolas took it in turns to stay with her and hand her damp cloths. The next day, the King again saw Cardinal de La Roche-Aymon and the Archbishop of Paris. He refused to speak to them, on the pretext that he could not string two sentences together. In the evening, his face appeared darker, and his voice showed the effects of the pustules in his nose and throat. Every time the word 'confession' was mentioned, he would say he was afraid the pus from his spots would get on to the host: it was a kind of obsession with him, which made his daughters despair. The day passed without any notable developments.

Early on the morning of the seventh, the King asked the Duc de Duras to send for Abbé Maudoux, his father confessor, who was waiting in the chapel, overcome with emotion. He received him for more than a quarter of an hour. As if he had calculated everything in advance, he regained a presence of mind which astonished those around him. He talked to Monsieur d'Aiguillon, then had his daughters brought in and asked them to wake his grandchildren, prescribing exactly how close to him they should advance. In fact, he gave all the necessary orders before again speaking to his confessor. At seven, the Dauphine and the Comtesse d'Artois were in the council chamber, the King's daughters at the door of the bedchamber, and the Dauphin downstairs. Only the servants, as well as La Borde and Nicolas, remained with the clergymen, who stood in a circle around the bed while the King received the holy viaticum.

'Gentlemen,' said the First Chaplain, the Bishop of Senlis, 'the King has asked me to tell you that he begs forgiveness of God for offending him and for the scandal he has caused his people, and that if God restores his health, he will make penitence, support religion and relieve the suffering of his subjects.'

From the bed came a rasping voice. 'I wish I'd had the strength to say it myself.'

On Sunday the eighth, the King's fever increased, his pulse quickened, and his face was an alarming sight. Nicolas realised that the end was near. At eleven, the Suttons, famous English inoculators, were admitted. They had a miraculous powder, an effective specific against smallpox. Refusing to divulge its composition, they were rejected by the doctors, who preferred not to trust the unknown, and dismissed as charlatans.

By Monday 9 May, the King was giving few signs of life. La

Borde, although exhausted, refused to leave his side, and Nicolas made sure he brought him enough food to stop him fainting with hunger. The King was given an especially strong potion, but it had no effect whatsoever. At about ten, it was decided to give him the last rites. Visitors could now be admitted, and the doors were opened. A crowd, which Nicolas noted indignantly was dominated by mere onlookers and by those whose presence was justified more by etiquette than by sentiment, came running in. The King's body was disintegrating, and a repugnant odour came from the room, even though the windows were constantly open. He was surrounded by candles that lit up his bronze, mask-like face, like a huge Moor's head, the features not distorted but enlarged, the eyes covered in scabs, the mouth open. All night, the First Chaplain and the confessor recited the prayers for the dying. From time to time, the King would answer the prayers and utter a few incoherent words. The fever remained very strong until early on the morning of the tenth. The King would sometimes suffer such violent convulsions that his body would be flung into different positions on the bed, which had now been moved towards the windows. The doctors had not given up, and they constantly made him take one remedy after another. At about midday, his death agony began. A little after three in the afternoon, just as Cardinal de La Roche-Aymon had uttered the words *Profiscere anima christiana*, Louis XV expired in the arms of Monsieur de La Borde. The candle in the window overlooking the marble courtyard was extinguished. The Duc de Bouillon came to the door of the bull's-eye antechamber and solemnly announced the King's death. A great noise was heard in the distance, like a regiment charging, or a roll of thunder: it was the crowd of courtiers deserting the apartments and running to greet the new monarch.

Nicolas went out into the park. A light wind, full of the scent of flowers, rustled the big trees. Crowds of people were on the paths. As news reached them, voices rose, and there was laughter. He heard one worker say to another, 'What difference does it make to me? We couldn't be any worse off than we already are.' He felt a tightness in his throat, as if the grief he felt were stuck there, made all the stronger by the general indifference. He realised that his fists were so clenched that his nails were digging into the flesh of his palms. He returned to the palace at about five, in time to witness the departure of the royal family, the new King and Queen for Choisy and the old King's daughters for La Muette, in sixteen eight-horse coaches. A large and already forgetful crowd filled the square and the avenue, erupting in cheers as the carriages passed.

In the deserted apartments, the Duc de La Vrillière was making an inventory of the objects found in the King's bedchamber and office. The First Gentleman, the Duc de Villequier, had given orders to Monsieur Andouille to proceed with the opening and embalming of the body. Nicolas heard the surgeon laugh.

'I'm ready, Monsieur. You can hold the head while I operate, as your duty demands, and in forty-eight hours we'll both be dead.'

Nobody insisted. For Nicolas, the two days that followed were like the road to Calvary. They were content to wrap the King's body in large aromatic sheets before placing it in a lead coffin coated with a compound of lime, vinegar and camphorated brandy. The coffin was then soldered shut and placed inside another coffin made of thick oak. Priests, missionaries and Franciscan and Cistercian monks remained in the chapel of rest, praying, until the time came to transport it to Saint-Denis.

Thursday 12 May 1774

The funeral cortege was due to leave at about seven in the evening, as darkness was falling. Naganda had asked Nicolas for permission to go with him and pay his last respects to his monarch. The two men climbed into Monsieur de La Borde's carriage. La Borde seemed to have aged several years. All three remained silent. The coffin was placed inside a large coach covered in black velvet. Two others were to carry the Gentlemen of the Bedchamber, the chaplain and the priest of Notre Dame de Versailles. These carriages were the same ones the late King had used for hunting. The French Guards and Swiss Guards sounded the salute. A group of pages stood as far as possible from the coffin, holding handkerchiefs over their noses and playing pranks with their torches. As they rode along, the convoy was the butt of the onlookers' jokes. Occasionally, people cried 'Tally ho! Tally ho!' as Louis XV had often done while out hunting, and sometimes they sang, 'Here comes the ladies' man, here comes the ladies' man!' With foresight, the King had built the Révolte road, which made it possible to get from Versailles to Saint-Denis by way of Porte Maillot without having to cross Paris. They reached the old basilica about eleven. After a few blessings, the coffin was lowered into the Bourbon family vault and a small brick sarcophagus was immediately erected around it.

Soon, only a few monks were left at the foot of the altar, praying, in the declining light of the candles. Near a pillar, La Borde, Nicolas and Naganda stood in silent meditation, the Indian as unshakable as a statue. They heard someone weeping near them. It was Monsieur de Séqueville, who had appeared as if from nowhere. The man whose life had been devoted to ceremony was on his knees, chanting in a low voice and describing, amidst sobs, the protocol of an imaginary funeral.

'Alas, my master, how they have treated you! Once the mass was said, they should have proceeded to the last acts of burial. Twelve bodyguards lift the coffin and lower it into the vault. The chief herald removes his coat of arms and his hat, throws them on the coffin, along with his caduceus, then, moving three steps back, cries, "Heralds of the arms of France, come and fulfil your function!" The officers approach the opening of the vault and in their turn throw their caducei, their coats of arms and their hats. The chief herald speaks again and orders the servants to lower the royal ornaments, the dead man's honours, the two sceptres, the pennon, the spurs, the shield, the coat of arms, the helmet and the gauntlets. The Grand Chamberlain, obeying the call of the chief herald, moves the flag of France towards the vault. Then, as grand master of the royal house, he cries, "The King is dead, the King is dead, the King is dead," adding, "Let us all pray to God for the peace of his soul." Everyone bows and prays silently. The Grand Chamberlain raises his staff, which he has lowered towards the vault, and cries, "Long live the King!" three times and adds, "alas, alas . . ."'

Monsieur de Séqueville got to his feet, raised his hands towards the dark ceiling and cried out, wakening the echoes of the necropolis and causing a few trapped pigeons to fly off in panic, '"Long live Louis, sixteenth of that name, by the Grace of God very Christian, very august and very powerful King of France and Navarre, our most honoured lord and good master, may God give him a very long, very happy life."'

Then, in the old church, a moan was heard, almost like a child's: an Algonquin orphaned by France was weeping, beside a loyal Breton, for his dead King.

XI

ILLUMINATION

> To them, we are like a broken vase which is thrown away and no longer used.
>
> SAINT BERNARD

Friday 13 May 1774

That night of affliction ended with a silent return to Versailles. La Borde, whose functions had ceased immediately on the death of the King, invited Nicolas and Naganda to have something to eat and drink in his apartments, which he would soon have to leave. Then all three, accompanied by a tearful Gaspard, set off again on the road to Paris. The deserted palace seemed like a great ship abandoned to the cleaners who were now preparing the apartments for the return of the new King and his Court once the quarantine was lifted. La Borde told them that Madame du Barry had been taken the day before to the convent of Port-aux-Dames at Brie, in Champagne, ten leagues from Paris. Amongst other details, he indicated, looking particularly at Nicolas, that she was in solitary confinement and did not have authorisation to receive visitors for the moment.

'What are you going to do?' asked Nicolas.

'I'm going to stay in Paris. It's been too long since I abandoned my studies, my work and my own affairs. It will help me to forget, and to bear what the future has in store. I'm going to deaden my grief with music, writing and women. That's what everything boils down to . . . We just have to accept it. You'll see, we'll become the "old Court"! Our devotion and loyalty will be considered of no account. People will pretend not to see us, few will greet us, most will turn their backs!'

'You seem very sombre and bitter.'

'You're still young – I'm a little older than you . . .'

'In the old days in my land,' said Naganda, 'when a chief died, all the warriors were killed. They were supposed to serve him beyond the grave.'

'Let us thank God we're not Micmacs,' replied La Borde, smiling weakly. 'Although . . .'

'We will show our loyalty to the King,' declared Nicolas, 'by serving his grandson.'

'Of course. However, the near future is going to be difficult. Condemning the King's true servants, settling old scores, scrambling for honours and positions, and provoking exiles and departures, that's what respectable people will spend their time doing. I've heard that Choiseul has already returned to Paris from his pagoda in Chanteloup, his *lettres de cachet* having been revoked, and intends to see the King at the Château de la Muette.'

'So,' remarked Nicolas cryptically, 'some travelling will soon be imperative.'

'I doubt the new King will show any interest in Choiseul. But then there's the Dauphine, I mean the Queen, who owes her marriage to him. We can't really be sure of anything. And what of you, Monsieur, what are your plans?'

'I'm going back to Brest tomorrow,' replied Naganda. 'From

there I shall set sail for the Americas. I received some letters yesterday informing me that the events I predicted are coming to pass. A cargo of tea was dumped into the sea at Boston last December. The English have decided to impose a blockade and the colonists are intending to defend themselves by force of arms. It's said that regiments have already set sail from a number of ports in England.'

'I hope,' said La Borde, 'that won't be a boon to Choiseul's plans. He's a great adversary of the English, and would dearly like to take his revenge on them for our past defeats.'

La Borde's carriage dropped Nicolas and Naganda in Rue Montmartre. The household was in turmoil. Two days earlier, Catherine, who slept little and often stayed up late, dozing by the stove, had been drawn from her torpor by Cyrus, who was unusually agitated. She had followed the dog, who was moaning and growling, as far as Nicolas's apartments, where she had surprised a masked stranger searching through his bed and his linen. She had not forgotten that she had been a canteen-keeper in the King's armies and had occasionally had to do the work of a soldier. Armed with a cast-iron frying pan, she managed to put the burglar to flight, having first inflicted a number of violent blows on his head. She was helped in this by a furious Cyrus, who tore a piece from the intruder's coat. The man hurtled down the hidden staircase which led to the courtyard and fled. Hearing all this, Nicolas felt a shiver go through him. He rushed up to his room and, with a trembling hand, laid waste to the row of books. The box was still there. He worked the mechanism, and collapsed in relief on his bed: it still contained the purse and the letter. Deciding that he would not let them out of his sight from now on, he placed the box in the inside pocket of his coat, then went back to Naganda and Catherine, who had been left speechless by his disappearance.

'So,' said Catherine, 'did he steal anything? Personally, I don't think he had time. And I promise you his head must still be ringing from the knocks I gave him!'

Naganda was introduced to Monsieur de Noblecourt, whom he charmed with his manners, his erudition and the elegance of his speech. The former procurator questioned him about his people and their customs with all the enthusiasm of a schoolboy. Unfortunately, the young Micmac chief had to get back to Versailles. He took his leave amidst a chorus of friendly words. Monsieur de Noblecourt gave him as a gift Montesquieu's *De l'esprit des lois*, a rare gesture from a man who loved books so much that he rarely parted with them: Nicolas whispered in his friend's ear how generous a gift it was. In return, Naganda gave Monsieur de Noblecourt a sachet of dried bear meat, reputed to be a perfect remedy for rheumatism when used in soup, and two bear's teeth of the finest ivory, which the beneficiary immediately placed amongst the other treasures in his cabinet of curiosities. Poitevin called a carriage and Naganda, surrounded by the whole household and watched curiously by the young baker's boys, said his farewells and left Rue Montmartre accompanied by a unanimous chorus of wishes.

'This man honours all those who acknowledge themselves as his friends,' said Monsieur de Noblecourt. 'What New France might have become with such talents!'

He asked Nicolas to tell him about the death of the King. The account was detailed but omitted some of the more shocking aspects. Nicolas insisted that the King had been quite peaceful at the end, and had remained truly regal in his demeanour until the very last. Monsieur de Noblecourt listened pensively, showing no reaction, and Nicolas feared that he had depressed him. Was it wise to mention such things to the old man?

'There's something I have to tell you,' he said. 'It wasn't mere chance that my room was broken into. I am the holder of a secret—'

Monsieur de Noblecourt raised his hand in a gesture of denial. 'A secret that is yours and that I have no wish to know.'

'A secret,' Nicolas went on, 'and an object which may place me in great danger. I lost my keys, which were probably stolen during a recent mission. I have every reason to suspect a definite conspiracy behind all this. I'm going to give instructions for the locks to be changed on the carriage entrance and the door to my staircase. Caution demands it, especially as I have no desire to put the inhabitants of this house, including you, in danger.'

'I shall make sure it's done. Will you stay with us a while?'

'Not yet. There is a final task I must do: keep a promise I made to the King.'

He went upstairs to get ready. What troubled him were the orders that had been given concerning Madame du Barry's exile in the convent of Pont-aux-Dames. Would he even be received? He resolved to do all he could: the end would justify the means. Even if he had to lie or distort the truth, nothing would stop him. Thinking he might have to impress, he decided to take his commissioner's robe and his ivory rod, symbol of his authority, which he rarely used except for ceremonies at the Châtelet or the Parlement. He left Rue Montmartre at eleven o'clock, having first eaten two pig's ears grilled in mustard that Catherine and Marion had made for him while in the middle of preparing a head of pork in terrine for the dinner which Monsieur de Noblecourt, as church warden of Saint-Eustache, gave every year for the parish council. His last act before leaving was to instruct Poitevin to call in the locksmith. He walked along the dead-end street leading to the church, where he remained for a good quarter of an hour before retracing his steps and plunging into the dark Passage de la Reine de Hongrie, opposite Monsieur de Noblecourt's house, which took him to Rue Montorgueil, where he found a carriage. He harboured no illusions about these precautions, although his long experience of surveillance gave him a fairly good idea of where anyone following him might be likely to slip up. His first stop was police headquarters in Rue Neuve-Saint-Augustin, where he let it be known that he would be absent, without going into further detail. Monsieur de Sartine had just left for the Château de la Muette, summoned by the new King. Nicolas changed carriages, reached Vincennes and set off along the Lagny road towards Meaux.

He was riding through a forest, half dozing, when a sharp crack roused him. The carriage swerved and came to a halt. He got out and noticed that the coachman had his head on his knees. Had the fellow had too much to drink and fallen asleep? As he was trying to shake him awake, a shot rang out and he heard a bullet whistle past his left ear. This was no time to hesitate. Pretending that he had been hit, he fell to the ground. His tricorn was still in the carriage, and in the right-hand brim was the pocket pistol, a gift from Bourdeau, which he never let out of his sight. A rider was approaching from behind the carriage. In the position Nicolas was in, it was impossible for him to draw his sword. Lying near the ditch, amongst the horses' legs, he tensed all his muscles, ready to roll across the grass for a desperate attempt on his attacker. He half closed his eyes, and saw everything around him in a kind of haze. Everything depended on his enemy's intentions. He did not think much of his chances of survival if the man chose to fire a second time. If, on the other hand, he drew his sword, there was a small chance that he could turn the situation around. He heard the horse advancing cautiously, at a walking pace. There was a brief moment of silence, punctuated only by the beating of his heart. Nicolas was afraid his adversary could hear it, too. The horse snorted and tapped its hoof impatiently. The carriage horses responded by neighing. Silence fell again, then the gravel on the road crunched: the rider must have dismounted. Clearly he was taking the measure of the situation, on the lookout for any signs of life. Nicolas heard the footsteps slowly coming closer. Another shot rang out, from somewhere close by. Instead of being hit, Nicolas heard a muffled cry, followed by the sound of a body falling. Someone was running towards him.

'Nicolas! Nicolas!'

The voice was Bourdeau's. He looked up. The massive figure of the inspector loomed above him. Nicolas stood up and they embraced.

'That's the second time you've saved my life, Pierre. I remain in your debt.'

They considered the damage: the coachman was dead and the stranger was lying on his stomach, beside his horse. He had a red hole in the back of his neck from which issued a thin trickle of blood.

'Congratulations, Bourdeau. What a shot!'

'I did what I could,' said the inspector modestly. 'There was no time to lose.'

'One thing at a time,' Nicolas went on. 'What on earth are you doing here?'

'Oh, that's a long story,' said Bourdeau, sardonically. 'Monsieur Le Floch killed! That would have been the last straw. I would have had to account to Monsieur de Sartine, who would have stood there stony-faced and demanded satisfaction of me, all the while torturing one of his wigs. I can just see it! Anyway, to cut that long story short, it all began when Monsieur de Noblecourt sent for me regarding the attempted robbery in your apartment. Neither of us thought it was chance. There are too many things happening around you. The house was placed under surveillance, with Monsieur de Sartine's blessing. Apart from that, Monsieur de La Borde informed me this morning that you had been entrusted with an extremely dangerous mission, and advised me to have you followed . . . You didn't make it easy for me, though, with all your usual tricks for throwing a pursuer off the scent!'

'You taught me well,' said Nicolas, with a smile.

'At your service! Anyway, until I got to Vincennes, impossible to observe anything, there was too much traffic. But later, on the open road, I spotted a rider who looked suspicious. The most difficult thing was to keep the right distance: far enough away not to be spotted by him and close enough to protect you. This poor coachman was his first victim. At that point, your servant, seeing what was about to happen, went full tilt. I took a short cut through the trees and arrived just in time to shoot this criminal. I was in a cold sweat, I can tell you, thinking you were wounded or worse. But let's take a closer look at our man.'

They examined the body. The man was about fifty, very corpulent, with a greying moustache. Bourdeau leant over to get a good look at him.

'Well, I could swear I know the fellow. I'm almost certain it's Cadilhac.'

'Cadilhac?'

'Yes, a real gallows bird, always suspected, never arrested. He used to rob lucky gamblers on the way out of the dens. It was said he enjoyed protection. In my opinion, he was a creature of Commissioner Camusot, your colleague from the Gaming Division whose schemes you brought to light fourteen years ago. This Cadilhac and Mauval were two of a kind – you remember, the other bastard you dispatched so neatly at the Dauphin Couronné.'[1]

'Now there's a coincidence!' said Nicolas. 'And here's another one. Look at this.'

He removed the white woollen wig to reveal the dead man's bald head covered in greenish bruises: wounds which, it seemed to him, were likely to have a connection with a recent event.

'These bruises are instructive, Bourdeau. Judging by their colour, wouldn't you say they might be what's left of the blows good old Catherine inflicted with her frying pan on my untimely visitor the other night?'

With a grunt, Bourdeau tugged at the dead man's clothes, and pointed to the hem of the maroon coat, where a triangle of serge fabric was missing, clearly torn off.

'And that's the mark of Cyrus! For an old dog, he has good teeth.'

They continued examining the corpse. Searching the coat pockets, they found a dagger, a check handkerchief, a piece of chewing tobacco, a powder horn and a few bullets. The pistol had rolled on the ground. It occurred to Nicolas, who often used his cuffs to keep his black notebook in, to search Cadilhac's cuffs. He discovered a small piece of paper folded in four, bearing an address: *Rue des Douze-Portes, opposite the parchment seller's, fourth floor.*

'Now that's interesting,' said Nicolas. 'A clue at last!'

'That's all very well, but what are we going to do?' retorted Bourdeau, making a sweeping gesture that took in the whole scene of carnage.

'I'm on a mission, as I'm sure you've guessed. I won't attempt to conceal it from you: I need as soon as possible to get to the place where a certain lady has been exiled.' He thought for a moment. 'The simplest thing, my dear Pierre, would be for you to take over from the coachman and get the two bodies to Paris. We'll put them in the carriage. I'll take Cadilhac's horse, yours will follow you. Do what you can for the poor coachman and his family. As for this other fellow, to the Basse-Geôle with him, and make sure this is kept as secret as possible. I want the people who sent him to think that he's disappeared, or better still, that he's deceived them, that, having done away with me as planned, he decided to keep the fruits of his aggression for himself. To make it more credible, spread the rumour, through your informers, that I was attacked by a bandit and robbed. This rumour will get back to whoever was behind this and confirm the hypothesis that Cadilhac has made off with the loot. My poor Pierre, I'm sorry to entrust you with such an unpleasant task.'

'I'd rather be taking back these two than a commissioner!' said Bourdeau. 'From what you say, I deduce that you are carrying something valuable.'

'Nothing escapes you,' said Nicolas, his finger on his lips.

They carried the bodies to the carriage, placed them inside and carefully adjusted the curtains. Bourdeau's horse was harnessed to the frame of the carriage.

They separated, and while Bourdeau pulled the carriage off the verge Nicolas took possession of Cadilhac's horse. It was a fine white gelding, heavy and slightly lazy, but inquisitive and willing. He spoke in the horse's ear for a moment and stroked the soft skin of its nostrils. The animal's ears pointed forward, with interest and understanding. Everything was going to be all right. He leapt into the saddle and set off for Meaux at a spirited gallop, as happy as his mount to be riding with his nose in the wind, smelling the countryside, amidst clouds of dandelion seeds blown from the adjoining fields. He made an effort not to think about this latest of many attempts on his life, which once again had been thwarted by chance. If Bourdeau had arrived a few moments later, it would have been his, Nicolas's, body being taken back to Paris right now. The resurgence of a long-forgotten past was disturbing and anomalous: it seemed to pose a new threat and present him with yet more questions. What would they find at the address he had recovered from the assailant? Where was the investigation leading them?

He avoided Meaux, fearing that other would-be assassins might be waiting for him in the town. One question nagged at him: it was impossible for everything that had happened to have come about only because he was being watched. Someone had known about the mission entrusted to him by the late King. The treacherous, shadowy forces coiling like snakes around the throne had chosen him as their prey in a hunt that had begun months earlier, the starting signal for which had been the crime in Rue de Verneuil.

His destination was situated in a small valley near a village. It was a place where the ladies of the royal family always stopped on the way to Reims for a coronation. The massive grey buildings soon appeared. He came to a halt in a little wood and put on his magistrate's robe. Luckily, he had brought with him the safe-conduct signed by the King making him his plenipotentiary for his journey to England. It was of little value now that the King was dead, but anyone who glanced at it might still be impressed by the royal signature and seal. He got back on his horse and rode at a walking pace through the open gate of the convent. He entered a vast inner courtyard surrounded by dark buildings, including barns, woodsheds, press-houses and stables. The ground was paved with large, loose cobbles on which his horse slipped. One look was all it took to see how grim and dirty the place was, and Nicolas could well imagine the impression it must have made on the comtesse after the splendours of Versailles and Louveciennes. Clearly, the convent was not well maintained, and its prison-like aspect was more apparent than its religious purpose.

After tying the gelding to a ring, he raised the heavy knocker on the main door. There was no response to its dull echo. He noticed a handle sticking out of the wall, which presumably corresponded to a bell inside, and pulled it. In the distance, he heard the expected ring. Before long, the wicket opened and a shadowy figure behind the wooden grille asked him what he wanted.

'Sister,' he replied, 'I have an urgent message to convey to your mother superior, Madame de La Roche-Fontenilles.'

It was La Borde who had given him the necessary information during their return to Versailles.

'Who shall I say wants her, Monsieur?'

'Nicolas Le Floch, secretary to the King in his counsels, police commissioner at the Châtelet, and magistrate.' He had not skimped on the titles.

'Who sent you?'

'Monsieur Gabriel de Sartine, on behalf of the King.'

This was not an irrelevant point in a place like this, which was not only a convent, but a genuine State prison under the jurisdiction of the Lieutenancy General of Police, where women issued with *lettres de cachet* were sent.

'I'll go and see,' said the nun.

The wicket closed with a sharp click. He waited a moment, then the heavy door opened. Without a word, the nun, who was wearing a white robe with a wimple, a black veil and a scapular, beckoned to him to follow her. The interior of the convent looked even gloomier than the exterior. Water dripped to the floor from the old Gothic vaults, and oozed from mould-covered walls. Nicolas shivered, remembering his first visit to the Bastille. The nun opened another door and stepped aside to let him through.

The huge room was bare, its only adornment a large black wooden crucifix above a rectangular oak table, behind which stood the tall figure of the mother superior. He approached and bowed. There was no response.

'May I know, Commissioner, what brings you within these walls?'

'I have been entrusted, Reverend Mother, with a mission by the Lieutenant General of Police. I need to speak with the Comtesse du Barry as soon as possible.'

A look of surprise came over the mother superior's emaciated face. 'Are you unaware, Monsieur, that I have very specific orders to keep her in solitary confinement? They come from very high up and must be obeyed with absolute rigour. In addition, I consider it important not to disturb the poor young woman's rest and tranquillity.'

It was immediately clear to Nicolas that the mother superior had already fallen under the comtesse's spell.

'Madame, my orders are from the King, and I cannot shirk them.'

With a sweeping theatrical gesture, he took out his plenipotentiary letter and presented it to the mother superior at arm's length. Whether because she could not imagine it possible that he was not telling the truth, or because – as he strongly suspected – she needed glasses but, holy as she was, did not want to use them, or because the authority of the gesture confused her, she yielded.

'Monsieur, I cannot oppose the orders of the King. But, if it pleases you, I should like to be present at this interview.'

He acquiesced, only too happy that he had succeeded so easily.

She clapped her hands, and the door opened. The nun who had shown him in appeared and was asked to fetch the comtesse. A minute or two later, Madame du Barry entered. She was in full mourning: in black lace with a mantilla on her head. Nicolas was grateful to her for not choosing white, the mourning colour of the queens of France. Her eyes looked big and red, but her grief-stricken face, devoid of make-up, gave her a younger appearance. It was as if she had regained that freshness and youth that had so captivated the King. She returned Nicolas's greeting, and it was immediately clear from her expression that she had grasped the situation and that, as a woman who knew all about Court intrigues, she would make no objection.

'Madame, the reverend mother has given me permission to speak with you.'

He drew her away from the table, without Madame de La Roche-Fontenilles doing anything to oppose it or hear what he had to say to the prisoner.

'I don't have a great deal of time. The King entrusted me with something I was to give to you.'

He was standing in such a way that his wide magistrate's robe hid what he was doing. He gave her the casket, which she had no difficulty in opening: a sign that she was familiar with it. She removed the contents and gave the box back to him. Her hands were shaking as she broke the seal on the document. She looked at it and her expression changed. She screwed up the paper, then emptied the contents of the purse on to her palm: five grey pebbles. She clenched her fist in anger and he thought she was about to throw the stones in his face.

'Monsieur,' she said in a low voice, 'this is disgraceful! A blank sheet of paper and a few pebbles! You are mocking a disgraced woman and adding betrayal to her misfortunes.'

'Madame, I beg you to hear me. How could you possibly imagine that, having forsaken honour as you believe, I would then come and expose myself to your anger? I came here at great risk to my life, to keep the promise I made to my King as he lay dying. I lied and deceived Madame de La Roche-Fontenilles to get to you and fulfil my duty. How could you imagine I would betray the King's trust? Have I ever given you occasion to doubt my fidelity and loyalty? I would rather run on my sword than let you believe such a slander.'

He had raised his voice, and the mother superior was nodding her head, trying to understand the strange game being played between the commissioner and the comtesse.

'Monsieur,' Madame du Barry went on, calmer now, 'I am inclined to believe you. You sound sincere and your past services for the King speak in your favour. But you must understand my confusion . . .'

'I promise, Madame, that I will clear up this matter and recover the contents of this box. All I can tell you is that the King placed some diamonds in it, together with a document which, he said, would be a safe-conduct to the next reign for the person who possessed it.'

'Very well, Monsieur. I shall wait and pray with these saintly ladies that your quest reaches a successful outcome.' She hesitated a moment, then held out her hand, which he kissed. 'I should like to believe in you,' she murmured.

She withdrew like a shadow. Nicolas thanked Madame de La Roche-Fontenilles, who seemed uncertain what to think of the scene of which she had had mere glimpses. The visitor did not linger. He rode back to Meaux, where he had to requisition a horse at the post house: the white gelding, willing as it might be, was exhausted and would not have been able to take him all the way back to Paris.

It was already quite dark by the time he passed the tollgates. Throughout the ride, his thoughts ever more fevered, he had tried to make sense of what had happened. What had most affected him was the stain on his honour. He knew he would never forgive himself if he was unable to convince the comtesse that he had acted correctly. The first thing he had to do was question Monsieur de La Borde, the only witness to the scene between Nicolas and the late King: perhaps he could throw light on the hidden aspects of the mission.

His friend kept an apartment in town, a mezzanine in Rue de la Feuillade. Nicolas looked at his watch: it was already eleven. It was only with some difficulty that he managed to have the front door of the building opened to him. His friend greeted him in a nightshirt. Nicolas recounted his adventures on the road to Meaux and the torments through which he had passed since his discovery that the contents of the casket had disappeared. La Borde insisted that he knew nothing more of the matter. The King had not told him anything, and he knew only what Nicolas knew. As they were speculating on how the diamonds and the document could have gone missing, a servant entered and informed his master that a priest was asking to see him. La Borde asked Nicolas to excuse him and withdrew to his antechamber. He returned after some considerable time, a dejected expression on his tired features.

'Nicolas,' he said, collapsing into a *bergère*, 'steel yourself. What do you think of Gaspard?'

'A dedicated fellow, clever, helpful, pleasant – but, in my opinion, much too keen on personal gain to be trusted completcly.'

'A perceptive comment, which shows up my own stupidity. I always considered him entirely devoted and discreet. It was I who recommended him to the King.'

'What has he done for you to question your judgement?'

'He's been betraying us for a long time. The priest who asked to see me has just heard his confession. He's in a small room at the top of the house, where my servants live. He's been ill ever since we got back from Versailles. The doctor I consulted has diagnosed smallpox of the worst kind.'

'I seem to remember that, when the servants were asked to leave the King's bedchamber, he said he wasn't afraid, because he'd already had it.'

'He lied to us. Since witnessing His Majesty's death, he's believed himself to be doomed and wants to relieve his conscience. He asked the priest to speak to me, which is what I've just been doing. It appears that the man was spying on the King and reporting everything that happened around him. Being greedy by nature, as you observed, he was cashing in on all sides. He was being paid by both Choiseul's and d'Aiguillon's people. He didn't mind whom he spoke to. Unfortunately for him, he was given strict orders by his masters to remain in the King's apartments, even if it meant catching the disease.'

In a flash, Nicolas saw again the audience in the council chamber when the King, in the presence of Monsieur de Sartine, had given him instructions before his departure for England. Gaspard could not have been far away, since it was he who had come to fetch him after the mass. That presumably explained all the things that had happened to him on the way to London.

'Without any doubt,' La Borde went on, 'he was there when the King gave you the box, hidden behind the curtains in the bedroom. He came out once the King had fallen asleep. Do you remember? We were walking in the clock room before the King woke up and asked me to fetch Madame du Barry.'

'That's all well and good,' said Nicolas. 'But it still doesn't explain how the contents of the box were replaced. And if that had already been done, then why was I attacked on the road to Meaux?'

'It may simply be that there were a number of parallel conspiracies, and those behind one didn't necessarily know about the other. Be that as it may, he's asking for your forgiveness. He says you were always very good to him, and he regrets having done you any harm.'

'I hope he recovers. He can rest assured that, since I never trusted him in the first place, I don't bear him any grudge. But I would ask one favour. Let it be known that he's dead. That will protect both him and you, especially as we have no idea what the future has in store and what use we might be able to make of his revelations.'

'All right, I will. What are you going to do now?'

'Let you get some rest, you need it! Tomorrow morning, I intend to report everything to Sartine and ask his advice. Do you think I should let him in on the secret of my mission?'

'The King is dead. That doesn't release us from our vow of loyalty, but it does authorise us to reveal whatever may help his last wishes to be carried out. Besides, the Lieutenant General of Police had our master's full confidence, and knew all his secrets. Except this one, perhaps.'

Nicolas got back to Rue Montmartre to find Catherine waiting up for him. She immediately gave him the keys for the new locks which had been fitted that very day. While waiting for him, she had been baking tarts, using the first cherries from a tree in the garden of Monsieur de Noblecourt's house. He collapsed on to a chair in the servants' pantry. Seeing how tired he was, Catherine decided he needed something sweet. She cut a number of uneven triangles out of the leftover pastry and plunged them in hot oil, where they twisted and swelled as if animated by an inner breath. She recovered them with a skimmer just before they turned brown and placed them on a grate to drain before sprinkling them with sugar. Either because his nerves were on edge or because he was genuinely hungry, Nicolas gobbled up a good dozen of them, which he washed down, as was his custom, with a bottle of cider. Then he went up to his apartment and collapsed exhausted on his bed.

Saturday 14 May 1774

Early the following morning, Nicolas presented himself at the Hôtel de Gramont in Rue Neuve-Saint-Augustin. As he entered the building, he ran into Monsieur Durfort de Cheverny, former presenter of ambassadors, now governor of the Blésois, and a friend of Sartine's. He liked Nicolas, whom he had met at the King's little dinners and who had once helped him by solving a tricky case involving false bills of exchange.

'Commissioner,' said the comte, 'I hope your presence will cheer our friend. Before you go in, I must tell you that your devotion to His Majesty in his last days was a comfort to all those close to him. Now our master is gone, and for an insensitive nation that's an occasion for singing and laughter. When one reign ends and another begins, we know what we are losing but not yet what we are gaining. You will find Monsieur de Sartine in quite a bitter mood.'

'Did something unfortunate happen at La Muette, where he was due to see the King?'

'If you want to put it like that. Being his usual calm self, I fear he lacked presence of mind. The Dauphin – I mean the new King – is the best of men, but wearing the crown is a great burden. He is not sure whom he can trust, having no confidence in any of those currently in charge. His first concern was to ask for his Lieutenant General of Police.'

'It was a sensible move.'

'Of course, but His Majesty embarrassed our friend by drawing up an armchair for him and forcing him to sit down. He asked him a few questions about his post, then opened his heart to him and asked him to indicate which people he thought best able to run affairs. But . . .'

'But?'

'But Monsieur de Sartine dropped the ball. If, instead of saying that he would give his answer within two days, he had come prepared to speak knowledgeably on the various matters requiring attention by the government, the odds are that the young King would immediately have given him his full confidence. He would have become First Minister, instead of which His Majesty, not having found in him the support he had been hoping for, will now look elsewhere.'

Nicolas had been warned: the welcome he would receive from his chief would be the kind he usually received when the man was in a bad mood. And indeed Monsieur de Sartine replied to the commissioner's greeting with a low mutter and an absent air. He did not even seem interested in the wicker baskets, covered with labels, seals and string, containing the latest wigs newly arrived from the best manufacturers throughout Europe, but sat there, looking at his hands, without raising his eyes. Nicolas did not wait for him to ask questions. He recounted how he had attended the King with Monsieur de La Borde, the mission with which he had been entrusted, the events in Rue Montmartre and those on the road to Meaux, his meeting with the disgraced Madame du Barry, and Gaspard's betrayal.

As his story went on, he noted that Monsieur de Sartine's interest was gradually aroused, even though he did not manifest any reaction. He finally stood up and began pacing about the room. Then he sat down again, took a sheet of paper, wrote a few words, folded it and sealed it.

'Thank you, Nicolas,' he said, 'for having been where I was unable to be, due to my tasks here and the difficult situation here in Paris. I appreciate your loyalty. Now we have to trust in the new King. He has done me the honour of listening to me . . . or at least . . .'

He broke off, and gave a slightly bitter smile.

'And besides, he knows you, I think. This letter will allow you to approach him without hindrance. Do not waste a minute. And when you return, do not hesitate to come and report to me, even if you have to wake me. I have every reason to believe that the interests of the kingdom are at stake. We'll speak of that again. Intrigue is the order of the day as never before!'

Nicolas ran down the steps of the building, found a carriage and ordered the coachman to take him immediately to the Château de la Muette, which was situated on the edge of the Bois de Boulogne. On the way there, he thought again about his interview with Monsieur de Sartine. Only once before, in all the time they had worked together, had he seen events upset the precise mechanism of the Lieutenant General's thoughts and feelings in that way. He could not say whether it was a matter of the sorrow Sartine felt at the severing of the close ties he had established with his monarch during their weekly interviews, or the anxiety of a powerful man whose influence, unquestioned until now, could well, with the new reign, diminish and even disappear. This must be on the minds of all Louis XV's closest servants, Nicolas thought: La Borde had expressed the same fear in another form.

As he approached the Château de la Muette, he was surprised by the cheerful atmosphere that seemed to prevail amongst the idle crowd thronging the Bois de Boulogne. Stalls had sprung up, from which pastries and coconuts were being sold. He observed a vendor with a tin dispenser on his back and a cap adorned with plates of copper and heron feathers. Around his waist he had a white apron, and two silver cups hung from his belt on chains. The carriage having stopped for a moment, brought to a halt by the crowd, he heard the traditional cry: 'Nice and cool, nice and cool, who will drink?' A man refreshing himself from one of these cups suddenly saw it jump from his hands and fly away, spattering those around him with liquorice water: someone had walked on the chain and made it taut, thus producing this catastrophe. Some distance away, onlookers were crowding around a magic lantern. Its happy owner promised his prospective customers that he would show them 'what will never be seen anywhere else, the virginity of a girl from the Opéra'. With him was a fat woman who was taking advantage of the growing crowd to sell a box of fragrant almond biscuits hung round her neck on a strap. Despite his grief, Nicolas was not insensitive to the joy of this friendly crowd gathering around the royal residence in the hope, often disappointed, of seeing its occupants and proclaiming their expectations for the new era.

It was at La Muette that the Duchesse de Berry, the beloved daughter of the regent, the Duc d'Orléans, had died. In 1747, the late King had rebuilt it and transformed it into a boating and hunting lodge. Louis XVI and Marie-Antoinette were living there with a reduced staff. Nicolas encountered no difficulty in entering the chateau. The captain of the guards handed him over to the care of Monsieur Thierry, previously First Groom of the Dauphin's Bedchamber, who had now, with the accession of his master to the throne, taken over Monsieur de La Borde's functions. This discreet, courteous man took Monsieur de Sartine's letter, withdrew, then returned and ushered him into a drawing room. Two people were already there. One, wearing the purple mourning coat of the Order of the Holy Spirit, he recognised as the man he still, in his heart of hearts, thought of as the Dauphin, while the other was Monsieur de La Ferté, steward of the royal entertainments.

'Who are you?' the King was asking, looking down his nose at the steward and blinking his eyes.

'Sire, my name is La Ferté and I have come to receive your orders.'

'What? Why?'

Nicolas noted the somewhat abrupt tone. Monsieur de La Ferté shrank back, disconcerted.

'But . . . Sire, I'm the steward for entertainments . . .'

'What entertainments?'

'Your Majesty's entertainments, Sire.'

'Our entertainment is to stroll in the grounds. We do not need you.'[2]

He turned his back on the steward and, as he did so, noticed Nicolas. He did not recognise him at first. His eyes were clear and gentle, but vague: he was short-sighted and, without spectacles, moved in a blurred world which made him look totally lacking in self-confidence. Nicolas remembered the late King's dark, expressive eyes. He was struck again by the new monarch's size: he towered over Nicolas by a good head. But the whole was lacking in harmony, the legs were too thick, the face a little flabby, the teeth very irregular. Still irritable from his encounter with Monsieur de La Ferté, the King approached Nicolas and looked him up and down. At last, his face lit up in a friendly but not very graceful smile.

'Ah, Monsieur, did you know we had a good conversation with your Algonquin friend? Very interesting, in truth.'

Nicolas took Sartine's letter, now quite crumpled, from his coat.

'Monsieur de Sartine, in whom I have full confidence, urges me to hear what you have to say.'

He looked behind him. Realising that he was superfluous, Monsieur de La Ferté backed out of the room.

'We would have done so even without this,' the King went on. 'Our grandfather held you in great esteem, which fully entitles you to have access to our person. We are listening, Monsieur.'

This was said without hesitation and with real majesty, accentuated by the use of the royal 'we', which created a somewhat artificial distance. He sat down and invited Nicolas to do the same. Nicolas hesitated, but had to resign himself after a second, more peremptory gesture of invitation. He decided to get straight to the point, at the risk of seeming abrupt. He explained clearly and concisely what the late King had ordered him to do, as well as the exact circumstances in which the box had been handed over to him in the presence of Monsieur de La Borde. He next spoke about Gaspard's confession. The King did not interrupt him. From time to time, he took out an elaborate watch, more to observe its mechanism somewhat distractedly than because he was trying to show his impatience. Nicolas also evoked, in a succinct manner, the possibility that this episode might have some connection with a case that concerned him closely and because of which the late King had sent him to England. Louis XVI did not utter a word. He rose and tugged at a bell pull. Almost immediately, Monsieur Thierry appeared, and was told to fetch the Duc de La Vrillière, who was still Minister of the King's Household. The graceless little man appeared, bowed to the King and threw a casual glance at Nicolas, who was used to the minister's curt manner.

'Commissioner Le Floch has just revealed all to me,' said the King. 'That doesn't surprise you, I suppose?'

'Good, good. He's one of us, a man of honour. It could not be otherwise.'

Nicolas did not understand anything of this exchange. The King started laughing, positively shaking with mirth. Nicolas, whose grief for his former master was like an open wound, was shocked. But then he recalled that the Dauphin was not yet twenty.

'Monsieur,' the King went on, 'our grandfather was very fond of you. But he also loved the kind of action in which secrecy is everything and prevails over what one owes to the human instruments one uses, even their rights. Carry on, Minister.'

'Very well,' said La Vrillière, looking at the ceiling. 'It was the King who had those stones and that blank sheet of paper placed in the box that was entrusted to you. It was all a ploy to flush out those who wished to seize the box and its contents, by setting them on your trail.'

'But, Monsieur,' said Nicolas, astonished, 'how could the King foresee what was going to happen to me?'

'How? How? Please don't imagine, Monsieur, that you are the centre of all intrigues and the only victim of these plots. We had been aware on several occasions that information to which only the King and a few of his associates were privy had been leaking out. For a long time, we had suspected that it was one of the servants, those who are always around the King and are so much part of the furniture they are no longer noticed. Who this traitor is, we may never know.'

'Wrong,' said the King. 'Monsieur de Ranreuil has just revealed the culprit. A page by the name of Gaspard.'

'Well, well,' said La Vrillière. 'The chapter is closed, then. Commissioner Le Floch remains at your service, Sire, I recommend him to you. This affair proves his loyalty once again, if proof were needed.'

Nicolas had the impression that it was all going to end like this, but he could not agree to it. What of his honour? What of the promise he had made a fallen woman to find the objects entrusted to him by the King? Was he going to remain silent, thus surely earning him the mistrust and contempt of the Comtessse du Barry? He could hesitate no longer.

'Monsieur,' he said to the minister, 'I can understand the King's precautionary measures, but with your permission, Sire, I should like to know what was supposed to happen to the real box.'

'Ah!' said La Vrillière. 'I was supposed to hand it over to the lady after the King's death.'

'And . . .'

'And, Monsieur, to satisfy your curiosity, I did not do so. I considered that, as my master was dead, my service ceased immediately and that there was no further need to carry out his orders. His successor would have to decide whether to revoke or renew them.'

'Nevertheless,' Nicolas said, raising his voice, 'I gave my word to a lady in distress. What must I say to her now?'

'There is nothing to say to her,' La Vrillière replied curtly. 'She should count herself lucky that the King has been so lenient.'

Nicolas was dizzy with indignation. But then he noticed the King looking at him intensely. It was as if a cloud had settled over his face. Was he or the minister the cause of it? Could it be that La Vrillière's fate had been sealed? Was everything now in the hands of this awkward giant, who, for all his easy-going ways, had a good deal of knowledge and common sense, as Nicolas had already seen demonstrated?

'Monsieur Le Floch is right,' Louis XVI said at last. 'A man of good breeding does not lie. Here, Monsieur.' The King took out the little sealed red velvet purse and handed it to him with a smile. 'You may check the contents, Monsieur.'

'Your Majesty is mocking me. You know I would obey the King with my eyes closed.'

'That's good, Monsieur. Here is a letter for the abbess. We have such confidence in you that we anticipated your visit. As for the lady in question, tell her from me – my word is worth more than any scrap of paper – that the respect we have for our grandfather's memory precludes us from behaving in an unseemly way towards her. She needs to be patient, and make sure she is not spoken about. The unfortunate woman is more to be pitied than many of those who have abandoned her.' He cast a sideways glance at La Vrillière. 'In any case, she can rest assured that never – I repeat: never – will Choiseul, whose vengeance I am well aware she fears, return to office. Now, Monsieur, go to cleanse your honour: it is dear to me.'

Nicolas knelt before the King, who raised him up while the minister looked on expressionlessly.

On the return journey, Nicolas forced himself not to think and to concentrate on the spectacle of the street. His first reaction had been to accept and understand the former King's final precautionary measure. He told himself, nevertheless, that a more honest procedure would have been just as effective and would have made it possible for him to be more aware of the risks inherent in his mission. He would then gladly have agreed to be used as bait. But his life was of no account in this affair. The bullet aimed at him had missed him by a whisker and, without Bourdeau's intervention, his corpse would now be rotting in some shady copse in Brie. In truth, he no longer knew what to think. He remembered La Borde's words during those terrible days of the King's agony. Their master, in so far as his condition allowed it, had been tirelessly pursuing a long meditated plan. The firmness of purpose with which he had done so had astonished even La Borde. He had calculated everything, arranged everything, without saying a word. He had only asked for the sacraments when he was convinced he had no other recourse.

He recalled other, more bitter words: those of Bourdeau. The inspector, although as devoted as ever to his task, no longer nourished any illusions about the gratitude and consideration of the powers that be. Gratitude was, in his opinion, the only wealth of the poor, and consideration an illusion of those who thought they enjoyed it. 'That's what the great are . . .' he would say, raising his eyes to heaven. He nevertheless continued to serve his masters without unnecessary qualms. Nicolas vowed to follow his example. The years inevitably brought disappointment. The lessons piled up, but you never learnt from them. In this age of dissipation and corruption, did devotion and loyalty amount merely to naivety? Despite everything, he could not convince himself of that. There was more honour in keeping to one's own rules than in abandoning oneself to the failings of the century. It was with this reflection that he entered the Hôtel de Gramont.

Monsieur de Sartine was just finishing lunch – rather late, as he had been delayed by a number of urgent matters.[3] He came running, his table napkin in his hand. Nicolas reported his audience with the King, word for word. Sartine listened to him icy-faced, without interrupting. A long silence followed.

'So,' he said, 'the Duc de La Vrillière knew right from the start about the mission with which the King entrusted you?'

Another silence fell. When Sartine opened his mouth again, it was as if he were speaking to himself and Nicolas could barely catch his words.

'I understand him only too well . . . Where I was stupid was in misjudging him despite being such a close friend of his . . . What vanity, to mix sentiment with business . . . And that's not the half of it! Well, I've been servile for twenty years, and proud of it, so why should I be surprised now if I feel a certain disgust? This moment is a decisive one . . . Let's forget elegance, and may clarity take the place of reason.'

He looked up, as if suddenly discovering that he was not alone. His face regained its usual impassivity.

'If such is the case,' he went on, 'it is up to me to inform the King. Here are my instructions: that Commissioner Le Floch – you, Nicolas – after visiting the convent of Pont-aux-Dames, return promptly to Paris. That, aided and abetted by Inspector Bourdeau and by the full apparatus of the police force, he reopen the file on the murder of Madame de Lastérieux. That he place under arrest those witnesses so far protected by the powers that be and duly interrogate them. That the elements of the original investigation, once gathered and matched, be used as the basis of a formal and – I will request this if need be from His Majesty – secret judicial process. For that purpose, a commission over which I shall preside, along with the Criminal Lieutenant and a person of quality whom the King will appoint, will meet to hear you present your evidence and decide how to proceed with the case. I want to throw complete light on this series of events, which I am convinced are linked to hidden political intrigues. Monsieur, your duty is clear. Go.'

Monsieur de Sartine, his face flushed with new-found vigour, left the room, beating his calves with his table napkin, as if thrashing a pair of hunting boots with a riding crop.

Once he had passed Meaux, the sun flooded the road and the surrounding countryside. Through the lowered windows, scents of wet grass and flowers and the uninterrupted chirping of birds were borne in on the wind. The cloudless sky added to the serenity of this new journey on which Nicolas had immediately embarked, happy to complete his mission and impatient for the coming actions, which, he fully expected, would finally allow him to reverse the bad luck he had for too long been suffering.

He reached the convent of Pont-aux-Dames just before vespers. He could feel the difference in the welcome reserved for him. No doubt forewarned, the mother superior was lavish in her attentions. He had to agree to attend the service. Madame du Barry, in full mourning, her face bent over her Book of Hours, was like a heavenly apparition that had stepped out of a stained-glass window. Despite their reserve, the younger nuns stole glances at her out of the corners of their eyes, while the older ones looked on sternly. Madame de La Roche-Fontenilles had not been sparing in her praise for 'the poor young woman', vaunting her gentleness, her charm, the crystalline sound of her voice, the elegance of her manners, and even her passionate piety. The comtesse then followed him into the cloister. The spring air was driving out the dampness and mustiness of the vaults. The abbess stood back, observing them discreetly with a benevolent smile on her face. He reported the King's words and handed over the velvet purse. She did not bother to check the contents, but clasped it to her heart with a sigh.

'How can I express my gratitude, Marquis?'

He remembered another of the King's mistresses, also in peril, who had called him that.

'By remembering me, Madame, as a faithful and loyal servant of the King,' he replied.

'I pray heaven, Monsieur, that one day I will again have recourse to your help.'

'You will have it.'

She asked him to wait a moment. When she returned, she handed him a gold snuffbox decorated with guilloches, its lid adorned with a miniature portrait of Louis XV.

'This is all a poor woman can do to show her gratitude.'

He bowed. He was not so moved as to prevent himself smiling inwardly, hearing the comtesse, whose fortune was immense – a fortune to which he had just added by bringing her five diamonds, the last gift of an old lover – talk about her poverty.

'Madame, please believe me when I say that I shall never forget this moment.'

He took his leave of the two women and set off back to Paris, still overflowing with ardour. The crime and treachery weaving their snares around him would meet their match. He would bring down the hydra in whose clutches he had been trapped since Julie's death. Just as the sun disperses the shadows, so light and justice would unmask the guilty. Rays flooded the inside of the carriage, spraying the threadbare velvet of the benches with shimmering ripples. In these days when everything was uncertain, his happiness swelled with a new determination, freed from sadness and dread.

XII

THE BATHS OF JULIAN

In life, all is a mixture . . .
Nothing is one, nothing is pure.
CHAMFORT

Sunday 15 May 1774

After a night of dreamless sleep, Nicolas woke refreshed, his mind alert. He accompanied Marion and Poitevin to early mass at Saint-Eustache, abandoning himself to the reassuring sound of the prayers and chants and the smell of incense, which, in this stormy weather, served as much to disperse the insidious odours rising from the crypt, where the inhabitants of the parish continued to be buried, as to honour the Lord. It was in this same church that he had attended the funeral of Rameau – here, too, he recalled, Madame de Pompadour had been baptised. Then he reproached himself for becoming distracted, as he had so often done at school, and concentrated on his prayers, imploring heaven to help him see that justice was finally done. A pastoral from the Archbishop of Paris, relating the death of the King, was read in the pulpit. The piece, which was eloquent and full of solace, ended with an account of the Dauphin's gesture of distributing alms to the poor and beseeching them to ask heaven to preserve his grandfather's days. A fervent murmur rose from the crowd of worshippers.

Back in Rue Montmartre, the smell of hot bread from the bakery revived his appetite, reminding him that he had not eaten the previous evening. Catherine, a freethinker who usually derided church services and the schemes of priests, greeted them mockingly, her hands on her hips. This attitude saddened old Marion, who was trying without success to convert the former canteen-keeper whom she loved like a daughter come to her late in life. Nicolas sat down to a mountain of brioches and a steaming pot of hot chocolate.

Despite the sacred character of Sunday, he decided to go to the Châtelet. He wanted to look through his notes and examine his little black book, to bring together all the various elements of the case and try to find a connecting thread. As the weather was increasingly heavy and humid, he went on foot, glad to have donned a white coat of lightweight twill: he hated perspiring. Old Marie did not seem surprised to see him: he had long ago become accustomed to his chiefs' unpredictable hours. In the duty office, Nicolas was pleased to discover Bourdeau, who was sweating blood over a report.

'Good,' he said, 'your presence will save me a good page of writing. I didn't know you had come back from Meaux. I was doing the best I could for your sake.'

Nicolas briefly summarised the latest events: his audience with Monsieur de Sartine and his meeting with the new King, leaving until last the unexpected orders which again set them on the trail of an unknown adversary.

'That at least has the merit of being clear,' said Bourdeau, approvingly. 'Our motives now coincide with the wishes of the Lieutenant General. No more scruples! I brought the two bodies back to Paris. The coachman's, made to look presentable, was handed over to his family with a decent sum of money which will assuage their legitimate hunger for explanations. The other body was examined at the Basse-Geôle. The bumps and bruises do indeed come from Catherine's frying pan. There's someone who hasn't lost her touch since Fontenoy! In order not to panic the household, I gathered Cyrus's testimony in the garden, offering him a piece of biscuit as an incentive. When I showed the brave animal Cadilhac's clothes, he bristled and foamed with rage. I've never seen him in such a state.'

'So Cadilhac was definitely the person who broke into my room?'

'There's no doubt about it. Finally, I dispatched a whole host of spies under Rabouine's direction to Rue des Douze-Portes. The traps have been set. Right now, I'm waiting for Tirepot. He's really one of our best informers: his paraphernalia is so visible, it no longer attracts attention.'

'That's all well and good,' said Nicolas. 'But to attend to the most urgent matters first, we have to put Balbastre and Madame de Lastérieux's notary Master Tiphaine under lock and key at the Châtelet, and keep them in total confinement. There's another move I thought of, which we'll have to discuss with Semacgus: couldn't Awa talk to Julia, the slave Casimir's companion? She might do better at getting the poor girl to talk than we would.'

'I think that's a good idea,' said Bourdeau. 'It may help to explain some of the things Casimir said that don't tally with other observations. You're right to want to take everything from the beginning. A new look may reveal the whole story.'

Nicolas took a bundle of papers from a cupboard and spread

them on the table. Then he opened his little black notebook and started examining it closely. Meanwhile, Bourdeau seemed to be drawing up a list from which he occasionally crossed out a line, his brow tense with concentration. It was while they were thus engaged that Tirepot surprised them. He entered, pursued by an indignant Old Marie, who did not understand how anyone could have the effrontery to bring into such a temple of the law the self-evidently foul instruments of his daily trade, those two buckets linked by a bar and covered with a wax cloth beneath which anyone could sit down and relieve himself for a few *liards*. To provoke him, Tirepot was singing in a throaty tone his eternal 'You all know what you need to do!'

'Peace, my lambs,' said Bourdeau, trying hard to contain his laughter. 'What did you do to Old Marie, you rogue, to get him so flushed?'

'He was trying to stop me coming in with my gear, Monsieur Pierre, saying it was disgusting. Well, it's my bread and butter, and I've been shouting myself hoarse telling him that, all too aware of the honour you've granted me, I emptied my buckets and rinsed everything in the river before coming here. The whole thing's so clean you could eat your dinner off it. And anyway, I left my convenience at the bottom of the stairs. It's Sunday, it won't bother anyone there.'

'Come now,' said Nicolas, 'make peace, you two. Old Marie, bring four glasses of your cordial for us to seal it, as friends and Bretons.'

The usher puffed at his clay pipe and seemed to think for a moment. 'Only because Tirepot is a Breton, and from Pontivy . . .'

He went to fetch the glasses.

'What's the news?' Nicolas said at last, addressing Tirepot.

'There's so much that Rabouine was worried I might forget some of it,' Tirepot replied. 'He made me promise not to leave anything out. I'm delivering it still hot. I've been repeating it to myself on the way.'

'I'm listening.'

'In Rue des Douze-Portes, opposite the parchment seller's, there's a house which is neither rich nor poor. On the fourth floor a man lives on his own, apart from an elderly-looking maid, who arrives every morning and leaves at about one o'clock. The man's habits are somewhat irregular. Since we've been watching him, he's been coming and going at all hours of the day and night. He often has his meals in a little tavern nearby, but never talks to anyone there. He always uses roundabout routes, as if he's afraid the men of the watch are after him. He's harder to keep track of than a needle in a haystack. But the fact is, all his wanderings regularly lead him to the d'Aiguillon mansion.'

'Good work!' said Bourdeau.

'Definitely,' said Nicolas, boiling with impatience and downing in one go the glass of cordial Old Marie handed him. 'But you've forgotten the most important thing. Who is this man? Did you find out his identity?'

'You know him, and so do I,' replied Tirepot. 'It's Camusot, who used to be the commissioner in charge of the Gaming Division. The one who was in league with La Paulet. A shifty character you had a brush with once before, Nicolas. He nearly did away with you, thanks to his crony Mauval, that thoroughly bad lot you dispatched at the Dauphin Couronné.'

'He was convicted of abuse of authority and suspected of much more,' said Nicolas. 'Mauval was his henchman, but the only punishment Camusot received was to be removed from his post at the head of the Gaming Division. I thought he'd retired to the country.'

'Not a bit of it,' said Tirepot. 'Rabouine asked me to tell you that the First Minister uses him to do his dirty work for him. He has his own little agency all set up, prepared to do whatever they're offered provided it's handsomely rewarded.'

'If Camusot's involved, anything's possible,' said Bourdeau. 'He knows the way we work better than we do.'

'Rabouine thinks as you do,' said Tirepot. 'That's why he's changed his plans. His people are keeping more of a distance now, and he's using old men or children to draw less attention. Rue des Douze-Portes, which is at right angles to Rue Saint-Pierre, is completely locked in. The ends of the street, leading to Rue Saint-Louis and Rue Neuve-Saint-Gilles are being watched by our men, who are installed on the upper floors of buildings. A servant in our pay at the d'Aiguillon mansion is keeping us informed. We just have to tighten the noose.'

'Good, Jean,' said Nicolas. 'I'm pleased with you.'

'There's nothing I wouldn't do for such a generous countryman!' Tirepot said, winking and letting his tongue hang out. The commissioner understood the meaning of the gesture, searched in his pockets and took out a few *louis*, which he slipped into an already extended hand.

'Go and seal your peace treaty with Old Marie,' he said, 'and wait for a message for Rabouine. The most important thing is not to ruin what I'm doing: tell him from me to make sure he follows my instructions. Bourdeau and I are going to establish our campaign plan.'

Delighted, Tirepot left the office. Nicolas and Bourdeau were silent for a moment. It was the inspector who spoke first.

'I think,' he said, 'we have to try and connect the man on the road to Meaux with Camusot. This Cadilhac was already working with Camusot fifteen years ago. He tries to kill you and we find Camusot's address on him. Don't forget that Camusot doesn't yet know his hired man is dead – at least we hope so.'

'Let's try and put ourselves in Camusot's place,' replied Nicolas. 'Presumably informed by Gaspard of my mission for the late King, he has me followed. Several hours have gone by since I was given the box and left for Paris. I'm tailed, and quite naturally an attempted theft follows. But Catherine saves the day. We know what happens next: the road to Meaux, attack, failure and death. But Camusot doesn't know the last part. He hasn't heard from Cadilhac. What can he possibly be assuming? If the necessary secrecy has been observed, he has no reason to suspect that his hired killer is dead. The rest follows naturally. He assumes that his accomplice has been bought for a higher price or that, aware of the value of his find, he's run off to take advantage of the loot. Camusot is well enough informed to have heard the rumour, spread by us, that I was robbed on the road to Meaux.'

'Cadilhac was no fool,' said Bourdeau. 'After all, he was privy to Camusot's tricks for years. Camusot must have assumed he's grabbed the diamonds intended for Madame du Barry and . . .'

'And,' continued Nicolas, 'he also thinks the man found a document which is likely to be worth even more if he negotiates its return with some highly placed people. You see what I'm getting at. There's apparently nothing to connect Camusot to the affair, apart from the fact that his address was found in Cadilhac's coat. We have him under close surveillance. Let's say we find a way to lure him out, he responds and we nab him. With a little luck we may be able to follow the chain of this plot back to its instigator.'

'Good,' said Bourdeau reflectively. 'But what kind of trap can we lay? He's not small fry. He'll be all the more suspicious if he knows you're in the vicinity.'

Nicolas did not reply: his eyes half closed, he was thinking. He went out for a moment, paced up and down a little, then came back and sat down opposite the inspector.

'We still have to put ourselves in Cadilhac's skin. What would he do if he really was in that situation? Of course, he might be content with the diamonds. But I don't think so. He knows that what he has in his hands is the opportunity of a lifetime, the big break he's always dreamt of. But he has to play a subtle game. He could for example put an advertisement in *Le Mercure* or *La Gazette*, something like "Object lost on the road to Meaux handed over for reward." An obvious objection is that he'd be exposing himself to discovery when he delivered the text.'

'In addition,' said Bourdeau, 'there's nothing to guarantee the advertisement would even be read.'

'In that case . . . in that case . . .' Nicolas murmured, feverishly. 'Let's say Cadilhac sends a messenger to Camusot's lodgings when our man is out, that the letter is handed to the maid and the emissary disappears immediately. Camusot gets the letter, which informs him that his creature is rebelling, and wants to make a deal, with him in the first place, given all they've shared in the past, but if he doesn't bite then he'll go and knock at the door of a certain pagoda whose master has just returned to his mansion in Paris. Monsieur de Choiseul would no doubt be delighted to get hold of a document which I strongly suspect implicates him.'

'That's better,' said Bourdeau. 'Let's see what happens next. To perfect our plan and ensure the safety of our false Cadilhac, we need to specify that the first meeting will be a mere formality, devoted to a preliminary laying-down of conditions. We should also make it clear that the original of the document is in a safe place, together with a denunciatory letter addressed to whom it may concern in case Cadilhac doesn't come back at the appointed hour to collect his papers.'

'Objection,' said Nicolas. 'The person who comes to the meeting has to be recognised by Camusot. If he doesn't see him, he'll suspect something's not right and that's the end of our plan.'

'We'll arrest him immediately, that'll solve the problem.'

'I've got it,' said Nicolas. 'This is how I see things. Cadilhac doesn't want to negotiate directly, so he sends one of his friends. It could all happen in a church, which would be suitably dark.'

'Camusot won't deal with a stand-in.'

'Please, let me finish. He'll deal with a stand-in if the original is there, a few steps away, inaccessible but near. On an organ gallery for example, letting himself be seen. I can imagine him waving his hand in a mocking way.'

'Are you planning to raise him from the dead?'

'No, but I know you well enough, Pierre, to be sure you've carefully saved Cadilhac's clothes. The lowliest of our spies, or you, or I, can play the part of Cadilhac, in the shadows and at a distance.'

Bourdeau was rubbing his hands with enthusiasm. 'Sounds perfect to me. We still have to decide on the wording and the place.'

'We have to find something intriguing, something like "Cut stone doesn't bring in much. More demand for the paper, which will go to the highest bidder. To find out more, come on Tuesday 17 May, at seven in the evening . . ."' – Nicolas thought for a moment – ' "to the great hall of the thermal baths at the abbey of Cluny. Come alone and unarmed. We will be on our guard." '

Bourdeau shook his head, unconvinced. 'The content is fine, the form much less so. It sounds like something written by a commissioner at the Châtelet, not by Cadilhac. It has to be redrafted.' He took a sheet of paper and a quill, and started writing, crossing words out a few times. 'There you are. I just hope you like it. "To be honest, stones from Meaux, once divided up, won't keep my milk boiling for long. There's much more of a demand for paper. I'll give it up to the highest bidder, for there are some very interested customers, men of the highest taste, who even like pagodas. Come this Tuesday, 17 May, at seven in the evening, to the great hall of the baths of Julian. And no tricks."'

'Yes!' exclaimed Nicolas happily. 'That's really good! I still have to find suitable paper and a clumsy hand.'

'And poor spelling,' said Bourdeau. 'Old Marie will do it.'

'Impossible. Camusot used to work here. He'd recognise the handwriting.'

'All right. We'll find someone. Now we could just send the letter through the post.'

'There's a risk it would be opened, or wouldn't arrive at all. We must be sure it reaches its destination in time. The trap must be foolproof. The purpose of this encounter isn't to arrest the man but to try and follow the chain to the main link. We'll have to reconnoitre the place in the evening, at the same hour as the one we've chosen for the meeting. This is a real puppet show, and we have to play it properly.'

'Who'll play the role of Cadilhac?'

'I will,' said Nicolas.

'That's a very bad idea and I won't let you get involved. What if our man recognises you, even at a distance, and shoots you down, eh? How would I explain that to Monsieur de Sartine? Besides, you're the only person who has the whole of this case in his head. Anyway – and this seems to me the clinching argument – you don't look anything like Cadilhac.'

'I sense a criticism in your words. Don't worry, you'll know everything . . . when I'm sure of my facts. As for your argument, I accept it, though reluctantly. Who to turn to, then? Our people won't be up to it. Rabouine, perhaps?'

'No,' said Bourdeau, 'he's also known to Camusot. We mustn't neglect any detail. The man was about fifty, quite sturdy, with a grey moustache. With a toupee, I could do it. Don't worry, I'll wear a breastplate under my doublet, which in any case will give me more of a paunch and make me look more like him.'

Nicolas thought this over for a moment. 'I don't really like it,' he said at last. 'But it seems as if I'll have to resign myself. We just need to be very careful, and leave nothing to chance. We'll visit the place, preferably in disguise. There must be some old rags in our stocks here that'll make us unrecognisable. In the last resort, I think only you and I should be inside the hall itself. On the other hand, we'll need a tight ring round the area defined by Rue Saint-Jacques, Rue du Foin, Rue de La Harpe and Rue des Mathurins. Nothing and no one will be able to enter or leave without immediately being reported. Those who leave will be followed. I'm going to write to Pelven, who used to be a sailor and is now the doorkeeper at the Comédie-Italienne. He's an old associate of mine. He'll have you admitted there, and one of the members of the company will help you to make yourself up so that you look exactly like Cadilhac.'

'But the theatres are closed for a month because of the King's death.'

'He'll find a way, you can count on that. Take him a plug of tobacco and a bottle of brandy from me.'

'Let's not forget something,' said Bourdeau pensively. 'We're taking all these precautions, but our adversaries may well be taking them, too. I might be followed myself after the meeting. We'll have to keep an eye open for that.'

'Your carriage will go down Rue des Deux-Portes to Rue Hautefeuille. A haycart conveniently overturned after you've passed will do the trick.'

'And you?'

'I'll be there to back you up. I'll get there some time before you, in order not to arouse suspicion. My other concern will be to see if there's a second criminal watching everything in case Camusot doesn't appear. He may not want to enter into negotiation unless he's certain Cadilhac is really Cadilhac. Either he comes himself, or he sends someone who knows Cadilhac to make sure of the blackmailer's identity.'

'You'll have to make sure you don't get there too soon before the meeting. You'd risk bumping into the person you want to unmask.'

'It's not very likely. In fact,' said Nicolas, 'I'll sleep there on the night of Monday to Tuesday.'

Bourdeau looked puzzled. 'Isn't that too soon?'

'The sooner, the better. We have to get them in a panic. The only thing that might happen is that the messenger doesn't get to Camusot, then we'll have to hold off until another time. But I imagine he's on hot coals, anxious for news. He's sure to go home. We'll have to send someone who's unknown at the Châtelet, and he'll then have to go to ground for a few days. If there are any problems, he can say he was approached by a man with a grey moustache who paid him handsomely for the errand. I don't think I've forgotten anything. How about something to eat?'

As they walked to their usual eating place in Rue du Pied-de-Bœuf, not far from the Grand Châtelet, they talked about the news of the day, the main item being the publication of a letter from the new King to Monsieur de Maurepas. Bourdeau, again adopting his acrimonious attitude, mocked the tone of it, which he described as ingenuous. What was the point, for a monarch, of admitting that he did not have 'all the knowledge necessary to his state'? Nicolas, on the other hand, found this modesty moving, and they argued about it at some length. The commissioner mocked his deputy's inconsistency: he usually criticised the absolute power of the monarchy, but now, caught off guard for once, he resented not being able to deploy his usual jibes against the young King.

But the dish of calves' sweetbreads they were served by the tavern-keeper united them in praise. They demanded enlightenment, claiming, as was their custom, that the account doubled their enjoyment. It was a good way to please their host, who sat down at their table and accepted a glass of white wine, nicely chilled to wash down the sweetbreads. What you had to do, he said, was lard them with thin strips of bacon which had previously been rolled in a mixture of herbs, then wrap them in fresh bards and cook them lightly, moistening them with a mixture of white wine and thick stock, and adding salt, pepper, *bouquet garni*, a few slices of lemon with the pulp and pips removed, and, finally, a mixture of gooseberries crushed in a dash of vinegar. As a finishing touch, a little light caramel was just the ticket. The whole thing had to be cooked very slowly for no more than three quarters of an hour. At the end of that time, the sweetbreads were taken out, and you continued cooking until there was almost nothing left of the sauce except a thin, shiny layer at the bottom of the saucepan. Then, and only then, did you roll the sweetbreads in it to give them a glaze. The dish was served on a bed of sorrel heated in the same saucepan. Their feast ended with a few glasses of a kind of ratafia which the host made himself from brandy, saffron, cinnamon, bitter almonds, cloves, orange flowers and sugar – an excellent digestive, he claimed.

They separated before the Apport-Paris. Bourdeau would deal with the letter to Camusot and his own disguise, for which he would have to collect Cadilhac's clothes from the Basse-Geôle. They would meet again at four o'clock to disguise themselves before going to reconnoitre the great hall of the baths of Cluny.

Monday 16 May and Tuesday 17 May 1774

Everything had gone according to Nicolas's plan. A boy had given the letter to Camusot's maid, who had assured him that her master would see it the same day. The doorkeeper of the Comédie-Italienne, delighted that Nicolas had thought of him, had seen to it that Bourdeau had been transformed into a very acceptable Cadilhac. Tirepot having conveyed the commissioner's orders to Rabouine, the widened net was in place. Nicolas and Bourdeau, both unrecognisable, had surveyed the baths on Sunday evening and finalised their preparations. The house in Rue des Douze-Portes and the d'Aiguillon mansion were under constant surveillance by a large number of spies, including a number of priests, some delighted local women, some twenty fake blind people and cripples, and other hired helpers.

Nicolas persisted in his plan of going to the place well before the hour arranged for the meeting. He had disguised himself so well that even Rabouine, who had come for his instructions, took him for some fugitive from Charenton or Bicêtre and would have thrown him out the door if Bourdeau had not intervened, roaring with laughter. Nicolas would spend the night in the thermal baths: that way, he would be sure to detect any hostile presence and be able to intervene in time if the inspector's life was in danger.

And so, on the stroke of seven, a strange-looking individual hobbled down Rue de la Harpe, a dark narrow passage where two carts were sufficient to block the way and where the intrepid pedestrian who ventured in had to choose between damp walls and the threatening wheels of the carriages. Making sure that he was not being observed, the beggar pushed open the iron gate of the thermal baths and entered the great hall. It was a place of ill repute, much used for clandestine assignations. A hanging garden, like those in Babylon, built over the solid Roman vaults, still crowned the hall: another had collapsed in 1737 along with the vault that had supported it. Nicolas felt once again the awe he had often experienced, faced with this huge, majestic hall with its roots in the distant past.

Despite its bare appearance and the height of the vaults, the bases of the boldly projected arches were supported by consoles shaped like the prows of ships. The eye was drawn to the fineness of the archivolts, arcades and recesses. Nicolas felt as though he had been plunged into an unimaginable world. There were fragile buildings of cob representing farmhouses, sheds and cabins. Against the wall was a raised platform, accessible by a stepladder, on which was a kind of hayloft, collapsing beneath the weight of mildewed hay and abandoned firewood. It struck Nicolas that this would provide an ideal vantage point. He climbed the stepladder. There was straw in profusion here, burst crates and all kinds of barrels. He had a good view of the whole hall, including the main door and the buildings of the abbey. Of course, there was no way out from here, but the position was easily defensible and would allow him to repel an attack if it came to that. Bourdeau had ordered Rabouine to wait for a few minutes after he himself had left in his carriage. If Nicolas did not appear, the whole force would storm into the great hall to give him aid and assistance.

After making sure that he was alone, Nicolas set about erecting a kind of shelter from disparate elements. When finished, it reminded him of a charcoal kiln. He made sure he provided himself with an opening through which to enter and exit, and a revolving plank which created a kind of loophole similar to the one the Marquis de Ranreuil used when shooting mallards from a covert built by a pond near the chateau. As a finishing touch, he strewed the shelter with a lot of branches and hay. Catherine had provided him with a substantial *pâté en croûte* and a bottle of cider. He had with him his miniature dark lantern and miniature pistol, both gifts from Bourdeau, and his sword. To pass the time, his choice had fallen on a book of moral reflections by Marivaux entitled *Le Spectateur français*. He liked its style, and its uncommon insight into the workings of the human heart. It was like a simple philosophical system that you could dip into at will. The author was able to paint virtue in attractive colours that made you love it and vice in colours that scared you away. Nicolas settled down comfortably on a jute sack.

The abbey bell had just tolled nine o'clock, and Nicolas was reading peacefully when he heard heavy steps pacing up and down the great hall. A worker in a black woollen bonnet and a shiny jacket was walking towards the gates, a bunch of keys in his hand. Soon afterwards, Nicolas heard in the distance the creaking of the gates being closed and the turning of a key in a lock. So everything was closed up at night: he could hope for a peaceful evening. But that was to reckon without the insidious columns of ants, which he could only get rid of by constantly killing them or by leaving them pieces of food. That was the price to pay in a city where the countryside was still very present. Attracted by the smell of these same leftovers, mice next arrived, soon followed by rats, whose aggressiveness worried Nicolas until a little black and white she-cat appeared, lifting its paw in a begging gesture and miaowing softly. He won her round with some meat from the pâté and made himself an ally against the rodents.

Again he heard footsteps. The watchman reappeared with a lantern, escorting a couple whom he left alone with the light after being paid. It was clear that the clandestine activities which took place in the baths of Julian were profitable for the man who guarded them. Nicolas had to endure the simpering, the vows, the supplications, the woman's resistance, and finally the noisy conclusion. This was repeated several times, until late into the night. One couple, thinking the hay on Nicolas's platform might be more comfortable, climbed up. The ardour of their love-making almost dismantled his finely wrought edifice. It made him laugh, but the little cat was scared and hid as deep inside his old rags as she could burrow. Once the episode was over, he at last fell asleep.

He woke to birdsong: the whistling of blackbirds, the tenor notes of nightingales, and the amorous cooing of pigeons, echoing around the vaults. The day passed without mishap, its monotony broken only by the occasional visitor, a few loving couples who were less bold than the ones at night, and a peasant who came with a cart pulled by an old nag to collect armfuls of firewood. The wait was beginning to weigh on Nicolas. He started to make anagrams, first out of the names of those closest to him – Bourdeau, Sartine, Noblecourt, La Borde, Semacgus – then from Balbastre, Camusot, Müvala and Cadilhac. His efforts produced some not very satisfactory results. But one of the names, when rearranged, filled him with amazement. Had he stumbled by chance on the beginning of an explanation of what he had suffered since the start of the year? He could not believe his eyes and repeated the operation several times. For a long time, he reflected on his discovery, which was still too incredible for him to tell anyone. If his supposition was right, the missing link in the whole affair had suddenly emerged, like a sign, out of a chance attempt at mental distraction. He tried bringing in other elements, and they all fitted, like pieces in a jigsaw puzzle. Much suddenly became clear . . .

He pulled himself together. No, he decided, his long wait was making him think like a madman. He had to keep a cool head, wait, and hope that other elements would emerge to either confirm or invalidate this absurd theory. His mind must be wandering: as they said in Brittany, 'he was looking for sloes in the brambles.' Making an effort not to think, he returned to his surveillance.

The day dragged on, and he grew increasingly impatient. Some market gardeners came to find tools. A group of boys playing hide and seek almost discovered him, and it was the little cat, proving herself a definite asset, who saved him: coming out of the refuge they shared, her back arched, her fur bristling, she snarled and spat at the boys, who ran away in terror. Nicolas was more and more weary of being cooped up like this. He finished his provisions, sharing them with his companion. A few more visitors came, including lovers who, given the hour, did not go very far with their endeavours.

At about six, he gave a start. Bourdeau had appeared, looking, in Cadilhac's clothes, more real than the original. The inspector placed himself in plain sight on a platform opposite the one where Nicolas was. At seven, a man appeared, dressed all in black. Nicolas could only see his profile. Suddenly the man turned, and he recognised one of the young men who had been playing cards at Madame de Lastérieux's house on the fatal evening of 6 January. Bourdeau advanced to the edge of the platform. The stranger saw him immediately and took a step forward. It was then that the police spy who had been chosen to negotiate appeared. A few words were exchanged. Nicolas guessed the words by reading the movements of the lips: ransom figures for the stolen box, warnings to be careful, a new meeting fixed. There followed a long explanation from the police emissary, indicating that if, unusually, in the hours following the meeting, Cadilhac or his representative were not in a position to go to a particular place, everything would be revealed to the concerned party. Now the action sped up. The young man raised his hand in farewell and withdrew, after a last, intent look at the enigmatic figure of Bourdeau. The spy fled towards the abbey cloister where it had been agreed that he would wait in a remote room, out of sight of those who were surely waiting for him. Nicolas smiled, thinking of the two groups outside: the agents of the Châtelet and the assassins. Fortunately, the spies all knew each other. Some had as their one task to hinder any adverse move.

Bourdeau-Cadilhac quickly left his lookout post and rushed outside to his carriage. Everything had been arranged to throw off any possible pursuers. As for Nicolas, he would melt into the crowd, a beggar amongst beggars. The hardest thing was to be separated from the little cat, which was convinced after their night together that she had found a master. She used all her charms to convince him. Much as he would have liked to take her, her efforts were in vain: Cyrus would never appreciate this young creature in the house. Abandoning the last remains of his pâté, he took advantage of the greedy cat's inattention to silently withdraw. But when he reached the gate, there she was, looking at him questioningly with a mixture of impishness and puzzlement. He could not resist any longer, seized her quickly by the skin of her neck and put her in his beggar's pouch where she fell smugly silent.

Nicolas slipped outside, and crouched for a moment in the corner of the entrance, surrounded by a smell of urine so heady that Mouchette, as he had chosen to name her, stuck out her little head and sniffed in disgust at the odour. He set off in the opposite direction to the Châtelet, then, through narrow alleyways, made his way back to Quai des Grands Augustins. There he found a boat which took him to the Apport-Paris, in the stinking silt on the banks of the river. He was pleased to see the usual congestion around the royal prison. The street vendors were folding their umbrellas and putting away their stalls. Despite the dirt and the proximity of the sinister theatre of justice, the animation and gaiety of the place tempered the horrors of the foul-smelling area which began as soon as you got off the Pont au Change.

He made his way through the crowd to the gothic entrance and slipped inside the old fortress. The duty office was empty: ideal for changing his clothes. Mouchette carefully inspected the premises, taking cautious little leaps and looking generally disgusted. Finally, she jumped on the table, stretched herself, rolled into a ball and fell peacefully asleep. Nicolas had many long hours to wait before his men showed themselves.

*

Suddenly, he was struck by a thought. He was even surprised that it had taken so long to occur to him. Had he been so involved in the practical aspects of the meeting at the baths that he had lost his usual ability to analyse? Now, though, it came to him with blinding clarity: the fact that one of the young men who had been invited to Julie's party had come to the baths as Camusot's envoy proved for the first time beyond a doubt that there was a connection between the crime in Rue de Verneuil and the political intrigues surrounding the King and the Comtesse du Barry. He immediately placed this basic fact within the overall picture he had recently been building up. It tallied exactly with what he had been thinking, even though he did not yet dare formulate a conclusion.

A commotion drew him from these reflections. An excited Bourdeau appeared, still dressed as Cadilhac, but without the moustache. The corridors were filled with police officers and men of the watch, leading three prisoners.

'Look what the latest tide has washed up!' cried the inspector jovially.

'Tell me everything in detail,' said Nicolas.

Bourdeau sat down heavily. 'I left the baths after that little conversation in which our emissary named a price, laid down the conditions and warned against any kind of trickery. My carriage was immediately followed into Rue des Deux-Portes by a cabriolet. Fortunately, the haycart worked wonders, allowing me to get away without my identity being discovered.'

'And the young man from the baths?'

'Hold on, you're going too fast for me! He was duly followed. As for me, I went and took up position beside the Samaritaine fountain, a centrally placed and very busy spot. Messengers kept coming one after the other to inform me of the enemy's movements. That way, we were able, little by little, to tighten our grip around the part of the city we were interested in. Our man entered Notre Dame just before the doors were closed. He allowed himself to be locked in. Our people had slipped in discreetly after him, and were watching his every move. They were able to signal to us from a gallery. The cathedral was soon surrounded. After half an hour, three men came out through a side door. One of them was Camusot. I ordered him to be followed and, as soon as his destination became known, arrested – which he was, a few yards from the d'Aiguillon mansion. As for the other two, they took a cab, after closing the door leading to the cloister and Rue des Chanoinesses. Locking the door behind them, I should say.'

'Balbastre?'

'It seems very likely that he provided them with a key. Who would be more likely than the organist of Notre Dame to have the keys to the cathedral? As for our two customers, they proceeded to Rue du Paon, where they entered a house. Arriving there soon afterwards, I had the two ends of the street leading to Rue Saint-Victor and Rue Traversine closed off. There was no way they could have escaped. They were in a garret at the top of the house. They didn't put up much resistance when we went in, and we soon had handcuffs on them.'

'Who are they?' asked Nicolas.

'A nameless young man and someone you know.'

'Müvala?'

Bourdeau gave a kind of hiccup of surprise. 'Nicolas, you never cease to astonish me!'

'Did you find any useful evidence?'

'Less than nothing. They must have been moving from one hiding place to another. Just some pistols, some swords and a ring with a ribbon.'

Bourdeau handed it to him. Nicolas took it and examined it before stuffing it in his pocket.

He went out to examine the prisoners. An older-looking Camusot looked him up and down provocatively. The unknown young man from the baths bowed his head. Müvala stood impassively with his eyes closed and did not even open them at the approach of Nicolas, who looked at him for a long time. It was too late to start the interrogations now. Orders were given to place the three men in solitary confinement. Nicolas gave firm instructions to the jailer. He was obsessed by mysterious deaths in prison, which were not always suicide, as the poisoning of Casimir had recently shown. It was important, therefore, not only to take away any objects they could use to take their own lives, but also to forbid all contact with the outside world. Nicolas went back to Rue Montmartre. In his room, he put the sleeping Mouchette down on the tiled floor, then himself sank into a deep sleep.

Wednesday 18 May 1774

The cat was introduced to the household without Nicolas having to do anything. Cyrus, who had come to see his old friend early in the morning, discovered Mouchette just waking up. Nicolas had to admire the little creature's seductive skills. She was not at all scared. With a serpentine grace, miaowing softly, she sheathed her claws and stroked the intrigued Cyrus's nose. After a while, the old dog, becoming aware of his responsibilities to this young creature, took her delicately by the neck. Panting and purring, she let him do it. They left the room together.

Once he had finished washing, Nicolas found them both in the servants' pantry, where Cyrus was watching attentively as Mouchette lapped up the milk which Marion and Catherine had poured for her. Questioned by the two women, he explained the animal's presence. They were delighted, having long hoped for feline support in their daily battle with rats and mice. Informed by Nicolas, Monsieur de Noblecourt grudgingly agreed to admit the intruder into his house on the express condition that she did not enter his apartments, in return for which she won herself, after a brave struggle over the hours that followed, a privileged place on the former magistrate's lap. As for Cyrus, he seemed rejuvenated by this new presence at his side.

The following days were devoted to the reopened investigation. Camusot threatened Nicolas, saying that a powerful person, whom he refused to name, would react angrily to his arrest. The nameless young man refused to say anything, as did Müvula. Nicolas was loath to resort to torture, always preferring to trap the guilty through the subtlety of his reasoning rather than the use of force. Balbastre, who was by now a crushed man, had been arrested and imprisoned. Master Tiphaine, warned by a mysterious party, had been apprehended at the gates of Paris while attempting to flee to an unknown destination. In his statements, he had said as little as possible, merely admitting that he had received a will but had not been especially scrupulous about verifying its authenticity. As for the terrified organist of

Notre Dame, it was impossible to get any admission from him at all. The date of the prisoners' appearance before the commission presided over by Monsieur de Sartine was fixed for 31 May.

Tuesday 24 May 1774

In the carriage taking him back to Paris from Vaugirard, Nicolas thought over the long conversation he had just had over dinner with Semacgus, sitting under a big lime tree whose fragrance filled the night air. He also reflected on the imminent hearing of the commission of inquiry. Three magistrates would be presiding: Monsieur de Sartine, Monsieur Testard du Lys and Monsieur Lenoir, counsellor of State, who was being spoken of for the stewardship of Limousin to replace Monsieur Turgot, now that the latter had been appointed to a government post by Maurepas. His participation in the commission had been decided by the King. Claiming to be a lifelong friend of his, Sartine had confided in Nicolas that Lenoir had enjoyed the trust of the late King, having been asked to deal, not only with the affairs of Brittany, but also with some letters of the monarch's that had been stolen from an unknown lady. He was accustomed to secret matters. Nicolas did not find that very reassuring: he was convinced that Lenoir was closely connected with Monsieur de Maurepas – a rising power and the cousin of the Duc d'Aiguillon – and with Monsieur de Saint-Florentin, the Duc de La Vrillière.

He would have to play things close to his chest, not reveal too much, attack through suggestion, not mention famous names and reconcile irreconcilables. It would not be an easy task. Nevertheless, he considered himself a match for that learned assembly, in which he had an ally in the form of his chief. Monsieur Testard du Lys also liked him, although he had a tendency to fall in with the decision of the majority. But if his demonstration failed and the hearing did not result in certain defendants being charged, the case might be closed and he would never rid himself of the suspicion that hung over him. Whenever anyone talked about the murder in Rue de Verneuil and the subsequent events, they would revive the rumours about him, which would spread to both the Court and the city.

He still had a few cards up his sleeve, however. What Semacgus had told him about the conversation between his African cook Awa and Madame de Lastérieux's maid Julia threw an interesting new light on the affair – provided Julia agreed to repeat her confidences before the court. In addition, there was what the navy surgeon, questioned on a specific medical matter which had intrigued Nicolas, had revealed to him. His friend had thought about the question, and had then turned his library upside down until he had found one of the old campaign notebooks, wrapped in oilcloth to protect them from sea water, in which he had jotted down his operations, his ports of call, and his remarks on the flora and fauna of the countries he had visited. According to this particular notebook, he had spent one whole night in Madras in 1755 in conversation with a group of Indian healers, Buddhist monks and an Arab doctor. Nicolas's question had awakened his memories, especially of a surprising fact that he had learnt in the course of that night. He explained it in detail to Nicolas, who immediately drew his own conclusions from it, though he was not sure how exactly he would be able to use it at the hearing.

XIII

THE SEAL OF SECRECY

Oh, Caesar! these things are beyond all use
And I do fear them.
SHAKESPEARE

Tuesday 31 May 1774

The hearing of the commission having been fixed for ten o'clock in the morning, Nicolas proceeded to the Grand Châtelet on foot: a necessary exercise for him before the ordeal of his appearance in court. On his arrival, Monsieur de Sartine introduced him to Monsieur Lenoir. He was a man of average height, and although he was not excessively corpulent his figure was in marked contrast to Monsieur de Sartine's leanness. He had a plump, florid face, with a hooked nose and gluttonous lips, but very gentle brown eyes. On closer examination, a curious asymmetry became noticeable: depending on which profile was presented, the face could appear either kindly or stern. His left eye, deep-set and still, seemed to pierce those he looked at. His natural hair had been combed back from the forehead and fell on either side in three rows of curls. He spoke softly, as if holding something back.

The hearing was being held in the same room as the Lieutenant General's weekly audience. Monsieur Testard du Lys entered and walked towards his colleagues, hugging the wall. He greeted them and threw a friendly glance at Nicolas, whom he had known for a long time. He was naturally shy, and his evident embarrassment was no doubt due to the fact that he now found himself between two of his predecessors in the office of Criminal Lieutenant. Monsieur de Sartine ordered the doors to be closed before he began speaking.

'I hereby declare open this hearing of the extraordinary royal commission which has been given the task of throwing light on the murders of Madame Julie de Lastérieux, a slave from the West Indies named Casimir, and Monsieur du Maine-Giraud, and on the various attacks committed or attempted on the person of Monsieur Nicolas Le Floch, commissioner at the Châtelet, secretary to the King in his counsels, assigned by us to special investigations. The documents, information, testimonies and other observations gathered by our commissioners, inspectors and officers are and will remain under the seal of the most absolute secrecy, taking into consideration the interests of the Crown. Commissioner, you have the floor. We are listening.'

Nicolas bowed and took a deep breath. In a flash, he relived all the doubts and anxieties of the past few months. He became aware that, for the first time in his career, he was not acting merely as an investigator and prosecutor. In trying to elucidate this case, he hoped not only to avenge the memory of a woman he had loved, but also to defend his own honour and prove his innocence. The cries and noises of the city, coming in through the open window, brought him back to reality.

'Gentlemen,' he began, 'it may seem surprising to you that a man so closely involved in an intrigue whose consequences have been highly dramatic and who was suspected from the first of having played a crucial role, should, on the orders of the King, be called upon to present evidence and sum up the case before you. I did not ask for this fearsome honour. It has fallen to me because of the confidence that both His Majesty and the Lieutenant General of Police have in me. That said, let me come to the facts, which I intend to relate to you as fully as possible.'

Monsieur de Sartine was straightening the curls on his wig, Monsieur Lenoir was writing, and Monsieur Testard du Lys was looking attentively at the speaker.

'On Thursday 6 January 1774,' Nicolas resumed, 'after an exchange of words with my friend Madame Julie de Lastérieux, I left her house in Rue de Verneuil at about six thirty in the evening. Present in the house at the time were Julie, her two black servants, Casimir and Julia, Monsieur Balbastre, the organist of Notre Dame, Monsieur von Müvala, a native of Switzerland, and four young men who were unknown to me. I decided to go to the Théâtre-Français: Commissioner Chorrey can testify to the fact that he saw me there. Then, having calmed down, I took a cab at about ten o'clock in order to return to Rue de Verneuil. I gave the coachman such a generous tip, I'm sure he remembers me. Having a key to the house, I let myself in. Let me be clear about what happened at this point. The party was in full flow and, humiliated at being treated as of no account, I decided to leave again but, before I did so, went into the servants' pantry to recover a bottle of wine. There, I was seen by Monsieur von Müvala and on my way out by Casimir, whom I bumped into. I left the house for the last time and returned to Monsieur de Noblecourt's house, where, feeling ill, I fainted. That was about midnight. The next day, 7 January, at two o'clock in the afternoon, I woke and learnt the news of Madame de Lastérieux's death. As for what had happened between ten fifteen and midnight the previous evening, I really do not know what I did or where I went.'

'So you admit you have no proof?' said Lenoir. 'That seems strange.'

'Monsieur, when I got back I was covered in mud, and my clothes stank of brandy. The next day, Monsieur de Sartine advised me to lie low in Monsieur de La Borde's apartments at Versailles, with the collusion of a page named Gaspard. A double took my place, and I disguised myself and accompanied Inspector Bourdeau on his investigation.'

'I hope this does not mean,' said Monsieur Testard du Lys, 'that the Lieutenant General of Police allowed an officer of his who had been implicated in a murder to participate in this masquerade. That's something I couldn't accept.'

'You will have to, my dear fellow,' said Sartine. 'You need to realise that this was the only way to ascertain the veracity and sincerity of our commissioner's assertions. I wanted Inspector Bourdeau to keep a close eye on him and see what his attitude indicated as to his guilt or innocence.'

'Ah, I see!' exclaimed Testard du Lys, raising his arms to heaven.

'This subterfuge,' Nicolas resumed, 'made it possible for me to be present at a preliminary visit to Rue de Verneuil, where the scene of the crime had been left as it was, awaiting further investigation. The corpse presented evidence of a terrible death . . .' At these words, he had to break off for a moment. 'We discovered Julie lying on her bed in her nightdress. Contrary to her custom, the windows were closed. Bourdeau and I found a plate of chicken in a sauce from the West Indies and a half-empty glass containing a whitish liquid. We also found some sticks of green wax and muddy prints on the floor. Bourdeau observed that these prints exactly matched the boots I was wearing.'

'Are you saying, Monsieur, that the prints came from those boots?' asked Monsieur Lenoir, sharply.

'No, Monsieur. I had two pairs, one of which was in Rue de Verneuil, where I kept a number of things.'

'And where was that pair?' asked Sartine.

'They had disappeared from the closet where they were usually kept. Someone clearly wanted to make it seem as though I had come back to see Julie that same evening. Let me remind you that it had been snowing and the ground was muddy. Only Julie and the two servants knew that pair of boots even existed. The autopsy performed on the victim proved that she had been poisoned, and also raised a number of interesting questions. As was her custom, she had eaten nothing solid. So who was that chicken wing for? Obviously, once again it was there to suggest that I had been in the house, that dish being my favourite of those prepared by Julia and Casimir. The practitioners' suspicions eventually fell on the liquid. Further examination confirmed this supposition. If the chicken had not been poisoned, the liquid was. There too, I was in the firing line, since I often prepared eggnog for Julie. In fact, it was on the subject of eggnog that we had had our very public quarrel earlier that evening.'

'Do you know the nature of the poison?' asked Monsieur Testard du Lys.

'Alas, no! Fragments of crushed seeds were found, which suggests that a vegetable poison was used. However, another hypothesis emerged, which was that these fragments might have been intended to conceal the existence of another poison, which although powerful may be difficult to detect.'

'And what was the aim of this ploy?' asked Monsieur Lenoir.

'To put the blame on someone who was familiar with the house and knew that the two slaves had brought spices with them from the West Indies and used them in their cooking. After all, I could easily have had access to those spices. The suspicions were piling up, made even worse by a letter of denunciation from Monsieur Balbastre claiming that I had been in the kitchen on the evening of the tragedy. He couldn't have known this himself, so he must have been told by Friedrich von Müvala. Monsieur de Sartine then revealed to me the special role Madame de Lastérieux had played as an agent of the police, using her residence as a place to gather information, and even on occasion testing the loyalty of the King's servants.'

No one batted an eyelid at this revelation, except Sartine, whose thin lips tensed.

'Balbastre, questioned by Bourdeau, and somewhat driven into a corner, confirmed this and confessed that it was he who had been given the task of bringing Julie and myself together. He was clearly very afraid of someone important, whose name he refused to reveal.'

Nicolas judged it prudent not to mention the hypothesis that Balbastre belonged to some mysterious Masonic lodge.

'Was it by any chance you who asked Balbastre to do that?' Lenoir asked Sartine.

'Certainly not,' replied Sartine curtly. 'We have no idea whose initiative it was.'

'Meanwhile,' Nicolas resumed, 'Monsieur von Müvala had vanished, but before doing so he, too, had found the time to send a letter of denunciation to the Criminal Lieutenant.'

'Of course,' said Monsieur Testard du Lys, 'it would have been preferable in every respect if the contents of the letter had been kept from the prime suspect. Then he could have been arrested, taken to a place of justice and duly interrogated, tried and—'

'Sentenced and hanged!' said Sartine. 'Fortunately, my dear fellow, the late King judged otherwise, or you would now have a miscarriage of justice and the death of an innocent man on your conscience, and I know how much you care about having a clear conscience. I prevented that happening to protect the reputation of the law and the good of the State.'

Monsieur Testard du Lys sighed and muttered something under his breath.

'I should add,' said Nicolas, 'that this new informant proved to be something of a mystery man. There is no record of his having either entered or left the kingdom. All we knew of him was a remark from Balbastre to the effect that he was interested in botany, and my own observation that he played the pianoforte proficiently. I ask you, gentlemen, to remember these two points. As I said, the man disappeared, and all our efforts to find him proved fruitless. At that point in the investigation, a wise old friend of mine remarked to me that Julie's murder probably concealed more than one thing. There was a great deal of truth in the observation.'

Monsieur de Sartine raised his hand. 'Gentlemen,' he said, 'Commissioner Le Floch will now go into some detail about a series of events so private and so closely involved with the interests of the throne and of the late monarch that I think it necessary to bind you to the most absolute secrecy regarding what you are about to hear. We are listening, Monsieur Le Floch.'

Nicolas cleared his throat. 'Advised to distance myself from the scene of the drama, I was entrusted by the late King with a secret mission to London. Madame du Barry, informed somehow of my departure, crossed my path at Chantilly. There followed several attempts both to kill me and to steal the papers I carried as the King's plenipotentiary. Miraculously, I escaped these attacks. Returning to Paris, I learnt that Madame de Lastérieux had named me in her will as her sole heir. In addition, there was a letter from Julie, posted by her servant Casimir on the night of 6 to 7 January, implying that a reconciliation was possible between us.'

'I must say that letter doesn't quite fit in,' said Sartine. 'If we assume that there was a plot against you, and that somebody was trying to make everyone believe you were jealous, surely the letter would seem to remove any motive for violence, thus proving your innocence.'

'Provided I had received it in time! Of course, Monsieur, your argument is a reasonable one, and I myself have given the matter a great deal of thought. However, there is much doubt as to the authenticity of this document. A master in the art of detecting forgeries will so testify before this court. Now, if this letter is indeed a forgery, then the man or men who were trying to get me condemned may well have hoped that again suspicion would fall on me. After all, who knew Julie de Lastérieux's handwriting better than me? Who had more examples of it in his possession? There was even a phrase of Molière's, inserted in such an artificial manner that it could not help but attract attention. If we add that the will, too, is a counterfeit and contravenes the legal rules, then the very falsity of the two documents could just as easily have been used against me.'

'Do you mean,' asked Lenoir, 'that both the letter and the will are forgeries designed to throw suspicion on you?'

'That is precisely what I mean. It also appears from Doctor Semacgus's researches in the Jardin du Roi that a drawer containing a spice from the West Indies known as *piment bouc* was emptied of its contents by a visitor not long before Julie de Lastérieux's murder. It so happens that this visitor, Monsieur du Maine-Giraud, lived in Rue Saint-Julien-le-Pauvre in furnished rooms belonging to Monsieur Balbastre, one of the parties to the drama in question. Our discoveries must themselves have been discovered, and this young man was horribly murdered and his death made to look like suicide. There are two suspects to this crime. One, who went in disguised as a Capuchin, left the house in the shape of a young man, the other, who was recognised as Balbastre, went into the house and came out a short time later to take refuge in the private mansion of . . .'

Sartine threw him an imperious look which made the expected name die in his mouth.

'. . . of a highly influential individual. You should also know, gentlemen, that we discovered some bloodstained shoes and a Capuchin's robe in Monsieur Balbastre's house. Last but not least, the famous boots belonging to me, which had disappeared from Rue de Verneuil, reappeared miraculously in the bedroom in Rue Saint-Julien-le-Pauvre.'

The three magistrates looked at each other. They seemed

dismayed by the turn Nicolas's presentation of the facts had taken.

'I was amongst those who had the unfortunate privilege of attending His Majesty the late King in his final illness,' he went on. 'Just before his death, he entrusted me with another mission. I was to deliver a box containing a number of precious stones and a document to Madame du Barry at the convent of Pont-aux-Dames. This object I kept first at Monsieur de Noblecourt's house in Rue Montmartre, from where, gentlemen, there was an attempt to steal it. It was then that I realised why my keys had been stolen during my journey to England. It explained, on the one hand, the strange message which led us to have the Seine dragged at Pont Royal to find an empty jewel box, and on the other hand, how a stranger was able to enter my apartment in Rue Montmartre. In the first case, they wanted to make it seem as if I had disposed of the keys to Madame de Lastérieux's house, and in the second, they were trying to misappropriate those things entrusted to me by our dying master.'

'This story of yours, Monsieur,' said the Criminal Lieutenant, shaking his head, 'is becoming less and less credible as it goes along.'

'Then you will be even more surprised, Monsieur, by what happened next,' replied Nicolas. 'I was attacked on the road to Meaux, and only owe my life to the foresight of Inspector Bourdeau, who killed my attacker. This turned out to be Cadilhac, a low criminal and the henchman of former Commissioner Camusot. He had a paper in the cuff of his coat with Camusot's address on it. I'll pass over Comtesse du Barry's surprise on discovering that the box was filled with pebbles and a blank sheet of paper. It was the King himself, gentlemen, our new King, who revealed to me the precautionary measure taken by his grandfather. I was a kind of decoy. His Majesty was in possession of the diamonds and the document all the time.'

'And how does all this end?' said Monsieur Lenoir.

'We needed to track down the person who had tried to get hold of those things. We tricked him into thinking that he had been cheated by his emissary Cadilhac. Thanks to this trick, which involved a meeting arranged at the thermal baths, we were able to arrest three suspects: Commissioner Camusot, Friedrich von Müvala and a young man who has so far obstinately refused to give us his name.'

'Evidence, Monsieur, evidence!' cried Sartine, leaning towards Nicolas.

'I shall do my best to give you satisfaction. First, you will hear witnesses whose words will confirm my arguments. Then, I shall interrogate the suspects and, with God's help, try to convince you of their guilt and make them admit their faults and crimes.'

One by one, Julie's notary Master Tiphaine, Master Bontemps, senior member of the Company of Notaries, Monsieur Rodollet, public letter-writer, then the Châtelet agents Bourdeau, Rabouine and Tirepot, and finally Doctor Semacgus were introduced and questioned by Nicolas and the three magistrates. Master Tiphaine came out with the same excuses he had given before, but remained silent about the reasons for both his journey to Holland and his second, abortive departure. Master Bontemps, wrapped in a tunic of cat skins despite the heat, destroyed his fellow notary's reputation in a few scathing words. Monsieur Rodollet expounded his observations on the documents that had been submitted to him – in such detail as to leave the members of the commission in an even greater state of perplexity. Bourdeau gave an account of his investigation, Rabouine and Tirepot described the surveillance and the events following the meeting in the thermal baths. Finally it was the turn of Julia, Casimir's companion, a small dark form wrapped in shawls. Nicolas walked up to her.

'Julia,' he said gently, 'could you repeat for us—'

Monsieur Testard du Lys interrupted. 'I consider it unseemly for a black slave to be heard before our commission. Monsieur Le Floch seems to be invoking some kind of technicality, and I cannot be a party to it.'

The three magistrates began conferring. It seemed to Nicolas that the exchange of views was a lively one: he saw Monsieur de Sartine underline his arguments by hammering with his fist on the table where the commission sat.

'Please continue,' he said at last to Nicolas. 'The majority wish to hear this witness.'

'Julia,' Nicolas resumed, 'I'd like you to repeat what you told Awa.'

'Casimir was very angry with Madame Julie,' the young woman said, in a slightly lilting accent. 'She didn't keep her promise to free us when we got to France. She changed her mind. He didn't know which way to turn. He nearly told Monsieur Nicolas, who was so kind to us. Not like Madame, who was hard sometimes.'

'Why didn't he tell him?' asked Lenoir.

'He said it was because the two lovebirds were so close, it

would never work. When the other man, the younger one, started coming to the house—'

'Monsieur von Müvala?'

'Yes. Casimir talked to him about it. One thing led to another, and the gentleman suggested a deal. He was in love with Madame. He wanted a potion that would help him . . . you know. In return he promised a very large sum of gold, enough to get away. Casimir hesitated for a long time, then decided there was no harm in it. The night Madame died, he prepared eggnog, adding some powder provided by Monsieur von Müvala. That gentleman also asked for a plate of chicken, then told Casimir to say that he had posted a letter from Madame, during the night, without asking any questions. Another man came during the night and threatened him if he didn't say that he had seen Monsieur Le Floch in the kitchen. We didn't understand. It was only after we found Madame dead that we started to get worried. Casimir made me promise not to say anything. He said he would never admit he had seen Monsieur Nicolas. I don't think he did.'

'A man?' said Nicolas. 'Another man?'

'Yes, in a big cloak and boots.'

'Would you recognise him?'

'No, I didn't see him. I just heard his voice. It was an old man's voice.'

'Monsieur Balbastre?'

'No, his voice is very shrill.'

'Do you have anything else to add?'

'You can find the money hidden in our room, under the tapestry.'

'May it please the commission,' declared Nicolas, 'tubes of

louis were discovered, still wrapped in strips of paper from the Comptroller General's office.'

He gave a signal, and two officers emerged from the corner of the room, approached the magistrates' table and placed four heavy tubes of gold coins on it. Monsieur Testard du Lys, who, as Sartine put it, always thought after speaking instead of before, looked at them and exclaimed, 'In your opinion, what does it mean that these *louis* are still wrapped in strips of paper from the Comptroller General's office?'

Sartine was staring at Nicolas.

'Monsieur, I enquired of the cashiers from that office. Gold coins are usually supplied to the great ministerial departments wrapped in that way.'

'And what do you deduce from that?'

'Nothing. I merely make the observation that, unless it came straight from that office, the money given to Casimir by this unknown man must have come from a ministerial department.'

Julia was shown out and Balbastre was called. Nicolas found him unrecognisable. All traces of the powdered, would-be dandy had vanished. Sloppily dressed, bare-headed and unshaven, his face grey, the organist was the very image of wretchedness, like someone whose life had suddenly been thrown off course.

'Monsieur Balbastre,' Nicolas said, 'are you prepared to reveal to us in complete honesty all you know about the murder of Madame de Lastérieux and its consequences, and about the murder of Monsieur du Maine-Giraud, who was your lodger? I call your attention to the fact that your statement will be heard by three magistrates who have been appointed by the King to pronounce on this matter.'

Balbastre turned a distraught face to the members of the commission. 'I have no idea why I'm here,' he stammered. 'Allow me to express my surprise that a person suspected of an odious crime should be the one given the task of questioning me before you. I protest . . . I am the organist of Notre Dame, a composer, a well-known virtuoso, harpsichord tutor to—'

Sartine raised his hand. 'I command you, Monsieur, to avoid mentioning illustrious names, which have no place before this commission. Monsieur Le Floch has been cleared of all charges, by order of His Majesty. He is conducting this case, and I would be grateful to you if you could reply as candidly as possible to the questions which are put to you.'

'What did you do,' asked Nicolas, 'after you left Madame de Lastérieux's house on the evening of 6 January?'

Balbastre, still crushed, refused to answer any questions, including those concerning his presence in Rue Saint-Julien-le-Pauvre at the time of Monsieur du Maine-Giraud's simulated suicide. One again, Nicolas sensed that the musician was haunted by the threat hanging over him. Would they ever know what exactly Balbastre was afraid of?

'I ask that the suspect be held for the moment,' he said. 'I haven't quite finished with him yet. One last formality will be necessary. Let Commissioner Camusot be brought in.'

The man who appeared was quite unlike the man with whom Nicolas had crossed paths at the beginning of his police career.

They had never confronted one another directly, but he knew that Camusot had tried several times to have him killed by his henchman Mauval. Once tall, he was now stooped, his sparse, yellowish hair revealing the bald patch on top of his skull. His deeply lined face was impassive. Nicolas knew this was going to be difficult. There was no direct charge against the former commissioner. An address in a killer's pocket, an encounter in Notre Dame, his frequent visits to the d'Aiguillon mansion: these were not crimes. It would be impossible to confound Camusot simply through questions and answers. He would have to use another stratagem, one to which he had given a great deal of thought.

'Monsieur,' said Nicolas, 'I know you only too well, and have known you for too long, to think for a moment that you might tell me the truth, so I'm certainly not counting on that.'

Camusot raised his head. 'Well, it would be difficult for an innocent man to respond to such an insolent introduction,' he replied. 'Nevertheless, I am enough of a prophet to predict that you and those controlling you will soon be ruing the day you arrested me so unjustly.'

'Monsieur,' said Sartine, 'be careful what you say. It is scandalous that a former commissioner such as yourself should offend the King's magistrates.'

'What were you doing at Notre Dame,' Nicolas asked, 'with Monsieur von Müvala and a young man who claimed to be your envoy? Why did we find your address in the cuff of Cadilhac's sleeve after he had tried to kill me?'

'Believe it or not, I was praying in the cathedral. In fact, I was so absorbed in my prayers that I was not even aware that the hour had struck for the place to close. As for this man Cadilhac, I don't know him. Bring him here, and we'll see who's lying.'

Nicolas bit his lip. It was clear that, even though Camusot had been held in solitary confinement for two weeks, he had somehow got wind of his hired man's death. The rest of the interrogation produced no results. It was like walking on quicksand, every step taken merely adding to the uncertainty.

'I could produce dozens of witnesses proving that Cadilhac was a frequent visitor to the commissioner's lodgings,' said Nicolas, 'but what would be the point? Gentlemen, if you'll allow me, I'd like to perform a little experiment.'

Bourdeau, sitting a few yards behind him, stood up and brought him a pair of boots.

'Look at these boots,' said Nicolas. 'A fine pair, from an excellent bootmaker. They're mine – or were mine. These boots, gentlemen, turn up again and again in this story. After the death of Madame de Lastérieux, they disappear from the place in Rue de Verneuil where I was in the habit of leaving them. But they leave fresh prints – wet, muddy prints – on the floor. And is that the last we hear of them? Not a bit of it! Miraculously, they are found in Monsieur Balbastre's furnished rooms where they seem to play their part in the terrible struggle between Monsieur du Maine-Giraud and his attacker. A tack has been stuck in the sole of one for some time, and here, too, the floor is streaked and scratched where the murderer has moved. It might be supposed that they are now still attached to whoever possesses them. Not at all! Here they are, neatly put away in a closet, where Bourdeau finds them, newly cleaned. Monsieur Camusot, would you please be so kind as to try on these boots?'

'No, I won't. This is absurd.'

'Guards!' cried Nicolas. 'Seize the defendant and put these boots on him.'

It all happened very quickly, with a great deal of force and resistance, accompanied by cries of rage. Two guards seized Camusot from behind and laid him down on a bench. Two others held his legs. Once the boots were on, Nicolas approached.

'It appears, Monsieur, that they fit you perfectly. We take the same size. We could swap boots in the future. Get them off him, and take him away.'

A long silence fell over the court. It was broken by Lenoir.

'Commissioner, perhaps you would like to inform us, poor ignorant fools that we are, as to the purpose of this unpleasant scene? You seem to be groping in the dark along a path known only to yourself.'

'Monsieur,' replied Nicolas, 'what is interesting is not so much that the boots fit him perfectly, what is interesting is the contrary.'

'You'll just have to get used to it,' Sartine said to Lenoir. 'Monsieur Le Floch loves coming out with these enigmatic phrases. He always approaches the truth in concentric circles, and he's never closer to the centre than when he seems the furthest away.'

Monsieur Lenoir shook his head, unconvinced.

'Bring in Monsieur von Müvala,' said Nicolas.

A tall young man in a grey coat strode in and greeted everyone politely.

'Monsieur,' said Nicolas, 'please state your name.'

'Friedrich von Müvala.'

'It appears you're from Switzerland.'

'That's correct. I was born in Frauenfeld, in Thurgovia.'

'You speak French very well, without an accent. Why is that?'

'I was educated by a French tutor.'

'What about your parents?'

'They died when I was a child.'

'And what is the purpose of your visit here?'

'Study and pleasure. I wanted to get to know and enjoy Paris.'

'I've heard that you're interested in botany.'

'Amongst other things. But my major interest is music. Especially the pianoforte, as you know.'

He spoke easily and with each answer turned and looked at Nicolas with a kind of ironic condescension.

'Are you ready to answer the questions I wish to ask you on behalf of this commission?'

'I would have preferred someone else to ask those questions, Monsieur. However, I shall reply with all the respect I owe the authorities of this country.'

'Good. What was your position in Madame de Lastérieux's house?'

'A shared taste for the art of music had brought us together. I dared to flatter myself that she was not indifferent to the discreet tributes I paid to her intelligence and beauty. Our frequent encounters had led her to trust me and she had got into the habit of confiding her sorrows and torments to me.'

How clever all this was, thought Nicolas. It would lead gradually, he foresaw, to slanders and insinuations designed to implicate him, the accuser. Müvala's smooth voice, full of apparent candour, continued with its insidious little music.

'She wasn't happy. Her current lover – you, Monsieur, I believe . . .'

The tone and the words were so insulting to Julie and himself that Nicolas clenched his fists. 'Please go on.'

'Her lover, as I was saying, was harassing her with his constant reproaches. He was becoming increasingly jealous, as manifested in endless violent words and actions which she did not dare describe, but which I could guess at. In short, she was afraid of him.'

'Are you insinuating,' asked Monsieur Lenoir, 'that she feared her lover would resort to physical violence?'

Sartine, whose wig was drooping dangerously, did not seem to appreciate this intervention, judging it ill-timed.

'It's hard to say,' replied Müvala. 'But she sometimes gave me that impression.'

'Monsieur,' said Nicolas, 'perhaps you could tell us your version of what happened on the evening of 6 January 1774.'

'I was invited with four friends of mine.'

'Friends?'

'Acquaintances. It was the kind of evening Madame de Lastérieux was so good at organising. Imagine a mixture of freedom, insouciance, light conversation, music, and games. One of those very special occasions that so displeased this gentleman.' With a movement of his chin, he indicated Nicolas, who remained impassive. 'Four of my friends were playing cards. Monsieur Balbastre, the famous composer, was talking, coming out with all sorts of stories and anecdotes. I was playing the pianoforte and Julie was turning the pages for me. It was such a pleasant moment, and she seemed really relaxed. Then this gentleman arrived and disturbed the atmosphere with his sour tone and increasingly violent words and gestures. He left the place in a raging temper. Everyone was glad to be rid of him and to be back amongst good company.'

To Nicolas, these venomous words were like so many dagger thrusts.

'And what happened after this troublemaker had left?' he asked, coldly.

'Julie was saddened, but her guests were so merry at dinner that her melancholy soon left her. As I've had occasion to remark before, I met this gentleman again . . .' He once again indicated Nicolas with his chin. '. . . lurking with an expression of such concentrated rage on his face that it still makes me shiver.'

'And what was this "gentleman" doing?'

'He was rummaging in the servants' pantry, looking for something, or so it seemed. The servants were a little over-stretched, so I had offered to fetch a bottle. I remember perfectly well how startled he was when he saw me. He was hiding something under his cloak, I have no idea what. On the way out, he bumped into Madame de Lastérieux's black servant.'

'How detailed this all is!'

Monsieur Lenoir tried to intervene, but Sartine put his hand on his arm to silence him.

'Monsieur, please continue with your account of the evening.'

'It finished quite late.'

'What do you mean by late?'

'About eleven. I then accompanied Madame de Lastérieux to her boudoir. She wanted to show me a new perfume. We exchanged some small talk and I left ten minutes later.'

'Again, very precise. You're a remarkable witness and I do not doubt that your powers of observation will allow you to answer my remaining questions.'

'I hope, Monsieur, that I can always anticipate what will please you.'

He gave a quick bow, like a dancer, which Nicolas thought out of place and provocative.

'Perhaps you would be able to please me, then, by telling me more about the perfume.'

'It was a fashionable perfume.'

'Of course. As a matter of fact, I already know the answer. Julie had a passion for Eau de la Reine de Hongrie. I assume that's what it was?'

'Yes, she sang its praises to me.'

'The bottle is unusually elegant.'

'The most exquisite Parisian taste.'

'With a very colourful label.'

'Yes, indeed.'

'I suppose,' Nicolas went on, 'that as was her custom she sprinkled it all over herself. I sometimes reproached her for using it too freely. It was very heady, quite disturbing to those around her.'

'How right you are, Monsieur. She threw it all over her nightdress.'

There was a silence.

'Her nightdress? Surely you mean her gown? It's an understandable mistake, I suppose, you may be confused about the hour or . . . something else.'

For the first time, Müvala's arrogance faded, and he was finding it hard to control his emotion, although it was not entirely clear what that emotion was. Nicolas decided to push the point home. The first skirmish had achieved its aim: to break down the defendant's smugness and put him in a difficult position before three attentive magistrates.

'If I understand correctly,' Nicolas went on, in a chatty, amiable tone, 'after talking about perfume for a few minutes when Madame de Lastérieux was already in her nightdress – no, her gown, please forgive me, her gown – you left Rue de Verneuil. Oh, one thing, though. For your information, Julie hated blended perfumes. She used essential oils, bergamot or citron, dissolved in alcohol. Monsieur Gervais, the apothecary at La Cloche d'Argent in Rue Saint-Martin, who enjoyed her custom, will be able to testify to that. She only put on perfume in the morning, never on her neck and only a little on her arms. I should also point out, for the benefit of the court, that this perfume comes in a damascened silver bottle with a crystal stopper surmounted by a crystal swan. It can be found on her dressing table.'

'So you claim,' retorted Müvala. 'A man over whom a great deal of suspicion hangs, and who is in a position to twist evidence and testimonies to suit him.'

'I'm sure, Monsieur, that the magistrates will appreciate the implausible aspects of what you've told us. Where did you go after you left Madame de Lastérieux's house?'

'To my hotel, in the Marais.'

'Which one? The police found no record of your stay at any hotel. Any more than they found records of your entering the country.'

'I've forgotten. I changed hotels frequently, staying under borrowed names.'

'Why all the mystery?'

'As a foreigner in this city can so easily fall prey to all kinds of crooks and swindlers, it is best to be on the safe side and keep one's identity a secret.'

'And then you disappeared.'

'No, I've been travelling around your beautiful country, visiting monuments and collecting plants.'

'You must have been to Picardy, then? I'm sure the beautiful church at Ailly-le-Haut-Clocher drew your attention.'

'No, I went through Burgundy, Clamecy, Montbard and other places.'

'And yet we haven't found records of your stays in hotels there either.'

'Being of a very sociable character, I was always invited to private houses. I also ate in restaurants.'

'Again I will leave the court to judge. What were you doing in Notre Dame?'

'Praying. I was accidentally locked in.'

'I seem to have heard the very same story from someone else. But let me go on. What were you doing in a squalid garret in Rue du Paon?'

'I was staying with a friend as impecunious as myself. I'd used up all my money playing faro and was waiting for a bill of exchange from my banker.'

'And of course this friend was praying with you in Notre Dame! For his luck to turn, perhaps. What devotion!'

Müvala did not reply.

'One more thing. How is it that Inspector Bourdeau found this when he arrested you in the garret in Rue du Paon?'

Nicolas showed the defendant and the court a ring attached to a ribbon of blue satin.

'I have no idea what that is,' replied Müvala.

'Let me enlighten you. This ring and this ribbon were given to me by Madame de Lastérieux for me to put my keys on: the keys to my lodgings in Rue Montmartre and those of her house in Rue de Verneuil. The ring, ribbon and keys were all stolen from me during a nocturnal attack at the tavern in Ailly-le-Haut-Clocher. And here they are in your possession. Do you have any explanation for that?'

'A conjuring trick! Anyone would think we were at the Saint-Victor fair!'

'I beg the accused to moderate his language,' said Sartine. 'I also note that, for a foreigner, he is well acquainted with our customs. Only old Parisians know the Saint-Victor fair and its attractions.'

'You forget,' replied Müvala, 'that there are guide books for the use of foreign travellers, which describe the sights of the city in some detail.'

The man had an answer for everything, Nicolas thought. He gave another signal, and the boots were brought back.

'One last formality, Monsieur,' he said. 'I'd like you to try on these boots, if you don't mind.'

Müvala gave Nicolas a blank look, took off his shoes and tried to put one of the boots on his right foot.

'Clearly, they're not my size,' he said. 'I have too large an instep.'

Bourdeau stepped forward and confirmed this.

'Good,' said Nicolas. 'Take him away. We'll resume his interrogation later. We haven't finished with him yet.'

'Anyone would think we were in a bootmaker's shop!' remarked Monsieur Testard du Lys, sourly. 'Are these repeated exercises in keeping with the dignity of this court and the majesty of the law?'

'More than you may think, Monsieur. You will see for yourself very soon.'

Sartine got to his feet. 'I must now intervene before letting Commissioner Le Floch continue with his demonstration. We all have this case and its various elements in our minds. The young man arrested with Monsieur von Müvala, who was at the baths to serve as an intermediary between Cadilhac and Commissioner Camusot, bears an illustrious name.' He sighed. 'I have been urged repeatedly to spare the honour of a family. You know our custom with regard to such things. I have been unable to escape the influence of these entreaties. The man made a statement in my presence, and as we speak he is on his way to Lorient, where he will set sail on a ship heading for our colony in Senegal. We can only hope that there he will mend his ways and settle down honestly. The commissioner will summarise for you the substance of his statement, to which I most particularly draw your attention.'

Nicolas took a deep breath. 'Gentlemen, this young man, of whose appearance in this court we have been deprived because of his name and the influence of his family, a fact which I can only deplore . . .'

Sartine shifted uneasily in his chair.

'. . . this young man, as I was saying, told us that on the evening of 6 January he was asked by Monsieur von Müvala to follow me. That is why he knew my whereabouts and movements that night better than I did, and was able to accuse me without fear of contradiction. I recall to this court that that part of my night had remained a blur until then, such was my state of distraction and despair.'

'Please note, gentlemen,' observed Sartine, 'that this testimony completely exonerates Monsieur Le Floch, in case any of you had ever doubted his innocence.'

'We would have preferred to hear the original,' said Testard du Lys.

'Does that mean that you are challenging a testimony which I myself received, Monsieur?' said Sartine, rising to his feet, his cheeks suddenly redder than Nicolas had ever seen them.

'Not at all, not at all!' stammered the Criminal Lieutenant, beating a retreat. 'Let's not say any more about it.'

'What happened next is just as enlightening,' Nicolas resumed. 'The young man told us that the disappearance of Müvala corresponded to the period during which I left Paris for London. Last but not least, he offered us an entirely new vision of the murder of Monsieur du Maine-Giraud. Everything had been so cleverly arranged that our spies were deceived. This nameless young man did indeed visit the house disguised as a Capuchin monk, and came out without his robe. But there was someone else in the house. We discovered, thanks to his testimony, that Monsieur Balbastre owned several furnished rooms in the building. When Bourdeau found the victim's body, the murderer had not left the house. He was hiding in another room, waiting for the commotion following the discovery of the body to die down. We must assume that he is a person of foresight who is well acquainted with the habits and customs of the police. He suspects that the street is under surveillance. He knows he mustn't show his face in any way. He realises that if the simulated suicide doesn't convince the investigators, suspicion will immediately fall on the nameless young man, the Capuchin monk or both. He therefore leaves behind a pair of boots he wore when he was committing his crime. He doesn't know where I am, but he wagers that, if I don't have an alibi, these boots will implicate me in another crime. Chance being on his side, that will confirm what has already been observed of the crime in Rue de Verneuil. Admire the wealth of detail! What a diabolical intelligence!'

'And who do you point to for this accumulation of compliments?' asked Monsieur Lenoir.

'It's still too soon to unmask him. A final verification will be necessary. I promise you, though, that you will not leave this room without knowing his identity. I should add that sending Monsieur Balbastre to that house was a particularly perfidious touch. He was already being blackmailed. How much greater was the threat to him now, when his presence at the scene of a crime could well lead to his being accused of it himself, if necessary.'

'And those mysterious young men?'

'You mean the ones who were present in Rue de Verneuil and have never been found again?'

'Precisely,' said Monsieur Lenoir.

'Monsieur du Maine-Giraud's correspondence with his sister, which we seized, has enlightened us on this matter, leading us to suppose that a life of gambling and debauchery, with the debts that entailed, had made them ripe for blackmail, too, and that they were being used like puppets by men to whom they were bound hand and foot. The city is an abyss in which many innocent young people find it impossible to resist temptation. I ask that Monsieur Balbastre appear again.'

Bourdeau carried a small table and a chair into the centre of the room. On the table he placed a quill, an inkpot, five sticks of green wax and one of red wax, a sheet of paper and a lighted candle. Finally, the pair of boots made their reappearance. Balbastre was just as pitiful as before.

'Monsieur,' said Nicolas, 'please try on this pair of boots.'

His body shaking, the musician did as he was told. They were much too big for him, and he stumbled when he tried to walk in them.

'All right,' said Nicolas. 'Now sit down at this table. You have before you a sheet of music paper. Would you oblige us by filling the first stave with a melody of your own choice, then writing these words: 'The last wishes of Jean-Philippe Rameau.' Then fold the paper and seal it with the red wax.'

Monsieur Balbastre obeyed, writing a line of music and the words he had been given. Nicolas ordered the paper to be brought to him and the defendant to be taken out.

'Talk of the Saint-Victor fair and conjuring tricks!' said Testard du Lys. 'What's the meaning of all this?'

'I hope you will soon be enlightened, Monsieur. I once again call Monsieur von Müvala.'

Before Müvala entered, Bourdeau took away the stick of red wax. The young man had regained all his arrogance. Nicolas asked him to do the same things as Balbastre, emphasising that he should seal the paper with red wax. In no time at all, the line of music and the words had been written. Just as quickly, Müvala took the stick of green wax, heated it and let the melted wax run on to the paper.

'But look what he—' began the Criminal Lieutenant.

'Monsieur, please!' Nicolas immediately interrupted.

He thanked Müvala and had him led out. Monsieur Rodollet was then summoned to appear. He sat down behind Nicolas.

'Gentlemen, it falls to me to throw light on a series of events marked by three murders, several attempts on my life and a desire to appropriate State secrets. This is how I see things. Madame de Lastérieux, an instrument of the secret police, is being watched by the factions who are agitating behind the scenes in expectation that the King's days are numbered and a new reign is coming. Commissioner Camusot, who is in the pay of the leader of one of these factions, orders Balbastre to arrange for me to meet Julie. They suspect that I am often entrusted with special missions. Balbastre is clearly being blackmailed over some past fault, and such is his terror that he is only too ready to obey. Not only does he introduce me to Madame de Lastérieux, but he is also responsible for Monsieur von Müvala gaining a foothold in her house. Alas for her! We must remember that Camusot has hated me ever since I exposed the abuses with which he had been compromising his career. He is hoping to lay a trap for me, to ruin me in such a way that I will never recover. Madame de Lastérieux means nothing to them. He and his accomplice will use her and then coldly murder her. They take a great number of measures to make sure they succeed, such as the use of the slave Casimir as the innocent tool of their Machiavellian schemes. They take so many of these measures that some of them have the opposite effect from what they hoped.'

Nicolas was pacing the room, his eyes closed and his hands together.

'Where they go wrong is in not really knowing Julie's habits. That plate of food in the bedroom – something she would never have tolerated – is one of their mistakes. So is the closed window. And there are others. But all that trying on of boots which so intrigued the Criminal Lieutenant proves that, besides myself, only Commissioner Camusot could have worn them and left footprints in Rue de Verneuil on the evening of 6 January. Which also proves that Monsieur von Müvala was not alone in the house that night. What then of that surprising remark by the person in question – I'm sure it won't have escaped you – about what Julie was wearing? I persist in thinking that no true connection, other than the coquetry of a woman trying to make her lover jealous, existed between her and her killer. Yes, her killer. He saw her dead, in her nightdress. How else could he have known what she was wearing? She would not have received him half dressed. That is the first point we have established.'

'And the second?' asked Sartine.

'Müvala falls into the trap I laid about Julie's perfume and ties himself up in knots. The third point is that we know he had Monsieur du Maine-Giraud steal some seeds of *piment bouc* from the Jardin du Roi in order to conceal the use of a strong poison, the nature of which is still unknown. The fourth point: my attacker in Picardy steals my keys, again with the intention of getting me into trouble. The box thrown in the Seine, so easily recovered by dragging the river, doubtless contained the key to

Madame de Lastérieux's house. The keys to my lodgings in Rue Montmartre are used to get into Monsieur de Noblecourt's house in order to search through my things for the box entrusted to me by the late King.'

'It is rumoured,' said Monsieur Lenoir, 'that there were other attempts on your life during your journey to London.'

'There was a price on my head, according to our English friends in Whitehall. Two factions were pursuing me, Monsieur. For a long time I thought that an indiscretion by Madame du Barry had set this pack on my trail. In fact, we now know that the day the King, in the presence of Monsieur de Sartine, entrusted me with my English mission, one of his domestic servants was hiding in the former wig room, listening to the conversation. It was the same person who overheard the King giving me that box and asking me to take it to Madame du Barry. He was hiding in a room off the recess in the King's bedchamber. That servant's identity is now known to us. He was one of the King's pages, and he was supplying information to the two rival factions, who were both, for opposing reasons, interested in the result of my mission to London, as well as in the document which the late King wanted me to give to Madame du Barry. The connection between these secret political intrigues and the initial murder is clear. One of the factions tries to kill me on the road to Meaux in order to obtain a document which would prevent Monsieur de Choiseul returning to office. Then this same faction, through the intermediary of Camusot and Müvala, does everything it can to recover the document, which has supposedly been stolen by Cadilhac – who in fact is already dead and buried.'

'Commissioner,' said Lenoir, 'we are following you with great attention. But why did these people go to such absurd lengths to implicate you?'

'I was coming to that,' replied Nicolas. 'The hatred I inspire in these two culprits is so strong that they will do anything to make me look guilty. Hence all these excessive tricks, the forged letters, the fake will, even the box thrown in the Seine. That can only be explained if their hatred for me has its roots a long way back in the past, a past I thought had been forgotten.'

'That's all well and good. But so far you've presented nothing but suspicions, certainly serious ones which seem to hang together. Where is the evidence, though? You're impugning the honour of a young man and a former police commissioner, but it's your word against theirs.'

'Please be patient a little longer, Monsieur. May I remind you that this case has lasted five months and that everything has been done to make it unusually complicated. I'd like to call Monsieur Rodollet.'

The public letter-writer got to his feet. He did not seem unduly impressed by such a formidable audience.

'Monsieur Rodollet, this morning you confirmed to us that a number of documents were forgeries. Here are two sheets of paper with music on a stave and a written phrase. You once told me that the forger might have been a musician or someone accustomed to copying music. Which of these copies could have come from the hand of the guilty party? I again give you the originals of Julie's handwriting to facilitate your judgement.'

He handed him the papers written and sealed by Balbastre and Müvala.

Monsieur Rodollet approached the window and held the two

sheets and the originals up to the light. The examination took so long that Monsieur de Sartine was nervously adjusting his wig and Monsieur Lenoir was drawing little hanged men in pencil, arranging them in rows of five, by the time Monsieur Rodollet walked back to Nicolas and handed him the sheet with the green seal.

'Here you are, Commissioner. The person who wrote this is undoubtedly the person responsible for the forgeries. The details, the hand movements, it's all quite unmistakable.'

'Thank you, Monsieur,' said Nicolas. 'You may go.'

He turned to the magistrates.

'Remember the testimony of Madame de Lastérieux's maid, Julia. Casimir was drawn into the scheme and forced to state that he had posted a letter. Now this letter – a forgery, as we know – was not written and sealed in Rue de Verneuil. Madame de Lastérieux only kept sticks of green wax, green having been her favourite colour. Somewhere else, I don't know where, it was sealed with red wax and thrown in a post box in the Rue de Verneuil area. And this is what our handwriting expert – this Monsieur Rodollet, whose knowledge and insight are recognised at the Palais de Justice – tells us: here is the sheet of music paper written by the forger, the one who forged the letter and the will.'

He waved the paper above his head.

'Written by a man who copies music and plays the pianoforte, one of Madame de Lastérieux's killers: Monsieur von Müvala.'

'It is not uncommon for there to be errors in the field of handwriting,' said Lenoir. 'You should be careful not to commit yourself overmuch and—'

'I'm sorry to interrupt you,' replied Nicolas, 'but please let me finish my demonstration. Why am I so sure that these forgeries are from the hand of the supposed killer? My belief is based on something else. You all heard me ask Monsieur von Müvala to seal the paper with red wax, and you all saw him pick up the green without any hesitation. Why? Why didn't he notice that he didn't have any red wax? He immediately grabbed the wrong colour, just as, on two occasions, forging a supposed letter from Julie addressed to me, and drawing up a will making me Madame de Lastérieux's sole heir, he used red wax, the most common colour, the one which comes most naturally to hand. The very colour that Julie de Lastérieux would never have used. It was a serious mistake, if the intention of both these documents was to implicate an innocent man beyond a shadow of a doubt. How could such a clever man make such an obvious mistake? The solution, gentlemen, came to me in the course of a conversation I had with Doctor Semacgus, the navy surgeon. I was talking to him about this question of colour, when he remembered a discussion he had had in Madras with some Eastern doctors. Both the ancient Persians and the Arab physicians discovered that a particular defect of the eye prevents some people from distinguishing the colour green from the colour red or related colours.[1] I believe that Monsieur von Müvala is one of those people.'

'Perhaps,' said Monsieur de Sartine. 'It's certainly an ingenious argument. However, while it is obvious that Camusot hates you because of the past, how do you explain that this young man should have pursued you like that, to the point of murdering Madame de Lastérieux in order to compromise you, unless he was simply a mindless tool in the hands of the former commissioner?'

Nicolas smiled. 'Gentlemen, I am now in a position to reveal to you the essential point on which my demonstration rests and which authenticates my conclusions. During my long wait at the baths, I started playing a game from my childhood, the game of anagrams. How blind I had been, and for so long! Müvala . . . the foreignness of the name deceived us. All we had to do was change the position of one letter, just one, move the final *a* to before the *u* and it gave us MAUVAL. Obvious, isn't it? So obvious that it never occurred to us. The reason for Monsieur von Müvala's hatred of me is that he is the younger brother of Mauval, a hired killer working for the brilliant and influential Commissioner Camusot, head of the Gaming Division, whom I was responsible for removing from office fourteen years ago. This Mauval I killed in self-defence in the drawing room of the Dauphin Couronné, where he had been sent by Camusot to kill me. The supposed Müvala was born in Montbard, in Burgundy.'

He took a piece of paper from his pocket.

'Here is a copy of the parish register where his birth is recorded. He had the audacity, a few moments ago, to mention the name of his native town. It must have come into his mind spontaneously. He was born in 1751, and lost his parents at a young age. After their death, his brother became his guardian. Then, when his brother died, Camusot took care of him, gave him a respectable education, but inculcated in him the one overriding idea that one day he would avenge his brother, so unjustly killed by a certain Commissioner Le Floch.'

'Why didn't he simply kill you or challenge you to a duel?' asked Lenoir.

'He would probably have done so in the end. But the obsession instilled in him by Camusot was to destroy me and see me go to the gallows for a major crime. Poisoning, for instance. It so happened that our paths crossed at Madame de Lastérieux's.'

'Was she his mistress?' asked Testard du Lys. 'The report of the autopsy would seem—'

'We will never know. I owe it to the memory of a woman who was dear to me to banish the thought from my mind. In conclusion, gentlemen, Camusot and young Mauval killed Madame de Lastérieux, then Casimir and finally Monsieur du Maine-Giraud, whose indiscretions they feared.'

'Bringing the culprits back in again seems unnecessary,' said Sartine.

The three magistrates conferred for a moment in low voices.

'The Criminal Lieutenant and the Councillor of State wish for a last appearance,' Monsieur de Sartine announced, in a weary tone.

Camusot and Müvala were brought in.

'Camusot,' said Sartine, 'we are convinced of your responsibility, as well as that of Monsieur von Müvala, in the deaths of Madame de Lastérieux, the slave Casimir and Monsieur du Maine-Giraud. You will therefore be handed over to the criminal chamber and subjected to torture. As for you . . .' – he turned to Müvala – '. . . the younger brother of Mauval, as Commissioner Le Floch has proved to us, you will answer for your crimes and suffer the same fate as your brother once the law has taken its course.'

Nicolas would long remember the young man's terrifying reaction. It was as if his brother's face had reappeared – that half-angel, half-devil face – reawakening in Nicolas the nightmares of a dead past. Insults spewed from the man's mouth as if from the mouth of hell, promising the judges eternal damnation. He screamed so loudly that even Camusot looked scared. He described Madame de Lastérieux's death agony with a wealth of horrific details, and cursed Nicolas until the commissioner had to put his hands over his ears to stop hearing this litany of hate. If any doubt had still existed, young Mauval's reaction would have dismissed it. The two culprits were bundled out of the room, leaving all those present in a state of shock. At that moment, a man entered, dressed in black riding clothes, and handed Monsieur de Sartine a large letter with the seal of France. Sartine opened it, read it, and looked up, pale and displeased.

'Gentlemen,' he said, 'this letter informs me that the Duc d'Aiguillon has resigned. It also orders me to suspend all further legal proceedings against Commissioner Camusot and Monsieur von Müvala and banish them from the kingdom forthwith. Monsieur Balbastre is to be freed. The order is signed by the Duc de La Vrillière, in the name of the King.'

'Monsieur—' Nicolas protested.

'That's enough!' Sartine cut him off. 'As defenders of the law and magistrates of the King, we have no choice but to bow to this decision, however painful.'

Monsieur Lenoir and Monsieur Testard du Lys withdrew immediately, bowing formally to Nicolas. Monsieur de Sartine walked up to him and put his hand on his shoulder, an unheard-of gesture coming from him.

'You've read Montesquieu, Nicolas. There's a sentence of his running through my mind: "But it was thought prudent to cease the pursuit, for they ran the risk of finding a great enemy whose enmity had to be concealed, in order not to make it irreconcilable." You have handled this case with real authority and have nothing with which to reproach yourself. We are the pillars of a State which some are trying to weaken. This affair is yet more evidence of that. As for the culprits . . . Stay on your guard: one day you will meet that villain again.'

EPILOGUE

Must scruples still undo us in the end?
But here comes Atalide, now all will mend.
RACINE

Wednesday 24 August 1774

Nicolas was summoned to the Hôtel de Gramont early in the morning. The place was unusually busy. Servants were going up and down the stairs, carrying heavy wicker trunks. The courtyard was filled with overloaded carriages. Someone seemed to be moving house. He was admitted to Monsieur de Sartine's office, and found his chief supervising the packing of his beloved wigs into boxes of fine leather. When he saw Nicolas, he stopped.

'I'll be brief,' he said. 'The King has appointed me Minister for the Navy, to succeed Monsieur Turgot who's been made Comptroller General. My place will be taken by Monsieur Lenoir, whose name I myself put forward as my successor. The Duc de Chalabre is renting me a house nearby, in his gardens: you will always be welcome. I have to go to Versailles forthwith. I hardly have time to tell you all I'm feeling . . .'

He snapped the clasp of one of the boxes several times.

'. . . or to tell you . . . Well, anyway, I've recommended you to my successor. Go and see him immediately: the first hours are crucial, and those who do not push themselves forward then are ignored forever after. It is too early for me to consider finding you a job with me at the Ministry of the Navy, for the moment at least. That doesn't in any way mean that I won't call for you one day. Of course I shall. Goodbye, my friend.'

And he went back to packing his wigs and taking the servants to task for their clumsiness. Nicolas withdrew, stunned, amidst the general hustle and bustle. Thus, in a few seconds, a working relationship begun fourteen years earlier had come to an end. He appreciated Sartine's restrained emotion. Whether it was equal to all the devotion, fidelity and loyalty he had shown the Lieutenant General over the years, through many trials and tribulations – of that he was not entirely convinced. He decided not to go to the Châtelet: there was nothing urgent he had to do there. Much better to give himself a day to reflect. He would go home and spend the hours reading in Monsieur de Noblecourt's library, thus escaping the late summer storm that was threatening Paris. The day would be heavy, like the weight that burdened his heart.

He knew only too well what was going to happen. He was already 'old Court', as La Borde had put it. A policeman known to be loyal to the late King, forever marked, whatever had happened, by the stigma of an affair which had leaked out to the outside world, but of which respectable people knew only one side, without any inkling of the hidden mysteries, Nicolas did not rate the chances of his career continuing. His former position with Sartine, now ensconced in ministerial glory, would not count for much, and he would be made to feel a hundredfold the acrimony of having been his ally, even though he had been careful not to abuse his power and influence. The services he had rendered, he knew, aroused more ingratitude than gratitude. As for Monsieur Lenoir, would he wish to keep him in that unusual role, with responsibility for special investigations? At best, Nicolas would be placed under observation before his fate was decided. At worst, he would be shunted aside and confined to minor tasks. His loyalty to Sartine would be of no account and would even be considered a flaw and a disadvantage.

When he reached Rue Montmartre, he found a carriage and horses waiting at the entrance. The sweaty, red-faced coachman had taken his coat off and was drinking chilled cider served by Catherine. The baker's boys stood around, merrily chatting away about this extraordinary event. The oldest of them told him, with much mirth, that they had all lent a hand heaving a fat lady upstairs. Her face, the boy said, was smothered in make-up, patches of which fell off like the floury crust from a cob loaf. His curiosity aroused, Nicolas ran up to Monsieur de Noblecourt's apartment. He stopped outside the door of the drawing room, surprised by a rasping voice that he knew well.

'This beverage, Monsieur, is so smooth!'

'Smooth?' said Monsieur de Noblecourt, anxiously.

'Oh, yes! It flows into the gullet with a smoothness that reminds me of an old ratafia our Nicolas used to love. And these spicy lemon buns! They're so soft! I should tell you I have something of a sweet tooth!'

Nicolas risked a glance through the half-open door. He saw La Paulet, a mass of violet satin and purple ribbons, slumped in a *bergère*, her flesh overflowing the sides. Her face, as covered with ceruse as ever, the cheekbones spotted with rouge, had gained a kind of dignity and calm, doubtless as a result of her services to the poor, to whom, in spite of her infirmities, she now devoted herself. Monsieur de Noblecourt – with Mouchette sleeping on his lap and Cyrus at his feet – sat there in a black coat and a large Regency wig, playing the role of a father confessor with that air of polite affability that hid his ever-alert, ever-keen mind.

'Madame,' he said, 'to what do I owe the honour of this visit?'

'You're so understanding, Monsieur. Just think, I really dithered about coming to see you. I actually had to force myself. "Go on, old thing," I said to myself, "where's the harm in talking to this gentleman Nicolas has told you so much about?" I was worried sick wondering if you would agree to receive a former brothel-keeper. Just think, you a procurator! Well, here goes. I've entrusted the care of my house, the Dauphin Couronné, to one of my former residents, La Satin. What I should tell you is that many moons ago—'

'Nicolas's friend.'

'Oh, you know everything! I like it better that way. There's always been a little something between them . . .'

'A little something?'

'Yes, you know, a feeling, a passion that comes back every now and again. I've retired to Auteuil, you see, but whenever I have something big on, I get one of the maids to come over from Rue du Faubourg Saint-Honoré to help my cook. She's a nice girl, this maid, and very talkative. Thanks to her, I stay up to date with what's happening in my establishment. She told me that our Nicolas met a young man there. The way he reacted shows that he must have been struck by the young man's resemblance to himself.

And that must have started him wondering. La Satin found out, and now the poor girl is sick with worry.'

'He's their son.'

'That's right! Louis, his name is. She always hid it from him, out of respect, and a sense of tact. I mean, how could you have a relationship between a commissioner – a marquis, they say – and a lady of easy virtue? The child has been very well brought up, educated by monks and all that! He'll be all ready for a good career.'

Nicolas did not listen to the rest of the conversation. His heart was pounding and a wave of joy swept over him. Nothing else mattered any longer. He had lost his old King, Monsieur de Sartine was flying off to high places, and his own future was looking grim. It was likely that he would encounter a great deal of bitterness and resentment. Despicable sycophants, who had wormed their way into Court and were pushing themselves forward through intrigues, would do everything they could to humiliate him and drive home the loss of his protectors and influence. But what did it matter? Something else was weighing in the scales of his destiny now. Just a few yards from where he stood, La Paulet was singing his son's praises. What more precious gift could fate offer him? Life, like the boundless ocean he had contemplated as a child from the beach at Batz, took away and gave back. Anguish and sadness abandoned him like the water receding from the shore before the twelfth wave, the one that carries everything away. Just when luck seemed to have deserted him, he had been given a son.

La Marsa, June 2001–May 2002

NOTES

CHAPTER 1

1. The barracks of the Regiment of Musketeers were situated on the corner of Rue de Verneuil.

2. Françoise Marie Saucerotte, known as Mademoiselle Raucourt (1756–1815): actress at the Théâtre-Français.

3. A Brazilian tribe.

CHAPTER 2

1. Mansion rented by Monsieur de Sartine and used as police headquarters.

2. See *The Man with the Lead Stomach*.

CHAPTER 3

1. A building in which costumes and sets from Court celebrations were stored.

2. A fashionable tavern in the outlying district of La Courtille.

CHAPTER 4

1. See *The Phantom of Rue Royale*.

2. Marc-Antoine Laugier (1713–1769), a Jesuit, later a Benedictine. He was a diplomat and the author of works on art including *Essai sur l'architecture*.

3. This facelift was eventually carried out in 1779 during the hundred weddings celebrated in Notre Dame on the occasion of the birth of Madame Royale, the first child of Louis XVI and Marie-Antoinette.

4. See *The Phantom of Rue Royale*.

CHAPTER 5

1. Madame de Pompadour.

2. See *The Man with the Lead Stomach*.

3. Madame du Barry had a house here.

4. One of the nicknames given by pamphleteers of the time to Madame du Barry.

CHAPTER 6

1. Popular card game of the period.

CHAPTER 7

1. This magistrate, Monsieur Vermeil, in fact proposed this form of torture in 1781.
2. Henri Louis Duhamel du Monceau, French physiologist, agronomist and general inspector of the navy (1700–1782).
3. A plant-derived remedy recommended by Homer for combating sadness.

CHAPTER 8

1. See *The Châtelet Apprentice*.
2. The modernity of the institution of the Farmers General during the *ancien régime* is still quite striking.
3. The Comptroller of Finances, responsible for the State's coffers.
4. This experiment with a diving suit is a real historical event. It took place on 20 January 1774 beneath the Pont Royal, in the presence of a commission from the Academy of Sciences.
5. See *The Châtelet Apprentice*.

CHAPTER 9

1. An oblong beetle, green and gold in colour. Its dried powder was used externally as a vesicatory, and, in pastille form, as an aphrodisiac with remarkable health benefits.

CHAPTER 10

1. The King presided over the going-to-bed ceremony in the show bedchamber, then went to his real bedchamber a few rooms away, which was where he actually slept.
2. Arab doctor and surgeon, also known by the name Abulcasis (936–1013).
3. The same debate on the expulsion of the then mistress, the Duchesse de Châteauroux, had caused a scandal during the King's illness at Metz in 1742.
4. It was reported that Madame du Barry had introduced a young girl into the King's bed and that it was she who had given Louis XV smallpox.

CHAPTER 11

1. See *The Châtelet Apprentice*.
2. This is a real incident which became widely known and caused much mirth amongst Parisians.
3. Lunch was usually eaten at about eleven o'clock in the morning.

CHAPTER 13

1. Colour blindness was scientifically demonstrated by the English doctor and physicist Dalton a few years later, in 1791.

ACKNOWLEDGEMENTS

First, I wish to express my gratitude to Isabelle Tujague for her competence, care and patience in preparing the final version of the text. I am also grateful to Monique Constant, Conservateur Général du Patrimoine, for her encouragement and her research into the period. Once again I am indebted to Maurice Roisse for his intelligent and detailed checking of the manuscript and for his helpful suggestions. Finally, I wish to thank my publisher for the confidence he has shown in this fourth book in the series.